SHADOWSPEAK

RAVEN ECKMAN

RAVEN ECKMAN

SHADOWSPEAK

FOX POINTE PUBLISHING

This is a work of fiction. Names, places, characters, and incidents are either a product of the author's imagination or are used fictitiously. Any resemblance to actual events, places, organizations, or persons, whether living or dead, is entirely coincidental.

www.foxpointepublishing.com/author-raven-eckman

Library of Congress Cataloging-in-Publication Data
Eckman, Raven, author.
Farr, Chelsea, editor.
Hudson, Becca, designer.
Shadowspeak / Raven Eckman. – First edition.
Summary: A young woman with special powers must rescue a prince and reckon with the shadows of her past.
ISBN (softcover) 979-8-9938504-9-8
[1. Dark Fantasy – Fiction. 2. Occult – Fiction. 3. Mythology – Fiction.]
Library of Congress Control Number: 2 0 2 0 9 2 5 9 3 5

Second printing February 2026

Cover design by Becca Hudson
Interior illustrations by Nicole Deal

This book is intended for mature readers, ages 17 and older.
The reader's discretion is advised.

To my grandmother who never stopped believing in me.

THE LAND OF BEASTS
FRUMLAND
THE RIVER KVOL
THE UNKNOWN FOREST
OPEKKTI SKOGURINN
THE MISLA SEA
WRAITH VODIHR
VILLAGE OF LAUS

DÝRA
THE ISLE OF UTLAN
ARDEN
N
RIKI SKUGGA
REALM OF SHADOW

~~BYRJUNIN~~

THE BEGINNING

Once there was a girl who spoke to shadows …

The rain goes from something violent to a slow steady drizzle.

Securing the drenched moth-eaten cloak more firmly around my shoulders, I keep my head down in a display of learned obedience. The action conceals my fear, even as the shadows beckon me to play.

My toes curl self-consciously, my thin boots disturbing the wet leaves beneath me as Papa's muttering grows in volume. He had dragged me from bed around midnight, throwing my cloak and boots at my feet as I blinked sleep from my eyes.

We've been walking for hours, dawn teasing among the folds of rain. The path has long since grown uncharted, our clothes laden with rain. Fear prickles its fingers along my spine at the first etching I see, dug deep into the bark of an old pine tree.

Það horfir. It watches.

"Papa," I try, finally breaking our long silence, only to flinch when his voice rises with distress.

"Skuld, it always comes back to the *debt.*"

Only a handful of times has Papa slipped back into his ancestral language over the years, a language that I held close and buried deep because something told me I wasn't supposed to know it. Mama never spoke it, nor Anik.

"Ég lék mér með skugga, Papa—"

The hand pressed against my lips took me by surprise. I had been telling him, or trying to tell him, about playing with my shadow friends today.

Wide-eyed, I watched the fear turn to anger as Papa dragged me from the doorway and back outside.

Skuggar peaked out from the tree line of the forest. One waved and I waved back. Papa grunted. "Stop it, Rune."

My hand falling to my side, I started fiddling with the muddied skirt of my dress, digging my toes into the dirt.

"I'm sorry," Papa said then as he crouched before me. His face twisted in apology. He couldn't see the shadows like I could; he'd told me so. I wished he could; then he'd understand and not be so afraid of them—of me.

"I don't ... I don't understand." I kept my gaze on the tips of his scuffed boots. He hadn't always been this way, or so I thought. Sometimes when I dreamed, there were two different Papas and a beautiful woman who sang to me when the skuggar spoke too loud and demanded too much.

"I know, sá litli," he soothed. I loved when he called me 'sá litli,' as I often felt I was no longer his 'little one.' The older I got, the more his irrationality grew. When he'd disappear for days at a time, I was lost. I needed him even though I feared his anger and distrust.

His hand came up to cup my cheek and I leaned into it.

"Remember, though, you cannot speak the language of the old gods

in our home, nor mention the skuggar—the shadows—to Mama or she will get upset."

"But why? I don't understand."

Papa's sigh ruffled my hair. "Rune—"

"Rune, come here."

I fight the urge to cower like a small child at Papa's snarled command. At the age of ten, I am no longer able to hide behind Mama's skirts—not that she is here for me to do so now, nor has she ever let me do so before.

Mama and my older brother, Anik, are at home, blissfully warm and dry. They usually don't come with us when Papa takes me out. Perhaps this outing is another boat trip to Arden, the main port city of Utlen—a wet and soggy land full of lush green fields that are speckled with small villages. I remember my first glimpse of Utlen, then of Arden, the land itself long since settled from the clans of old. Our village, Laus, is on a neighboring landmass, Frumland. We are outcasts of Utlen's supposed glorious history.

When we'd visit, Papa would bargain for goods or play cards recklessly while I played thief or worked in a tavern kitchen for a hot meal—my mouth waters now at the thought of food. I hadn't had anything to eat before Papa rushed us out of the house. Anik would probably be eating breakfast now ... Maybe the porridge we'd gotten from the market earlier in the week. Or maybe he was able to save enough for a few scraps of bacon from the town's butcher.

Gnarled fingers appear, breaking through my thoughts of sizzling bacon. They wrap around a low tree branch inches to my left. I freeze, watching the fingers grow solid, their form strengthening under my gaze, their silver threads weaving patterns in the bark.

A litany circles my mind: *Please not right now. Don't speak to me now. Please not—*

"Rune."

Stifling the urge to run, I come to stand in front of Papa, not once looking back at the creature behind us. My eyes water. I know that crying and pleading are two things Papa loathes most; my fading black eye is proof of that.

Eyes prick at the nape of my neck. The skuggi still watches.

The skuggar, or shadows, are beings from The Unknown Forest, or in the old tongue, 'Óþekkti Skógurinn.' They travel throughout the earth, forbidden from crossing over without a guide to light the way. According to legend, they are remnant energy of the Other, a clan that had resided in the forest for centuries before being purged from the land.

I had read about them in an old black book at Grandma Bell's, but I haven't been able to find the book again after she caught me with it and took it away.

"What are you doing?"

I heard her voice before I saw her. "Reading," I answered, distracted by the crinkled pages and rough ink. The book seemed to groan as I turned the next page, anxious to see what new illustration would come to life before me.

At first I had spent a good ten minutes arguing with myself on whether or not to even read the book. I'd found it underneath the crystal cabinet while playing on the floor with my doll. Xavier kept hissing when I got too close. But it had whispered to me, covered in cobwebs and dust, and had gotten so loud I had to put down my doll to answer its call.

It was worth Xavier's bite.

A few more shadows appear, whispering louder and for me alone. Papa is staring hard at my face, but I can't answer him—can't hear him over the skuggar and the fierce grip of a memory.

"Reading wh—"

The sudden silence had me looking up from my hiding spot between the two large potted plants on her porch. The color was gone from Grandma Bell's face. Her hand was clutching at the wolf's tooth pendant around her neck.

"Grandma—"

She reached out and snatched the book from my hands. I bit back a cry at its loss, not understanding the ache it caused. When her eyes narrowed, I cowered, waiting for her correction.

I wait for Papa's blow, expecting him to punish me for seemingly ignoring him. Instead, he yanks my chin up. The movement causes my hood to fall back, revealing my uncombed mass of ebony curls. My head often aches at the weight of my hair, but Mama refuses to cut it, for she does not want to touch me or be too close. Am I such a wretched thing?

"She is a pretty thing, just like you promised," a male voice calls. Pretty? I jerk against Papa's hold, surprised at the invasion of our solitude. I feel more eyes assessing me, raising goosebumps where their gazes touch. I strain to see the newcomer, but Papa prevents me from moving, his fingers biting into my tender flesh in warning.

Papa's umber eyes are narrowed in a madness not even I knew he was capable of. He is looking at someone behind me.

I hold my breath.

"Not as big as I expected."

"She doesn't like to eat much." Papa's reply is curt, his head tilted to the side. He appears confused before he finally lets me go.

I rub my jaw, my cold fingers soothing some of the sting. In truth, there is never enough food to eat thanks to Papa's gambling. We often starve, regardless of the game Anik catches or the berries I forage or what either of us manages to steal from our neighbors. I like to eat just fine.

"She's obedient at least," Papa offers before twisting me around and nudging me forward.

Rune. Rune. Rune.

I stumble at the shadow beckoning from a tree inches from my face; my name is frenzied, unnaturally weighted in the air. Fingers grab for me as I step inside a circle crafted of decaying branches, an old ritual site left behind by the Others. The book said circles represented a sacred space to call their gods.

A robed figure kneels waiting there, anonymous under a cowl hood. I taste bile as a bitter floral scent stings my nostrils. It is familiar, yet not. Is it something Mama wears?

Tears return to blur my vision. The rain resumes its steadier beat from before, each drop hitting the earth, but not reaching my skin now.

How odd.

My brow furrowed, I reach out beyond the circle of branches. My palm meets resistance for a moment, and then I can catch the rain again. Drops fall into my hand, cold and unsettling. I draw my hand back quickly, hiding it in the edges of my cloak.

"Is that so, child?" the hooded man asks as he stands up. His words are slow, almost hesitant.

A new skuggi appears, then another, both studying the circle I am in. They join the first, all now stalking around the edge, eyeing it with revulsion as they whisper amongst themselves. Their forms are still translucent, shifting from pitch to gray as if cast by some flickering candle, their shapes human yet not. But the dead have no form—there is no existence after death—or so the new religion says.

Those who study the old ways know the truth.

I know the truth.

One shadow coughs, pink wisps of thread—the shadow's essence—falling from its mouth to twist in the breeze.

Does she know yet?

She can't. Too young, too soon.

One kneels, eyes with blown pupils in a featureless face snaring my shifting gaze—*Come to us, little one. Come play.*

I stare ahead, my lips pressing into a thin line. The skuggar flicker as if they can hear my racing pulse, sense my growing fear.

The first shadow reaches out, pink threads now dangling before me. Its taloned hand beckons.

The hooded man grunts at my prolonged silence before doing a thorough inspection of me from top to bottom. At one point, his hood slips back and I catch a glimpse of celadon-green eyes in a scarred, discolored face. He looks tense, unhappy. His gloved hand hurries to righten the dark material.

I feel like the old horse we'd had to auction off last month at our village's weekly market. My hair is lifted, then dropped. My hands are groped, my teeth studied. His touch is soft at first, but then more weight is added. My muscles tense when a wandering hand brushes across the slight swell of my breasts.

Don't touch me.

There is a pause, as if the stranger has heard my internal plea. I see a flash of revulsion, of disgust, before he backs away. His gaze is on something off to the side.

A lengthier silence grows between us until he nods briefly, then moves off to talk with Papa. And when their conversation turns heated, glances in my direction becoming more frequent, deep down I know what is happening.

I know what is about to be done.

"You promised that she'd go—"

The stranger holds up his hand, causing Papa to stop whatever he had been about to say. As the two eye each other, summing each other up, my head bows in resignation.

I hear Papa's vicious curse and glance up to see him shaking the stranger's now-outstretched hand. This is a game he has apparently not won and oh, how Papa hates to lose.

Visibly impatient, his fingers twitching, he grabs the coins being offered to him. I watch his expression twist from triumph to disappointment before finally settling on the familiar look of disgust I am used to. I look away at the clinking of coins; I don't want to see him counting his prize.

"She's yours."

Papa's words hit like the snap of a fresh-strung bow. The shadows blanch, dissolving at my panicked breathing. My heart bleeds, a blush darkening my pale face. He's really done it … After all the threats—all the years of taunts and abuse I have suffered—this is the end result.

Don't I matter at all, Papa?

Of course I don't—what a foolish question. My existence is a mistake; the result of a heated night that shouldn't have happened. My parents had only ever planned for—only ever *wanted* one child.

I stand there, recounting their late-night arguments and Papa's nonsensical drunken roars.

"What has she done this time?"

"Everything! She does everything and craves affection I cannot give."

"You can but you won't."

"She isn't mine to give—"

"Enough!"

The beatings had started on my seventh birthday; Papa had seen something in me that day and everything changed.

"Hún myndi hata mig fyrir þetta, fyrir það sem ég hef gert."

She would hate me for this, for what I have done.

The blood ran from the cut on my forehead and down into my eye. My birthday meal was left forgotten on the table behind me, my medicine untouched.

Everything had hurt.

Everything was red.

I wilt as Papa turns away from me, his shoulders hunched against the rain. Dimly, I realize he had never stepped within the circle. He retreats, oblivious to the hands that grab at him from the trees, to the shadows that skip in his footsteps.

It hurts too much to breathe.

A fourth shadow forms, glances at me, then focuses on Papa. I shift my weight, watching its eyes, gray and bottomless, light up with some sort of recognition, greedily taking in the sight of him. Then, it abruptly faces me.

Rune?

I shiver. "Papa! Komdu aftur, Papa!"

Please, come back, Papa.

Tears trickle down my cheeks, mingling with the fresh sweat dotting my upper brows and chin. Regret is suffocating me. I shouldn't have said anything about my portion of bread yesterday morning—shouldn't have complained. But my stomach had been cramping with hunger all night and when Mama had given me nothing but a small piece of bread with the beginnings of mold on it, I'd snapped and swept the plate to the floor.

I glance at the waiting shadows, my only friends in a world full of change and want and darkness.

Help. Please help.

The air in the circle grows thick as they press closer, seeking a way in. Their threads tangle and knot together, weaving among the circle's branches …

Nothing.

The gray skuggi presses forward in determination, clawing at the resistance between us; a bead of sweat trails down my spine at its lack of success—at the futility and hopelessness.

And then Papa turns back to me.

"Rune … a debt … I cannot pay." His eyes roll and I see their whites.

He speaks of the skuld.

A shadow snaps back, *She cannot know of it—not yet.*

Biting my lip to stifle the sob building, I try to make sense of his words—try to discern the truth in the lies that seep from Papa's mouth. It is no use. The damage is done. And not even the shadows are making sense now.

I watch Papa turn away a second time before he disappears into a blanket of rain and fog, his footsteps silenced by the morning dew.

I'll never forgive him.

There is a moaning sound and the creaking of limbs as the trees settle around us again. From the corner of my eye, I see the cloaked figure toss back his hood and remove his gloves; the shadows gather, mimicking his actions as they pull their threads from the circle's branches. Two hold up hands curled into fists. One begins to sob before fading away.

Rune.

"Child."

I turn at the man's voice, seeing that I am being beckoned to come further into the circle's middle. A sad smile crinkles his split lips as I obey.

He takes a deep breath, then begins to speak—"Once there was a child who spoke to shadows … "

A pale face with red lips appears in the fog as he speaks, pressing a finger with a long ragged nail to its lips when I open my mouth to scream.

Ssh.

From the branches of a nearby tree, a raven's beady eyes meet mine.

~~FANGI~~

CAPTIVITY

CHAPTER ONE

Six years later.

She watches me with holes for eyes, her mouth twisted in a snarl. She is a daughter of the Other—a feral thing the hunters stare at with childish delight as they circle her cage in the center of the room. When her face turns towards me, my throat closes. She is about my age, and yet older, infinite.

Her head tilts, her mouth tightening as she sniffs the air.

"Creepy, isn't it?" Keegan asks, his voice a whisper in my ear. "Creepy and pitiful."

I jerk forward, nearly spilling the wine jugs I'm holding. When I look over my shoulder to glare at him, he's studying the girl, his brow furrowed.

"I would think you incapable of remorse," I reply. "Afterall, you were the one who captured her—*it.*"

He tsks, snatching a jug from my hand and taking a long swallow. "Mistress Agata asked it of me. I was lucky to be given such a responsibility."

He sighs and I smell the sweet floral scent on his breath. I lick my parched lips. I need a drink, desperately, but I had promised Weylin I'd be careful. They've laced the wine and ale again.

"You say lucky … I say cursed."

"Elskan, darling, do you not agree with my choice of entertainment for the evening?"

Blanching at her voice, I grip my remaining wine jug with both hands and try to steady my breath—but I can't find the words to answer her.

"Elskan, you will answer when you are spoken to."

Swallowing bile, I manage a nod, my movements stiff as I murmur, "My apologies, Mistress. I was merely speaking with Keegan about her … its … unrelenting stare." I risk a glance to see if she has bought my lie.

Agata's rose-painted lips match the light blush on her cheeks—both are slightly wrinkled as she considers me through narrowed emerald eyes. I know she wants to make a spectacle, to entertain and draw more coin from the hunters and huntresses mingling about the room. There is a rumor that even one of Arden's royalty plans to be in attendance tonight. A private showing is a rare commodity and one that Mistress Agata undoubtedly takes pleasure in hosting.

Finally, she waves her hand, her manicured nails catching the candlelight. They reminded me of tiny stars, abandoned on her hands, trapped by her fingers … I have to shake my head to clear my thoughts. The muscles in my throat convulse.

"I see. Well, perhaps your opinions would be better suited

for another time. There is someone I'd like you to attend to immediately."

Keegan's face is sympathetic as I'm steered away. My hands start to shake. I scan the room, my feet following Agata's flowing dress of rose gauze weaving amongst the masked occupants. I catch a glimpse of Weylin, his eyes warning me to behave before he turns to smirk at the huntress he's feeding grapes to. When she reaches to touch the inside of his leg, I force myself to look away.

I'm passing the center of the room, the cage itself, when something wraps around my wrist and yanks me to a stop. The hairs on my arm raise as iron-colored threads slink across my wrist and up into my fingers. Fresh blood soon follows. My lips part and I look up.

The captive Other is even more ragged up close. Naked, covered in dirt and shallow wounds, a handful of leaves still in her unkempt hair the color of flame.

"Papa, tell me more about the Other." I burrowed deeper within the folds of my blankets. The wind howled outside, unrelenting.

Papa leaned back, a tired smile on his face. "What of them, sá litli?" he asked, rubbing at his eyes. He had been gone for most of the day and I felt a little guilty for keeping him here, but I had missed him terribly. He was gone so often.

I frowned, bringing my ragged doll closer, trying to remember what I'd heard that day in the village.

"Do they eat children?" I asked this first because it was my most pressing concern. At the ripe age of eight, I'd been learning more and more from Anik about the monsters of our land and how many of them had a penchant for eating children. I would rather not be eaten, of course.

Papa chuckles and I catch a whiff of mead on his breath. "No, *they don't.*"

"*Do they really walk around naked?*"

The Other is speaking to me: "Hjálpaðu mér."

I glance to see if Agata is watching, but she has disappeared.

"I can't," I manage. Old scars wreck her face and body. Claw marks run across her chest and left breast. There's a wildness to her that stirs something deep inside me; a buried call I won't answer—refuse to, am frightened of.

"*Papa?*"

"*Yes?*"

I bit my lip until it nearly bled. "*Do the Other speak to the skuggar, too?*"

He froze in the act of blowing out the candle by my bedside. I saw the turmoil in his eyes before he blew once, and my room was cast into darkness.

"*Only to those who answer, sá litli.*"

"Hjálpaðu mér," she breathes again before pulling her threads back, an ability I envy. She stalks back to the corner of her cage. She does not cower. She remains defiant, even when trapped.

Help me.

Her words haunt me as Mistress Agata reappears, a beautiful middle-aged woman at her side. I put on my best smile and bring the woman's outstretched fingers to my purple-painted lips, bowing my head as I do.

The woman laughs in delight.

Help me.

CHAPTER TWO

I wake to the rhythmic and ever-present *thud, thud, thud* on the wall at my head. The eyeless face watching me from the tree line begins to fade from my mind as I blink away sleep. I bury my face deeper into the pillow I hold—a whiff of dirt greets me, and I frown, pulling back.

There are muddy fingerprints smeared across the white satin.

Thud, thud, thud.

I thump once on the wall above my headboard, ignoring the moan that answers me and sit up with the sheets wrapped tight around my naked body. I see it's not just the pillow: the entire bed is covered in dirt, dead leaves, and little clumps of grass.

Trying to control my breathing, I suck in another breath and register the sour taste of ale on my tongue. My blood runs cold. Did I drink last night?

I bring an unsteady hand to my forehead, ignoring the dirt that is crusted there. Some flecks off and falls in my eyes; I squint.

Last night: the beautiful woman and her outrageous demands, Mistress Agata's steady gaze, a stolen, frenzied kiss with Weylin during a trip to the kitchens …

Hjálpaðu mér.

"Help me," I whisper aloud. The words sting my cracked lips as the Other's face reappears in my mind. She is wailing, reaching for me from the trees—

I stifle a scream when the door to my room bursts open. Two guards, utterly expressionless, drag me from bed. They lift me between them, dangling like a dead thing destined for the spit. One of them at least has the decency to stop and secure the sheet still wrapped around me, tucking the end into an oddly neat fold.

Shadows seep from the walls, pooling onto the floor in a frenzy. They watch me, curious, concerned. One lets its navy blue threads come just a hair closer before being forced to retreat from the guards' heavy treads.

Some of Mistress Agata's 'pets' mimic the shadows' stares, gathering as I'm hauled out of my room. I look for Weylin, for Keegan's purple hair among the onlookers, but they're not there. The pets scatter when I struggle and am placed on my feet.

"What—"

A painful squeeze on my arm is enough to silence me.

Down the steps we go, my feet slipping and sliding against the polished wood floors—then I'm blinded by sunlight.

My senses explode with the usual activity of Vodihr: a woman laughs, a child shrieks in play, a dog barks. Yet the sudden silence that comes on is equally painful.

All eyes turn on me as I'm dragged down the path toward the heart of the city. Little rocks cut at my bare feet—more scars for my flesh.

"I don't understand … " My words fade as I'm shoved to the ground.

Pulling the now-tattered sheet more firmly around me, I lift my eyes up, brush my hair away to see.

Mistress Agata stands before me, with an empty cage slightly off to the side. Behind her stands Vodihr's only shrine, a tribute to the old gods that some still worship.

A memory whispers, an unseen shadow's threads slinking closer to me from the cracked slate stones surrounding the shrine. I get a glimpse of a woman's gray eyes, a small smile, before Agata crushes the threads beneath her feet. She steps toward me.

My vision swims. Blinking, I don't have time to duck before her palm smacks the side of my face. My cheek stings and I hear a muffled laugh from the crowd.

"Why?" Agata asks.

"Why what?" I retort, spitting at her feet.

Her eyes widen and I brace myself for another hit. Someone boos at our backs and I watch her expression twitch. "Oh Rune," she whispers before all her anger is replaced by fake sorrow. She turns to address the growing crowd—"It would seem our gift from the gods has been released."

The crowd's murmurs mingle with my growing unease and I glance to the cage, one of many she owns, that is glaringly empty in the light of day. It is all just for show. But why?

I look for Weylin in the crowd.

For Keegan.

I'm alone.

"We had been given a gift, a gift from one of our own … " She lets that hang there for a moment before she continues. "And yet, that gift was taken from him—*us*." Again she faces me. "Was it jealousy, Rune? Did you have to have the girl for yourself? We all know how you like to tease … "

I gape at her. "What?"

She sniffs, shaking her head. "Don't play dumb, elskan. You were seen."

"By who?"

My question goes unanswered and I'm yanked to my feet, the sheet ripped from my body. I go to cower, to cover myself, but the guards take my arms and lead me to a lone post that stands before the shrine's altar.

"Please, I didn't," I whisper, my eyes slamming shut as the ropes appear, my wrists cracking against the speckled stone. Goosebumps spatter my forearms.

I watched as Weylin was led away, the huntress on his arm beautiful and alluring. His eyes met mine, but I couldn't hold his gaze for long.

I pushed past the woman I had been entertaining, past the doorway where Keegan leaned with his arms caging in a finely dressed hunter with dirty blonde hair. His eyes darted to me, but I waved him away.

With a nearly full jug in my hand, I walked toward the supply closet by the kitchen. When I opened it, I found it already occupied. At the scandalized gasp I received, I snarled. The two occupants scattered, leaving some of their clothing behind.

Exhausted, I slammed the door shut, locked it.

I brought the jug to my lips.

In my mind, I see myself walking back into the now-empty main hall. I'm grasping the lock of the cage as the creature stares at me from the corner. When the lock clicks open and falls to the ground, the Other's smile is all teeth. She steps forward—

The scent of bellflower overwhelms me as Agata circles my post. Her eyes dance, her joy visible for me alone to witness. She leans in closer to press a kiss beneath my ear—"Elskan. Elsssskan."

Darling. Darling.

Through blurred vision, I see a figure watching me from the trees. Her empty eye sockets bore into me.

"Hjálpaðu mér," I whisper.

The first lash strikes across my back.

CHAPTER THREE

I don't understand," I mumbled, watching as my blood dripped onto the shrine's altar. Each sizzle and hiss caused my heart to beat just a little harder. I was scared. In awe. Mesmerized.

My open palm shook before she closed my fingers and gave my fist a squeeze.

"I know, ljúfa stelpa—my sweet girl." She released my fist and quickly opened my hand to wrap a piece of cloth around my wound. I could see little wisps of thread, like the ones the skuggar have, before she tied the cloth and stepped back.

"Why must we pay our respects to the gods if they are dead?" I asked, watching as she cut her own palm and gave her hand a squeeze. Like my blood, hers also sizzled and steamed when it touched the altar.

"Who told you they were dead?"

The sharpness of her voice surprised me, and I frowned. But before I could reply, fear flashed across her face.

A shiver went down my spine; skuggar were at my feet, their threads tugging in urgency.

"Rune, you need to—"

"Rune, you need to wake up," a voice beckons to me, firm and unrelenting.

I fight against consciousness, instead reaching for a memory that is already just out of reach.

"Rune, wake up," a second voice says. It's Weylin.

I reach out, unseeing, to grasp for him, and when our hands connect, my senses come back to me. A sting shoots across my back, bringing bile to my lips. I barely turn my head in time before heaving. Again and again, I gag. I try to curl into myself and escape the fire raging across my back.

"Það er allt í lagi, andaðu," Weylin whispers in my ear. I feel his hand move to hold back my hair, his other hand still tight in my bruising grip.

'It's okay, breathe.'

"How can I breathe when everything hurts?" Snot mixes with my sweat and tears.

He doesn't answer, just waits for me to calm down. From beneath the dresser, a pair of yellow eyes is watching me. They blink once, then twice, before a furry black face appears—"Xavier."

The cat acknowledges me with a sniff before moving away to groom himself. The cheeky bastard.

At last, the fire fades and a coolness rushes in. The gagging stops as well and I force myself to shift positions, my forehead pressing into the mattress. I drop Weylin's hand, letting my own hang limp, fingers almost touching the worn wooden floor. The silence is too much.

"Anyone want to tell me what happened?" I ask.

Fingers probe along my back and I growl. My head is then turned to the left and I meet Embela's eyes. "You don't remember?"

Her worry gnaws at me and without thinking, I say, "Grandma Bell, what's wrong? Don't be sad."

My eyes widen at the childish lilt of my voice and my choice of words. I don't have a grandmother ... I see panic on Embela's face before she looks away.

She releases my chin and my face is suddenly back on the mattress. The sheet is teasing my cheek and my nose; I desperately want to scratch the itch but moving isn't an option right now.

"When was the last time she had her tonic?" Embela asks.

"I-I don't know," Weylin answers, his voice rough and unsure.

I turn my head and get my first good look at him since waking up. The redness lurking in his eyes, the dirt caked under his nails, the tear in his shirt ... The blood in dried patches all over his arms. Was it mine? Or had the beast taken control when he came to the shrine and saw what was happening? But had he even been there? I vaguely remember screaming his name, begging him to come, and yet I wasn't sure what had occurred after I blacked out.

I go to speak again only for a familiar floral scent to burn my nostrils as a mug is shoved in my face. I press my lips tightly together, trying to avoid the thick sludge I know I have to drink.

"You need to take your tonic, Rune."

I glared from beneath the bed. "I don't. I'm not sick."

"Oh, but you are," Mama crooned before reaching under and dragging me out by my hair.

"Rune."

Eyeing the mug, I sigh and open my mouth, choking on the

liquid as it goes down. A warm weight settles in my chest; Embela must have put a sleeping tonic in it as well.

As everything becomes static, hazy, and my eyes close, I hear, "She needs to leave—soon."

CHAPTER FOUR

Pain. It curdles the air, ripens and slivers as if alive.

I don't want to be here.

Agata appears, tossing back her cloak and rolling up her sleeves. At her side is her latest apprentice, who likely will be dead in a week. She already has the bruising about her throat—that's how it starts.

Four talas are coming up the hill, bowls in their hands.

Green eyes meet mine before Agata speaks. "Today is the first step of your rebirth. Of your test to see if you are truly worthy in the eyes of the gods."

"The gods don't exist anymore," a boy mutters, his accent hard to understand.

I wince.

"That may be true," Agata says. "But their creatures still do."

From the end of the line a girl begins to scream, and we all crane our necks to see why. A being has appeared from the circle of Vodihr. All I see is the blood dripping from her elongated nails.

An apparition of darkness.

"What is that?" I ask, my voice hushed.

Agata glances at me. "The Zila."

The screaming begins anew.

"The Zila is said to be a creature from the time of the gods. She will test your will, your worthiness, of becoming a true member of Vodihr." There is a murmur of unease when the screaming stops. From the corner of my eye, I see a body drop to the forest floor. "The old gods demand only the best for their offerings, and I must appease them."

Screaming starts again.

"When the Zila gets to you, you will not say anything. You will not look her in the eye. If you fight, try to run, try to speak, the guards at your backs are free to do with you what they want."

Another thud of a body hitting the forest floor. My mind is racing. Are they dead? Is this part of the test?

The fourth boy, Matthias, tries to run and I cringe at the sound of a whip. It's been a week since I let the Other go. I'm barely healed and cannot afford to disobey right now.

The skin stretches taut over my back.

"If found worthy, we will take you to the river to bathe again, a second washing to further purify your intentions."

Our intentions ... We'd been ripped from our beds in the predawn, taken to the city's shrine, and forced to line up single file. One by one, we were then stripped and bathed. Sage forced into our faces, an order to breathe deep. The remains of the bundles were still burning on the makeshift altar a few feet away. At some point, a cup had been forced against my lips, the liquid thick and murky. It burned on the way down.

There is a whisper of sound beside me and the hairs on my arms raise.

Not even the shadows have so far dared to find me this morning.

"Elskan, are you ready?"

"Darling," she cooed, her lips an inch from mine, "are you ready to play a game?"

I blinked against the fogginess in my mind. "What game?"

Someone snickered behind me. "Oh, yeah. She's ready."

There was a flash of bone, of a twisted antler, before Agata's face swam into sight again. "Good girl."

I was shoved into a room and all eyes fell on me.

Agata's lips press against mine now. She nips my bottom lip, then pulls away. "Behave."

There is a whisper of movement, a brush of air that has my eyelids fluttering shut. I squeeze them tighter to resist opening them. "Don't look," I mutter to myself. "Don't look."

Look.

The word whispers through my mind. Fingers trail lazily across my cheek. The touch is so soft, so gentle, that tears come to my eyes.

Look.

My head snaps up.

Hello, child. I've been waiting a long time for you.

I scream and scream.

CHAPTER FIVE

I still reek of sage. My skin is covered in oil, which causes my dress to cling uncomfortably to my breasts and hips. My ears pulse from the beat of the lone drum in the corner, the laughter of the gathered crowd.

The party is in full swing when we are permitted to enter. We had been bathed, dressed in colors Agata chose—I in pink to match her—and now the pre-Bloodletting ceremony truly begins. Our stories are in place. Our lines are memorized. If we are spoken to, we must reply. And as this year's offerlings, we can be touched but not harmed; a bellflower is pinned to our shoulders, symbolizing our importance.

I hover in the corner, nodding at those who approach but ultimately unwilling to entertain conversation. I try to stop my fidgeting, to keep my head up.

Inside, I quake.

I see the Zila's eyes. Feel the soft caress of her fingers.

Then I'm screaming as she yanks individual threads, plucking them from my core.

The crowd cheers and I jolt, smiling a little when a huntress blows me a kiss in passing. Before me, a hunter stands on a raised platform. He is drunk, wobbly, and roaring with laughter as he fumbles around. Dressed in blue velvet, he stumbles another step but recovers to wrap his arms around a woman pressing against his side.

His eyes meet mine for a moment, and I swear the brown flashes with recognition, a sheen of tears appearing behind his blue mask. But then he turns to the woman clinging to him and they kiss. I can feel the heat, my cheeks flushing.

Shifting at the odd feeling in my chest, I scratch at my arm to distract myself from the show on the platform, the catcalls and whistles. My entire body is itchy from the delicate, diaphanous dress I'm wearing. I despise the color pink. To add additional offense, it glitters like trapped stars when it catches the lanterns' light just right.

Resigned, I take a step forward and am swallowed by the crowd. I know Agata will punish Weylin if I stay inactive much longer. She knows that's the best way to force me to behave.

His freedom and mine are at stake.

"Ru."

The nickname is breathed in my ear and a bare hand wraps around my forearm. I'm frozen in disbelief. I haven't heard that name in such a long time.

My nose stings from the alcohol invading my senses. He reeks of it. "Anik?" I don't turn around. I feel the velvet of his sleeve brush my arm.

There is a sniff, a watery cough before he answers, "I've finally found you."

I go to reply, to turn and embrace him, but stop. Agata is watching. She looks from the boy—no, *man*—at my side, then back to me. Her brow furrows further and there is a brief flick of her wrist—Keegan starts to make his way towards me.

"Go," I whisper through a smile. "Go away, leave."

"Ru—"

"Shut up," I breathe, yanking my arm away. I press my hand to my chest, laughing loudly.

"No," he slurs, and another whiff of alcohol clogs my nose. Underneath the ale is the scent of henbane and my stomach sinks further.

"Anik, please," I say. Frustrated, panicked, I reach out to a passing pet and take a gulp of the drink in his hands. He scowls at me and moves away. "You need to leave."

"Not without you."

"I cannot go with you." I'm desperate. Keegan's getting closer.

"Now isn't the time for games, Ru."

That hurts more than I want to admit. He has no idea what games I've been forced to play in the six years we've been apart. "There is nothing but games in Vodihr," I manage, twisting when my brother reaches for my arm again. "You are drugged. You need to leave."

"Is there a problem?" Keegan's voice is smooth, unhurried at my back.

"No," I answer at the same time Anik says, "Yes."

Keegan's brows raise. "Which is it?"

I glare at Anik. "He is upset because he cannot have a private show so close to the Bloodletting." When he goes to speak, I wave my hand. "He is drunk as well—confused. I've got it handled."

I push past them both and disappear back into the crowd.

CHAPTER SIX

e are in a new line, the seven of us—the oldest of us has had nineteen summers, and the youngest, me, only sixteen. Any of the offerlings younger than me are dispersed among the businesses in need of extra hands. On the sidelines, the talas stand, arms full of white shifts for us to wear once the ceremony begins.

I stand here, swathed in gray as the masked hunters and huntresses survey me with predatory intent. Their smiles do nothing to ease my thundering anxiety. I press a hand firmly against my stomach to still the rising nausea. Their eyes speak of promises I don't want to make—am not ready to make. Each brush of their hands—some gloved, some uncovered—leaves a festering sting in its wake.

Not ready.

Mistress Agata had promised that I would be free, would be able to take Weylin and go. Just one more night. One more game...

"Elskan, what do you want most?"

"To be free."

Her head tilted to the side. Was she considering my words? Truly? "You can be—your lover, too—but at a cost."

"And what is the cost?"

She smiled. "Willingly participate in the Bloodletting. No arguing or resistance."

It was too simple. Too easy of a way out. But I didn't hesitate to agree to her terms.

I try to comfort myself, tell myself there will be no more unwanted touches after tonight, no more being blamed for their lack of control. How I hate their triumphant smiles when I'm reprimanded before them for some incident that is not my fault. How I hate being punished for refusing to submit.

And every one of my cries has gone unanswered—but no longer will I be a victim. I only have to survive tonight, the final test of obedience to the gods of Vodihr. I will obey Agata one last time.

I must.

For me.

For Weylin.

The hunters and huntresses in tonight's sacrificial game walk up and down our line. Our fear makes them preen and strut and grin. They whisper amongst themselves and occasionally to one of us, the Bloodletting's offerlings. They ask for a smile, or to touch our faces to see how soft our skin is. One girl has to undo her braids so a huntress can see how long her hair is.

How degrading it is to be a sacrifice.

To know that after tonight, even with the gods' approvals, they'll become nothing more than pets. Not me. That *won't* be me.

I snag on a pair of brown eyes and wince. But Anik isn't here anymore. He's safe. I made sure of it.

"You left me," he sniffed, his arm around my waist. He was pressing further and further into my side like a frightened child.

"I didn't," I denied, tightening my grip on him when he tripped over a stone on the path. "We are almost there."

"Where?" he breathed. "Home? Did I bring you home, finally?"

Tears slid down my face when the circle appeared a few feet in front of us.

Squirming as another hunter passes by, I dig deeper into the hole in my mind I've created for myself—it is quiet, so quiet. I fiddle with my sleeves to distract myself from the pain in my chest.

Oh, Papa would love to see me now, how I sell myself to escape a world that doesn't even want me.

"I'm sorry, Ru," Anik said in my ear.

"For what?"

"For taking so long."

I remind myself again that he is safe—taken away by the Zila before Keegan found me, dragged me back to the House, and locked me in my room. He hadn't gotten Agata and that still confuses me; I check the crowd for him, but he is not here.

A pair of hunters stops before me, making note of my flaws on the stupid little white cards they were given before the bidding began. The bellflower crowns printed on the backs of the cards mock me as the printed gold lettering flashes in the firelight.

I will not break.

I straighten my spine, hold my head higher, and study them right back, trying to keep my face impassive.

They are fools.

The clearing spins briefly as I adjust my very own crown of bellflowers, the customary symbol of beauty and rebirth. It had been delicately placed on my head right before the blockade opened to admit the hunters and huntresses for the silent auction.

I feel each individual thorn prick of my crown, one digging deep enough to draw blood on the side of my face, though the mess is hidden under my hair. I used to think bellflowers didn't have thorns, but Vodihr's do. Agata's do.

From the corner of my eye, I see a partially formed skuggi, its mouth opening to form a silent cry, its eyes finding mine through the darkness. I blink and she's gone, replaced by a raven that watches from a bare tree branch, its body black and white streaked with silvery-gray.

It is a gift from the gods to see the skuggar and interact with their world, to lift the veil, and to my knowledge, it is one only I and the Other have been given. I could speak to the skuggar. See the memories they shared. The gods had chosen me for something, or maybe they had doomed me from the start.

It wasn't a gift.

It was a curse.

And in Vodihr, only curses survived.

When one of the hunters laughs, I draw back into myself. I crave my fix. I'd only been given some henbane three hours prior, but it is already too long. I fight the urge to shake and fidget.

Little beads of sweat dot my brow. The tang of spice and flowers weighs down my tongue and I swallow.

In and out, breathe.

As Mistress Agata begins to chant, I force a serene expression and bow my head. We have been warned that none of the hunters or huntresses here tonight like boldness in their prey.

Weylin had said—No. No, I can't think about him. Not now.

I bite my lip hard enough to draw blood.

Shadows begin to form around my bare feet, fingers caressing my skin—one grazes a rope burn above my ankle and I hiss.

A huntress pauses in front of me, frowning for a moment before moving on.

It has been whispered amongst the offerlings that some who attend the Bloodletting hold higher positions of power in their respective villages and cities. But I believe the whispers are just childish gossip—a means to get over pre-performance jitters by pretending that being taken by a duke or a marquess makes one worthier and more precious to the gods.

The hunters and huntresses wear identical masks, hold identical cards. And while the quality of their clothing may mark some of them as upper class, the lot of them are nothing more than drug lords, harlots, cheating husbands, shrews, and other creatures of filth.

I notice one of the hunters fumbling to fix his skewed mask and swallow a near-hysterical laugh. Amateur.

The Bloodletting's simple burgundy masks may cloak their identities now, but later, once the ceremony is finished and we are distributed to our highest bidders in secured locations, the masks will come off.

In the end, the hunters and huntresses will reveal themselves as the fakes they truly are—usually in the heat of passion…Or so Weylin has explained.

Weylin.

I flinch again, picturing his face. Where is he?

A masked hunter, a brute of a man, stops to hover in front of me. His callused hand traces my features with eerie familiarity as his breathing grows quicker with excitement. My own breath catches in the back of my throat.

The low thumping of the drum, the watching shadows, and the chatter of the crowd all fade.

My eyes meet umber ones.

"Papa?"

"Whatever you do, don't fight."

"I thought you'd be dead by now," I whisper.

His eyes dilate behind his burgundy mask. His breath holds the scent of spice and my nose twitches. "My lítil stúlka, my little girl is all grown up."

"Five minutes," Agata's voice rings out. "Five minutes until your cards must be returned and the ceremony begins."

I watch as he walks to Agata, their heads close together as they speak. Papa hands her his card, then disappears into the tree line.

CHAPTER SEVEN

óðir, please. Can you read it again?" I begged, holding my doll close to my chest.

She laughed, reaching out to tug the end of my braid. "Ljúfa stelpa, you must sleep. Papa comes home tomorrow."

With a big sigh, I flopped back against the pillows. "I know! But I want to know what happens. You always stop reading before the end. So does Amma."

Her smile was patient but a little strained. She closed the black leather book in her hands, and I caught a whiff of old parchment before she slid from the bed to her feet.

"One day," she whispered to me, "one day you will know the end."

With that, she blew out the candle at my bedside and left the room.

I jerk awake, immediately clawing at my bindings when I can't sit up; kicking and screaming and wailing the more coherent I become. My mouth is dry, and the taste of ash and blood are on my tongue.

I remember standing with the other six offerlings, dancing with them. The pounding of the drums. The crackle of flames. Someone was crying. Someone was screaming.

The slice of a dagger on my palm and the sizzle of my blood landing in the bowl held before me …

And then I remember.

Papa.

"Papa, why are you here?" I whisper, finally stilling. He stands, his face covered by a deer-antlered mask of skull-bone. It's crude, with deep carvings that run over the bleached white. It is the old language—there are symbols even I can't decipher.

I struggle against the bonds that tie my wrists and ankles to the bedposts. My skin stretches and breaks under my movements.

I'm sprawled out, humiliated.

I'm in the House. My designated room.

Where is Weylin? Agata?

There is a sigh before he responds. "Hush."

Then he just stands there and watches me. His eyes are narrowed behind the slits of the mask. His head tilts to the side. "She isn't who I want."

"What?" I yelp when he steps closer to the bed. His collar is undone. His cape is thrown across the chair by the door. "What do you mean?"

"She's dead." He eyes darken as he says this.

"Who is?" He just chuckles, and I begin to struggle against my bindings again. "Papa, who are you talking to?"

His hand comes out and grabs my chin, his wedding band catching my lip and tearing the skin as he jerks my face down.

"I've missed you so much. Why are you fighting me?"

I rear back and spit in his face. "Will you just get it over with already? Stop the game and be done with it," I manage, my voice tight. "I have better things I could be doing with my time than pleasing you."

Like finding Weylin. Demanding of Agata that she keep her word. Leaving …

Dots dance before my eyes, my lip throbbing.

A bead of red slips from Papa's eye and touches the mask. My skin crawls when the mask absorbs it. I swear I can hear a slurp.

I try to fight when a cup is forced to my lips. The metal stings.

Soon there is nothing but the taste of floral on my tongue as the cup moves out of view. A sigh of relief slips out before I can stop it. I nearly melt into the bed; my head fills with static.

"Do you remember our wedding night?" Papa asks, his words almost hesitant. "I was afraid to touch you. Afraid to believe I'd defied the gods."

My head feels too heavy for my neck. It flips backward onto the mattress and my vision fills of wooden rafters. Papa's hand comes to touch my collarbone.

"Þetta er ég. Það er Rune. Papa, takk."

His hand stills at my garbled sentence. My tongue feels too thick for my mouth.

"It's me. It's Rune. Papa, please."

Papa shudders, a moan escaping his lips. When his eyes close, mine do, too.

"Goddric."

We both flinch at the woman's voice.

"Goddric."

I turn to see a shadow, see-through, standing by the window. Her features are unclear, hazy. I blink sweat from my eyes when Papa stifles a sob.

"You're dead."

The shadow nods. Her gray eyes flitter to me and I see her expression soften.

Papa follows her gaze and looks at me.

There is a flicker of light in his eyes. A flash of pain before he rips the mask from his face and flings it into the corner. His hands go to his head, fingers digging into his hair.

"I'm sorry. So sorry."

Before I can reply, he's rushing from the room. I turn my head, coughing.

There is a whisper of movement. A creak of the floorboard and I groan, rolling my head back to rest against the pillow. Through blurred vision, I see the flash of a dagger and shriek, jerking away from the hands coming to grab my wrists. I'm still fighting when a second flash of the dagger breaks the ropes at my feet.

"Rólegur." *Quiet.*

My stomach rolls when I'm tugged to my feet. I sway, swallowing harshly. "What ... ?"

"Rólegur," the Other repeats and I can only stand there, staring at her—at the eyeless holes in her wild face. She shoves the dagger at me, "Hlaupa." *Run.*

"I-I can't," I whimper. My fingers loosely curl to grip the dagger's handle. I see the bright red gem in the handle and blink. How had she gotten this? "This is—"

"Hlaupa!" the Other snaps. She pushes me toward the door.

I'm reaching for the handle when the knob turns and the door slams open and I jump back.

"Weylin?"

CHAPTER EIGHT

eylin, please. Just a little bit further. Anik says his ship is waiting." I'm dragging him at this point, both of us covered in blood and sweat and dirt.

The skuggar are howling, urging me—us—faster, faster as we race through the woods towards the cliff's edge. Everything is a blur of sound and smell, fresh pine at war with stale copper. The Other is back, running with us; a blur among the trees.

"Weylin?"

His reply was a slur, one I couldn't untangle.

I glanced behind me, but the Other was nowhere to be seen. I looked back at Weylin and saw his pupils were dilated, each nearly taking up the whole eye.

"What happened? Weylin?"

He was unresponsive, a leash still clipped to his collar. He slumped towards me—a guard was prodding him forward from the doorway.

"I see she hasn't come for you yet," the guard said.

My feet stumble over a branch and we go down in a tangle of limbs, landing in the stream we've been running beside. I take an elbow to the face before I register what has happened. Bits of rock and shell cut my palms; water is seeping into my boots.

The guard kicked off his boots, reached for his belt. "She always did want you all to herself." He grunted. "Never told us why you were such a special pet."

I'm numb.

Weylin slumped over further and I saw the blood staining his shirt. "What did you do to him?" I snapped.

"I was keeping him entertained—he only killed two this time— making sure he didn't try to come for you." The guard sneered at me.

"You bastard."

He slapped me across the face. I felt blood trickle from my nose. "Such a mouth on you. Maybe that's why Agata wanted you so much."

My nose is bleeding again.

Nearby, Weylin is gagging. Between heaves, I make out the choked sobs. I quickly get to my feet and move to his side. He's shifting, moving from his elbows onto his hands and knees, his stomach forcing him to expel its contents. I'm surprised it's taken him this long to vomit with the amount of henbane and ale that's likely in him.

At my silence, the guard snickered. "Such a shame really, that this is your last night." He nudged Weylin aside, dropping his leash.

My fingers on the dagger's hilt at my side felt tense, ready.

"Weylin … " I place a hand between his shoulder blades and wince at the intense heat that greets my palm. I want to say it'll be okay, that we will make it to the ship and—

A branch snaps above us and the Other reappears, her mouth open, a flash of teeth. Whatever she first says is lost to the shouts that fill my ears. She points forward, trying again.

Hurry.

Hurry.

The Other stepped from the shadows that had cloaked her so well. I was sure she'd gone out the window, but no. She had not left me.

The guard's eyes went wide at her appearance, his mouth opening to shout. Using her as a distraction, I stabbed him in the shoulder with the dagger, then kicked him in the groin.

He crumpled at my feet, the air gone out of him.

I grabbed Weylin's leash and yanked him from the room.

My hands grasp Weylin's shoulders and I tug him backward and up to his feet. Water sloshes around us.

Blood smears across my skin as he turns, angling his body to face me, his hand fumbling to cup my cheek. His lip is split. The bruise around his right eye is darkening with each slow blink.

We made it to the stairs when Keegan opened the door to one of the rooms. He took in my appearance, then Weylin's.

From my room, the guard was heard cursing through his moans.

I gripped the dagger in my hand tighter. If he yelled for Agata …

"Leave without me."

I bite back a sob. "Never."

And then I'm urging him to run.

Again the trees become a blur, the air thick as mud. I hear the breaking of twigs, the crunch of decaying leaves, catch a faint glimpse of the Other as she follows us while we slosh through the water. The shadows' whispers are becoming fainter—whether that is good or bad, I don't have time to think about.

Soon the cliff is in sight and I drag him up the small slope that lies between us and the edge of the forest.

Close, so close.

I jerk at the sudden stinging in my side. My hand finding the wound, I can feel metal in the puckered skin, the arrowhead buried deep beneath. Agata had never intended to keep her promise. Even if I'd behaved perfectly, she still wouldn't have let us leave.

"Rune—"

Weylin slips and I tug him up. "Keep moving, Anik said he'd be waiting."

One breath. Two.

Together we break through the tree line at last. I waste one second hesitating, one breath on a crazed laugh.

I look at him, taking in the bruises, the blood and sweat. "Kysstu mig." *Kiss me.*

He does, and I move us to perch on the cliff's edge; we watch rock and dirt fall and fall. I count the seconds.

I'm hesitating, wasting more time. The shouts of the guards are getting closer and yet I can't bring myself to—

There is a rush of air behind me, a hard blow landing between my shoulder blades.

My feet leave the ground, Weylin with me, and we are freefalling into the waiting sea below.

From the cliff's edge, the Other stands, her hands still outstretched.

"Megi guðirnir gleyma þér."

May the gods forget you.

Her words haunt me as I fall—something keens in the distance.

~~BROTINN~~

FRACTURED

CHAPTER NINE

Three years later.

"What can I get you?" I ask, covering my mouth to hide a yawn. I look in disinterest at another drunk, just one of many tonight.

The earlier crowd has long since dispersed outside where acts of the Revelry continue to ensnare Arden's people. This means it is just reaching the time when I no longer care about proper manners and barmaid etiquette. I have seen too many costumes, heard too many crooning liars, to care if I make that extra coin or two from tips. Hensley owes me for this big time anyway.

Birgir is still asleep at my feet but I see his ears twitching at the sound of my voice. Affectionately, I nudge the wolf with the toe of my boot, causing him to chuff in annoyance before stretching and settling again.

At the lack of an immediate response from the patron barely managing to stay upright in front of me, I smirk and go back to methodically wiping mugs clean. If he isn't ready to order, I'm not going to pretend to be interested.

There is a rather nasally laugh then that makes my skin crawl. The patron teeters forward to lean on the bar between us, his eyes on my chest. "Honey, you can give me anything you want."

"'Anything you want?' I can't say I know a drink by that name," I reply. My hand curls into a fist around the cloth I am using. "Perhaps I can get you something else." I give him a half-second to respond before dismissing him, shifting to fill up a regular's drink who has had to shoulder the drunk man aside.

Slavin, known as 'Vin' to the tavern employees and locals, eyes me with brief concern. I hand him back his drink and shake my head. The scars on Vin's face wink at me when he smiles. He waggles his eyebrows at the drunk's back, and I snicker, waving him away.

I briefly entertain the idea of splashing this drunk with the bucket of cleaning water behind the counter, but the last time I did that, my boss, Hensley, had cursed so loud and so long that my ears rang a solid hour after his lecture. It isn't my fault some men are just disgusting, especially this one; he has yet to even look me in the face.

Birgir brushes against my leg. He has shifted to lay facing the bar with his head tilted up.

I paste on a smile, leaning my hip against the counter. My position change causes the drunk to groan at the now-unsatisfactory view of my cleavage. The pathetic dullard looks annoyed at being unable to see down my low-cut corset—a torture device I despise but that Hensley forces me to wear every shift without fail.

Wheezing with sudden laughter, he finally looks at my face.

"Whatever you say. Just give me something nice." His shirt has ridden up a bit so his girth hits the counter with a nauseating splat when he leans closer. He's trying to get a better look at my breasts again. "Maybe you could give me—"

I slam a mug of ale down in front of him before he can finish. He goes glassy-eyed as he grabs it up, his hat flopping down to cover his face; he's only a coin away from passing out.

With a drawn-out gulp of appreciation, the glass clanks back down, his dirty hand wiping his chapped lips dry.

"Another one?" His sickly yellow Revelry mask slips the more he smacks his lips.

From the back doorway, Hensley appears. He scans the room and rolls his kohl-lined eyes when his gaze finds mine and he sees the mess I'm having to deal with. I just shrug.

Other barmaids would have cut this patron off and sent him packing by now, but I really don't care what happens to him after he walks out The Wild Rose's doors. All that matters is the coin.

"Elskan—darling—it is always about the coin. You please them, you do whatever they want. But never let them walk away without getting your due."

"I-I want to go home."

"Unfortunately, your debt has yet to be paid."

I shudder at the memory, paling as phantom silk hands cup my own, nails biting into my palms as she turns with a flourish, leading me to the red-painted door at the end of the hall.

The hallway stank of incense and sweat. From the doors we passed, sounds of pain and pleasure mixed together to the point I couldn't tell the difference anymore.

I caught a flash of dirty blonde hair up ahead.

I produce a second mug of amber liquid, nearly breaking it as I slam it down. The patron hoots with glee.

"Here you go, sæti." I cough. "Cutie." It doesn't matter; he isn't paying attention. Even if he had been, he is already far too drunk to care what tongue I am using. The new world order is just as vile as the old, even if the new one considers the old one to be taboo.

I pull back quickly as dirty hands brush against my fingertips when he reaches for the glass, and I bite down hard on my lip in revulsion. I hate being touched.

"Touching is part of the game, elskan. Let them."

This mug of ale disappears as quickly as the last. I try to stay in the moment, no matter how unsavory it is, but this persistent memory keeps tugging at my consciousness. I can feel the scratch-iness of the sheet, taste the floral and spice on my tongue. Feel pain as they place the thorny bellflower crown on my head.

From beneath the bar, Birgir whines. I nudge him with my foot to calm him … and myself.

The man sucks back the last dregs of his drink, belches loudly, and then promptly face-plants into the bar. I motion for the city guard posted by the door and he dutifully starts making his way over. The drunkard's snores have me rolling my eyes; I shove him to the side and wipe up his drool with a rag.

Only three more hours of this until I can go home.

Nearby, Vin and his buddies chortle. Sticking my tongue out at them, I catch sight of Hensley making his way upstairs to his private quarters with a vision in teal at his side; his hand is wandering lower as they climb and a giggle reaches my ears.

I forced a giggle, "Stop, that tickles!"

The man smirks, stroking lower. His teal sleeve is bright against the dark sheets.

I reach down to stroke Birgir's back, my fingers curling in his coarse top layer of fur.

***

Slipping out The Wild Rose's back door with several empty bottles in my arms, I take my first full breath of fresh air in hours … only to choke on the stink of incense. I snort a cough. Here I am, trying to escape the smoke-filled, sex-tarnished interior of The Wild Rose, only to enter a smoke-filled, sex-tarnished alleyway.

"Perfect," I mutter; Birgir huffs at my side as he pushes by.

Dumping the bottles into the overflowing basket by the door, I close my eyes and rest against the cool stone wall.

Everything hurts, from the balls of my feet to the tips of my fingers.

Rune.

Rune, come and play.

I watch two shadows form near the base of the building across the alley. Their fingers are little more than wisps, still mostly un-formed. Their threads unravel, spooling around Birgir's paws as he walks through them unfazed, though he knows they're there.

"Papa, what are the skuggar?" I asked, my gaze on one that was wandering through the trees.

"Shadows are just shadows, Rune."

"No, they aren't."

Papa turned to face me. I could tell by his expression he was surprised at my tone. He hesitated. "They … are shadows that no one can see—should see."

"I see them."

He hung his head. "I know."

At the sound of approaching footsteps, the threads recede. I press myself against the wall, half-wedged between the Rose's door and the alleyway arch. Birgir moves his bulk to my right side, his fur prickling through my skirt.

My confidence wavers for a second and I bury one of my hands in the raised hackles of Birgir's neck. Grounded again, I peer out into the darkness to find a drunkard taking a piss just a few feet away.

He is singing as he makes his way back into the Revelry's crowd. There is a shout of glee, a roar of triumph, and I tumble into the past again as the scent of urine assaults my nose.

"Rune, are you okay?"

I sniffed, burrowing further into the blanket I had wrapped around my shoulders. I took a deep inhale of earth, grass, and sweat before tilting my head back to look up at the stars. They winked at me, cold and bright and so far out of reach. I ached to touch one, to hold it and be reminded they weren't always infinite—stars die too. Stars can be trapped too.

"No," I finally answered, looking to see Weylin standing there with his Revelry mask hanging at his side. His costume was bright red and so at odds with the darkness inking his blue eyes.

I was humiliated.

Defeated.

The smell of urine teased my nose, another whiff of my disgrace.

In the distance, I could hear the returning Revelry performers' crows of joy.

~~AÐ UPPSKERA~~
TO BE REAPED

The scent of death hangs heavy in the air, suffocating them with such pleasure it makes them shiver. Panting heavily, muscles tremble in victory; a kill had been their prize from the beginning.

Disappointing, a voice whispers in their mind.

They sit back, looking at the corpse with bloodshot eyes, and suddenly feel … dismay, so at odds with the lingering shivers of ecstasy. The mask—the voice that speaks to them—is right. It *is* too neat, too tidy. There is no blood, no chaos, nothing to leave a lasting impression. This isn't as satisfying as the others had been.

"L-L … " A small voice tries to speak before devolving into whimpers.

"Shut up," Reaper snaps, not bothering to look in the small voice's direction. The bone mask seems to tighten on their face.

Criticisms form on the back of their tongue now, one being the most aggressive: *too neat.*

Violet eyes wide open, unseeing and unfeeling at a caress on the cheek. Those eyes would only remember a smile of satisfaction before the kiss of a needle touched the skin above her heart.

Their orders were, *'Don't make a scene, take the prince and return—quickly.'*

Still, it is theirs: a kill is a kill.

The mask always whispers for a kill.

The child's choked cry interrupts the Reaper's giggle, denying them their not-yet-reached physical release.

Shame, comes the voice again as the mask continues its mocking, the voice further whispering that their Mistress—no, the gods—are not fully pleased with this kill.

"The boy will make up for it," Reaper mutters. "The boy is to be reaped, the Mistress said so."

Disgruntled, they still waste a moment to tenderly brush a piece of corn-yellow hair aside, a piece that had stubbornly stuck itself to the dead maid's lips. Her death still means success, even if it is only a small part of the game being played.

Soon. Soon, the Mistress will no longer think I'm a fool.

Still a fool, the voice chimed in.

Annoyed by the taunt, Reaper commands the boy, "Come."

The boy—the youngest prince of Arden—continues to cower away from the body of his dead nursemaid. Why this child of eight didn't just run still perplexes Reaper—so naïve, so innocent. So very like a young girl from their past.

"I'm afraid to touch her."

A laugh was followed by a soft reassurance. "Don't be, she won't break."

Reaper jumps to their feet, barely able to muffle their cry as whispers of memory breach their reality and assail them.

"She looks just like—"

"She isn't."

The child whimpers, burying his face deeper into his palms, a gold mask forgotten at his feet.

Too slow, the voice reprimands.

Reaper straightens their own mask before picking up the boy's from the ground. The prince's gold mask, rich in texture and detail, is placed back on to hide his distress and his distinctive royal face.

"Come." They yank the prince into their arms. The boy's struggling is weak, but still enough to make Reaper stagger. A blow to the boy's head stills him.

Pausing at the alleyway's entrance, the scent of sea beckons to Reaper.

You're forgetting again, the voice says dryly.

With reverence, a simple white card with a thorned bellflower crown blazing on the front is placed between the dead nursemaid's hands. The bold burgundy emblem causes another delightful shiver to streak down the killer's spine. Next come the flowers, put on display on the windowsill above the body.

Too slow.

With one last look spared, Reaper and the unconscious young prince disappear into the Revelry's crowd of masks.

CHAPTER TEN

une.

Come play.

Disoriented by the shadows dancing at my feet and crawling up my legs, I watch as Birgir joins in with their playing, nipping at the threads between his claws and growling when one darts away.

Turning, I take in the distant glimmer of the sea before eyeing a crowd of masks that only the Revelry can produce. I can't control the shiver of fear.

Is she here?

Had she come for me after all this time?

The lost pet that had wandered too far …

A woman from the crowd laughs and comes closer and I shift back, moving further into the alley's dark embrace. The woman's mask drops glitter to the ground below as she dances for a growing audience of jesters, wolves, foxes, clowns … There are so many different designs this year.

My mask last year had been the worst; bleached-white satin lined with lace that caged my entire face. The rash lasted for three days. Thankfully, I talked Hensely out of making me wear one this year.

Another laugh from the street pulls me back from the brink of madness. I barely register my shaking hands or the wheeze of my breathing.

Focus, Rune. Focus.

Will it always be like this? Will I never escape my memories of Vodihr? I fear the answer. The Revelry is celebrated everywhere, and with the Revelry comes my past.

Once a year, the Revelry's caravans come by sea from Vodihr to entertain the kingdom. It is an agreement between Vodihr and all the cities and villages of Riki Skugga, but Utlen's port city, Arden, is a favored spot for the performances—they have the best of the best from drink to wealth to sacrifices.

The only requirement of the event: masks. Some are intricate and beautifully made. Some are hand-crafted to be ugly or terrifying. Some are simply potato sacks with holes cut for the eyes. Regardless of the style, there is a mask for every person, from the beggar seeking coin to the nobleman with his nose buried in ale and flesh.

The capitol city dances the night away under the pretense no one will remember anything in the morning.

"Why must they wear these?" I asked, my hands full of masks of all sizes, shapes, and colors. I knew I shouldn't have when I saw her eyes flash.

"The mask is meant to keep private the patron's identity. It is all part of the game, elskan."

I sidestep the puddle of piss near my boot, my nose wrinkling until Birgir's muzzle probes my knee. I roll my eyes at his next nudge, gripping the sleeves of my blouse, pulling at the fraying edges. I need to get home before—

"But why?"

"Because no one can know who they are." Her smile was as sharp as her words.

"It's all part of the game," someone repeated from behind me. I fought to keep from smiling as I turned toward him.

⚜

I am almost home when a scream disturbs the Revelry's final song. The crowd pauses and I find myself stuck between the performers and prostitutes and townspeople. Keeping my head down, I push past sweaty bodies as tension heats the smoke-hazed atmosphere.

And the whispers of speculation begin: Angry lover? Shrew of a mother? A discovery of something missing? Theft on the night of Revelry, whether it be an item or coin or person, is by no means uncommon.

Birgir dodges a scrambling crow-masked woman as she jumps toward the nearest booth. A man selling ale frowns when she trips over her own feet and jostles one of his jugs. She giggles at his glare, adjusting her corset before belching.

When she turns a greenish hue, I grab Birgir's scuff—ignoring his snap—and give him a quick tug to return to the path.

I breathe a sigh of relief when my boots touch the pebbled

path that leads down to the docks, branching off then to a rougher path that follows the shoreline to where my cottage resides.

"Should I finally break open the mead or maybe we can—"

My words falter when a touch ghosts across my shoulder. I snarl, thinking it is a shadow determined to get my attention, but instead I see the edges of a cloak, a flash of gold. A figure hurries off into the darkness, their cloak's hood pulled down low. They look to be carrying something heavy. Perhaps supplies for a ship?

Birgir growls, positioning himself in front of me, his hackles raised. I catch a musky scent that's vaguely recognizable, yet foreign all at once. I can't see anything save for the flicker of lights on the water and soon the sting of the salt in the air blurs my vision.

Perhaps I should return to taking my tonic … Perhaps old demons are too close to home and I'm seeing things again. Maybe I really am sick and need it—Anik still urges me to take it whenever I complain of memories that aren't my own. But it's been three years since I stopped making the tonic I can no longer find the ingredients for.

A child's wail comes from among the creaking of the wooden docks and the lapping of waves.

My shoulders hunch all the way to my cottage door.

CHAPTER ELEVEN

I t was the nursemaid from the castle."

"She was poisoned."

Someone snorts. "Nay, she was caught up in a bout of feminine ... uh ... hysteria."

"Nay! She was killed by ... a ghost dagger."

"A ghost dagger? Are you serious? Vin, you old dullard! You need your head examined."

A smile comes and goes from my face as I listen to the mindless chatter of The Wild Rose's morning regulars. It makes marking the daily stock counts for Hensley less tedious.

"I do not! The card was there. The one with—"

A hand enters my field of vision, tugging away the papers I'm holding with persistence. The charcoal smears on the last number I'd just written, but my swear is drowned out by: "Rune, we need to talk."

Twirling the charcoal piece in my hand, I take in his black

attire, the lingering scent of oil and sea salt. "Anik, to what do I owe the pleasure? It is past your bedtime, after all."

"Ru. Not now."

My hand's movements still, the charcoal dropping to the bar top. My brother's face is gaunt, lacking its usual devilish smile.

"Ru. Not now."

"But Anik, you said that hours ago. You promised to play with me if I stayed quiet." I nudged my brother, trying to peer over his shoulder at the project he had been hiding all morning. "Anik, you said—"

"Shut her up before I do, boy."

I tensed. Papa was swaying in the doorway, the sun falling across his slumped posture. "Papa."

"Ru?"

My eyes squint against the glare coming through the Rose's dirty, streaked windows, I'd have to clean them later.

My brother's hand curled around my wrist, giving it a squeeze of reassurance when Papa stepped closer.

When my brother clears his throat, I become aware then that one of my hands is gripping the other's wrist. Embarrassed, my cheeks flush and I let my hands fall to rest against the bar top.

"Goddric, come taste the stew. It's almost done," Mama called from the other room.

The tension remained. Papa looked at me, his eyes narrowed, and I braced myself for a slap, but instead he reached over my shoulder and snatched a tiny wooden ship from the table. I watched as he studied it, turning the carved figure in his hand.

"A replica of an Arden trading vessel?"

I felt Anik flinch beside me. "Yes, but I just—"

Papa slammed the ship onto the table.

As little pieces broke off and fell to the floor, I got angry for Anik and pressed closer to his side, protective, defensive. "Papa, that wasn't—"

"The Hel with it," he slurred at me, pointing his finger in my face, then Anik's. "Take your sister and get out of my sight."

I wanted to protest but felt Anik's hand give my wrist another squeeze. He tugged me past Papa and out into the late afternoon sun.

"He didn't mean it."

"He never does," I whispered.

A firm weight leaning against my right leg has me sucking in a breath. "Did you say something?"

Anik studies me, his hand partway across the worn wood to grab mine. I shake my head, eyes narrowed in warning. He waits a second longer before leaning back and taking a seat at the counter.

An awkward pause starts, then lengthens—one that has me gritting my teeth. "I don't have time for—"

He stops playing with the silver ring on his thumb. "You've heard the latest, I'm assuming?"

I blink at the oddness of his words but shrug. "The old sea birds over there filled me in." I motion to the rowdy table of haggard fishermen that are already sloshed from spiked coffee. "Just another castle servant that got too carried away in the Revelry. It's happened before and it'll happen again."

"Us old sea birds have ears, Miss Rune. Be kind to us!"

"Love you too, Vin." I blow him a kiss that has the others around him cackling.

My brother's stool creaks, his hands stilling their nervous fidgeting as he shifts closer. "Rune, it wasn't an accident."

I run a hand over my hair, noticing my braid is already coming undone. "Don't start in with your merpeople theory again, Anik. I didn't believe you then and I—"

"She was the nursemaid for Prince Larken." He pauses, his eyes darkening. "Who's missing."

I debate how to respond. Something is wrong; a familiar ring of warning murmurs in my ears. The shadows who've been sleeping in the corner begin to stir, to creep closer.

Anik reaches forward, his face grim as he takes hold of my hand. He tugs the material on his palm down. "Just watch."

When our eyes meet, a single light teal thread seeps from a scabbing cut on his palm and tightens around my skin.

Blocking out the innkeepers fretting and the weeping of the maid, he moved to study the victim. One of the guards shook his head but said nothing when Anik poked the body with his foot.

"Anik, what are you doing?" another guard asked. Someone elbowed the guard and he grunted.

"Can't you tell? He's snooping again. It's probably one of his crew who went out for a night of fun. Or maybe he lost a bet, had to check out the body without throwing up."

Anik ignored them, entranced by the girl's wide violet eyes that gave nothing away. He assessed the oddly neat area of dirt the girl laid on, the bright flower display on the windowsill above her head, and of course, the girl herself.

He cursed, taking in the torn lace of her corset. He reached out to reveal a small "x" hidden among a bellflower with thorns, a tattoo above her left breast.

He felt his gut sink.

As he stood back up, a third guard stepped up to intercept him, taking in the pallor of his face. "Is it … ?" she started to ask, only to fall silent at the glare he gave her.

Looking exhausted and grim, the king's healer appeared and shooed Anik and the guards out of the way. Kneeling, letting her satchel rest on her knee, the healer took hold of the small white card inside the girl's curled hands. There was a moment's hesitation before she put it aside. Even the poor yellowed light of the guards' lanterns was not dim enough to conceal the recognition on the healer's face.

Anik watched as she forced herself to take a deep breath and look back at the body, her shoulders tense.

"There looks to be no evidence of a struggle. Though, look at her nails, perhaps she clawed her attacker … " She scrambled for a piece of charcoal before beginning to scribble down notes.

Meanwhile, knowledge of the card had already travelled down the alley. The innkeeper and maid weren't of much help, and the guards were growing restless—Anik grew restless, too, as the minutes slowly passed.

His hands clenched, unclenched, clenched at his sides. The repetition caused the cut on his palm to reopen.

The healer turned her attention back to the card. Flipping it over, she took in the thorny bellflower crown boldly embossed in burgundy on the front. Her hands shook as she flipped it back over again, and Anik peered over her shoulder at the cursive words written there:

All debts must be paid in blood and sorrow to the god who waits.

Guilt hardened Anik's features. Gael had arrived at dawn, frantic, looking for his brother. Surprised at his appearance, Anik had cut his palm while sharpening his blade. Standing up to intercept him on the docks, Anik had told him to wait on the ship, that he'd go look in town. Now that he knew what had happened, he wasn't sure how he was going to tell Gael.

"We're going to have to think of something to tell the king," the healer spoke, her voice low. She glanced at Anik, who had unconsciously kneeled by her side at some point.

"What's going on?" a voice demanded from the alley's entrance.

Anik jumped to his feet, his expression twisting as he watched the emotions flitter across Arden's eldest prince's face: shock at the sight of the dead woman, followed quickly by anguish. His eyes frantically swept what little of the alley was visible.

"Where is he?"

Silence. Confusion.

A guard coughed. "Who?"

"My brother."

I rip my hand away, the lone teal thread dropping across the wood. "You promised you wouldn't do that anymore."

"I had to, you needed to see—"

"No, I didn't."

The shadows are motionless, hovering by my knees. One covers Birgir as he watches me, golden eyes unblinking through the threads that hang in his face.

"That's unfortunate," I say then, my throat tight. I can still see the prince's panic, the warring emotions on my brother's face.

And the girl—the girl with a matching mark.

Anik scoffs, tugging his piece of haphazard bandaging back into place. "An understatement. The royal family is frantic."

"I wouldn't know how that feels, no one came looking for me." I want to take the words back as soon as they leave my lips.

Any color left in Anik's tan face drains away, and his work-worn fingers curl into fists on the bar.

He *did* look for me, for years, and eventually he found me—brought me here.

"I-I'm sorry. I didn't mean … " The rest of the apology won't come.

More silence until he sighs. "I need a favor, Ru."

Now it's my turn to scoff to cover my building fear. I hunch my shoulders, tugging my corset just a bit higher to cover my chest more. I see Anik's eyes cut to the top of the corset's lace fringe.

"They marked you?" he asked, his eyes darkening when he saw the little 'x' on my skin among the thorned flowers.

My cheeks flushed in embarrassment, in anger. I tugged up my corset, snapping, "Of course, how else are they supposed to keep track of their pets?"

"Ru?"

"What is this favor?" My words are strained under the weight of his stare. It's only when I reach to clean a nearby glass that he finally looks away from my mark, back up at my face.

"I need you to take me there—to Wraith—or Vodihr, I mean."

The glass shatters.

A red-painted smirk. A thumping headboard. A whip falling on already-ruined skin.

The shadows wail, or maybe it's me.

Vodihr.

CHAPTER TWELVE

eylin.

I flinched, picturing his face. Where was he?

A masked hunter, a brute of a man, stopped to hover in front of me. His callused hand traced my features with eerie familiarity as his breathing grew quicker with excitement. My own breath caught in the back of my throat.

The low thumping of the drum, the watching shadows, and the whispers fading away into nothing.

My eyes met umber ones.

"Papa."

I wake up choking on a scream of terror. Half-wild, I spring up, my frantic hands moving over my body. I can still feel calloused fingers around my jaw.

"Whatever you do, don't fight."

I cry out as a shadow's hand touches my ankle, still kicking at it even after it moves away. Then a low whine gets my attention.

I turn to see Birgir's watchful golden gaze at the end of the bed. He's laying on his stomach, his ears twitching at my panicked breathing.

"I thought you'd be dead by now," I whispered.

"My little girl is all grown up."

I laugh, feeling the sting of tears. At least the madness is ebbing, the shadows retreating further to watch from the fireplace and the cracks in the floorboards.

"It's okay."

I'm not sure who I am reassuring: myself, Birgir, or the skuggar. I run a hand through my sweat-soaked hair, cringing at the snares and tangles of small braids. I should've known the nightmares would come. Should've prepared a tonic to prevent them. They always get worse during Revelry. The memories do, too.

Birgir clearly doesn't believe my empty reassurances, if his drawn-out sigh is any indication. Hel, I don't even believe myself. My chewed-down nails are digging jagged crescents into my palms.

This is all Anik's fault.

I toss aside my threadbare sheets—they'd need to be washed today—and stretch. Mid-stretch, I hear the wind chime I'd placed along the path to my cottage ring out. A moment later comes the sound of footsteps.

Any greeting or threat I had been about to yell out fades as I catch a glimpse of myself in the sea-glass mirror Anik had given me for my birthday two years ago; it had been my only possession for the longest time and it was one I still cherished.

Throat tight, my reflection mocks me the longer I sit there staring. There is the ever-present purple under my eyes, smudges that tell everyone I rarely sleep between my nightmares and my long shifts at The Wild Rose.

"Elskan, I can help you sleep. Do you trust me?"

There are wrinkles from frown lines and a single dimple that winks on the rare occasion I laugh—I can see it now if I squint hard enough. And then there are scars, semi-hidden at my hairline, inflicted by thorns I still can't escape from …

The cottage door shudders under the bang of a fist, little specks of paint falling from the already-cracked wood. Lovely.

My reflection grimaces, looking ancient and worn, pale skin sickly against the long mass of black curls that hangs below my shoulders, teasing the line of my waist. I should cut it.

"A caller complained of your hair again, saying he had gotten more in his mouth than what pleased him."

I scoffed at Keegan's chuckle. "Well he requested it down, and he was a biter. So, it was his fault, not mine."

"You should just cut it."

"No."

Keegan's eyes narrowed before he shook his head. He stretched out a hand to touch my hair. "Nevermind. Your lover likes it this way, I bet. Likes to pull and tug and—"

"Shut up."

I hunch into myself, the shadow rushing to cover my legs, tangling me in threads emitting love and warmth, reminding me I'm not there, that I am safe.

I look tired.

I am tired.

But is this woman really me? Am I the gaunt figure in the sea glass? Have I really gotten to this point?

"Rune."

I tense as the door swings open. "Oh yes, please come in. How rude of me to not answer." At his silence, I turn to look at him. "Anik, I really don't want to see you right now. I understand that the young prince has been taken, but that isn't my problem, and you can't just barge in … " I blink against the morning light.

It couldn't be. He had left. He had returned home to his tribe, his family.

He … was standing in the doorway beside my brother.

"Weylin."

CHAPTER THIRTEEN

Well ...fate strikes again," I muttered to myself. *Was it really too much to ask for, having a nice, quiet day of filching at the market?*

Three men, two of whom were guards, had wandered in from the end of the street, coming to a stop right in front of the baker's stall I had been about to snatch a meat pie from.

Muffling a curse, I watched as the third man—well, really just a boy, probably no more than three summers older than myself—had his arm seized by one of the guards. The boy gave the guard a harassed look, and I noticed his eyes dilate. Mesmerizing. Was it possible for eyes to be that pale a blue?

I could just make out the play of emotions across his face before his expression settled into one of friendliness. He yanked his arm away.

Shifting back into the safety of the alleyway, I debated whether or not to slip back the way I had come. This wasn't my fight.

My stomach growled in protest.

I just wanted a meat pie. Mistress Agata had started the fasting for the Bloodletting and we were all being made to suffer, even though I should've been allowed to take my meals still. I wasn't yet of age to partake in the sacrifice. At fourteen, I still had two years to go.

Lucky me.

The boy casually slipped his hand underneath the folds of his fur-trimmed cloak. "I'm waiting for my elskhugi, my lover. She's late as usual." Smiling like he was letting them in on a joke, he continued, "She takes forever. I swear, one night I had to wait two hours just for her to pick out a dress and do her braids."

Typical of any of the girls under Agata's care.

I barely managed to cover a sound of amusement.

"Yeah, the women do like to worry about their appearances," one of the guards agreed. He cast a meaningful glance at his fellow guard, a bald man with a unibrow. In unison, both guards stepped forward. "Perhaps when she arrives, we can keep her occupied for you." Letting the offer sink in, his voice then lowered to a fake whisper, "I love it when they scream."

I stopped myself from removing the dagger I had stolen from one of Imire's callers and instead imagined aiming the tip at the guard's—I gritted my teeth, hard.

The skuggi that had been watching from over my shoulder moaned at me as I stepped into view.

"There you are. I have been looking all over for you. You didn't wait for me at the house." Keeping my tone light and chiding, my hand came to rest upon the boy's arm. Craning my neck to look at him—for even in my borrowed boots, he towered over me—I waited. When he did glance down, I kept my face neutral.

Silently, I begged him to play along. There would be Hel to pay if he screwed this up now. Despite the muscle I was feeling under his shirt, I didn't think we'd be a match for two armed guards.

Thankfully, he got the message. Though his eyes were still constricted with rage—and oddly streaked through with red?—outwardly, he relaxed. I was caught off guard when he pulled me against his side and placed a soft kiss on my forehead. My skin crawled at the feel of a stranger's lips on my skin.

"Took you long enough." Pausing, his gaze slowly surveyed my attire, taking in the faded cloak, the visibly worn blouse and skirt, the scuffed boots too large for my feet. Laughter flickered in his eyes. "But you do know exactly how to please me, elskhugi."

I managed a tiny smile, tried for a casual shrug. While the guards exchanged a confused glance, I risked a solid elbow to the boy's midsection. Even though my elbow felt sore from it, I took great satisfaction in the resulting "oomph."

To cover his reaction, and mine, I laughed loudly. "Maybe I was hoping you would forget your city business for tonight if I took long enough and … " I licked my lips and raised an eyebrow, something I had seen the others do time and time again before they disappeared behind their marked red doors.

As the silence grew and the still-watching skuggi inched closer, I began to question my mental stability.

"Well, gentleman, you can see that my plans for the evening have changed. It would seem I'm needed for the night." Giving them a wolfish smile, he maneuvered me to be slightly hidden behind his lanky form.

Suspicious, I caught the flash of amusement in his eyes right before he turned and slid his hand down dangerously close to my arse. When I looked up to protest, his lips came down on mine.

Pulling back quickly, I glared. Perhaps he needed another elbow but lower this time.

"Isn't she a little young for you?"

"Not for me, but definitely for you," was the boy's retort.

One of the guards growled.

There was a raven's caw before everything went to Hel. I was pushed aside as one of the guards leapt forward. Wincing as my fake lover rocked back from a blow to his jaw, I scrambled to my feet, ducking under the other guard's arm as he reached for me.

Pushed forward by his own girth, his balance was thrown off and I kicked him in the gut. I fumbled for my dagger.

"They really need to teach you guys better," I mocked. "Maybe a diet would do you some good, too. Just go to Mistress Agata's, she is all about the starving."

The guard blanched at Agata's name; I knew he would. Using this distraction, I lashed out again, clipping his jaw with a malformed fist. I groaned at the crunch of my fingers, cradling my hand to my chest.

I rallied and was aiming for a groin shot when I was yanked away and dragged running through the market, stalls whipping by in a blur.

"What the Hel—" A hand covered my mouth. I was pressed back into the alley's entrance and up against a wall.

The sounds of labored breathing and footsteps rushed past seconds later. I let out a breath I hadn't known I was holding and waited for the boy's calloused hand to drop away. When it did, I merely raised my eyebrows in question.

The boy fumbled, his blue eyes a little cloudy still with adrenaline and hints of red. "Uh ... hi."

"Hi," I greeted, right before kneeing him and sprinting away. The skuggi who'd followed us cackled.

CHAPTER FOURTEEN

The memory of when I first met Weylin makes me want to laugh, and that makes me angry.

I had been young and stupid; Weylin was three years older and so much more intriguing than what Vodihr usually had to offer in the way of young men. He'd been taken from his tribe and was a new arrival to Vodihr as a Bloodletting sacrifice. Since the boys and girls were kept separate by Agata prior to their Bloodletting, with the boys living in another house in an entirely different part of the village, it was only by pure chance I had met him that day.

The anger turns to a throbbing ache as I take in his familiar features—defined jaw, pale eyes, tanned skin. But I prefer the anger. "Just stopping by out of the goodness of your heart or did you want something, too?"

Weylin's mouth parts, surprise flaring in his eyes. Had he just expected me to fling myself at him in gratitude for returning?

"Rune, let me—"

I hold up a hand as Anik begins to speak. "No wait, let me guess." I look at Weylin. "My dear bróðir told you about the young prince's kidnapping and you rushed here to be the willing volunteer to take them back to Vodihr." I purse my lips. "But that isn't right either, since you should be a sea's distance away with your tribe. Which means you were either here and didn't bother to stop by or … "

My vision grays. One breath. Two. I nearly wheeze on the third as panic edges in. They both move forward, but I jump back, tripping over Birgir who lingers by my legs. "Get out."

"Rune, would you just let me explain—"

I glare at Anik, outrage coloring my cheeks. "Get. Out."

Without thinking, I step forward and place a hand on both of their chests. My intent had been to shove both of them out the door and onto their arses. Instead, I shudder at the familiar warmth of Weylin's chest under my right hand. My fingers curl around a leather cord partially hidden by a coarse wool shirt. If I move my fingers, if I tug the shirt a little lower, I'd see it— Vodihr's mark.

Pale blue eyes meet mine, hard and unreadable.

His skin continued to leach of color; he gagged, pink water bubbling at the corners of his lips.

"Stay with me," I whispered. "I can't lose you."

Someone clears their throat and I jerk away, turning toward the doorway to see a third man standing there. His smirk is a little out of place on his haggard features, but he's trying, I'll give him that.

"Did I miss anything? The guards really weren't happy to be left waiting at the top of the path, but I didn't think we'd all fit into this … lovely little cottage."

Recognition clicks in my mind. "Bloody Hel, Anik," I curse. "You brought Prince Gael here? Are you crazed?"

My idiot brother shrugs. "Well, he wouldn't wait with the guards."

An hour of arguing passes with the occasional joke from Anik, some intense staring from a silent Weylin, and no small amount of hovering by a cluster of anxious guards outside the windows.

I just want to take what's left of my honeyed mead and go back to bed.

"I'm telling you, the best way to get to Wraith is with the *Tempest*."

"No one just *goes* to Vo—to Wraith, Anik. You of all people should know that," I say as I braid my hair again. This is my third attempt and my hands won't quit shaking.

Prince Gael slams a fist onto the table and I flinch, my eyes closing, my hands coming up to protect my face. Just as quickly, I put them down, forcing my back to straighten. When I do, I see that Weylin is crouched in front of where I sit, a thin blade's grip in his fingers.

I shift forward, my fingers hovering over Weylin's nape. I suck in a breath. The scar is barely visible beneath the longer strands of hair.

His gaze was on me as I made my rounds, stopping to smile or laugh at appropriate times, or flirt when a caller showed more than a brief glance of interest. Whenever I turned, he faked disinterest and murmured to the woman on his right. His face was set in a frown, his eyes narrowed as they swept the crowd almost restlessly.

With the next caller, I stayed a little bit longer than necessary, running my hand down the man's arm before moving towards the doorway, my tray empty and my nerves smarting.

I stopped to hover in the frame before darting to the kitchen.

Seconds later, when a hand wrapped around mine and I was tugged into a corner, I went willingly, my head falling back, a smile already on my lips.

"Not much longer till this party is over."

At my silence, Weylin took the tray from my hands and hastily set it on a nearby counter.

"You seem to be enjoying yourself." My words were cruel, a little jealous.

He just leaned in and pressed his lips against mine.

My hands trailed up his chest, stopping at his neck. I wrapped my fingers in the loose strands of his hair and tugged. His arms came up to press against the wall, framing my face—caging me in. I felt the pucker of raised skin, still healing, on the back of his neck.

An apology hovers in the air, mingling with fading lust from the memory.

The anger the prince is radiating grabs my attention. I see my brother's hand hovering above the prince's wrist on the table. Interesting.

When Weylin stands, Anik's eyes seek mine out. "The Bloodletting is in a week."

"I know, Anik." My hands drop to my sides.

"You'll begin fasting today," Mistress Agata called out. The room

went silent at her appearance. The unassigned pets, this year's offerlings, had all been gathered into the main hall. "One week from today, the hunters and huntresses will arrive, and you will be reborn into a new role—a new life with the gods' favor."

Meaning a new life either with a new master or with Agata.

But not me. She'd promised.

"So, you'll help me get him back?"

"No."

"No. I can't."

Imrie threw her hands up in exasperation. Her black-painted lips twisted into a snarl, so at odds with her whispered words. "Please, Rune. I can sneak you out, no one will be able to find you."

I looked out at the closed red door across the hallway. I could hear the whimpers from here, the hiss and crack of the whip as it hit skin, followed by the creak of a wooden bed frame. "I can't leave him."

"He'd leave you if he had the chance."

"He wouldn't."

"What?" The word is spoken at a mild roar by the prince. He looks like he wants to stab me, and I can't blame him.

I have to stop myself from shaking. The press of memories is causing an ache to form behind my eyes.

"He's only eight," the prince thunders on. "He can't possibly survive the ritual."

I turn my back, blocking out the prince's desperation and the looks of disgust on the guards' faces as they listen. "It is quite possible he's already dead."

"So you condemn him to rot in Wraith?" This comes from a guard who has come halfway through my front door, one hand already on the grip of his sword.

A dagger lands an inch from the guard's cheek and embeds itself in the door frame. I barely manage to hold back a laugh at his yelp of fear and the shock blooming on his boyish face.

"Seriously, Weylin? You come into our—*my* home," I clear my throat, "and you're already doing damage to the property?"

He shrugs, his ash-brown braids and small ponytail bobbing as he settles back into his seat. He still doesn't speak, and I find myself longing for the rough tone of his voice; the feel of his hands on my skin.

"Tell me what you want, Rune."

My breath mingled with his, our lips mere inches apart.

"I—"

Someone cleared their throat and I squeaked in surprise, turning to see Keegan in the doorway, an unreadable look on his face.

Weylin's hands tightened on my hips.

"Is it riches you want?" the prince asks, shaking off my brother's hold on him and bringing me out of my memory.

My head's a mess and I rub at my temples.

Looking up, I see the prince stalking towards me. I blink to clear my vision, focusing on watching the shadows claw at his feet, unnoticed by him. Their threads shimmer in tones of red, of warning.

"I'll give you access to whatever you want in the treasury, anything."

I ignore him, instead moving my focus to my brother. A skuggi is sniffing at his ear. His face is downcast, his shoulders hunched.

"How can you ask me to go back?" I hate how small my voice

sounds. I hate that I even asked him in the first place, but my emotions are bubbling up too fast.

I feel trapped.

"I wouldn't if I didn't think we could do this," Anik whispers. He casts a look at the prince who nods once. It's almost like the prince knows with these next words spoken that he will win, so when Anik looks up at me, I brace myself. "Rune, I-I owe him a debt. This is what he is asking for as repayment."

"A skuld I cannot repay," I said, repeating Papa's words.

Agata nodded. "You owe me a skuld now, elskan. You're mine."

"But what is my debt?"

She smiled, patting my cheek. "You'll see."

I gasp, finding my face pressed against a solid surface. My breathing is raspy, ringing in my ears amid the whispers of the shadows. A hand is cradling my head. Another is rhythmically running fingers through my hair, snagging on snarls as it goes. I register the tears on my face first and embarrassment soon follows.

I push at the chest that holds me, my fingers burning at the graze of a thin leather cord. My legs are shaking and I hesitate to move further away even as I twist backward.

I see red-painted doors.

I smell blood and ale and incense.

Stilling mid-twist, I then let the hand, now on my neck, tug me closer. My head throbs to the beat of my frantic pulse.

"H-how long have you had this skuld?" I don't know what makes me ask this. My words are partially muffled by my hair, by Weylin's skin and clothing. I still force my head to turn, to look at my brother.

"Three years."

My vision narrows. The length of time it's been since I escaped Vodihr in the first place.

"Elskan, elskan, where are you hiding now?"

Birgir whines, shifting closer.

I hear the cries.

I'm tangled in silk sheets.

"No," I breathe out and push away to stand on my own. I face my brother, the prince, the guards, and even Weylin. I force my gaze to meet each person in the room before I direct my answer to Anik.

"I will not go back. I'm sorry."

"Rune, please—"

My hands reaches for Birgir. "Get out."

CHAPTER FIFTEEN

efore I even got through the doorway, I knew something was wrong. The walls were hushed but watchful, the floor devouring every step I took and leaving me soundless. While everyone was out at the ceremony—the induction of a new priestess into the city's fold—I had slipped away before the cutting began.

Hesitant, I walked up the first flight of stairs, passing closed doors that blurred the faster I moved. It wasn't until I reached the third floor—my floor—that I paused again.

The door two down on the right was open just a sliver, some light spilling into the dark hallway. I saw a skuggi already seeping from the doorway. It was new—a muted imprint joining the already-stained structure that housed Vodihr's most wicked delights. Its threads were a sickly green that twisted and grappled the air. The threads were searching for something. Someone.

I already knew what awaited me, already suspected what had occurred. Yet, I still took the steps to the door; felt the wood against my *palms as I pushed it open.*

She laid in a pool of blood, naked and raw, her wrists still weeping.

Swallowing back bile, I found myself moving to kneel at her side, to check for a pulse that was no longer there. Her eyes were open, sightless. I felt like they still met mine—still watched and waited for my response.

The floorboard creaked behind me and a voice said, "I couldn't take it anymore."

Turning, I saw Imrie standing there, weeping wrists and all. Her hair fell to cover her breasts, her hands tangling in the split ends we had planned to trim later tonight. It was—had been a nervous habit of hers to play with her hair.

"I know." I wasn't sure what else she wanted me to say. I had known for weeks that she was planning to escape. That she wanted me to come, too. I just hadn't known this was the route she'd take.

"I'm not a coward, Rune." Her words were a hiss. Her form wavered and a little piece of me fractured. We had been friends, or as close to friends as Mistress Agata would allow among her pets.

"I know" I repeated tonelessly, my voice flat.

Only after she faded away and took her sad smile of painted, bruised lips with her did I turn back to her body, close her eyes, and weep.

⁂

I stare blankly at the stars high above, water nipping at my toes. Birgir plays in the waves that crash ashore a few feet away. He growls at an incoming wave, then yips as it sloshes around his legs. I shiver in the cool breeze, the sand sticking to my bare feet. A wave crashes and I shift my weight.

The *Tempest* sits in the distance, quiet. She is resting near Arden's main dock.

My shoulders tighten, knees half-buckling against the crash of another wave. I palm the dagger I had unearthed earlier that evening from beneath the floorboards of my cottage. Its red gem catches a flicker of starlight.

"I'm not a coward," I say, echoing Imrie's last words to me aloud. The shadows that have gathered murmur in agreement instead of calling me out on my lie.

⁕

I find Anik and the prince together, standing on the quarter-deck of the *Tempest*. Stopping by the dock, I watch them from a cluster of rocks sunk deep in the sand. Birgir moves a little ahead of me before lying down, resting his head on his front paws. His ears twitch as he follows the sounds in the night.

My brother, brown-haired and dressed all in black, is leaning against the rails, nervously tapping his fingers on the wood. Myself and the prince at his side bear witness to the misery clear on his face.

His gaze is on the stars and I wonder who he talks to tonight.

"Anik, do you think they are listening?"

"Who? The gods?"

I nodded, pressing myself closer to his side.

"I-I think so," he admitted. "It is easier than believing no one is there at all."

At age seven, that was a little hard to understand. But I nodded again, asking, "Then who should I talk to tonight?"

For years, Anik and I would look up to the night sky for help. Talk to gods who may still have been listening. Then I was sold and Anik started drinking. I had seen the toll on him when I left Vodihr.

"Anik, please. No more," I begged as he took another sip. His eyes were half-lidded and dark.

The others at the gambling table peered at us over their cards.

"I can't. I can't stop." He took a gulp and played his next hand.

I thought he was doing better, but now I'm seeing him reach for a bottle at his feet. Before I think better of it, I'm rushing over the dock, up the gangway, up the short steps to the quarterdeck, and reaching for the full bottle he holds loosely in his fingers.

Anik stares at me, his mouth open in surprise. Gael stiffens, eyeing me with suspicion. I briefly wonder where the prince's guards are, but it doesn't matter.

"I thought you stopped," I say, my eyes narrowing on Anik's pale face.

The amber liquid sloshes when his hand twitches.

Birgir growls at my distress and creeps closer, nearly crawling on his belly. He dislikes the *Tempest*—I'm surprised he even braved climbing aboard in the first place.

Determined, I reach for the jug again. My fingers brush something sticky and everything shifts, my present falling away.

He had cheated, he'd admit that now. He had cheated and bullied his way into winning the card game, and his opponent was too drunk and too sloppy with his earnings to notice.

As the alcohol whispered to Anik, his stomach churning, he had demanded a final bet—his life for the ship. At the time, his desperation was too great to realize the stakes and when the game had started … it was too late.

So he'd had to cheat.

Had to win the boat and his life.

Earlier in the day, and already half drunk, he had stumbled into a conversation about a girl with gray eyes and a wicked tongue in the city of Wraith. She would be a special Revelry act in the new year—if she survived her initiation in two weeks.

The more the traders spoke—her gray eyes, her pale skin, her long ebony hair—the more he knew it was her. He had finally found her. It was just ironic that she was in the one village his father made him swear to never visit or he'd face the wrath of the gods.

"Rune," he whispered aloud, his head bowing.

And so he drank more ale and plotted how to get to the city that no woman or man was allowed into unless the gods approved of it. Later, he found himself taking a blade to the ornery captain's throat, demanding the ship when the man hesitated to hand it over. After blubbering and pissing his pants, the deed had been placed in Anik's hands.

It was only after Anik stood staring at his new ship that reality set in. He vomited once at his feet, the dock groaning beneath him. Then again over the dock's side, chest and stomach heaving, too sick to notice the creeping up of two men before they were already on him.

Dazed from a blow to the jaw, he slipped and fell on his arse in his own vomit. A kick to the ribs followed, then one to the head.

The dock swayed beneath him, sweat dotting his brow and lips and neck. He curled tighter around himself, waiting for the next blow.

There were brief sounds of a scuffle, a shortened cry—then silence.

"They're gone," a voice called out eventually.

Looking up, Anik took in the blurry features of a young man, his hand hovering outstretched, reaching for him.

"I don't need your help," Anik snapped before hacking up a bit of blood. He was humiliated even further when it gracelessly dribbled down his chin.

The man grimaced, his nose turning upward in distaste. "I think you do."

"Don't."

Shrugging, the man's hand dropped to his side, the buttons of his winter coat gleaming in the moonlight.

Panic spread through Anik when the man turned to leave. His vision rolled with his stomach. He wanted a drink. He needed to find Rune.

"Wait," he wheezed, "don't ... don't go."

I rip my fingers from the bottle, my eyes wide. Looking down at my hands, I see a smear of blood on my fingertips.

Anik's face hardens in anger, his reddened fingers reaching for mine.

His face blurs.

The Tempest *rocked, the waves lapping at her sides. Anik stood up, shifting his weight to keep his balance, the bottle at his feet forgotten. It had been for Gael anyway—Gael who was still muttering to himself, rolling and unrolling his shirt sleeves. He stopped suddenly, hands reaching to grip and tug at his hair.*

"You said she would take us."

Anik felt the shame burn hotter in his gut. "I thought she would've, I didn't—"

"Do you remember how to get into Wraith?"

"No."

"Will the other one—Weylin—will he take us?" At Anik's silence, the prince of Arden moved to lean against the railing. Their hips brushed and Anik's skin flooded with a different kind of warmth.

"I can't-I can't lose him. I won't."

Warm feelings quickly dissipated and Anik's eyes stung. Gael's desperation was all too familiar. But Rune had been found, saved, taken away from that awful place. And yet he expected her to go back?

"We will find a way, Gael. I'll look for Weylin." Anik made to leave, to begin heading for The Wild Rose, but stopped as a hand wrapped around his wrist. Blue-green eyes stared at him, bright with tears. The bottle at his feet skidded a little as his foot bumped it.

"Don't go."

And I am myself again. Throat tight, I step back and Anik lets me go. We both stiffen as Gael moves closer, clearing his throat. The scent of bellflower and kryd spice drifts on the breeze. I feel a phantom tick begin in my jaw; saliva pools around my tongue as the need builds. Oh, how I've craved—

"I-I changed my mind."

"Ru ... " Anik starts, then falters.

The prince speaks before Anik can say more. "We leave tomorrow."

CHAPTER SIXTEEN

The dock rolls under my feet and my stomach rolls with it. I suck in a breath of salty air, wanting nothing more than to turn around and go back to my cottage. I make myself walk along the deck instead.

Feeling returned, bringing with it the full force of the sea's annoyance. Waves battered and churned around me as I broke the surface and swallowed foam. Coughing, I treaded water, or tried to. I then realized Weylin was nowhere to be seen.

I screamed before a wave took me under again. The salt stung my eyes; my sense of direction was hopeless even under the best conditions. I soon welcomed the pull of the cold; the tangle of seaweed tickling my calves.

"Weylin!" I screamed for him one last time.

The sea wailed her scorn for me and dragged me back down.

A lone raven cries from above me, its black and white wings ruffling in the breeze, sunlight glinting off streaks of silvery feathers. Birgir huffs at my side, ears low as his eyes follow the bird's movement. It seems to study the dock and shoreline near the port, then makes another sweep overhead. I can feel the intensity of its gaze, full of questions, before it becomes a speck amongst the engorged clouds. Thunder rumbles overhead.

Heat radiates from behind me and I tense. Weylin and I haven't spoken since last night; in fact, he hasn't yet spoken at all after his first fumbled attempt. Was he punished by his tribe? Had he lost his tongue as well as his place as the leader's youngest son of the Beastlanders? I don't know much about his family or Dýra—I want to know what happened but my own anger and unease keep me from asking.

"Well, I'll be damned," a woman's voice calls out. "As I live and breathe, I didn't think I'd ever see Rune Hansen back on a ship after we dropped your sorry self in Arden. Did you lose a bet? Drink too much of that fancy mead I smuggle in for you?"

A slap to the face was what forced me to wake next. There was a pressure in my lungs and my head was rolled to the side seconds before I threw up buckets of foul saltwater.

It seemed to go on forever; the ache, the pressure, the random slaps to the cheek or pounding on my chest and back. Finally, I flopped back exhausted. My eyes pried themselves open to see the sky—a black dot circling above—before a bronze face filled my vision and I was overcome by the sweet scent of coconut.

My eyes quickly find the lithe figure lounging against the rail up ahead. From her threaded and gold-charmed dreads to her leather vest and matching boots, Ailith is unmistakable. I can't help but grin at this force of nature.

"Or I missed you so much I was willing to suffer from your horrible sense of direction and likely die at sea just to see you again."

Ailith scoffs. "Well, you certainly aren't any nicer."

"Like you would want me any other way."

"I should've known Anik's sister would be just as stupid as he is." She paused and cast a glance over her shoulder at me. "I'm Ailith."

I move towards her and give her a quick hug, taking in the scents of sea salt and coconut. The ship rocks beneath us. Birgir's more cautious as he half-crawls to join us, stopping to lean against Ailith's legs for attention and comfort. She grins, kneeling to ruffle his fur.

I blink away the sudden weariness I feel and turn, looking for Anik. The flashes of memory are getting more frequent, and I suspect it'll only get worse when we get to Vodihr.

I couldn't sleep. Couldn't eat. Couldn't breathe.

From the steps leading down into the belly of the ship, I watched Anik as he manned the helm. He was guiding us toward Arden and the fear nearly strangled me. We'd slowed down twice so far. Lost a full day of travel when a storm had hit.

I'd discovered I hated the sea. Its temperament. Its choppy waves. The never-ending sting of salt. The cries of the gulls as they circled overhead incessantly.

But the pride on Anik's face gave me pause. My agitation quieted. His smile reminded me of all the wooden ships he had made and hidden from Papa. The stories he'd shared after visiting friends whose fathers were merchants or fisherman. He had always wanted to be on the sea. To sail far away on adventures we could only pretend to imagine the likes of.

He had changed. Was older, sure. But there was a worldliness about him I couldn't describe.

And I could only think on the past.

"Are you okay?"

The tremors that hadn't stopped since I climbed from the cot below deck were worsening. I turned and walked into Weylin's arms.

There's a creak, a wooden groan, and now excited chatter. I glance up to see the sails opening to gather wind.

Ailith and Birgir are watching me. Ailith's brow is furrowed, pronouncing the line of inked dots under both her eyes. I wave away her concern as she stands up and gives Birgir one last pat on the head.

"Ailith!" Anik calls to her from where he stands at the helm. "Can you stop flirting with my sister long enough to tell me where you hid the compass? I'd like to read the map again and make sure someone," my brother looks at me pointedly, "hasn't given me the wrong coordinates."

His first mate's lips quirk into a half-smile. "You wouldn't do that, would you?" She doesn't give me a chance to answer—she already knows I would. I had only given Anik wrong directions once before, after a petty disagreement when we were kids trying to sneak into town. That was a long time ago, but it was a story Anik loved to tell and would never let me live down.

With Birgir at her side, Ailith bounds over to where my brother and the prince are fighting over who gets to take the wheel first.

"Some things never change."

"What? Anik's determination to keep his toys to himself? Or his inability to remember where he puts things?" My words are light, but one of my hands has reflexively curled into a fist over my pounding heart. I haven't heard Weylin's voice in nearly a year. I'd forgotten the way it used to make my stomach flip. It's rough from disuse now, but it's still so familiar—I hate it.

Weylin moves to crowd my space, both of us turning to look out at the sea that coaxes us forward. I take in his profile from the side; the new muscles in his arms that stretch the material of the clean wool shirt he has on. There's a fresh scar that clips his right brow in half. I also notice there's a new tattoo just behind his ear, partially covered by his braids.

"Why are you doing this? You don't have to go back. This isn't your debt to pay."

He shrugs. "It isn't yours either." He keeps his gaze on the sea's green-gray waters.

I growl, my hand moving to grasp his forearm. My fingernails dig little half-crescents into his flesh. I want to shake him, to yell at him. Too much is building again, memories and feelings I've buried so deep I'm not even sure what is real and what isn't. And then the neckline of his shirt gaps just enough for me to glimpse a leather cord around his neck and a small purple bellflower tattoo containing a tiny "x" within the design.

It stops me cold.

"You didn't say goodbye," I blurt out, surprised at my words and the prick of tears that accompany them.

"I didn't know how," he whispers back. "I had thought you'd get—"

"Stop." I start to shake from the cold wind whipping at my thin skirt and even thinner blouse. Or maybe it's from the shadows stroking their fingers down my arms and neck. One sniffs at my tears before flicking its tongue across my cheek.

Birgir appears at my side, a whine caught in his chest as I bury my hand in his fur. He eyes Weylin warily, moving to insert himself between us and I choke on a laugh.

"That isn't good enough," I manage to say and turn to leave.

"W-what did you name him?" His words are so soft I barely catch them.

I keep my back to him as I answer, "Birgir." The wolf's ears flicker at his name. Weylin's eyes meet mine and I can see the strain on my face reflected in his gaze. Unsettled, I add, "It means 'to save' in the old language … because I needed something to hold on to after you left."

I leave Weylin staring at the sea, his hands gripping the rails. I slink below deck to nurse old memories of stolen kisses and forgotten promises. I hope Ailith kept some of my mead stocked—it's going to be a long trip.

CHAPTER SEVENTEEN

The first day, it rained. And I dreamt of a beast lurking around a fire.

The second day, it rained. And I dreamt of the night I lost my virginity at fifteen.

"Is this okay?" he asked, and I shivered as his hand teased just above the strings of my corset. I felt each press of his fingers while he tackled the knots, my skin aflame.

"Are you sure?"

My back arched, my hands impatiently fumbling for something to hold on to. His pale blue eyes bored into mine, still waiting for an answer.

"Yes."

The third day brings more rain, a new haircut, and a hangover after having broken into the galley the night before in search of Anik's personal emergency stash of liquor. It's midday and still I taste honey.

Now I sit in the galley again, a deck of cards in my hand, my eyelids drooping as I stifle a yawn.

Twice now, I've reached to brush my hair aside only for my hand to meet nothing. It is still long, brushing at my breasts, but not at my waist where it had been. My head feels lighter but my heart is heavy. I'd treasured my hair for years, until last night when I suddenly became sick of it.

"Cut it. All of it."

Ailith eyed me, the scissors in her hands. We were sitting, surrounded by empty bottles. A red gleam caught my eye but I smacked the dagger hilt further away, sending it skittering over the floor.

"Do it. Or I will." It was an empty threat. I was too drunk to even hold my hand up without accidentally slapping myself.

"Okay. Just, uh, stay still."

I watched as chunks fell around me. Agata would've hated this.

Nearby, the galley storage door with the replaced lock mocks me. I wonder if Ailith cleaned up the bottles I'd left behind … and all the hair.

Shifting in my seat, I smother another yawn. My jaw pops.

"You know, you could have told me."

To my right is a naked—*almost* naked—Anik, who may or may not be losing on purpose.

"Told you what?"

My brother is a master at cards and yet he has lost every hand so far. I'm suspicious but too tired to pry.

"That Weylin left. I would've kicked his arse for you."

"I did tell you," I snap.

"Not about how he left."

"It isn't my fault you didn't ask more questions."

Anik shifts in his seat, a slight flush crawling up his neck and into his cheeks.

I sigh. "I-I'm sorry. I didn't see a point."

"So you suffered alone, again."

I shrug and look at him, my cards forgotten. Some girls would say he is handsome, with the scars he wears and the perpetual light scruff on his face and his windswept hair haphazardly tied back. I've had to deal with a fair number of girls over the past three years, swooning over his muscles and tan and the brood he's got going for himself.

When we'd first gotten to Arden after escaping Vodihr, it had taken weeks for us to be comfortable around each other again. At first, I had wanted my old Anik back and looked for him everywhere. I wanted the fourteen-year-old who built tiny wooden ships, snuck me extra slices of fuzzy cheese, and hid in the empty bathtub with me after I was disciplined. But especially after Weylin left, I was too afraid to lose another person. I grew to accept this new Anik, demons and all, and I held on tight.

Anik groans, grabbing my, and the prince's, attention. He lays down his cards and takes a gulp of his ale.

From the corner of my eye, I see a slight shift from the prince, his eyes darting to my brother's bare chest, his calloused hands, then back to his own cards.

I sit back and take in the prince's cropped blonde hair—a trademark of the royal family—and his eyes, the same blue-green as the sea said family has dominion over. He is tall, at least six foot, and equal in stature to Weylin.

He notices my stare and another flush colors his freshly shaven cheeks. He hides behind his cards, the red tips of his ears still visible. I nudge Ailith beside me—she saw it, too.

"Wimp," she mutters when I fold, stealing a sip of my mead; she can have it. I'm sure if I take another sip, I'll be spilling the meager contents of my stomach on the galley table.

Of course she'd say this, considering out of all the players at the table, she is the only one still fully clothed. Minus her boots, which I believe she took off only out of pity for the rest of us.

Another round begins, followed by grumbles from the two crew members and two soldiers who each lose an item of clothing. The prince also discards his shirt and I blink at the scars I see. One in particular catches my attention; it runs in a jagged line along his right rib cage.

I hear a growl and turn to see Weylin glaring at me from across the galley. Innocently I blink, pretending to be unfazed by his jealousy. Why should he care anyway? He can move on, but I can't?

"What was it tonight? A prince? A pirate? A—" My teasing stopped as I took in the trashed room—the torn pillows, the ripped bed curtain, the fist-sized hole in the mirror that's now in pieces on the floor.

He was huddled in a pile of silk and shards. Carefully, I skirt around the glass and move to crouch in front of him.

"Weylin?"

"They wanted a prince."

I took no offense at the curtness of his voice. Instead, I got to my feet to grab a cloth to wipe the sweat and makeup from his blank face.

His glare fades just a bit, his attention pulled back to his own card game.

Birger's cold nose brushes against my bare foot.

After cleaning Weylin's face and hands, I grabbed a brush for his matted ash-brown strands. Ignoring his winces and grunts, I got out most of the knots before braiding his hair the way he liked it.

His eyes met mine in the fractured glass of the mirror. "What do you want, Rune?"

My hands curled around his shoulders and I pressed a kiss against the nape of his neck. "You," I whispered helplessly. "Just you."

Two shadows blink out of focus near the wall. They disappear so quickly that I may have imagined them. An unease settles in my gut; they're new shadows—ones perhaps lost at sea or to the cliffs—we're getting close to Vodihr.

"Rune, it's your turn."

A wet nose tickles my knee. I find a smile and take the offered cards for the next round. One of my hands disappears under the table to stroke Birgir's muzzle; he shifts closer.

Keeping my gaze on my cards, I feel Weylin's eyes return to my face. This time I flush and bite my lip. Gods, I miss him. Why did he have to go?

I breathed deeply, pressing a kiss to his shoulder when I felt tears wet my breast.

"Mundu eftir mér," he begged against my flesh, shifting to rest his weight on his elbows as he hovered above me. He averted his eyes. "Remember me."

I fisted my hand in his hair, tugging until his gaze met mine again. "Ég mun alltaf muna eftir þér."

In a world full of masks and rituals and games—in acts, in passion, in pain—we only had ourselves, our hidden truths that we buried deep down to protect.

And so later, once we were entwined together and hidden under the cover of blankets and darkness, I whispered again, "I will always remember you."

But the Bloodletting was to begin at dawn, and I worried I would not be able to keep my promise.

I had to get us out.

Shaken, distracted, I look back at my cards to find I'm armed with a flush. I watch as everyone but myself, my brother, the prince, and one of his guards folds. The guard's eyes narrow in my direction when I wave away an opportunity to exchange cards. My fingers begin to tap a slight beat against the table. Laughter fills the galley, followed by the whistled tune of a familiar sea ballad.

The prince places his cards on the table—I hum, then lay my cards down.

"Son of a bitch," the guard mutters, throwing down his cards.

Ailith laughs and tosses aside a sock.

"Ah well. I was getting hot anyway," is my brother's reply before his hands disappear under the table. He shimmies for a second before his breeches appear and are casually tossed away.

I smirk at the scandalized look on the prince's face. It's priceless.

"You cheated."

My humor falters. The galley goes silent at the accusation.

His breath was hot against my neck, his body pressing me uncomfortably into the frame of the door. I should've known cheating in the card game would cause trouble. I wasn't supposed to be in the social room yet anyway. With the Bloodletting only two weeks away, I couldn't afford to mess up. The gods demanded purity and I had already given that away.

"You cheated."

I bit back a whimper. One of his hands travelled lower while the other one toyed with the ties of my blouse. Wet lips nipped my shoulder before his tongue licked the spot. I wanted to throw up. To punch him. To cry out.

Instead I admitted my crime—"I did."

The hand at my laces stilled. Fingers now crept up to wrap around my neck. The fog of his breath touched my cheek then settled over my ear.

"I don't like cheaters."

This time, I couldn't stop my whimper.

Shifting in my chair, the wood biting into my backside, I size up the guard who watches me with greed. I'm familiar with the look. He doesn't care about the cards or the money. No. He wants me and has wanted me since he walked onto the *Tempest*'s deck. If Mistress Agata had taught me anything, it was to know when lust took hold.

My silence makes him bold. He leans closer, where I can smell the acidity of his breath mixed with his body odor. He wants to intimidate me, but I won't give him the satisfaction of even so much as a flinch. When he licks his lips, my hands worry at the material of the pants I stole from Ailith.

I'm reaching for the knife hidden in my boot when two things happen. The guard's hand comes within inches of cupping my cheek—I can see the dirt coating his skin that highlights his chipped nails. Then, he's screaming, his hand turned at an unnatural angle.

"Weylin," I whisper, seeing the red haze take over the blue of his eyes.

Birgir is on his feet; he circles the guard, hackles raised, teeth bared.

My chair shudders as I jump to my feet.

The bedroom door shuddered once, twice, three times before it burst open. I grabbed at the ties of my blouse—

But Weylin already stood in the doorway, his eyes shadowed with red streaks.

Dazed, I reached for him.

I'm hauled back into the arms of the patron. Stupid. He was no match for the beast that was before him.

"Get out. This one is mi—"

Before I could blink, Weylin had the man pressed against the far wall. The patron's legs were dangling, his face turning a shade of purple that matched the plum wallpaper. He fought, hitting Weylin's arms, chest, sides. All the same, his movements soon became sluggish and his bulging eyes began to close.

Stop him.

The shadows whispered, urging me from my frozen state. Numbly, I nodded and walked forward to place my hand on Weylin's arm.

"Let go."

A growl.

The patron shivered, his threads starting to pool on the floor below.

"Weylin," I whispered. "Let go."

Blue eyes still fragmented with red turned to me. "No." His voice was a guttural growl, unrecognizable now as his familiar tenor. I hid my fear, knowing the beast was attempting to take control. I'm surprised

Weylin was even able to respond to me.

"Please." I squeezed his arm. "He didn't hurt me, I'm safe."

I watched as his hold loosened just a fraction; the man, nearly unconscious in his arms, was suddenly flailing to take a deep breath. There was a slight pause, a brief squeeze of Weylin's hand, before the patron fell to the floor in a tangle of his own receding threads. I watched as they sank back into his exposed skin.

Blocking out his wheezed curses, I moved closer to Weylin. His hands clenched at his sides. A shudder ran through him and I knew I had to get him outside before the heaving started.

I was guiding him toward the door when I heard a choked voice. "Freak."

I froze. There was a pressure building inside of me. The shadows answered my unspoken call. Freak. Freak. Freak. I could see Mama's disgust as she uttered the word over and over before walking away from where I was sprawled on the floor.

Weylin was already halfway back to the man before I could grab him and wrap both hands around his middle. I ignored the shadows at my feet, the heat under my palms, the goosebumps that were rising on my arms.

"Rune." Weylin's voice was stiff, pleading.

Nodding in understanding, I pulled him away and guided him to the door. His weight shifted closer to me as the red in his eyes receded. He told me once, when I first met the beast, that he didn't want to kill. He didn't want to give Agata the satisfaction that he had slipped.

His curse was an ancestral one. In his tribe, it was an honor, something to take pride in. Here in Vodihr, though, it was nothing more than a source of entertainment for Agata and her whims—something he could neither control nor escape. She spiked his food often to force him to change.

He was already bending over, swallowing against the rising nausea, when we reached the door. I kept my eyes on him, my one hand pressed solid on the small of his back. My other hand dropped to flick my wrist—

The shadows jumped forward from my feet and exploded from the walls.

The patron laid paralyzed on the floor—his mouth open in a silent scream as the skuggar's threads leaked into his flesh.

I smiled as my feet touched the first step of the stairs.

Freak.

There is a buzzing in my ears. The shadows rush from the galley walls to gather at my feet. They are ready, already whispering to me, reminding me of the headiness of power I've only experienced a few times before. My head is bowed. I try to breathe through the lust.

Freak. Freak. Freak.

I throw a punch without realizing it, my knuckles catching the guard's nose. My stomach gurgles at the crunch and scream that follow. The entire crew turns to face the remaining guards in the galley. They look to Anik for a sign, for permission. His gaze is on me as he dresses.

The tension mounts; the shadows slither their way up my thighs. I feel their weight against my skin, their threads vibrating with a want that mimics my own.

I'm almost lost to the sensation, just like the first time.

I stepped into the room and saw the girl weeping in the corner, wrapped in a torn bed sheet. I took in the flecks of blood, the dagger discarded on the floor near a rumpled pillow.

"Your time is up." I didn't even recognize my voice. My vision was tunneled, darkening.

The patron who'd been lounging naked on the bed rose to his elbows, unfazed by my words and presence. His eyes cut to the ceiling, his mask still on but askew.

"I want more time."

I nearly choked on my breath. "No."

His lip curled. "Ask your Mistress."

My blood slowed, my pulse skipping. I looked to the girl in the corner, to the walls where the shadows watched—some were laughing, some were screaming.

All of them waited.

"No."

At my denial, his body stiffened, and he angled towards me. I didn't give him the chance to speak, didn't allow the words to form.

With a flick of my wrist, the skuggar attacked and I watched as the man withered in agony, his screams silent. Threads crisscrossed over his face, neck, arms. From the corner, the girl whimpered, her hands coming up to cover her eyes.

It was over in a matter of minutes. I watched as his spasms subsided into nothing—a trickle of blood escaped his nose.

I watch a trickle of blood trail down the guard's face.

"Go, Rune." Ailith's eyes are watchful, wary. She nods towards the galley door.

"No." I'm not even sure why I'm fighting, who I'm fighting. My voice is low, a warning. Her eyes flash; she doesn't want this escalating any further.

Some of the skuggar leave me, breaking away to sniff at the fidgeting guard.

Anik invades my space then, his leather-booted toes coming to rest in front of my bare ones. We share a look, one that tells me it's okay, I'm okay. I'm caving until the guard moans and starts cursing about how I broke his nose.

'Ask your Mistress.'

Birgir snaps his jaws inches from the guard's thigh.

My hands tighten on the threads I hold, the shadows moving higher, hovering around the guard's knees.

Still waiting.

One thread sinks into his skin, he shivers, his face twisting in discomfort.

I let go and bolt for the door, scrambling up toward the deck.

Feet and nail-clicks pound after me.

The night air caresses my face in welcome, cooling my heated flesh. I'm drawing in deep breaths, trying to; acid is stuck in my throat as I fold myself over the railing—the twinkle of the water below blinks in and out of focus.

Something warm brushes my hip.

My head spins.

"Let it out. Don't fight it," I reassured Weylin.

He heaved again and again from his position on the forest floor. We'd travelled to the outskirts of Vodihr, the city just barely still within sight through the trees. I squinted at the lightning that flashed across the sky, thunder responding in kind.

"I hate this," Weylin rasped, still fighting the tremors that shook him.

I sighed and moved to kneel next to him, placing my hand against his tensed back. I felt the bones and skin shift underneath my touch. The dew of the decaying leaves seeped into my dress—Mistress Agata wasn't going to like that I had ruined another one.

"Let it out, don't fight it."

I heave and heave, the bile scorching my throat. When it finally stops, I take a deep breath. "You stole my line."

Weylin laughs at my side; Birgir sits on the other. "Well, it usually worked for me, so I figured I'd give it a try."

After one last spit, I shift upright, my elbows connecting with the railing. My head stays bowed. I run a hand through my hair, and frown at the stickiness and grime I feel from lack of a proper bath. At least I'd have less to clean later, now that I'd cut it. I nudge Birgir with my foot, telling him I'm okay.

"You can control it now. You learned how," I whisper, surprised. I remember every time the red began to seep into his eyes. Remember the times where he roared and raged and attacked whoever was in his way—myself included. Mistress Agata's dosing only added to the intensity and mindlessness of his rampages.

"Damnit, Weylin," I shouted and dodged a fist.

He roared.

"Focus!" I sucked in a breath. "It's me!"

An elbow brushes mine and I know without looking that he's leaning on the rail beside me, mimicking my exhausted pose. I feel his eyes touching the side of my head, trying to see my face through my curtain of hair.

He eventually replies, "I did."

"When you were home?"

"Yes." There is a pause, and we both look to the cloudy sky for answers.

I'm seeing him laugh at one of my jokes.

I'm seeing him hover above me, his voice hesitant as he asks again if I'm ready; if I'm sure I want this—want him.

I'm seeing him broken, surrounded by gore, his gods-given gift as much of a curse as mine is. We yelled at the gods together that night.

I'm seeing him leave again, watching the ship sail away with a young Birgir at my side.

His voice is gruff when he starts to ask, "Do you remember when—"

"I remember a lot of things I wish I didn't."

A light rain starts to fall. My lips fight against self-deprecating thoughts and snarls I want to unleash. Here I am with Weylin, something I've longed for since he left, and all I can do is fight off memories of the past. For a split second, I crave the spice-and-floral drug. Want my medical potion from childhood to be able to forget everything.

"Rune, what is it?"

His warmth was behind me; he pressed closer but didn't touch me. I cowered away, my arms wrapped around my middle. My gaze stayed on the fire, on the figures dancing within. I was seeing things again. Hearing snippets of conversation. Watching a little girl fall, over and over.

"I can't stop it."

Each night, the dreams were stronger. Lingered well into the day. We were trying to create our life in Arden, but I was defective. Spiraling. Not for the first time, I wondered if the medicine I had taken was actually one I needed. I had stopped once we'd arrived in Arden as the supplies to make the tonic were not readily available.

A woman with gray eyes smiled at me from the corner. I started to shake.

Maybe I was insane. Sick.

A freak.

"Rune."

I can't stop myself from looking at him. I don't want to see the pain—the shared emotions between us. I don't want my heart to twist, my blood to warm. "Weylin, I—"

A short howl shatters the stillness between us. My gaze drops to Birgir, his muzzle still raised; I swear the wolf grins at me. *Cheeky dýr-beast.*

I allow the tension to tighten, to build again before I whisper, "goodnight," and slip away like the coward I am, biting my lip until it bleeds.

CHAPTER EIGHTEEN

The tri-colored raven was back, watching from above as we neared the cliffs where Weylin and I had made our escape three years ago. At first, the bird was just a black speck in the still-moody sky. When it flew lower, it cried out a lament of warning and agony and goosebumps pricked along my arms. It circled us once more before disappearing.

Waves battered and churned around me as I broke the surface and swallowed foam.

"It's an omen," Ailith comments at my side, her gaze fixed on the sky; I blink. "A death omen from the gods."

My mouth goes dry. I've heard the stories, the tales of woe that follow the sighting of a raven—stuff of nightmares to scare young children:

There once was a young girl who spoke to shadows ...

"Lucky for us then the gods don't exist anymore." Anik's smirk falters just a bit at my glare, but he shrugs it off. I watch him make his way toward the helm where Weylin and Prince Gael seem to be having a heated discussion. The wild gestures of the prince continue, and his watching guards stand at the ready for anything.

"You broke his nose," Ailith remarks, briefly glancing their way.

I see a mess of tape on his nose and bruising under one of the guard's eyes. "Good."

At the guards' feet, shadows dart in and out of focus and I sigh. I'm still protecting Weylin, even without realizing it.

"You know, it's getting stronger," I find myself saying. Ailith stiffens at my side, her skygazing forgotten as she turns toward me.

It's easier to say out loud than I expected—"The skuggar. They're impatient."

Silence meets me for a time, and I can't help but shift my gaze back toward the looming stone. Each wave sends foam lapping at the cliffside, the rocks below gleaming with broken pieces of ship ... and threads.

Rune. Rune is back.

Home. Rune came home.

"Do they speak to you?"

I suck in a breath, blocking out the dancing shadows along the cliff's edge that preen at my attention. They peek at me, long fingers curled around the dirt and grass; creatures without flesh that sway in the slight breeze.

Ailith and I have never fully discussed my curse.

And we never would.

I made the mistake of confiding in Ailith once before. She'd later given me a diluted version of my tonic in a bottle of mead she'd smuggled in. I'd been sick for days until she confessed. She'd thought it would help.

"No. No, they don't."

From her expression, she knows I'm lying.

I snap my fingers and Birgir's ears twitch in my direction. He joins me from his position under the crow's nest. I walk across the deck to head below. Behind me, the shadows' whispers continue.

Rune, play with us.

Come play. Don't you remember us, Rune?

As I walk away, I crush errant threads beneath my boots.

⚜

I spot the footprints as soon as we ascend the incline leading to the woods. They are blurry, coming in and out of focus depending on where we step. If I stray too far, deliberately at times, shadows come out to poke and prod my legs. Sometimes they pull my hair, sometimes I'm gifted with threads showing bits and pieces of their lives. It would be amusing if it didn't remind me so much of the games I'd played as a child.

"Break time!" someone wheezes to my right.

I hide a grin. One of the guards is bent at the knees, taking in huge gulps of air. I can't resist turning to Prince Gael and saying, "It would seem your guards are a little out of shape, Your Highness."

Satisfied with the guard's curse I get in response, Birgir and I move on a ways until I find a smoothed rock to plop down on. A touch of dirt puffs up when I adjust my weight, my legs falling to dangle toward the ground.

Nudging Birgir with my boot, he sighs before moving away to sniff at something buried in the dirt. His tail lifts at a particular patch of ground, which he promptly flops down on, rolling to his back and wiggling in ecstasy.

After the child strayed too far from the path, a wolf soon appeared. The child saw amber eyes gleaming with hunger from a gray face hidden beneath foliage. And the child was filled with fear. This is what happens when one …

A nursery tale comes to my lips, but I swallow the words and tune. Now isn't the time to conjure more shadows.

A twig snaps, alerting me. Weylin hovers just at the edge of my line of sight, watchful as always. I can feel the tension from here—my own tension pulsing to match his. We hate being back, not knowing how much of us will be lost again to Vodihr.

And I hate that I want him closer.

I wish you had stayed gone.

Tears burn my eyes. Of course I don't really wish that, but the pain of his leaving still lingers. I constantly have to fight against the desire to hold his hand. I want to pick up the pieces of the dreams we had created during the twilight hours when we had to listen to the screams, creaking, and moans that surrounded us.

His eyes meet mine and reflect to me all that is left unsaid.

"Are you sure, Rune?" He swallowed, his hand tightening around the material of my skirt. "I don't want to hurt you again."

I reached up and tugged his head to mine. "Yes."

"Uh, Rune? Your pet is growling at me right now and I'm not sure why."

Anik waves at me, motioning to where Birgir stands, fur bristled, amber eyes gleaming. I smile a little at the bits of dirt in his gray fur. I'm reminded briefly of the nursing rhyme from earlier as I slip to my feet, ready to intervene. But Birgir isn't staring at Anik—he's staring at the shadow that is slowly taking shape to Anik's left.

The little girl blinks, then sighs. Her sightless eyes, void of color, shift to each member of our group—Anik, Prince Gael, Weylin, the guards—before settling on me. Her cracked lips pull into a smile of broken flesh and chipped teeth. Keeping me in sight, she tries and fails to walk. Birgir growls again when her threads scatter too close to his paws. She waves her hand his way, throwing the wolf an unimpressed look, before gazing back at me.

Each step she makes brings her more into focus: a torn yellow dress, bare feet, long braided straw-colored hair. Blood decorates her entire face from the gash above her brow. The wound is ghastly for one so young—she's perhaps six summers at the most.

Hello, Rune, she whispers into my mind, for my ears alone. *Do you remember me?*

I shift uncomfortably, feeling like a child about to be reprimanded. "I'm sorry, I don't."

The forest grows muted in sadness, matching the girl's crestfallen look.

"Who are you … ?" Anik's words fade into a buzz.

The shadow looks impatient now, older and more intelligent than she should be. *That's okay. It's been a long time.*

Her head falls to the side and I see some skin that hangs loosely from her neck; I wince.

More shadows crowd around us, seeping from the trees, the earth.

The girl holds out her hand. I reach for it without thinking but I'm scared. Something feels wrong. My limbs are heavy and there is a hum in my ears—whispers I can't quite make out. My eyes itch and I desperately want to rub them.

Something cool but solid wraps around my outstretched hand and I shiver. I feel each press of the girl's fingers as her threads melt into my skin—happiness, love, loss, hope. I feel her weight against my leg; she's closer than I remember her being a second ago. She suddenly giggles, shifting away and giving my hand a tug.

Come on, silly. Mama and Papa are awaiting.

~~AD HORFA~~
WATCHING

They crouch, watching her from the safety of the trees, the roots and leaves covering their body. A sneer creeps up at the panic visible on the faces of her lover and her brother; the delicious confusion on the guards' and prince's faces.

One, the lover, is approaching her from behind, shadowing her steps while she walks forward with her hand outstretched and loosely curled, the other hand limp at her side. Her wolf sniffs at the ground where she had been standing, whines, then joins the lover in his pursuit.

She is talking, humming, and skips once before falling into a fit of giggles.

"I forgot Mama wanted us to stay close today. Do you think we will get in trouble?" Her head tilts and a nod soon follows. "But Papa ... " She stops and sighs. "Fine. Just this once."

Her brother tries to speak again, his face pale. "Rune. "

The prince, equal in height and pride, steps forward and puts a hand on the brother's shoulder. "Don't touch her." He ignores the glare he gets in return, his free hand gripping the sword at his side. "She's in a trance of some sort—look at her eyes."

"So we just let her wander?" The anger in the brother's voice makes Reaper grin. The mask croons to them.

Yes. Let her wander.

Let her come.

Reaper tilts their face upward and sniffs the air.

CHAPTER NINETEEN

y footsteps become the footprints I saw before, my feet falling into the path as I'm guided by the child before me. She chatters about pointless things, greeting passing shadows, remarking on the forest animals that scurry at our approach. She tells me of her day; how her older brother still likes to pick on her about her fear of worms—I can relate—and how her mama is always fussing with the knots in her hair.

What if I don't want bows in my hair? she asks me then, looking over her shoulder. Her left eye has started to roll back into her head of its own accord. Thankfully, her eyelid has begun to drop as well, blocking the sight.

"Perhaps you should tell her that," I find myself saying.

Oh no. Mama would be very upset. I'm her little girl after all.

I don't have anything to say to that. My mama had never bothered much with me, let alone put bows in my hair.

Then, as if pulled taut by an invisible string, the young shadow jolts to a halt and I stumble forward to gain my balance. There is a whisper of touch against my shoulders, but my attention is on the child and the sadness that make her features more drawn.

More and more shadows are appearing. Their fingers pick at the dirt and tree bark. I can hear their whispering again, urgent, full of warning.

Someone is watching us.

The Reaper watches.

I shiver when the little girl focuses on the shadow furthest from us, a smile of recognition on her face. I see the outline of a woman, the whiteness of her night gown. She is standing above on the slope of the ravine I'm steps away from slipping into.

Rune, I forgive you. I know you didn't mean it.

"For what?"

"Rune, it wasn't your fault."

I ripped my arm away, moving to stand by the fresh mound of dirt. "It was. I shouldn't have brought them out to play."

The sunflower fell to land atop the grave and I turned away, glaring at the shadows that had gathered. Sunlight reflected off the fresh grave marker. Her etched name was too bold, too new for the weathered stone.

Tillie—

"I miss you," I whisper, the words coming from somewhere deep within me. I mean them. It isn't fair. I don't understand.

I hold her hand tighter, fighting tears. My boots knock bits of dirt and rock loose, sending them tumbling below.

The little girl's eyes roll backward, both this time, and I watch in horror as her mouth drops open on a silent scream. She tilts forward into the ravine—

And then vanishes from sight, exploding back into the bright buttercup-yellow threads she's made of.

Confused, I flounder, grabbing at the threads as they flutter past. They are warm, like sunshine, and so soft. I nearly fall over the edge myself when I try to catch one last dangling thread.

A hand grabs my arm and yanks me back.

The buzzing in my ears is fading. My eyes sting and tears stream down my cheeks. I rip my arm away to wrap it around my middle.

"What … ?"

"Rune," a voice urges, "Rune, can you hear me?"

My head flops forward; I nod, or I think I do.

Slowly, my surroundings come back into focus: the trees, the barely visible gray sky, the concerned faces of my group. Birgir is whining, his nose against my knee. And Weylin … Weylin is grabbing my shoulders, his palms warm and steadying against my cool skin. I move closer, a sob breaking free before I can stop it. My forehead connects with his chest, his pendant digging into my cheek.

Prince Gael steps forward. "What happened?"

I don't answer right away.

"Did one of the creatures—"

"They aren't creatures," I snap, rage momentarily distracting me from the crafted wooden circle a few yards away. I feel the pull of it before I see it, the yearning and fear and disgust. My blood burns.

It's moving closer, has a mind of its own. To others, that would be unsettling, but in Vodihr, nothing is impossible.

The circle is hungry.

It's waiting.

"Weylin."

"I know," he whispers.

I move away, my hand grabbing his to stay steady. It's the same as I remember; the wood is still somewhat crooked in places where someone had tried to arrange it in an artful manner ... or had maybe tried to rip it apart. The grass still clings just around the edges, reaching for the dirt inside the circle, but ground bathed in that much blood and rot can never be saved.

It is always the smell that gets me, though—the lingering scent of rotted flesh making the air metallic and putrid, choking anyone who dares to breathe too deeply.

And she is there, watching.

Red lips smile. "Hello, Rune." Her hood is firmly in place, the rich earthen-colored cloak billowing in a breeze no one else can feel.

Anik starts at the feminine voice, his hands going to the blades strapped to his hips. They jerk free, the steel reflecting the little light falling through the canopy of trees caging us in. I'm surprised he can see her, let alone hear her. But everyone must, based on their sudden fighting stances.

The keeper of Vodihr beckons with a slight curl of her finger.

I want to tell Anik and the others that the Zila, a forgotten creature forced into servitude by the old gods, could break their necks with a snap of her fingers. Her story is still grand to me, despite being diluted from the retelling of it over and over. She had always fascinated me when I lived in Vodihr. Of course, she had terrified me, too. Weylin and I had once seen her rip the threads out of a would-be patron when he had failed to provide sufficient payment for Vodihr's admittance fee.

Most patrons and traders were able to come and go with an offering of some of their own blood, or maybe a small animal, but the Zila could ask for anything as fee, and if you couldn't pay it, you'd pay with your life.

And everyone had to pay a price. It was always a risk, coming to or leaving Vodihr—one usually only taken by the desperate, the deranged, and those addled by lust and greed.

"The gods don't exist."

"That may be true," Agata admitted. "But their creatures do."

One of the girls started to scream. Someone—something—had emerged from the circle of Vodihr, the gateway to our secluded little world. It looked like a woman, but it most certainly wasn't. Blood dripped from nails like talons as she approached. Fear clenched my gut and rooted my feet to the ground.

"What is that?" I whispered.

Agata looked back at me, smirking. "The Zila."

And the screaming began anew.

Should I warn them? But Anik is already tinted green under his tan, a twist to his features that speaks of his unease. I don't want to make it worse … Besides, I know what she wants. What she usually demands as payment. I remember this lesson very, very well.

"Gael," I call, noticing the prince startle at the informality of his name. I hadn't called him anything other than his title until now. His guards have formed a semi-circle around him, weapons drawn, their eyes locked on the Zila. She looks bored, unaffected, and yet the weight of her unspoken curiosity is nearly smothering me.

Gael clears his throat, shifting his stance. "Yes?"

I drop Weylin's hand, my hand moving to tangle my fingers in Birgir's raised hackles. "What if your brother is already gone?" I ignore Gael's growl. "We should turn back."

The Zila tsks at me and shakes her head; I ignore her.

"Are you really such a coward that you'd abandon a young child to this place?" His question cuts deep but he knows this. His eyes are calculating as he watches my face react to his words.

"I was left, abandoned. What does it matter to me if someone else receives the same fate?"

Behind him, the Zila sniffs the air, feeding on our strife and fear.

I don't move, don't say anything else, just stare at Prince Gael and watch the emotions run amuck on his face. He settles on anger, his hands fisting at his sides. Good.

When I break eye contact and look back to the circle, I see that the Zila's hood has fallen back to reveal the ethereal beauty beneath. She is truly as beautiful as I remember. Her features are marred, ghastly and severe in their angles. Her eyes are of infinite night, only flickering with light once the entrance fee to Vodihr has been paid.

It is her lips that always scared me, though—the blood red that bleaches the rest of her face to the color of bone, the same red as her hair. Or maybe it is her torso, ripped open to reveal tendons and ribs, the hole framed by tatters of skin and the cloth of her dress; it is said she was ripped apart by mythical beasts before a god answered her cries for mercy. The rest of her dress drapes down around her feet, resting in the detritus of the forest floor.

"How much are you willing to give up for your brother?" I ask the prince then. My eyes are on the Zila's curved white nails speckled with dried blood.

Gael doesn't hesitate. "Everything."

The Zila hums with satisfaction.

Before his guards can react, before he can react, I'm grabbing him, dragging him toward the circle, ignoring the angry shouts that follow me. With a shove, he enters the circle first, the Zila moving closer after giving a wave of her hand toward the edge of the circle. I hear the crunch of twigs and moaning of wood.

Her nostrils flare when I step closer and I catch the earthiness of the prince's scent mixing with the stench of blood and rot. The Zila's black eyes meet mine again when I cough.

"Shit."

I glance back to see Anik, his hand hovering just out of reach—the circle is closed for the time being, just like I figured.

Weylin's red-speckled eyes are on me when I feel the scrape of nails along my forearm. Still at my side, Birgir growls in warning. I look up—

The Zila is too close, our noses only inches apart. She smells of incense, of decay, of soiled flowers. Of death.

"Please," I begged, hovering just outside the wooden circle, a dead rabbit at my feet. "Please just tell me what you need from me. How can I go home?"

She watched me, motionless in the moonlight. She was unmoved by the tears streaming down my face, by the bruise darkening my cheek or the rips in my dress—even by the blood covering my hands.

I squinted, unable to make out much more than the blurred outline of her body. "The others had said if I offered something dead, you'd listen to me." At her persistent silence, I shouted, "Answer me!"

"Þú getur ekki farið heim."

You cannot go home.

The words had the effect of a whip, much like the belt Papa used when I did something to displease him or Mama. I shifted closer to the path, a rock cutting into my bare heel. I almost kicked the dead rabbit in frustration. This was foolish. I should never have listened to the tales Keegan told when he was too far into his cups.

An apology was on my lips but instead I said, "Please—"

"You cannot go home," the Zila said again, interrupting me, "because in your heart, you do not wish it so."

"That's not true!" I wailed. "Why am I stuck here? What do the others give you?"

She shrugged. "Everyone has something to give up." Her head fell to the side. "How much are you willing to give?"

I shake myself free of the memory. Of my first failed attempt to leave Vodihr when I was only twelve summers. I didn't officially meet her—didn't see her in the daylight in all her terrible glory—until I was sixteen and being cleansed for the Bloodletting.

"Is it the usual payment?" I'm abrupt, to the point. I won't beg ever again.

"Three times now you've begged to leave," the Zila taunted. "How many more times will it take for you to break?"

"You listened the last time," I rasped. "Why not again?" I tightened my hold on Weylin, his head lolling to rest on my shoulder.

Her eyebrow raises in amusement, as there is no "usual payment," but the Zila nods anyway and steps back. I suck in a deep breath when her nails scrape against Gael's forearm and I wonder what memory she's making him relive first. Birgir growls once but I hush him with a tap to his muzzle.

"Great. Let's get this over with." I grab my dagger from under the folds of my cloak, ignoring the winking red gem, and raise it quickly to slice at my right wrist. The burn is familiar, as is the feel of blood oozing from the wound—a reopened one, one of many I've carved into my flesh over the years.

I let a few drops fall to the earth, ignoring the way they sizzle and steam when they hit the dead soil beneath us. The soil itself begins to churn, turns dark. I see bits of lost threads, bones, and roots. I nudge Birgir back when he shifts too close to the hole being created.

Somewhere below us, a god laps greedily at my offer.

Without asking permission, I slice Gael's closest wrist. He grits his teeth, hissing at the suddenness of my movement and the clarity of pain that follows. I'm unapologetic and turn his wrist to face downward, giving it a hard squeeze.

"Do you need the others to … donate as well or are we all allowed to enter?"

The Zila speaks to me alone, her words rasping as they leak into my mind: *What is your business in Vodihr? If I remember correctly, you were eager to leave and never return.*

"A debt," I say aloud, feeling sick. "I've come to fulfill a debt."

"But not your own."

Gael starts at the changed sound of her voice, grating now in its otherworldliness. All feminine softness is gone, replaced by the reality of what the Zila truly is.

Does she pity me? I hold back my agitation, my denials and protests. Why is she playing this game? She knows what I have at stake—I cannot hide anything from this creature.

Do you know what you are giving up? The price this time around is steeper. I warned you when you left last ... of what awaited you should you ever return.

When I don't answer, her expression empties and her eyes close as she whispers into the air between us, "Very well."

From behind comes the cracking of wood and rustle of leaves.

Soon, Weylin is at my back, his hand steady on my shoulder. Birgir nips at my uninjured hand but then settles to lean into my hip. Anik is hovering by Gael, who is wrapping his wrist with a piece of cloth one of the guards has given him. Both guards glare in my direction but aren't stupid enough to approach with me being so near the Zila.

There is a sudden feeling of vertigo, and from my half-lidded eyes, I see the Zila fading as the trees blur around us. Her eyes are open, dancing with light.

I hear the caw of a raven seconds before the spinning stops and a familiar path appears beside the circle. A laugh forces itself from my lungs as I step forward, a boot touching the first stone of the pathway.

I turn, feeling the brush of the others as they move past me and disappear. They don't seem to notice the dried blood on their wrists. The Zila must have taken payment from all of them after all.

A fog hovers now, creeping in, blotting out the trees and

muting the sound of the others' voices; silencing Anik's shouts for me.

The wolf must stay.

"No!" I reach for Birgir but my fingers meet resistance, a barrier I cannot see. Birgir whines, pawing at the air between us, the Zila towering over his shoulder. His shape wavers in and out of focus, but his amber eyes remain steady on mine.

My fingers just manage to brush his outstretched nose before I'm shoved back, hard, by a pressure against my chest. I see him lunge for me, but the Zila pulls him back by a collar that's suddenly materialized on him.

"He stays." Black eyes meet mine and then the Zila's gone, taking Birgir with her.

She croons, *Welcome back to Vodihr, Rune.*

The circle of Vodihr is gone.

I get to my feet and stumble backward, joining the others on the path.

"What did you have to give her?" Anik's voice is thick with apprehension.

"Where is your pet?" Gael asks. He sounds … sympathetic and I don't dare look his way.

The closest shadows dance in greeting but all I can hear is Birgir's last whine of goodbye—I've lost him, too.

~~ENDURKOMAN~~

THE RETURN

CHAPTER TWENTY

ven from here, I can hear the music and drunken laughter. Stale alcohol trails on the breeze with the scents of body odor, sex, and metal. Fog still hovers over the crumbling stone walkway, which is for the best. If I focus hard enough, I'll likely see bile and blood stains among the grayish-brown.

A stoic Weylin glances in my direction and I refuse to answer the question in his eyes. I refuse to acknowledge that my heart is breaking, too. "Nothing appears to have changed. That will make things easier."

Weylin straightens, eyes roaming for threats—his hand moving to hover over a dagger tucked in his belt. "Lucky us."

There is a silent consensus, one of shuffling feet and averted gazes—I am the one who must lead the way. I have to bite back my anger. Who is the coward now?

The first step is the hardest. I cannot smell the sea anymore, nor can I feel the sun's warmth, absent in this dead place. Birgir is gone ... But I step once, twice, and soon my feet are carrying me steadily onward. I force myself to not reach down to my knee, knowing my hand will grasp nothing but air.

Rune ...

Rune, come and play.

When we reach the first structure—past the crude warning signs and a decrepit graveyard full of failed offerlings and murdered talas—I hold up my hand for the others to stop. Before us stands a forgotten wreck of a house, rendered unnatural from decay. The shutters are all unhinged, dragging on the ground below the windows they once decorated. The door has been removed entirely—whether stolen to protect another home or destroyed by a storm, I can't be sure. The house has always reminded me of a cave, its yawning mouth providing a harsh comfort only the most desperate would seek out.

And seek it I did—many times.

"Are you sure?" I whispered, eyeing the house. My hands twisted in the folds of my skirt, a nervous habit that always got the better of me when stressed.

There was something about the house that had both called to me and repelled me. Twice now, I had passed it only to see memories of a past that didn't make sense, not in this place. A child playing. A woman singing in the garden.

"What's the worst that could happen?" Weylin joked, already halfway up the path in front. He sent me a wink over his shoulder.

"It could eat me," I said, more to myself than to him. My hands twisted tighter, the fabric strangling my fingers. In my mind, I suddenly saw a little girl screaming, a woman in a pool of blood before I blinked the image away.

Weylin's laughter trailed behind him …

… and the house laughed too.

I had once joked, after my third visit here, that all it needed was a fresh coat of paint to cover the grime, yet wildlife still creeps from within, over the bricks and out the windows and gaping holes. Paint is only one of the many things it needs.

Still, Weylin and I used to pretend we would move away from the center of the city, the watchful shrine, and make a home here. I'd resurrect the garden in the back for herbs and exotic fruits and vegetables. Weylin wanted a swing for the porch and a firepit where he could roast the meats he'd hunted or traded for. These were the young and foolish dreams of children who hated their circumstances, who needed some respite from the pain of correction and the touches of patrons.

On the really bad days, when I had forgotten my tonic and was further lost to the henbane in my system, I'd tell stories about a little girl that haunted the house.

I notice the light that flickers in the farthest attic window from a single candle burning—it can't be. Squinting, I see a black candle, one that looked undistinguishable to the one I had lit three years ago when rushing to stitch up a bleeding Weylin as we hid from the city's guards.

"Weylin, focus on my voice okay?" I begged. My hands moved to cover the biggest wound. Blood was still weeping from between the strips of my blouse and skirt I had used to wrap them with earlier. "It's going to be fine."

The cuts gaped at the edges, angry and red. Some would need stitches, need to be drained—things I couldn't properly do. In the distance, I heard the thrilled shrieks of the city dwellers.

My breathing was quick, panicked. Vision wavering from the sweat and tears on my face, I tilted his chin up to get some water down his throat. His skin continued to leach of color. When he gagged, pink water bubbled at the corners of his lips.

"Stay with me," I whispered. "I can't lose you."

The guards. The guards were coming. I had to work quickly.

A few minutes later, I was dragging him from the house, leaving a lit black candle in the attic window and a bloodied cloth on the floor with a rusty needle stuck in it.

From the second attic window, a shadow now watched us, her smile sad.

The silence lingers as we continue walking, strengthening with the smells and calls of Vodihr. Anik and Gael have fallen into their own silent communication—one full of hand gestures and subtle facial expressions. Whatever it is they're plotting— likely a plan to get the young prince back from the clutches of The House—it is beyond my interest. I only need to take them a little further.

My part in all of this was simple: direct them to the island, bargain with the Zila, and lead them to the heart of Vodihr. After that, I would be free to wait and bide my time with Birgir in the woods while everyone else played their parts.

Birgir …

I can't. I won't think of him. Not yet.

I stare hard at a rock until the press of tears lessens. Prince Gael's groan has my eyes flickering over to an animated Anik, his hands and arms swinging around wildly.

While I don't know the plan, I have my suspicions: the prince would be in costume, his guards as well. He would likely be a hunter entering in the annual Bloodletting ritual that was only a day from now. At eight summers old, the young prince would be ineligible for the Bloodletting. Instead, he would be rented out to a local business for labor or auctioned off as a servant, rather than a pet. The selling of underaged children took place after the Bloodletting, after the winning hunters and huntresses absconded with their chosen offerlings for a night of "passion."

Of course, if he was as unlucky as I had been, Mistress Agata would've taken a shine to him already and decided to keep him for her own crew. He'd then be hers until she either grew tired of him, he was eligible to participate in the Bloodletting, or ... he died. In most cases, death is the best option since being granted freedom or managing to escape is so unlikely. I had escaped only to end up right back where I started.

"I'm keeping her," a woman's voice crooned.

The old building groaned, slowly settling beneath me as I stepped through the doorway. My eyes downcast, I shivered at the light pressure of nails that first caressed my cheek before cupping my chin.

"That wasn't part of the—"

"She's mine."

I felt each nail imprint upon my chin as my head was yanked upward.

Shuddering, I shake my head to clear the memories away. Already, I'm slipping: focus ... *focus.*

Their plan ... My brother would likely haunt the local pub, The Banshee, for information on the offerlings and who the major hunters and huntresses were this season. He had been a hunter once, when he had come for me, but he cannot play the same role this time around. He had simply been too unforgettable.

A hunter in blue velvet was drunkenly cavorting about on a raised platform, an equally inebriated and merry woman glued to his side.

His eyes met mine for a moment and I sucked in a breath. His brown eyes seemed familiar, and he seemed to recognize me, too. Were those tears? Was he crying? But before I could make sense of his tears or his identity, he turned to the woman next to him and gave her a passionate kiss. I blushed.

I lost track of him in the crowd and decided I ought to start entertaining before I brought Agata's wrath down on myself, or possibly Weylin. As I stepped into the crowd, though—

"Ru?"

I faltered. "Anik?"

At least Anik's costume would be his own clothing this time, instead of that ghastly blue velvet attire he'd stolen from a wealthy traveler. I just hope he remembers to change his name while playing his part, gambling and flirting his way into the hearts of The Banshee's staff and regulars.

He plays the role of a drunkard almost too well, perhaps because he'd been one all those years I'd been away. Is still struggling with it, even now. He'd told me one night, when he had digressed after one too many cups of ale, how after I'd been "taken," Papa had grown even more inattentive, had left for even longer stretches of time, while Mama continued to dote on him obsessively. Five years later, Papa just left, disappearing for good. That was when Anik renewed his search efforts for me.

And as for Weylin ... he's the wildcard of the group. I'm not sure if he'll pretend to be a pet for Gael, who ironically looks like one of his former regulars, or if he'll be on patrol duty, making sure the city guards are distracted enough to pay us no mind.

Out of the two of us, I'm not sure who will be more noticeable; we had both been prominent pets to Mistress Agata and our absence hasn't been long by Vodihr standards.

"Are you … ?" My words to Weylin fade as a group of costumed performers appears on the road ahead of us.

Their macabre attire gives me pause, my gut clenching at the familiar burgundies and blacks and grays of their gauze and ribbons and too-tight cloth. The masks are worse this year, which I had noticed at Arden's Revelry. One is speckled in blood, while another looks like a human skull, almost too realistic in appearance to be fake.

All of us seem to notice each other at the same time, immediately sizing each other up. I wait, watch, and struggle to not reach for a weapon. Inwardly, I try to reassure myself that no one will recognize me, yet stupidly, I have done nothing to hide my features—none of us have. Involuntarily, my hand moves up to cover the marking given by Mistress Agata above my breast, the material of my shirt teasing the puckered scar tissue.

"A bellflower for my little flower," she whispered in my ear, her lips catching the lobe and biting down hard.

I yelped at the feel of her teeth and the press of the bed frame against the back of my thighs. "Yes, Mistress."

The performers shift. One—probably their leader—moves forward and bows low. His hat tumbles off and causes a bit of dirt to billow up and cover his pants. The bow itself holds a touch of mockery to it—mischief, as well. I manage to return it with a curtsy that shows a bit of cleavage, a little something to distract them from looking too closely at my face. Their snickers make the skin around my lips tighten, but I keep my pout firmly in place.

Please don't recognize me or Weylin. Please—

"First time visiting Vodihr?" the leader inquires in a smooth voice. "It's our second time attending, and I would be happy to—"

One of the girls snickers and the other chimes in, "Doubtful, the royal there has guards … and he's gotta be hungry for a new pet. The one at his side is too ugly and used-looking to be enjoyable anymore."

From the corner of my eye, I see my brother's hands twitch. I am torn between laughing—I suppose sea-weathered skin and a half-shaved head aren't considered as appealing here in Vodihr— and the relief I feel at seeing they don't know me.

Be careful, a shadow warns, materializing nearby.

The Reaper watches, another hisses.

My brow furrows at the familiar name. While in Vodihr, I had heard rumors of this "Reaper," a terror to be unleashed by Agata at whim. The being would supposedly be sent away with the Revelry to wreak havoc on unsuspecting towns across the land. Agata told me once that the Reaper was a gift from the gods, as was the ability to have such a creature at her disposal. But I never saw the thing.

It is hungry, a shadow sighs.

I bow my head to be more submissive, to hide my features— how I hate that I've fallen right back into my role.

And then a pet arrives: a pet always recognizes another pet.

When our eyes meet, I see him start, drawing himself up to his full height—a shade taller than six foot. He shifts on the soles of his boots; his eyes jump to Weylin and darken.

Weylin responds in kind, moving a hand to the small of my back, the hilt of a dagger pressing against my spine. I shift backward into him, my one hand hanging at my side—grasping for fur—while the other snakes back to wrap around the dagger. The familiar prick of warm steel, a single crudely cut red gem at the hilt's center, provides little comfort.

I wait for the inevitable. Keegan had always been a snitch and a bootlicker, working tirelessly like a good pet to earn treats from Mistress Agata. And yet he hadn't stopped us the night we escaped—had stayed in the doorway blocking the city guard who had gotten stuck pulling up his pants.

"*Come with us.*"

I don't know why I offered, why I couldn't just disappear after Weylin who had already stumbled toward the trees. My eyes were distracted by the blood on the path, the trail that would be too easy to follow, before I turned and faced Keegan in the doorway. I took in the fresh wounds on his bare chest, a mix of scratches and bites.

My eyes closed as I smelled sweat and blood.

"Go, Rune," his voice was deep, oddly pitched. Where was the crude remark? The flirt that suggested a quick tumble before our next round of duties continued? He was being too nice. Too serious.

"I—"

From behind Keegan came a sudden scream, a cursing guard tumbling into view on his knees as he hurried to right himself and pull up his pants.

"Go!"

I turned and fled, leaving Keegan standing in the doorway, his shoulders filling the frame, taking the lashes of the guard trying to get by.

"Ryker, the first set of acts is about to begin," comes a woman's voice. It is childlike and reedy, as if she's gotten stuck playing the role of the perpetual little girl—seductive to some, perhaps. Just the kind of thing one would expect in Vodihr.

Ryker, the man with the mischief and darkness in his eyes, sighs. His lips purse in annoyance and he bends to grab his hat. "Yes, I'm aware, Star." Brushing the dirt away, he beckons to Keegan who comes forward and leans down to offer his neck.

"I was merely trying to welcome them to Vodihr and offer my assistance if needed." As he says this, he pulls a leather leash from his cloak and clips it into place, the burgundy stark against the black collar around Keegan's neck.

Pets should not wander too far, a skuggi whispers, giggling.

Or else the wrath of the Mistress is not far behind, comes another, more solemn voice.

When one pet leaves, another must take its place, the first chimes in.

"Will we see you at the festivities?" Ryker asks me, his eyes roaming my body, his hand tightening on the leash he now holds.

I surprise myself with how calm my voice is when I say, "But of course." I cast my gaze around their group, taking in the joy on Ryker's face, the annoyance of the two women, the glint of rage in Keegan's eyes—"We wouldn't want to miss the fun."

Ryker is bolder now as he steps forward to offer his hand. "Shall I escort you there?"

My lips form into a coy pucker. I push the dagger back into Weylin's hand and step forward. "I'm afraid I cannot accept." I pause for effect before adding, "We have an appointment with Embela first."

The two women hiss; the men shudder.

"The witch?" Ryker's confidence fails him, and he takes a hasty step back.

The delight I take in their horror threatens to break my façade. Embela is still alive then, and based on their reactions, the old witch is still causing chaos. Excellent.

CHAPTER TWENTY-ONE

Only a few seconds of silence last while the performers leave, Keegan's eyes boring into mine. My hands twitch in the folds of my skirt before he's tugged away.

One ...

Two ...

Thr—

"Are we really going to go see a witch?" Prince Gael asks, intrigued.

"No," Anik snaps. "Then maybe ... I didn't even know the nornir still existed." I can feel his frustration and confusion from here, apparent at his use of our native tongue.

The nornir (witches), or norn (one witch), were no longer referred to as such. In fact, most people rarely referred to them at all, believing they were all gone.

"What was that all about, then?" Anik stands in front of me, his arms crossed over his chest, bracing for a fight.

I shrug. "You asked me to bring you here. You play by my rules."
I can practically hear his teeth grinding.

"Your rules?" he repeats. "I—we—had a plan. Your 'rules' now have us attending a ritual none of us but you and Weylin know anything about."

"And how exactly were you going to get the young prince again? Sorry, I blocked out your planning sessions on the ship." He glares and I continue. "But it doesn't matter. I bet you thought you could just charm your way into The House and expect a warm welcome." I scoff. "Gael blends in, can pass as a hunter with his guards, but he looks just like his brother, doesn't he? Someone is bound to notice that. Then what?"

He's silent, and I realize something. They don't have a plan at all. Not a real one. Between us not being disguised and Anik and Gael still arguing over what to do, they are clearly out of their depth. I glance at Gael; had he known that—that I would need to take charge?

And now Keegan knows we're here, too.

"You have no plan. Therefore you'll listen to *me*." I'm angry. Scared. "Besides it isn't my fault you were too drunk to attend the Bloodletting when you failed to rescue me in the first place!"

He raises his voice. "I was drugged! I had a plan then and I have one now. Whatever game you're playing is going to get us killed before we can get Larken and leave this gods-forsaken city. Your—"

"Enough," Gael interjects, causing my brother to gape at him. "Your sister is here because she knows what is at stake. How to navigate Wraith."

I hum, trying to hide my interest at the informality that grows more obvious between them.

"While I may not agree with her … methods, I trust her to see this through until we get my brother back."

Anik sucks in a sharp breath. "Fine." He fluffs himself up a bit and drags a hand through his hair before glancing down the path. "So, who is this norn, Embela?"

Weylin and I share a look. "A witch who bites," he says.

"But not too hard," I add in, winking at the antsy guards. "Unless you provoke her."

Anik curses under his breath.

With a laugh, I take the lead and unknowingly grab Weylin's hand. We share a look, and he gives a squeeze before I quickly let go.

Embela knows you are coming, child, a shadow rasps from the ground beneath my feet. I absorb her threads, basking in the comfort she gives me.

Beware, Reaper watches, another whispers, and I sidestep its reed-thin threads thrumming with disapproval.

I glance up to see a raven sitting in a nearby tree; its black feathers splashed in white and silver ruffle and it turns from my gaze.

※

The closer we get to Embela's, the stronger the mist nips at our exposed flesh and the louder the humming becomes—humming that everyone can hear, based on their collective unease. I remember the first time I had heard the humming—the soft, old lyrics I could barely decipher as I ran barefoot over rocks and roots. The soles of my feet had been a mess of blood and glass and dirt but all I could think about was hiding.

Wheezing, I fell over another root, my ankle twisting at the awk-wardness of my landing. I screamed then in anger, in fear and pain. Frustration choked me, as did the ties of my cloak. I hadn't meant to break the dish, hadn't meant to slap Mistress Agata across the face. But the longer they ridiculed me ...

Hearing the crunching of leaves, I jumped to my feet. Hot pain spiked through my ankle and I bit my lip to keep from screaming again.

I ran, hobbled, further into the woods. Branches stabbed at my body; roots seemed to rise up at random, trying to trip me; my arms wind-milled against foliage from every angle.

Desperate, I turned—and suddenly there was silence. No birds. No wind. Nothing. Stilling, I watched a thin mist creep closer. It tickled my feet, soaked the hem of my dress, and then stroked my cheek before receding.

But the silence remained.

Another step, another wheezed breath brought the little cottage into view. I took in the sight of an antlered beast's skull sitting on the porch railing, its bleached whiteness at odds with the delicate lilac shutters on the windows and the basketed floral arrangements that lined the opposite railing.

That's when the humming started; lyrics in a language ancient and forgotten followed.

Feeling soothed, needy, I abandoned the shadows watching from behind—forgot the calls of Mistress Agata and Keegan echoing from Vodihr.

The porch steps creaked under my weight as I walked up them and to the door. I thought it was odd that there were tiny bells, bronze, hanging from the doorknob amid the etched sigils on the frame of the door, but I couldn't stop myself from touching them, smiling at the sigh they made.

Abruptly, the humming ceased and the door banged open.

I fell backward onto my arse and found myself looking up at a wrinkle-faced norn.

We stared at each other, a frown on her lips, a small confused smile on mine. Her ruffled graying black hair frizzled down to around her hips, my black hair chopped off at the shoulders in an uneven line ... An old crone and a hapless maiden.

A black cat appeared at my feet, sniffing at my toes before its nose turned up in disinterest. Fascinated by its shining coat, I reached out to stroke its back, but it hissed at me and my hand dropped into my lap, fingers picking at my sleeves. The cat's yellow eyes narrowed to slits.

The norn cleared her throat and I looked up to see her smiling, her gray eyes crinkling into raven's feet at the edges. "Hello, child. I've been waiting for you."

"It isn't nice to dawdle, child. I've got the tea already started and you know how I hate cold tea."

I find myself facing that same old cottage. The lilac shutters are a little more worn, there are more flowers and odd plants cluttering the porch, and the antlered skull now has a small companion, but even with the absurdity and wariness it evokes, I grin.

"Embela," I call back, "I've brought guests."

I hear a snort from inside and make my way up the porch steps. I notice they now sag from use—or maybe I've just gained weight.

"I can see just fine, child."

My foot is on the porch before I realize only Weylin has followed me. He'd been to the cottage often for tonics—some for me and some for him. The House and even Agata herself were known to deal frequently with the last norn of Vodihr.

The others linger back by the trees. Prince Gael looks curious, like one of his royal nursemaid's tales is taking shape before his very eyes; his guards just look spooked.

My brother is the last one I look to, and I cannot help feeling a bit of pity at the roundness of his eyes and the slack of his jaw. It seems the ever-so-slightly exaggerated tales I told during my first few months back home are possibly replaying in his mind right now.

"Anik, are you—"

"I'd appreciate it if you'd stop gawking. It's rude to stare."

Whipping around at the closeness of the voice, I come face-to-face with one of the few kind souls in Vodihr. I hear my brother stutter an apology. My eyes are burning from the sting of tears. It's been so long, and I hadn't gotten a chance to say goodbye before.

"I know, child," she says soothingly, giving me a quick, efficient pat on the shoulder. "All is forgiven and all is well." Her milky blue-gray eyes study me, sussing out my reason for coming, then move onto my companions, lingering on Weylin, who greets her with a quick nod. "Come in, come in."

She disappears back inside, tiny bells tolling and the sound of a cat hissing from within.

"Hi, Xavier," I call into the darkness, knowing the ornery feline familiar is somewhere close. Another hiss sounds, accompanied by the scrap of claws on wood; I sigh before stepping through the door.

"Yes, he's in quite a mood today," Embela says from her place at the table.

I squeeze around two potted ferns, nearly step on a fallen map, and end up colliding with a small mountain of bird skulls with lilac-painted floral etchings before making it to the seat she's gesturing at. I catch a brief glimpse of a large black leather-bound book and pause. It seems familiar.

"Amma, read it—please!"

"This story isn't for young ears."

"I'm five now. That is not so young, is it?"

She chuckled and reached for the black bound book next to her journal.

Someone bumps into me from behind, interrupting this strange memory. "I think she is going to eat us," comes Anik's whisper into my ear. "I'm offering Weylin first. He has the most meat."

"Ah, but you have more salt from the sea, already seasoned and ready to cook!" Embela replies. She rasps out a laugh when he blanches.

He casts me a sheepish smile, then ducks, narrowly missing a hanging plant.

"Don't scare him too much, please. I'd rather not have to swaddle him before we … " I trail off because saying out loud the reason I'm here would ruin the happiness I've just found.

Here, in this small cottage full of odd trinkets and dead things, I could pretend just for a little while that I didn't have a part to play waiting for me. We had been seen. *I* had been seen. And Weylin. Agata either knows or will soon.

To Hel with Anik's plan.

"A debt … a skuld I cannot pay."

The echo of Papa's long-ago uttered words, right before he sold me to Vodihr, sends a shiver down my spine. If his voice is what I hear now, then the shadows are soon to follow—I feel a gaze on my face and meet Embela's eyes. The slight downward tilt of her chin confirms my fears; she can only keep them out for so long.

"Yes, yes, I remember you. Hello." Weylin is talking to Xavier, the cat practically climbing his legs in excitement to be held and doted on; I roll my eyes. The first time they'd met, it had taken a solid three minutes to get Xavier's claws out of Weylin's arm. Yet after his initial attack, Xavier decided Weylin wasn't all that bad and had clung to him for attention rather than in defense.

From the corner of my eye, I see Anik poke at something. The prince is at his side, studying a map of constellations tacked to the wall. The guards have chosen to remain outside, which is fine by me.

"Are you sure about this, Rune?"

I blink away the haze of lavender, sage, cinnamon, and witch hazel. The fact she used my given name ... "I'm sure," I whisper, and my eyes go to Weylin, his narrowing in suspicion. I offer a tight smile. "I have to."

Her bones creak along with her chair as she leans back and casually tosses something into the shimmering pot in the hearth. "Very well."

A few minutes pass in contentment; no one seems to notice the temperature dropping, the slight rattle of bones from the pile in the corner, or the dimming candlelight. All the while, Embela hums beneath her breath and stirs her tea.

"What is it?" I asked, my voice cracking from fatigue.

The norn's smile was gentle, soothing. "Just something to help with the pain, child."

I cast one last wary glance above the rim of the clay cup before taking a sip. Instantly, a pleasant heat warmed my stomach and spread. "What … ?" I was crying again, my eyelids drooping. The cup shook in my hand, or was it my hand that was shaking?

Something warm was wrapped around my shoulders, fingers—cool, rough—lightly patted my cheek. "Hush."

The sudden clap of hands startles me, and everything freezes: Anik is half-seated at my side, his elbow level with my eye. I tilt my head to watch the flashing of his eyes, the tightening of his lips, but nothing else moves—it can't. Prince Gael is still by the map, one hand hovering over the moon; his eyes are frantically moving from side to side. And from the window, I can see both guards leaning close together.

And then there is Weylin, who is seated on the floor, half-reclined beside an annoyed Xavier who glares in my direction before turning to groom himself.

Another clap and everyone's eye movements cease, too. They can no longer see or hear us.

"What am I to tell them?"

I drag my gaze from Weylin back to Embela. "That I have a plan. To wait for my signal."

White eyebrows arch. "And will they wait?"

"They must," I reply.

At her nod, we work quickly—I stuff my pockets with herbs, a small tonic, a bird skull to ward off negative energy. Embela goes to each of her other guests and forces their jaws open, pouring a cooling tea down their throats. She mutters each time before moving on to the next. I see each of their eyes close, their postures slumping.

I reach for a stray piece of paper and a charcoal pencil and begin to scribble—

So I did a thing.

Everything is okay, I'll be fine.

My plan is better.

Frustrated, I scribble something that I hope makes sense and jump to my feet. Knowing I'm running out of time, I grab Embela's gnarled hand as it hovers over Weylin and give it a squeeze. My eyes meet Weylin's, his pupils bottomless, unseeing.

"Take care of them for me."

Embela taps my arm until I turn to face her. Her eyes are nearly white with film. "Oh child, I wish I could. I can't keep them asleep for long, though."

Troubled by the warning her words hold, I smooth out the paper slightly crumpled in my hand, place it on the table, then turn and head outside, dragging in deep breaths as I go. This has to work. It must.

The same monochrome raven from earlier is watching from a nearby branch and I glare at it, coming to a stop on the bottom porch step. "Whoever your master is, tell them I will not be intimidated."

Its feathers ruffle at my words and I swear its head dips in acknowledgement. Amusement seems to tinge its beady quicksilver eyes before it caws and flies off. At my feet, a single white feather rests, tinged with black and gray.

I'm leaning down to pick it up when there's rustling ahead, the snap of a branch, and he appears. I take in his map of scars, his tousled purple hair, his smirk.

Keep your friends close, keep your bootlicking snitches closer, I suppose.

"How did you know I'd need you?"

"At first, I couldn't believe you were dumb enough to come back." Keegan shrugs at my snort. "You haven't gotten rid of your tick; it will be your downfall."

I curse under my breath. "Right. Well let's get this over with."

He chuckles and I push around him, the feather crushed in my palm before disappearing into my pocket.

CHAPTER TWENTY-TWO

On the edge of town, I stop to change into a costume haphazardly shoved into the hollow of a tree. The flimsy—dare I say see-through?—fabric in my hands is courtesy of Keegan himself.

I threaten, "Peek and be gutted," to an idling Keegan who's using one of his knives to clean the grime from beneath his fingernails.

He scoffs. "It isn't anything I haven't seen before, elskulegasti."

"Really? *Dearest* is the best you could come up with?" My dagger lands between his boots and his laughter follows me as I weave a few more feet away through the underbrush.

I'm nervous, shaking. Already, I can feel the gauze against my thighs, feel the cool touch of air on my exposed flesh. The costume itself is standard, one that all pets usually wear and modify as needed. It could be sparkly—I detested those the most because the sparkles went everywhere. It could be in an array of colors—each pet was assigned a color that fit their given role. Though, it really depended on the year and Mistress Agata's mood.

My color had usually been gray, a storm gray that hinted at the anger and pain just beneath the surface. Mistress Agata had said, *"It is an ode to the color of your eyes, because that is what first drew me to you."*

My given character story had hinted too close to the truth and made me cringe every time a drunk patron whispered it to me to let me know they had chosen my company for the night. Of course, my company only went so far. I was a special pet and, at the time, not of age.

"She hunts her men and basks in their ardorous gazes. A trapped young beauty, sold for the debts of her faðir. She seeks a revenge only the gods can provide. Can you tame her for the night?"

"Or will she kill you before you find release?" I recite my old scripted response for interested patrons, hearing my voice startle the still forest air.

"Good. At least you remember something."

My snarl at Keegan becomes lost among a swath of material. I wiggle my way into the constriction of the dress, tugging it upwards. First it touches my calves and I flinch at the ghosts of fingers. Next, it reaches my thighs, then hips; I feel the bite of teeth. Moving over my stomach, it caresses like the rough palms of the past. I'm panting by the time it smooths out around my neckline, the material hugging my breasts last and molding to highlight their curves. The bellflower tattoo over my heart is in full view.

"Hold her steady," Mistress Agata ordered as I squirmed on the bed. She pricked my flesh again, the burn traveling from the top of my left

breast all the way down to my navel. I whined at the feel of blood and renewed my struggle.

Slap!

Surprised, I opened my eyes to see her hovering above me; she was seated on my thighs, her upper body hunched over my struggling form. Two of her older pets held my legs and a third checked the ties at my arms. In her one hand was a needle covered in ink and blood—my blood. Her other hand held a cloth she'd been constantly dabbing at my flesh with, seemingly just to cause me further suffering.

"If you stopped fighting, this would go much faster."

I bared my teeth, a hiss slipping through as the needle connected once more with skin.

"Oh, elskan," she started, her painted lips twisting upward, "they are going to love you."

I stuff the tonic between my breasts and rip the dagger from the ground to hide it on my hip. I realize the bird skull is too noticeable to hide, as is my spare knife, and I end up tossing both into the bushes, hoping I won't come to regret the decision.

A throat clears from behind me and I whip around to face Keegan. His eyes start at the top of my head and travel slowly downward to where my feet peek out from beneath the dress. His eyes burn with hunger, but the rest of his face is unreadable. "Shall we?"

I surprise both of us when I take his hand.

We walk back to the path and it takes but a minute or two to reach the inner part of Vodihr. My senses overload with body odor, liquor, and woodsmoke first, then laughter and chanting. I see the horde moving from one vendor to the next, greedy for the pleasures being sold at every stall and storefront.

In the center of the clearing is the wooden stage where Mistress Agata will begin the Bloodletting celebration by slaughtering a prized shadow-wolf captured just for the occasion.

"Do you remember the year we angered the gods, and Agata, by slaughtering a cow instead?"

"Yes. I still don't know what happened to that year's wolf." My lips form a genuine smile at the lie.

I was already tired of being pushed and prodded from one place to the next as Vodihr filled with traveling merchants, performers, smugglers, and wealthy patrons. They bumped and stomped and shoved their way through the crowds, trying to claim dominance over a town that could not be claimed. My eyes blurred from the materials and goods being offered in every direction. My attention caught briefly on a leather cord, the polished bone pendant glittering under the painted nail it hung from.

The merchant's eyes met mine, a smirk on her lips before she looked away.

A few more shoves and finally I managed to find a spot to watch, out of the way of lecherous eyes and wandering hands. I tucked myself into an alleyway, my small lantern soon balanced between my knees. I sat and began to pick at a loose thread on my borrowed dress. The thing itched, a rash already forming on my elbow from the awful material. Absentmindedly, I rubbed at it, ignoring the scuffling from behind me until something hit me in the back.

I fell to the side, grabbing the lantern as I flailed. There was a flash of gray and a growl, then more shuffling. Torn between intrigue and fear, I moved closer, my eyes narrowing at the lantern candle's distorted light. Another flash to my right, the scrape of something dragging across rock and dirt between The Banshee and The Skull Joint—two taverns at war with each other over gambling parties, stolen patrons, and dis-appearing ale.

Biting back the "hello" on the tip of my tongue, I inched closer only to be met with a pair of amber eyes sunken in an elongated face. I saw the pain in them, the red of burst blood vessels and fatigue. I was surprised at the snout and fur that followed, the clip of nails scratching on the dirt-smothered stone below, tangling with the heavy chain that weaved around the creature's legs. I took in the spiked collar biting into the matted fur at its neck and I chewed the inside of my cheek in agitation.

Its growl stopped my hand midway to its neck. I stumbled back, slowly putting the lantern down to show I meant no harm. The shadows mur-mured in sympathy and I thought I heard a howl seconds before the wolf in front of me whimpered. When its head bowed in submission at whatever I deemed fit to do, now resigned to a fate outside its control, I wanted to cry.

The lantern light captured more blood, raw flesh, matted fur, and a lingering scar on its cheek, and my fear changed to anger.

Another howl from the woods caused the wolf's snout to raise to the air. It sniffed once and took a step forward: a jerk on the chain caused another whimper, one I echoed. This must have been the sacrifice Mistress Agata was boasting about at dinner last night. The wolf whose impending death she had described in gory detail: she would first slice its throat, then its belly—a grisly offering to the gods to mark the beginning of the Bloodletting.

It was pathetic-looking, sickly. I could see myself in its eyes and I was much the same—thin, bruised, and broken.

Raising both hands, I balanced on my knees. Each slight shift forward brought my hands closer and closer to the chain collar. Involuntarily, one of my hands rose to my own neck, my fingers brushing the still-unclaimed flesh of my neck.

No collar. Not yet.

I move closer for a better view of the stage, or rather, Keegan has to nudge me closer and by default I comply, resigned. A flash of a blush-tinted skirt has me tensing. She's close.

Keegan nudges my side again, hard, and I angle away, ready to melt into the growing crowd. A voice booms from the stage—"Ladies and Gentlemen, welcome to the 19th Annual Bloodletting."

The headache is sudden and intense. I'm dizzy and disoriented. I reach for Keegan's arm to hold myself upright. His lips are moving; the words are lost in the haze of pink suddenly dominating my senses. The shadows are agitated swirls around my legs. All I can see is the flush of skin against a low-cut dress, the taunt of a smile, and a mocking drawl—"elskan." She has haunted my dreams and waking memories for the past nine years.

I'm suddenly sixteen, thirteen, ten: the slash of nails, fingers wrapping around my throat, the lazy explanations of how to work a crowd and please my audience. Outfit changes, the binding of my breasts when I was too ugly, then when I was too pretty. The prick of a needle or a cup of drugged wine to make me more compliant. My tonic … always my tonic.

I think I may be dying; each breath is a gurgle.

Flowers bloom on my tongue, acid from a drink I haven't had in years.

"Rune," a pause, the voice pitching lower, more urgent, "Rune!"

Another flash of pink, the roar of the crowd as the sacrifice— an aging wolf that looks half-dead—is dragged onto the stage.

Teeth were bared inches from my face; saliva dripped onto my arm.

"Please," I begged in a whisper, another brush of my fingers against warm metal, eliciting another growl. "Please, let me help."

The ceremonial dagger, it's twin hidden underneath the hem of my dress at my hip. More pink fabric, too delicate a color for the act about to take place. Soft hands grip the wolf's chain, yank it closer.

Silence.

My voice must have soothed it, or its remaining will to fight vanished. There was a brief huff of breath, strong enough to toss back a few loose strands of my braided hair, before its snout dropped. The wolf shivered as I fiddled with the collar. I missed the clasp twice, scared now of being caught, still scared of being bitten.

I jerked hard and the collar snapped open, falling to my feet in two pieces.

"Go." I pushed at the wolf's side, feeling fur and blood stick to my palms. Its nose brushed my forehead, its eyes almost looked human. "Go!"

The swift cut of the neck—a ripple of delight from the crowd followed by a collective sigh as the wolf's belly is gutted next and blood splatters those closest to the platform. A heavy chain falls to the ground.

Tears stung my eyes as the wolf shot around the corner and disappeared, the street too busy with people too self-interested to notice a wolf running by.

I wished I could follow.

Silence.

Green eyes snare mine, serpentine, ready to eat me whole.

A bloodied hand, the dagger still cradled within it, is raised and the aim of the tip cuts through the crowd, landing on me. I'm unable to move, unable to fight, as the dagger beckons me forward, motioning for me to come to the stage.

Against my will, my feet are moving: one, two, three steps—the crowd whispers and parts for me. My low-heeled boots catch on the rickety stage steps and still I walk: one, two, three.

"Is that Rune?" I hear someone whisper.

I step over the wolf's body and find myself standing in the middle of the stage, dazed by countless lanterns, bombarded by catcalls and whistles as the crowd catches a new wave of hunger.

Green eyes gleam; there's a flicker of gray surrounding the shrinking pupils. Agata's head lowers, her lips hovering above mine. Her hand comes up to stroke my cheek.

This moment was inevitable.

She always found me. Would always find me.

The bark embedded itself in my palms, twigs snaring my clothes and pricking exposed skin. I crouched lower, cowering as the footsteps got closer. Covering my ears, I pleaded silently to whatever gods were listening—save me, help me.

Hjálpaðu mér.

A branch snapped in front of me and the shadows at my side scattered. There was a sigh, followed by laughter like a hiss.

"Hello, elskan."

I feel the tip of the dagger cutting into the flesh at my neck. She trails down to fondle the small "x," to tease the tip of a bell-flower petal.

"Hello, elskan."

My fate is sealed with an angry kiss and the clasp of a thin leather collar around my neck.

Hello, darling.

~~YFIRGEFNING~~

ABANDONMENT

The night sky brings little comfort as they lay within the folds of dry grass and soil-encrusted leaves. Vodihr waits in the distance—its calls full of drugged merriment, the scent of roasted flesh on the breeze.

It's a disappointment, an outrage.

No one knows of what they've done, of how they have contributed to the ritual this year.

Ale is spilled, kisses are exchanged.

And here they sit, lost in the dark and in memories of a family they never fully had. Of a childhood full of stealing and begging, lying and pain.

"She promised," they mutter to the stars, "she promised if I brought her home that I'd be free—be rewarded. Still she hasn't looked my way—has fondled and hoarded her prize since the girl's return."

The stars say nothing, merely blink at Reaper's words.

Perhaps you need to take what you want, the mask murmurs. Its voice fills Reaper, blotting out the ringing in their ears. *You complain and you beg, and she doesn't care. Has never cared.*

"I've been abandoned again."

Only because you are nothing.

They weep and so does the shadow that watches them.

CHAPTER TWENTY-THREE

My reflection stares back at me from cracked glass. I can still feel the press of Agata's sickly sweet lips against my own, the sting of her dagger against my throat. My cheek is still pink from her wicked claws.

"So, you've come crawling back to me," she whispered, circling me in the foyer of The House. From the doorways, her pets were listening.

I kept my head bowed, waiting. I knew she wanted me to plead, to beg. The words wouldn't come. I could barely stomach being stripped bare for her and her guards that circled the room. My dagger and tonic were gone.

Keegan had been dismissed shortly after we'd arrived, and I almost wished he'd return.

"Have you nothing to say to me?" Her tone was mocking, her smile cruel when I glanced at her and shook my head. She sighed. "I see. So why then has my little pet come back home to me? Was your freedom not all you'd hoped it would be?"

She moved closer as she spoke, her lips now hovering over mine again, the tip of her dagger at the base of my throat. She traced my neck with the point, fondling the collar I now wore. "I won't let you go again."

"I know," I managed to say.

She laughed and laughed, her nails raking tracks down my cheek.

And now I'm right back to my beginning—locked in a room, a dress waiting for me to change into by the door, and an entertaining story being written to proclaim my return.

"I'm sorry," I tell myself; the words are broken and rough, more a rasp than solid language. I rinse my mouth of the sweet ale I'd consumed, wash away the taint of unwanted kisses when I'd been passed around the party. I shiver at the room's silence, still naked, my hair covering my shoulders, touching the top of my breasts.

Sorry, sorry, sorry, the shadows repeat over and over as they form legs, arms, fingers, feet in the glass's reflection.

The temperature drops further as night takes hold, the shadows waiting, watching my hands clutch the brass basin I'm supporting myself against. My head bows, the ends of my hair now dipping into the cooling water that I'm supposed to be washing with.

"I'm sorry," I repeat to the emptiness. Pain roars through me, draining my skin of color, dotting my brow with perspiration. My knees buckle and I gasp, bending at the middle, the basin cutting into my stomach.

"Did you really think you could escape this, elskan?" she whispered in my ear as she wrapped me in a hug. We were putting on a show for the curious eyes that watched from around the stage as we greeted the hunters and huntresses that had arrived early.

"I—"

She tsked. "You were bad, my darling." Her nails pressed into my upper arms. She pulled back, her lips firmly set in a smile. "You ran away … left me all alone." Her eyes dug deep for the secrets I was keeping from her. She knew I wouldn't come back without a reason and she wouldn't allow me to deflect any longer.

"Me for him," I managed to say before we turned to walk off stage. Our pace was brisk, our dresses flaring much to the crowd's delight. They gawked and applauded as we passed. I felt their eyes on my naked back. We navigated among the outcasts, those unsure of their place in the festivities occurring, heading for The House.

"Who?" she asked, a picture of innocence. She was stopped frequently to speak with people, but her face darkened the further we got from the crowd.

"Keegan," she called, and he moved closer to her side. He'd been following just a few steps behind us.

"Stay, make sure the party continues to run smoothly."

"But—"

Her look was enough to silence him. He nodded, then turned and headed back towards the milling crowd. I had to clench my teeth to stop from crying out his name. Although there was nothing he could do to help me, I didn't want to be alone with her.

We were turning another corner, The House in sight, when she said, "I had to replace you eventually; he was the best choice. He's young. Pretty." She shrugged. "Tender."

I didn't respond. I was too surprised that she'd admitted to taking the young prince, then too disgusted. What of the repercussions? Did she think Arden would just let their youngest prince go?

Then again … it appeared so far they had done just that.

It was when we were steps away from The House's path that I was spun to face her. "You think you can just come back and offer yourself for him?" She eyed me from head to toe, her revulsion plain. "You are not worth it, not now."

Her hand reached down the front of my corset, yanking up and revealing the clear liquid tonic I'd hidden there. Next, her hand slipped under the slit in my dress, her fingers trailing over flesh before she gripped the dagger's cool steel and pulled—the material of my dress ripped further.

Guards stepped from the House's door.

"But you won't let me leave," I snapped, seeing lust and deceit swirl in her eyes at my reminder. "You said you won't let me go again."

She seethed, her eyes narrowing on me. "I do not like to lose, elskan. You cannot leave, nor can you have him."

"But I will."

A sob disrupts the memory, but it is not my own. My head lifts to take in the redness of my eyes, the gauntness of my cheeks … and the shadow forming behind me.

Another sob escapes the woman as she solidifies. Her dress is torn, an oozing gash across her stomach leaking down in a splattered mess on the white of her nightshift. She stumbles, her bare feet soundless on the floor. Her soft gray eyes take in the dress laid out on the chair by the door before they meet mine, the sorrow in them nearly choking me.

"Who are you?"

She sniffs, her hand reaching out. "My ljúfa stelpa, my poor sweet girl." Threads dangle, their blackness stark against her outstretched fingers.

I step just out of reach, alarmed at the realness of her. At how I can hear her aloud, rather than just in my mind. None of the skuggar have ever been this life-like, even the little girl from the woods.

"I didn't know this would happen," the shadow whispers. Her voice breaks on another sob. "I couldn't-can't stop it." Her gaze lands on my neck and she moans at the sight of my collar.

My blood freezes at her next sentence—"A debt … a skuld I cannot pay."

Her eyes travel back to mine before she fades, her wail ringing through the room.

I stare at the place she was just standing until there's a banging on my door, followed by a gruff, unknown voice. "Keep it down, would ya? Some of us are actually trying to sleep." Heavy feet shuffle off down the hall and I'm left in silence again.

Disoriented, I walk back to the basin, the cool water a relief when I splash my face. I'm hot and cold, my stomach churning. I keep telling myself it wasn't real.

But when I look up, she is back, crying in the corner, watching me. My hand shakes as I reach up and cover the glass—cover myself and whoever this shadow is.

Not real, I say firmly in my mind.

Her black-gray threads bleed across the floor.

❦

When I awake, it feels as if my entire body has been beaten—a feeling I'm unfortunately all too familiar with. I stretch slowly from my toes upward, working out the kinks and studying the bruises that cover me. My tattoo stings—a reminder I don't want—and I rub at the phantom pain before rolling onto my back. The sheets lay tangled around my legs and one arm hangs awkwardly off the bed.

There's a brisk knock on my door followed by, "Thirty minutes!" It's a cheery voice—unfamiliar, just like the one from the night before. I wonder how many new people grace the halls of Mistress Agata's establishment. How many more have fallen into her clutches? Any familiar faces I had seen last night hadn't approached.

Activity stirs in the hallway: doors opening and closing, hushed voices, rapid footsteps, a brief laugh, an angry curse.

Groaning, I force myself to sit up, my toes curling against the coolness of the wooden floor. The blanket I had curled up in, found somewhere in my fumbling before I made it into bed, falls to the floor as I stand.

The dress Agata had chosen for me is still there, still laid out on the chair by the door. It is pretty in a cruel and abusive sort of way, with its sparkles and see-through material. It's smoke-gray. From here, I can see at least one slit, likely coming up to my hip, and the patches of floral design that are just enough to ensure I'm somewhat covered: I snort.

"Twenty minutes!"

At the reminder, I waste little time getting ready. The dress slips on with ease, revealing makeup and shoes beneath. Resigned, I pick up both and make my way to the mirror to paint on the face Mistress Agata has decorated me with many times before. I had to look older most nights when the patrons arrived for entertainment.

Only a few liked them as young as I was, but it was still a few too many.

Lost in the cream, the rouge, the kohl, and the red lipstick that I almost stain my teeth with, I barely glance at myself. I finish the look by roughly running my fingers through my hair. I glance to see a small hair pin forgotten in the corner of the sink and laugh; there's not much I can do with such a small clip. I struggle to pin back a few curls from one side of my face, then let the rest fall freely where it may. It would've been worse if I hadn't had Ailith cut my hair.

I'm at the door, slipping on the soft calfskin boots I've been given, before I realize I've moved at all. Old habits die hard, and I don't want to be late—Mistress Agata doesn't allow tardiness and I still have to find the young prince and get a message to Gael.

I heard him before I saw him. He hovered just behind me, unsure of himself. As a prince who was likely used to getting what he wanted, his hesitancy was amusing. Birgir shifted at my side, his ears twitching.

"Yes?" I asked, breaking the silence.

"You know Wraith inside and out."

I choked on a laugh. "Well, yes. You could say that."

His expression hardened. He glanced behind him before stepping closer. "Can you get my brother out?"

"I thought you had a plan?" I kept my expression carefully blank, wondering where this is going, wondering what Anik had told him of my time in Vodihr.

Earlier, Anik and the prince had been sitting in the galley, their heads bent close together with papers spread out before them. After catching brief snippets of their conversation, I discovered they were still at an impasse as to how exactly the younger prince would be recovered.

"Can you get my brother out?" he repeated, his lips thinning into a hard line.

"Perhaps." I didn't know what else to say. I now had a feeling of where this was going but I still wasn't ready for his words—

"I want you to get my brother out … Do whatever you must, and I'll give you anything you want."

"Even if it means going against your plan? Betraying you? Anik? Killing someone?" I tried to keep my words light, airy. Inside, I was aghast at what he offered and sickened at the desperation crawling in his eyes.

I was even angrier that I wanted to take his offer. To leave Arden, move further into Utlen—be that much further away from Vodihr. Explore a world I knew only through stories heard at The Wild Rose.

"Anything?"

"Yes. Nothing else matters. Just get my brother out."

I can still do this. I'd known deep down Agata would find me eventually, even if Gael and Anik had actually had a plan. This collar on my neck changes nothing. I will rescue Larkin and we will leave this place together, no matter what it takes.

'I won't let you go again.'

She would.

My hand is outstretched for the knob when the door jumps open and Keegan fills the frame. I blink, letting my hand fall to my side. My lips part, a snappy remark on the tip of my tongue before I see what he holds in his hand.

"I won't."

He frowns. "You have to."

My hands press over my stomach, the dress crinkling slightly at the agitated pick of my fingers. "No."

A laugh taunts me from just behind Keegan's shoulder—I see a glimpse of pale pink. "If you don't want the boy hurt … " The words trail off and I hear a sharp cry. "You will."

I rip the crown—the Bloodletting crown only those participating in the ritual wear—out of Keegan's hands. The thorns and crudely wrapped vines bite into my hair and forehead, contrasting against the delicate brush of bellflowers weaved through the sharp green. I smell their delicate watery scent and nearly gag.

I don't know what I hate more, the color pink or the small purple flowers adorning my head.

Keegan steps back, his face grim, and holds out an arm. I can do nothing but grab it and hold on. From behind him, I see another flash of pink, then forest green, before we head for the stairs.

My door closes on whispering and a faint sob.

CHAPTER TWENTY-FOUR

awn has always been kind to Vodihr; it paints the sick, misshapen city in soft strokes of gold. Dancers gather near the edge of the clearing in a light mist that swirls at our feet, moving fluidly, mimicking the steps we take.

I'm in line, Keegan behind me. We are waiting for our customary markings that have been prepared at the city's shrine. The occupants of Vodihr, as well as a handful of hunters and huntresses, have stretched out on the stone-paved main road heading outward from the city's heart to the clearing.

Around us, buildings made out of pillaged material loom. The closer we get to the main clearing—which is already being prepped for the day's events—the less populated the streets become, turning from stone to dirt. From "civilized" to primitive. Each building reflects an attempt to control, to harness, and yet Vodihr consumes all.

I take a step forward and into another memory.

"What do they use for the markings?" I asked, straining to keep my voice calm, fearing I already knew the answer. Weylin hadn't mentioned it and I had never asked what he used on his face each time he was called away to perform with the Revelry, but knowing Vodihr, there was really only one thing it could be.

"Blood," muttered the boy in line ahead of me; his eyes were closed tight as gnarled fingers swiped from left to right, then down his face.

I jerked back and turned away, ready to protest, but was stopped when a sharp finger poked me hard between my shoulder blades.

Reprimanded, I looked over my shoulder to find eyes staring at me from beneath a white hood. "Next."

The costumed priests and talas stand in view, making swipes and swirls at random on whoever is in front of them.

"What do the markings mean?"

The girl behind me answered, "I heard it doesn't matter. The sigils have long since lost their meaning. Only the gods know now."

I wonder at the "who" underneath their hoods, their white capes a strong contrast to the wide array of colors decorating the clearing. Is it Caitlyn who used to talk to plants? Or perhaps Torren, who took great pleasure in guarding the city and cutting down anyone who tried to escape?

I'm next and I step forward, my boot treads stifled by the dirt beneath me.

The wolf carcass from yesterday's sacrifice lays beside a scattering of half-filled bowls a short distance away, and filthy daggers and cloth lay beside those.

Blood, cooled and congealed overnight, is swiped across my right cheek first, one-two-three lines under my eye. Next, fingers dab three quick dots on my left cheek, and finally, a combination of a line and dot on my forehead and down my nose to my chin. I get a strong whiff of its coppery scent, the rancid tang so strong I can taste metal in my throat as the priest's fingers hover over my lips. It makes my eyes water and I grit my teeth.

Lips, just barely visible under the low hood, twitch before a hand waves me away and the priest walks off to refill his bowl.

I head toward the growing crowd as the music starts. It will stay a low hum until everyone is ready, and then the dancing will begin. From my spot, I can see Mistress Agata standing with this year's of-ferlings, who range in physical stature, gender, and age. The youngest grabs my attention, the boy with blond hair and a slight frame. He is tucked under the arm of an older boy. I cannot see the younger one's eyes, but in my gut, I know he is the young prince and my heart sinks.

He is dressed in forest green.

"Being royalty doesn't even save you, it seems," a voice mumbles to my left before belching.

I raise an eyebrow in question at the old man who'd spoken. It's true. Though, Vodihr never did have such a royal sacrifice before. The visiting royals—those partaking as hunters and hunt-resses—would undoubtedly have frowned upon their own chil-dren being taken for such a purpose—to be the prey.

The old man shifts his weight from side to side at my silence. His eyes are slightly crusted. His features, rough and sagging.

"A debt is a debt. The gods don't forget."

My mouth opens, but my response is lost as the chanting starts. The words that follow are foreign, some gibberish that Mistress Agata had added years ago for effect.

The dancers move into position; they are Vodihr personified as they stalk through the fog to fan out and face the crowd in a semicircle. I latch my eyes onto the prince, keeping him in sight. When he doesn't leave the performers, my eyebrows raise in alarm.

He is too young.

He cannot be an offerling.

The crowd starts to sway, lost to the trance being created. An elbow hits my ribs, a foot on the insole of my own as I kick out a leg to knock them away.

Mistress Agata's head bows lower.

And so it begins.

"What if I forget the routine? What if I miss a step?"

The other girls and boys around me were silent but I could tell they were listening to me as I voiced my fear—their fear. The masked woman before me, her face that of a crow, glanced nervously at Mistress Agata who watched from the raised platform.

"Don't."

One command and we were motioned to begin.

The dancers are ethereal as the sun rises behind them, a crowning moment of renewal that will end tonight with their sacrifice to their city's past crimes, to the gods.

Disgust fills me.

I remembered the feeling of the music as it filled me, igniting something buried deep—kindling this spark I had forgotten from my childhood. My feet were flying, my limbs outstretched as my head tilted back and I shouted toward the sky. I twirled and spun and bent and stomped. I kicked and twisted and screamed and cried. I was one with the song, one with the dance.

I became nothing.

A low moan slipped out, the blood painted across my cheeks and lips cracking.

The dancers' feet are getting faster, all of them blurring into colors and movement. I've lost track of the prince now, not sure if he is dancing or not, and the music speeds up. The heartbeat of the sound calls to the memory of my own dance, my own awakening before my fall.

The horn blew a low steady note. I stopped mid-step, my head bowing. I fell to my knees. The other dancers mimicked me. We waited. One. Two …

As one, those gathered—the townspeople and hunters and huntress—move to weave between the dancers. Couples latch onto each other; strangers pick a partner or two. The song picks up in pace again, sounding cheerful but warning of pain—echoing of lost hope and of angered gods.

I'm spun first by Keegan, who is maskless, the sign of a pet. His hands fall to my waist as he yanks me forward. His breath is hot on my neck when he leans down to whisper, "To your right."

I don't have a chance to respond—someone else has already grabbed my hand, calluses rubbing against my own as I'm brought against a hard chest. His scent hits me first and my knees buckle as we come together, then spin apart. My feet act blessedly on their own, my body knowing what it needs to do. My breathing stutters.

Embela's spell should have lasted two days. It's too soon. What is he doing here? I need more time.

Tilting my head back, I take in the mask he wears; a brown wolf, the thick fur framing the hair hanging over his brow. The plaster snout is slightly dented.

Our breath mingles right before his lips crash against mine. I groan, my eyes closing. The mask's fur tickles my skin.

I give in. I've missed him so much.

"Weylin," I whimper, pulling back; the blood on my lips cracks—I taste the copper.

He starts to speak but I'm pulled away and into the arms of a stranger. I offer a blank smile at my new dance partner, his face and mask bland and banal in comparison to Weylin's. I crane my neck to search the crowd—there.

I go from one person to the next, and finally I'm back in Weylin's arms.

His grip is tight, unrelenting. He growls at a huntress who tries to cut in. Her eyes narrow on us before she spins away and becomes a blur among bodies. I know we don't have much time before Mistress Agata appears.

"You have to go."

He ignores my plea, countering with, "What have you done?"

From over his shoulder, I see the weaving of a dancer in pink—only Agata ever wears pink here—coming our way. Her eyes are gleaming, her smile wicked and expectant.

"Why pink, Mistress?" I dared to ask.

She stilled before the mirror, the dress held to her chest. "Because he loves it."

"Who?"

The dress dropped and pooled at her feet.

I step back, my hand going to brush against his cheek. "What I had to."

His eyes roam from the crown I wear to the collar around my

neck. Before he can reply, I give him a hard shove, pushing him back into the crowd that is now writhing in euphoria at the song's climax. He's swallowed up in its movements.

In a daze, I enter the arms of another, letting them pinch and caress as they please. My body grows numb and the music fades.

"What have you done?"

What I had to do.

ÞRÁ

DESIRE

"The lovers are in a quarrel, how cliché," Reaper muses to the drugged woman in their arms.

Nip her throat, just a little. I'm thirsty, the mask murmurs. Reaper's skin crawls at the back of their neck. They ignore the voice, for now.

The girl in smoke-gray leans in and there's a whispered comment; the boy's eyes darken, a scowl already on his features before they are swept apart.

Entertaining, yes. But not nearly as exciting as—

Reaper buries their face in the lax woman's neck and licks a bit of skin. The mask tightens around their eyes. Her smell is intoxicating, a perfect blend of the herbs and ale she's been supping on since the night before. The blankness of her chest calls to them, whispering of a night to behold and the kill that always follows.

She isn't one of them.

Isn't a pet.

Yes. Take her … I am hungry.

Their bodies move together as they watch, one intent, the other lethargic.

They are picturing the two of them slipping away, going back to The House, when their eyes are drawn back to the girl in gray. A voice within their mind growls something unintelligible.

The girl reunites with the boy from before, only for an angry demand and the girl to shove him away. Her caress of a goodbye has Reaper shivering. She enters the arms of another and the dance reaches its apogee before tumbling into the final note.

The music slows to a stop. People grow quiet and Reaper grunts, biting the inside of the woman's neck. She gasps, her lips parting. They taste blood.

The mask moans.

Their eyes snap away, wanting to keep tabs on the girl and her lover.

The game continues.

Fine, comes the voice within their mind. It is resigned. *Take her instead.*

Grinning, Reaper adjusts their mask of bone.

Take … Rune.

CHAPTER TWENTY-FIVE

ours later, I'm sitting on the lap of an elderly merchant whose jowls ripple every time he laughs. His hand on my thigh is a show of dominance and I have to hide my own laughter. If he only realized I was steadily pouring one of Embela's potions into the glass he cradled in his other hand. It was the same potion I'd used here frequently as a pet—it had still been hidden in the floorboards of my old room and would put a person right to sleep.

Squeeze, potion, squeeze and pat, potion and me gritting my teeth. He takes a gulp of his drink.

A slight tremor goes through his meaty hand; the next pat has a little less strength in it.

I curl around him tighter and purr, moving so that my breasts nearly smother him when he flops face forward.

The only thing in my favor—besides the potion finally taking effect—is that my spot in the clearing puts me in line of sight with the young prince rushing amongst the milling crowd. Agata has him serving roasted meats and wine.

I've waved him over three times now to discreetly check on his welfare. At first glance, he was fine—unharmed even. Second glance showed the dark circles under his eyes and the bitten nails on his hands. The third glance had me snarling—which sent him scrambling away in fear. There were bruises on his shoulders, some old and yellow, some fresh and dark. What more was his clothing hiding?

Disturbed and uneasy, my eyes sweep the crowd. There's a mask staring prominently out from among those gathered. It is smeared with grime and made entirely of bone—likely a skull from one of the kinds of deer that roamed on Frumland, judging from the antlers still attached. The light catches a bit of skin under the hollowed-out nasal cavity and my hand presses against my stomach in revulsion.

Our eyes meet and I nearly rip the material of my dress in agitation. My entertained patron grunts at my movement and sits up, blinking.

The Reaper.

The Reaper has come.

So that's him. The Reaper.

The shadows near him scatter as the Reaper's mask bobbles a bit when he nods, a slight tilt of his chin that I nearly miss, before he glances away. I see his eyes tracking the young prince …

More skuggar scurry from the creature's path when he stands and starts walking. I sit straighter to follow his movements around the bonfire—seeing the shadows' threads twisting and creeping through the ground.

The closest shadow to me bristles, its materializing fingers digging into the dirt. The tip of my boot touches its threads and I feel a moment of anger and fear besides my own.

Above me, a branch shudders and I glance up. The raven is there, watching me with strange silver eyes. Its beak shines with the stain of blood and I cringe.

"Perhaps we should leave ... "

Shifting, I glance down at the merchant leaning into my chest again. I take a deep breath, angling so that he hums in satisfaction before faceplanting for a second time. The snore that immediately follows tickles and I roll my eyes before shoving him away. His huff of protest is followed by a *thunk*, then a groan. His body oozes onto the small wooden platform his money has afforded him.

Dispassionately, I lift the hem of my dress and step over his prone form. "Thank you for such stimulating conversation," I say.

Another snore is my only answer.

The three beats in succession on the drum has me pausing on the last step of the platform. Is it that time already? My eyes shift to the sun in its downward descent.

For a moment, I'm drowning.

I'm not ready. I can't ...

Fingers of the past caress my skin, hands dig into my hair and pull. My knees quake, my breathing coming in pants. The pain, real but not, is clouding my judgement, my awareness.

Yet, it isn't time—night has yet to arrive. There should be another dance, and perhaps even a second animal sacrifice, before the Bloodletting truly begins.

The heaviness of the air deepens. The fog creeps back in and even the crickets give pause.

Focus. Focus. It's just part of the show.

The shadows soothe me with snippets of warmth only to then whine when Mistress Agata moves my way through the crowd. I see the young prince's arm is clutched in her hand. In her other hand, she holds some rolled parchment, a simple black string keeping it closed.

"What are you writing, Mistress?"

"Nothing to worry about, elskan." She barely glanced up at me when she spoke. Her charcoal scraped quickly across the stiff parchment. "Not yet at least."

She shoved me from the room and slammed the door shut.

Again, the crowd is hers to control. The awe and fear on the faces of everyone present is terrifying. How can one person have so much power? Why her?

The smile on her face doesn't reach her eyes as she comes to stand a few feet away, the young prince now pressed into her side, half-hidden by her ruffled dress laden with sparkling crushed crystals.

"Come closer, elskan," Agata ordered.

I had to pry my fingers from the doorknob, shuffling into the room. I kept my eyes on the floor, on the tips of my boots, instructed by the tala that sent me to not look up unless Agata permitted it.

"Closer ... "

From the open doorway, I felt the other pets watching me. This wasn't the first time I'd been to the Mistress's chambers. I'd heard the whispers of favoritism, of suspicion. Some were envious of Agata's interest in me, wishing she'd chosen them instead. Others knew better and pitied me.

"Look at me," she cooed and I squeezed my eyes tight, shaking my head. "Look at me, Rune."

My eyes snapped open at my name.

"It is time to read the names of this year's offerlings—each available for purchase following the Bloodletting inspection. If you haven't paid the fee to become a hunter or huntress for the night, please do so now." Her voice is deceptively cheerful—her emerald eyes still give her away for the liar she is. "Also, remember you are permitted only one pet for the evening. While I appreciate greed," the crowd chuckles, "I'm afraid I cannot allow it at this event."

"What do you see when you look at me?" Agata asked and I blinked. "Do you see youth?"

I shook my head. I didn't know the Mistress's exact age. Some said she was thirty-five summers. Others said forty.

"Beauty?"

Again, I shook my head. She wore pink for some reason. Cloaked herself in imported ruffles and crystal, all her dresses artfully crafted to expose skin but not much. She was more gaudy than beautiful. More deadly, too.

"Then what is it?"

"Greed."

Her hollowed cheeks puffed with laughter at my squeaked response.

Agata waits for the murmurings of the crowd to fall silent before continuing, "As you all know, this is our nineteenth Bloodletting—special in a number of ways. And through all the trials we've faced, through our ostracization for being different, for keeping to the old ways, we continue to demand respect. Our gods demand respect! And it is a debt to us and our gods no village or city anywhere has yet to fully satisfy."

Silence.

She shifted, tugging up her pink nightdress that had slipped to expose one of her shoulders. I could see how frail and bony she truly was.

Facing the mirror, she studied herself, pinching her cheeks and upper lip. "Greed is good," she answered, green eyes sparkling. Her hand rose when I tried to speak. "Greed means I'm still surviving in this world."

I could only nod, and then she motioned to her wardrobe. "Pick out my dress for tonight." She hummed when I stepped away. "Make me greedier, my elskan."

A tala rushes onto the stage, murmurs something to Agata, and then scurries off.

"But we know this. We know they owe us, and until we are satisfied, we will continue to take their children, men, women; continue to make them bleed."

Stamping feet, whistles, and cries erupt from the crowd.

"Will you ever take me to Vodihr, Papa?"

He froze, his hands going still in the braid he was making in my hair. His hands gripped my shoulders, roughly turning me around to face him.

"How do you know of Vodihr?"

I frowned and reached for the doll Grandma Bell had made for me. I would not tell him she was the one who told me of Vodihr when we talked of the old ways, of the gods. "Am I not supposed to know of the city?"

He shook his head.

"But why?"

"Vodihr—Wraith is a place no child should ever go," he started, his words careful. "Wraith is for the greedy, the corrupted—those who like the old ways. The city itself is angry, full of darkness."

I shrugged and he tugged me back around, resuming braiding my hair. Grandma Bell hadn't spoken of Vodihr in that way. I'll have to ask Anik later if he knows how to get there.

Mistress Agata holds up her hand and the blonde-haired boy at her side is forced to huddle closer, his face still hidden in Agata's skirts—I see a glimpse of a collar on his neck and the chain that tethers him to the belt on Agata's waist.

"Let's begin, shall we?"

The crowd's roar is all Agata needs, and I drown out the noise as she begins to recite the names in alphabetical order: "Aerie, Angus, Barthon … "

Only after she finishes does a voice shout, "What of the prince? We were promised a special prize this year." Murmurs and laughter spur the voice to add, "The Arden prince—he is here, is he not?" I recognize the voice now. It is Ryder, the man we'd met on the road outside Vodihr. The man who unknowingly forced my hand because of his pet.

Mistress Agata's eyes slice deep, but her reply is calm. "Yes. He is."

Before anyone can react or ask more—she must have kept him strictly in The House so he wouldn't be recognized—a wave of her hand starts the procession of offerlings. They are paraded back off the wooden platform and the young prince is freed from his chain to join the end of the line.

There are hisses, curses, praises … Sound taints the air and accompanies the stolen squeezes, pokes, and jeers the offerlings receive. One girl's crown slips and the crowd boos; she flounders to righten it.

I have to look away. That girl had been me once. All of them were once me, with their resigned and tear-stained faces. Their bellflower crowns that bind them all together.

When the young prince stumbles on the steps, a hand shoots out to catch him, wrapping around his forearm and preventing his fall. I see his eyes widen and I try to get closer.

"Damnit."

Prince Gael's eyes flicker toward mine, narrow, then move back to his brother. His two guards flank his sides, turning to protect the princes from any threats. I'm relieved that Gael had at least gotten my note. I hadn't been sure the boy I hired after the morning rite to deliver a message would be trustworthy. I notice then in Gael's hand there is a leash and the person it is connected to blocks my path.

My head snaps up. "Anik."

I see his anger at war with his happiness that I'm there, safe for the time being. But the happiness bleeds away as he takes in my appearance, the bite on my neck just visible beneath the collar I wear.

"We had-have a plan, Ru."

I shake my head and pitch my voice lower to say, "You *had* a plan that would've failed. We've already discussed that. This was my game to play, my rules to abide by."

He grits his teeth, the veins on his neck bulging as he struggles for calm. "You don't know that. You didn't bother to stick around long enough to know that."

I shy away from the ale on his breath, telling myself it's just for the part he is playing, not a relapse. But still, when his hand raises to my face, I flinch.

"I-I wouldn't," he stammers, his voice strained. He lurches to the side.

Saying nothing, I glance to see that the young prince—I believe Gael said his name was Larken—has already joined the others. He is fighting back tears. I can see how badly he wants to fling himself into his older brother's arms when Gael moves back into the crowd. My heart hurts for them both.

"Anik," I whispered, "you have to go."

He said nothing, only took my arm and dragged me through the crowd and out of the room. Clearly, he wouldn't let me escape a second time.

But I couldn't help but notice how much worse his stumbling and weaving had become. The smell of ale coming off him was stronger, as were the drugs in his system. He wouldn't be coherent much longer.

He stopped and opened his arms and before I could remember how much I hated to be touched, I was flinging myself into his chest.

"I've got you," he soothed, but I could barely hear him over my own sobs. I didn't have much time. I needed to get him out of there. But I was so tired.

"After this is over," Anik whispers, drawing my gaze back to him. I blink the memory away. "There's something I need to tell you."

I don't like the sound of that, but before I can reply, I notice we're starting to get curious looks and I dart away. My hands grab for Larken who was wandering back toward Gael. I latch onto his shoulders, my smile scorching as I ignore Gael's growl and Anik's whispered plea and steer the young prince away.

We walk fast toward the tree line, away from Mistress Agata who has strayed far too close. I feel a dozen pairs of eyes on me and catch another glimpse of an antlered mask before I dodge behind a cluster of trees.

Holding my breath, I let it go on a sigh and I kneel in front of Larken. His shoulders are shaking with suppressed sobs. I pause, unsure of what to say or how to comfort him. He doesn't know me—I've only managed to see him in passing in The House, and each time, he's been under Agata's watchful gaze.

He makes up my mind for me, though, when he flings himself into my arms. With his head buried in my shoulder, I can feel the wetness of his tears and I bite my bottom lip till it bleeds.

"It's going to be okay," I offer, even though I'm lying to him— to both of us.

He shudders, nestling himself closer.

"Hush. I've got you."

✶

The echo of a drum alerts me to the beginning of the Bloodletting. As the sun leaches from the sky, I know I only have a few more minutes before it begins. I've already dropped Larken off with the other offerlings, his face pale but void of tears. I can only hope he manages to keep up the façade for a little while longer.

With everyone moving into position, I weave my way through their swaying bodies and head towards where the lead tala prowls.

In my hands, I hold the customary white candle she'll need to give to Agata during the ritual. I'm inches from the tala when a hand grips my wrist and brings me a to a halt.

Turning, my stomach clenches. Agata. Of course it's Agata, all swaddled in pink. The crystal embedded in the notch between her breasts looks like it is sharp enough to slice skin.

"I need your help," Agata intones. Her voice is devoid of its usual twisted mirth. In her eyes is a madness I've only seen once.

"This Bloodletting is special," the Mistress informed us. "It needs to be perfect. Showy." She circled us, a finger pressed to her lips. "I want everyone to be on their best behavior, for we will have a special guest tonight."

"Who?" a boy of nineteen asked.

Mistress Agata's eyes flashed from green to gray, back to green. "A god."

Apprehensive, I start to protest, only to receive a hard slap across my face. Stunned, I step back, not getting far with her iron grip on my wrist. Her nails dig into my flesh.

"Yes, Mistress," I manage to say, unsure what I'm agreeing to.

Her smile oozes malice. "Good."

I follow behind her and once again am faced with the crowd, hungry for excitement, pleasure, and violence. They jostle each other and pant after us as we walk by. They reek of sex and sweat, their eyes glazing over. The Bloodletting lust is already upon them. Madness clogs their rationality.

Vodihr is falling.

Beware, a shadow whispers as I'm led in the opposite direction, toward the waiting offerlings.

Come and play, Rune, another chimes in.

Ignoring them, I numbly give up the candle to take instead the ceremonial dagger in one hand and the lantern—the candle now inside of it—in the other. The dagger is familiar in weight and appearance and for a moment I wish I had its twin still with me.

A pit forms in my stomach as someone rushes to light the lantern dangling from my fingertips.

"What—"

The tip of a cup is shoved in my face, the liquid thick and sour as it slips past my parted lips. Gagging at the taste of iron and ash, I shake. I'm suddenly stripped, my dress disappearing and another taking its place. I look down and the white material, innocent and pristine, fills my vision. I trip over a sigil-embroidered train that pools around my feet.

My head is swimming now, the scenery of the forest blending with the starless sky and the faces before me. Tilting again, I nearly drop the dagger when someone roughly yanks at my legs to remove my satin slippers.

"What … ?" I slur.

There is the buzz of voices, the murmuring of shadows.

Mistress Agata's face crowds my vision. I blink once, twice, to get her to come into focus. Pink lips. Narrowed green eyes. High cheekbones highlighted by tightly pulled-back red hair. It takes me a second to process her words—"Just hold the dagger and the lantern and do what I say when I say it."

Brow furrowing at the order, my head falls forward in what is meant to be a nod but instead, it feels like I've broken my neck.

A tala's ceremonial veil is placed around my shoulders, the hood yanked up to obscure my vision, and a leash gets clipped to my collar. I'm prodded and pushed toward the clearing's edge.

Silence.

Even the shadows are quiet, waiting to see what will happen; more are starting to form in the back of the crowd.

"For centuries, Vodihr has been scorned by those around it. We have been kicked and beaten and killed for our way of life, for our alleged crimes against humanity because we still worship the old gods," Mistress Agata began, nudging me forward. "We pleaded for mercy, stealing to survive, and then the gods answered our prayers nineteen years ago."

The crowd croons, whoops, whistles.

I swallow bile. This story is new. I don't remember it.

"Our pact is clear. To become invincible against the outside world, we must provide sacrifices, our beloved offerlings, to the gods that protect us."

"Kill them, kill them all," the crowd chants; their eyes on the offerlings that cower before them.

"These offerlings are from the very towns that used to mock us. But now they are the ones who seek mercy. Who come to steal from *us* to survive, to nurture their petty wants and desires."

Mistress Agata tugs my leash and I follow her, the lantern steady, the dagger clenched in my palm. Through my veil, I see her drink in their agony, their joy, their hunger and it feeds her, gives her life. The small hints of wrinkles around her eyes disappear, the shakiness of her steps smoothing out. Her eyes flare with specks of gray before melting to a dark emerald.

"Do you remember why? When it changed for Vodihr?"

My vision blurs further, but I can still make out the devoted rapture Agata's pulled from those gathered. Even some of her pets—older ones who have been through multiple Bloodlettings—seem interested.

"No? I'll remind you." She smooths a crinkled line in her dress. "At first, we wasted five years sacrificing our youth, our own children, to keep our pact, only for an outsider to take, then kill, our Leiðtogi's daughter and granddaughter."

Hisses follow her words.

She continues to weave her story: "The outsider took what was ours, leaving a broken family and a broken city ... Oh, how angry the gods were."

The crowd moans and a memory taunts the edges of my vision. But before the memory can take shape, a female shadow, dressed in white, motions for my attention, her gray eyes shining with tears.

"We cried at the injustice. We mourned. Our Leader killed himself in a fit of wild grief. The other cities hid this outsider, shielded him from us. And the mocking began again. We were ignored. Slighted." Mistress Agata pauses, her voice growing stronger when she starts to speak again. "But our gods answered us again and we grew in power. No longer would we be leaderless and weak. No longer would we grovel at the feet of outsiders."

The crowd's feet stomped a singular repetitive beat: *Ours. Ours. Ours.*

"We created a performance—our beloved Revelry—and birthed our vengeful Reaper. We took them out into the world to take back what belonged to us. Each city now gives us their most prized beauties of youth, and in return, we let them have their fill of us. They are outsiders still, yes, but we are in control."

She slows to a stop, her monologue finished.

She motions for the offerlings to line up. There's a whisper on the breeze before a drum begins—it sounds like a thunderous heartbeat, but so much slower than mine.

Thump, thump, thump.

Another drum joins the first.

"Tonight, we honor our losses, our hope, our sacrifices." Her eyes pass over me, her lips peeling back to show teeth. "Tonight, we demand more blood."

Thump, thump, thump.

A third drum starts a low beat, encouraging the crowd to join the procession of sound. Their stomping becomes more fluid, more rhythmic. I'm unsteady, sick, but I manage to hold up the lantern and dutifully follow Agata when she takes the dagger from my hand and begins the next phase of the ritual.

There is ash on my tongue, a hint of flowers and spice.

Thump, thump, thump.

One of the masked pets follows her with a bronze bowl, collecting drops of blood from the palms of each offerling. Desperate eyes meet mine as I walk. I see every wince, every clenched jaw, every errant tear, every gasp and snap of teeth.

Thump, thump, thump.

The scent of copper grows as we reach the young prince at the end of the line.

"He is too young," I murmur.

Agata's lips twitch at my words. "Just wait, elskan."

What for what? I hold back the question, pleading to the gods for Larken to stay steady, to not try to run.

His eyes hold mine.

Mistress Agata glances between us, then smiles. She surprises me by turning to address the crowd once more. "I almost forgot … " Her tone is apologetic as the drums slow and the stomping sputters in confusion. " … to introduce our special guest tonight." She pulls Larken from line.

He twitches and I reach for him.

"I'll need a little more from him, of course."

The crowd laughs.

"It is him. I didn't think—"

"He looks just like the Ardenian king … "

I fight the shaking of my vision and knees, try to block out the whispers around me.

My ears buzz with static.

"The Reaper was most fruitful in his search this year, finding us a prince from the family that mocks us the most—*Arden*."

The crowd snarls as one.

The shadows whisper, their threads trembling in apprehension.

"We will prevail, as we always do," Agata soothes before jerking the dagger across both of the young prince's palms. He cries out and the crowd's stomping starts fresh. Agata gives his hands a squeeze over the bowl before pushing him back into line.

We leave the offerlings holding their injured palms and make our way back to the center of the clearing where the fire waits.

Thump, thump, thump.

Bones—some animal, some human—circle the pit, mixed in with the outer ring of wood etched with weathered sigils that call to the gods. Bundles of the ceremonial bellflower are thrown in and I can smell them burning from here.

A shadow watches from the edge of the stage.

"Mōðir, what was your favorite gift from Papa?"

"On the night we met, he picked a Campanula from my mother's garden. It was so tiny, so fragile … "

I sighed, staring at her back as she bent to tend to another plant. "Mōðir, that doesn't sound like a very good gift. We have bellflowers everywhere—they are like weeds!"

Her laughter brought a smile to my face.

Disoriented, I look to see Mistress Agata stopping beside the pit, the masked pet from before dutifully kneeling at her feet with the bowl held up to her.

Agata slices her own palm then, her blood causing the bowl's contents to steam and swirl hypnotically.

My memory is forgotten at the first inhale of smoke.

The shadows' whispers grow louder.

Tainted, a shadow whines.

Another whimpers in reply, *Unnatural.*

A third speaks incoherently; I can only make out one repeated word—*Evil.*

I stop breathing when Agata lifts my veil and exposes me to the crowd that watches. From amid the whispers and stomps, I hear someone growl.

Thump, thump, thump.

The drums match my heartbeat now, fast and unrelenting.

Agata circles me, her fingertips outstretched—every place she touches burns.

"You betrayed me, elskan," she whispers into my ear. "The gods are angry."

"Lies."

Thump, thump, thump.

"Truth!" She yanks back my hair, the tala's veil slipping from my shoulders to land at my feet.

"The old gods are gone! They don't listen to us anymore, not even you."

She blanches at my words and I wonder if I am more accurate than I even expected. Have all the old gods disappeared? Had they abandoned their people as new cities rose?

Thump, thump, thump.

"You're just like her." The ceremonial dagger is pressed to my cheek, trailing down and cutting into the skin. I feel a trickle of blood first before her words sink in and the blade's sting registers.

"Like who?"

Weylin's moving to the front of the crowd, Gael and Anik flanking his sides. Gael's guards are at the edge of the crowd, fighting to follow him.

Thump, thump, thump.

There is another prick of the dagger's tip, now on my chest, another trickle of blood, before Agata releases my hair from her grip. I suck in a breath right before she brings the dagger down and slashes across my palm. The lantern I hold, my fingers numb from gripping the handle, quakes.

My eyes snare on my reflection in the blade that hovers inches from my face. I struggle to keep my eyes open as Agata's wrist snaps back.

Thump, thump, thump.

A gasp, my own, as metal caresses my cheek. At the shuffling of feet, I force my eyes open. Spinning around, I find one of the offerlings, an unnamed girl with mousy brown hair, in a heap on the ground, the dagger having sliced clean through her throat.

It's tip peaks out from the other side, her head slightly lifted from the ground where she lays.

Thump, thump, thump.

"The gods are speaking to me," Agata explains to the crowd. Some show fear, most faces hold confusion. She moves toward the prone body, yanking the dagger upward and free from where it was embedded. "They say she wasn't worthy to become part of Vodihr."

Two of the priests come forward and drag the offerling's body into the fire; the flames roar and cackle—the scent of burning flesh and hair is heavy on the air as her body is devoured.

And still the drums beat on: *thump, thump, thump.*

Calmly, Mistress Agata returns to where I stand and takes the bowl from the still-kneeling pet—one who smells of sweat and urine now—and grabs my bleeding palm, bringing it to hover over the bowl's rim, squeezing. My blood causes it to boil, turning it black before she tosses the contents into the fire. She hands the dagger to me and faces the crowd.

Red stains my fingers.

Thump, thump, thump.

"It is done," she screams, throwing her head back in a shrill cry that echoes into the night.

He comes, a shadow moans.

The crowd screams with her—their gurgles swallowed up by the shadows that watch and pace just out of reach. They form a circle around us, caging us in.

Thump, thump, thump.

On the edges of the flames, a shape begins to take form—black, solid. Faceless.

Thump, thump, thump.

Eyeless.

I'm nearly blinded by the lantern when it's ripped from my hold, then shoved into my face. I stumble at the push between my shoulder blades, glaring at the tala who hurries to escort me back to where the remaining offerlings are lined up for the final phase of the ritual.

It is now when they will be taken by their bidders to become consolations for their kingdom's sins; sacrifices to Vodihr's greed.

The beast in the flames is eyeless. Its head tilts side to side.

I quickly slip the ceremonial dagger I'm still holding into my sleeve and wiggle it to where I can slide it into the band of my underclothes.

As soon as I let my hands fall back to my sides, they're taken up by the offerlings on either side of me. Their grips are tight, and I tighten my lax fingers in response.

To my left is a teenager, at least sixteen, her hair is an array of colors. It's pretty, but I can't get the words out past my nausea and dizziness to tell her this. Her lips quiver before she turns to face straight ahead.

She reminds me of another girl I once knew—Tasha.

"If you pull the strings any tighter, I'm going to pass out," I warned. Tasha just laughed in response. Her green and blue hair whacked me in the face when she jostled around me to rework the ties again. "Tasha, why—"

She poked me in the shoulder. "Oh, shut up. Weylin is going to go crazy when he sees you."

I snorted as she gave the leather corset strings another tug. "The patrons will love it, too, since I'm serving tonight."

Another poke in my shoulder had me whining.

To my right is the young prince. Larken's eyes dart around, unable to focus on anything. His breaths are short and hurried and his grip on my fingers tightens. He gives a squeak, and I wonder if he sees Gael in the crowd.

Blinking back sweat, my head bows, and I try to block out the whispers and laughs that surround me. People are talking, someone is crying, and I just want it to stop.

Rune.

The hand in my left—that of the girl with the pretty hair—is ripped out of my grasp and I flounder, unmoored a bit at the sudden loss. She leaves, a huntress at her side.

Eyes peer at me from the trees; the fire beast ventures a step from out of the flames.

Rune, watch, a nearby skuggi commands.

"And these two are yours," I hear Agata proclaim smugly. "The gods have smiled on you greatly tonight. One to use for enjoyment, the other to kept for work."

When I lift my head, I see a mask of grime-covered bone. The sigils are black.

Rune, watch! the shadow repeats, more urgently this time.

The young prince has an arm around my waist, clinging to me, pressing against my thigh. I feel his body start to shake. He's crying. I look down, he looks up …

And Agata's words finally register. "W-what?"

Agata reaches under the slit in my dress and removes the dagger I had hidden minutes ago.

"That's m-mine. You gave it … But I'm not … " My tongue fights my words and I swallow thickly. "I'm not part of t-the—"

A feminine laugh cuts my slurs off. Mistress Agata is nearly quivering with glee. "Oh, but you are, elskan." Her grins grows at my obvious confusion. "You see … when you break the rules of Vodihr, you owe it something in return."

"If I do this again," the Zila said solemnly, *"then you owe me something in return."*

Agata's perfume—a sickly scent of dead flowers—fills my nostrils as she leans close. "And elskan, what you owe is simple … " She leans in even closer, until our noses touch. "It's you."

"Anything," I managed to say, my voice breaking. I held Weylin tighter in my arms. "I'll give you anything."

What was left of myself to offer that Agata had not already taken?

The Zila's head bowed and the circle shifted, allowing us to enter.

I feel spittle on my face and the brush of Agata's nose as she turns her head and places a light kiss on my cheek—I nearly throw up.

"Behave," she orders before flashing a smile at our hunter, the winning bidder. He stops at her side, head bowed.

I watch her disappear into the crowd.

"Rune," Larken whimpers when a leash is clipped onto his collar.

I blink when mine is hooked too.

At the continued silence, my gaze narrows. Our hunter is too controlled, too reserved. The calculation of his movements pick at me the longer his stare avoids mine. He should be boasting at his god granted privilege, describing the ways I'd be expected to please him or how he had landed a spawn of Arden to do his manual labor.

"D-do we have a name to c-call you by?" I finally ask, mouth still laboring to form coherent words.

Where is Weylin? Anik? Gael?

My eye twitches as a bead of moisture wets my brow, the sweat cooling on my forehead as the henbane coursing through my system fades quicker than I expected. I'm not so dizzy anymore, and the nausea is starting to settle down into the pit of my stomach, finally leaving my throat.

The eyes through the antlered mask meet mine and I'm freefalling as gray meets umber.

"Papa will do."

I don't realize I'm screaming. I don't see the guards rushing towards us, the others still in line waiting to be claimed, watching me with horror. I don't see Larken fighting to get away as he is pulled forward.

I catch a glimpse of Anik pushing through the crowd—a red-eyed Weylin too, though he is stopped by multiple Vodihran guards. Gael is being held back by his own men.

The collar on my next tightens and I choke mid-scream.

I'm terrified.

From a distance, Mistress Agata grins and gives a little wave of her fingers.

Papa?

Not real, it can't be real. Not again. I jerk away, try to run. Not for a second time—no, please …

"Papa," I whimper, and then I am smashed across the back of the head and I'm falling forward into Papa's waiting arms.

"Hello, sá litli."

Hello, little one.

CHAPTER TWENTY-SIX

The first thing I feel is anguish, washing over me in steady rolling waves. I choke on a cry; my lips are cracked, sticking together. Something is heavy on the back of my neck, liquid oozing down my nape. My hair is matted—the pin lost—and sticks to everything from my back to my cheeks to a few uneven strands underneath my armpits. Disgusted, I try to move, but my arms won't budge.

My eyes pop open, look to the right, then the left, and a moan slips free before I can stop it. The bindings chaff at my wrists, and I can feel the numbness already setting in. I give a hard tug, testing, before my fingers bend around the rope and I look down. I've been changed again, this time into a simple white shift—one that oddly resembles what the grey-eyed skuggi from earlier wore: it even has the high-collared neck with lace.

"Mōðir ... Mama, you are so pretty."

Her reflection smiled at me from the mirror as she made quick work of her wet black hair. She finished combing it and began to braid.

I giggled from my spot on the bed when one of the shadows started making animals on the wall. At Mama's good-humored sigh, I turned to see the braid finished and hanging over the lace collar that hugs her neck. I was reaching to give the long braid a tug when the door downstairs opened and a voice called out ...

Relief hits me swiftly as I realize my legs are still unbound; I kick at the blankets near my feet, fighting another memory I don't fully understand.

That can't be my memory, can it?

Who is the woman with black hair that I keep seeing?

Who is the girl? It can't be me. Mama never let me get that close to her.

"Rune?"

I turn to see Larken in the corner of the room, his wrists and ankles bound to a chair. His face is flushed, the dark circles even more prominent under his wide eyes. There is a fresh cut on his forehead and a bruise forming on his chin. I want to ask what happened but can't find my voice.

This wasn't the plan—my plan. The prince was to be sold for labor; I'd offer myself as a second prize for the night for pleasure. Weylin would track us and when we were in our secure location, I would distract the hunter or huntress until the others all arrived. The prince would be whisked away, the hunter or huntress killed. We'd then be on our way to the *Tempest* and—

The door opens, a whisper of sound, but I hear it and turn to see Papa in the doorway, bone mask in place. Is he the Reaper?

His cloak is missing, his collar now undone. He eyes me

briefly, then looks away and begins to roll up his sleeves. A dagger gleams from its spot at his hip. Red winks at me when the gem hits the light.

"Papa, why are you here?" I whispered, stilling for a moment. He just stood there silently, still wearing the antlered mask covered in ancient carvings.

I began to struggle again, and the ropes at my wrists and ankles cut into my skin, twisting and ripping it.

When he walks to the bronze bowl to wash his hands, I turn to Larken. "Whatever you hear, don't look and don't open your eyes."

He bites his lip, his eyes going to where Papa stands, methodically cleaning his dagger. "But—"

"Please." My voice cracks and I feel the pressure of tears I refuse to let fall.

Larken's head bows. He turns away and shrinks in on himself as much as the chair creaking under him will allow.

I close my eyes briefly, then open them to see two shadows hovering near the prince, forming into shapes around him. I see a head appear, teeth flashing. Hands. A torso.

Protect him, I ask silently, knowing they'll understand. Their threads weave around Larkin tightly, shielding him from whatever may come.

What about you? one asks.

Rune ... a feminine voice calls and I twist to see a third shadow flickering, a woman half-formed. She's gone in seconds, melting into the floorboards—her threads, now a muted black-gray, spreading across the floor.

"Hush," Papa soothes, now at my side; I whimper at his sudden appearance. He cradles the dagger, his features still hidden by the mask. I see fresh blood on one of the deer's antlers and gag. The markings from before are gone.

I reared back and spit in his face. "Will you just get it over with already? Stop the game and be done with it … "

"Papa?"

Red—blood?—seeped from Papa's eye and touched the mask. And then I heard a sucking sound, and the blood was gone.

I pull myself out of the memory—claw my way out.

Rune. Rune, watch, a skuggi demands.

My eyes open.

Papa is kneeling before me; Larken is humming brokenly in the corner to himself. The dagger is inches from my nose and blurs in and out of focus.

"I don't … " Papa begins to shake. "I can't … "

I drag another breath in, then out. "Papa?"

His free hand reaches up to remove the mask—it peels away with a suctioning sound and drops to land on the mattress.

I first take in his eyes: they are dark, unreadable. His skin has an unnatural pallor to it, and there's a hint of blackness in his veins on his neck and forehead.

"You're sick," I mutter stupidly, and he nods and closes his eyes.

The dagger shakes in his hands. "I-I cannot begin to ask you to do what I must. But I need you to know, this—" he motions around the room "—wasn't supposed to happen the way it did. Not now, not before."

Everything hurts: breathing, blinking, listening.

I wait for him to continue.

"Your mother was … was so beautiful and I couldn't … I needed her. I was lost without her." His words are fading, his eyes growing distant.

I'm shocked when a tear rolls down his cheek.

"D-did Mama die?" I ask, hesitantly. I had thought Anik was still in touch with her. Had thought he'd tell me if something had happened to her.

Papa shakes his head, a hoarse laugh escaping. "You don't understand yet," he says. "But you will."

"I—"

He slashes his palm and cups my cheek. His forest green threads latch onto my skin and I fall into his memories.

He was running, running through trees that reached for him. Mocked him. Vodihr was falling behind. But he needed to be further away. They couldn't catch him. But "they" who?

He wasn't sure why he was running, or whom he was running from.

His thoughts were a mess, his breathing harsh. His face hurt. Blood dried along his cheeks and nose. His hair tickled his ears.

He saw her face, her disappointment and anger and fear. Her love. For just a second, she had been back—alive!

What had he almost done in The House? What had he been sent there to do? And by whom? The people he was running from?

The cottage came into view, its door already open. The norn stood in the doorway, one of her hands pressed against her chest. A young man stood behind her, his eyes narrowed.

"Goddric," the witch called and he stopped at the sound of her voice. "Goddric, where is she?"

He began to shake. He saw his wife dancing under the stars. Laughing at a joke he'd made. Giving birth to their daughter. Dead in a pool of blood.

"Goddric," Embela was standing in front of him, the young man just behind her, "where is Rune?"

He saw Agata holding out a mask, asking him to wear it for the night. His daughter tied to a bed. He saw himself ripping the bone mask from his face and running away. He had almost—

"I left her."

The memory stops abruptly and when his gaze meets mine, I flinch. "I need you to kill me, Rune."

"No."

He touches my cheek again.

Embela stumbled back, half-turning toward the path he'd come from.

"You what?" the young man snapped. "You left her with Agata?"

Salvia pooled in Goddric's mouth. He rubbed his hands over his face. "I almost—" He stopped. "It told me, made me think—"

"They'll kill her," the young man shouted. "You left her to die!"

"Keegan!" Embela yelled, but it was too late. He was already a blur of movement as he ran towards Vodihr.

Goddric fell to his knees, heaving.

Rune. Rune. Rune.

Papa's hand drops from my cheek. "You must."

"I won't."

He cuts the binding on one of my wrists; it falls to land limply against the sheets. I cry out as pain hits the sensitive nerves. The humming in the corner grows louder, choppier.

"I-I don't deserve your mercy." He strikes again and the rope falls away from my other wrist.

I react fast, moving to thump against the wall at my back. My arms are still limp at my sides, but I force my knees to curl and fold beneath me so that I'm mimicking him, kneeling. What has he done? What had he just shown me?

"It hurts, everything hurts: to eat, to breathe, to drink. I cannot find pleasure in the gambling halls or in sleep."

My lips curl back in a snarl. "Good."

Papa gives a ragged wet sigh, another tear escaping down his cheek. "Please, sá litli." He winces. "Please … Rune."

I smell the rot on his breath.

No mercy. I won't.

I find myself moving to yank the dagger from his outstretched hand, avoiding his threads that still search the air, and I press the tip to his jugular. One of my hands grips his hair, pulling his neck back to further expose his decaying skin. I relish the position I have him in and give a tug, soaking up his hiss of pain.

"I can't do this anymore," he pleads. "The ignorance. The killing."

A black haze clouds my vision.

"Ignorance of what? Did you try to forget what you did to me, Papa?" I could drag this out, make him suffer for everything— every lash of the whip, strike of a fist; every cruel word he has ever spoken to me. Already, shadows are pouring into the room, swirling around the bed. They are hungry.

I am hungry.

Rune, a voice calls from the corner. I ignore it.

"Rune!" a voice shouts in the distance. There is the bang of a door, followed by the sound of rushing footsteps in the hallway below me.

"Rune," Papa begs, angling his neck closer, a bead of black blood forming beneath the dagger's tip. "It has to be you. Your gift … "

I watch in morbid fascination as the black in his veins spreads to his cheeks. The tainted blood trickles down his neck, lower and lower, leaving a small thread in its wake. It touches my finger and I see stars—an endless night sky—before the face of a woman appears. She is beautiful. So young. Her face turns towards me and—

"She looks just like me."

Papa lets out a sob.

"Who was—"

The door bursts open—there is a blur of movement as Gael rushes toward his brother while Anik, Weylin, and Keegan take in the scene before them. I meet each of their gazes—lingering on Anik's horrified expression a moment longer.

"Rune."

Umber eyes meet mine as I jerk the dagger across Papa's throat.

Blood spurts onto my face, my hands, my nightdress. I lean down to whisper in Papa's ear, "Það er búið, Papa."

It is finished, Papa.

His eyes close, his lips brushing my cheek before he slumps to the side. I watch as the color leaches away with the life that still lingers in his eyes. When they glaze over and more of his threads leak too close for comfort, I move to stand, pushing by Keegan and going to calmly wash my hands and the dagger at the bronze bowl. I don't want more memories right now.

When I look up in the mirror, two shadows are embracing in the corner, their threads weaving together and pulsing with such joy that I feel a prick of tears, of anger and confusion.

I tremble when a hand grips my forearm. I shrug it off and continue to watch the water turn pink. I wash and scrub and wash again and still the stains linger; still the water is only pale pink.

The dagger mocks me from the bottom of the basin. Its red gem blinking through each fresh splash of water. I reach for it, wrap my fingers around the hilt.

"Rune, we have to go."

The tears finally spill free as I look up at Weylin. "I had to," I whisper to him, unable now to look in the direction of my bed. My hands go lax, floating uselessly in the water.

He nods. "I know." His hands move to grab mine, saving them from the basin. I see a wink of a red gem from the basin's depths before I'm pulled away. "We have to go."

I'm led past Anik who cannot look at me. Past the guards who are grumbling for us to hurry; past Gael who holds a sobbing Larken in his arms. I pass Keegan last, who is looking at the bed with an unreadable expression. And when he reaches for the deer mask, I cringe.

My feet touch the first step of the back staircase; the alarm bell begins to sound.

CHAPTER TWENTY-SEVEN

awn approaches.

Roots trip me as I run, my legs burning. Above me, I see flashes of white and gray and black feathers amid the branches. Below, the shadows are nipping at my heels, staying close, whispering reassurances. The forest fights us, trying to claim us for its own.

Faster.

Faster, Rune.

The wail of the bell chases us from a distance, the pounding of feet and yelling pulling at my subconsciousness. I slip in and out of reality.

"Weylin, please. Just a little bit further. Anik says his ship is waiting." I was dragging him at this point, covered in blood and sweat and dirt.

Anik himself is nothing but an angry blur. Gael and Larken stick close, hand in hand. Weylin flickers between being an adult and an injured teenager at my side. This time he is dragging me, broken and unconnected.

The skuggar are howling, urging me—us—faster, faster as we race through the woods towards the cliff's edge. Everything is a blur of sound and smell: fresh pine at war with stale copper. The Other is back, running with us; an impression among the trees.

My feet stumble over a branch and we go down.

I'm scared, I tell the shadows, yanking myself from the memory. *So scared.*

Their silence is answer enough; not even their shared threads of comfort—of light—can save me this time.

My breathing shortens and I trip again.

We burst through the trees and back onto the path to the circle of Vodihr's entrance. I can only hope it hasn't moved. That the Zila is waiting. Listening.

Focus, focus.

We round the bend and the abandoned house is waiting.

From the corner of my eye, I see a flash of movement in one of the second floor windows. A shadow is holding a candle—both flickering in and out of existence.

Her smile is sad. She holds up a hand to the chipped glass, pressing her palm on the pane.

A white feather falls to land on the windowsill.

The candle sputters out.

"Rune!" This time Anik is reaching for me, pushing me faster.

More steps.

I notice Keegan lagging further and further behind but when I go to stop, he motions me onward. He gives a little wave, then turns and takes a step back the way we came. His head is cocked to the side as if he's listening to someone.

I let go of Weylin's hand.

One of Gael's guards nearly knocks me over before I pick up the pace.

Breathe.

Nearly breaking down when the circle comes into view, I see the Zila waiting, her eyes narrowing on me. Her gaze shifts and she's focusing on something over my shoulder. I see her painted lips part in surprise, then begin to move rapidly. I can't make out the words over the sound of my heartbeat and the baying of hounds.

I'm so close—

And I slam into a wall of threads, forced to a full stop.

There is a scream in the distance.

The others reach the circle's edge and step inside without issue. Anik folds over, gasping; Gael sets Larken down, one of his hands moving to bury itself in his brother's hair. He turns to my brother, reaching for his shoulder. The guards immediately cover them, blocking them from sight. Weylin enters the circle only to immediately turn and meet my gaze.

A fog rises, shadows at my feet wiggling in agitation.

Sorry, one whispers. *You can't leave, yet.*

"Take them," I whisper and turn, the skuggar nudging me back to the path. Their threads creep up my calves and I'm loaded with memories and emotions that are not my own.

I'm sorry, another shadow whispers. *He needs to see you ... to remember who he is.*

There is a hiss followed by a wave of energy and I know they have disappeared; I know my brother, the princes and their guards, and Weylin have all been allowed safe passage to the other side. Ignoring the goosebumps prickling my arms, the hair on my neck standing upright, I watch a figure step from behind a cluster of trees, his footsteps soundless. A familiar mask adorns his face.

The shadows' threads tighten around my legs and feet.

I know it isn't Papa: the stature is off, the color of his hair different. He looks like—

"Papa is dead," I say.

The Reaper hears my whisper and nods, causing the antlers to catch the remaining light the full moon spills down on us through the trees.

In his hands is a body—a guard from the looks of it—with a broken neck.

My skin burns. I flounder for a weapon only to realize I have nothing to protect myself with, so my hands burrow uselessly into the skirt of my ruined shift instead.

The masked figure suddenly shudders and steps back. He turns, looking in the direction of Vodihr. The body slides from his hands.

I blink—he's gone—only for the shapes of other men in the distance to replace him. The baying is louder, and I can see the hounds now, too. There is a flash of a weapon, the *thunk* of an arrow hitting a tree nearby.

Rune.

Rune, come.

Once again, I'm facing the circle. The Zila is back, waiting.

The threads that held me back earlier fall away and my feet pull me, trance-like, across the threshold of the circle. My steps are clumsy, laboring.

Everything blurs when I reach the inside of the circle, the buzz of energy almost too much to handle. The gods are angry. Or excited. I'm still not sure how the circle of Vodihr works and the Zila refused to explain the one time I was brave enough to ask.

My vision narrows to a pinpoint; I block out the yells and howls; a raven's caws. One of my hands is pressed to my chest, the other held outward—

"Are you sure?" she asks, her voice filling the void between us.

My lips part on a breathless "yes" and I try not to fidget.

Her lips quirk upward and one of her hands shoots out to grip my arm. She drags a cracked talon across the puckered flesh of my palm. The skin gives easily, and she throws back her head, nostrils flaring as copper scent hangs like a dead weight in the air. The lantern attached to her hip sways as she does, beginning to flicker when she hums a single unintelligible note.

There is only beautiful silence. No pull of a memory.

Then a rush of cool, fresh air; a shadow's wail.

The Zila's eyes flash in regret and I close my eyes as the world tilts.

"Hello, Rune," a voice greets, and my eyes snap open in surprise. "And here I thought you were going to be delayed a little while longer." The giggle is odd and out of tune but familiar.

Blinking against the first rays of sunlight, I'm pulled out of the circle and into the arms of a waiting Vodihran guard. Confused, I push him away and try to steady myself.

I see Anik and Weylin on their knees between a handful of guards. Weylin is angry, borderline on the verge of a shift, his eyes flashing red; Anik seems resigned to whatever's happening. Gael and Larken are untouched, flanked by their guards. Gael has his hand on Larken's shoulder, but his eyes are on Anik, worried.

And then I see who it was who spoke to me.

"What—" My mouth is dry. "Mama?"

"Jocelyn, this wasn't part of the plan." It is Keegan who speaks, coming out of the circle from behind me to stand at Mama's side.

Distracted by his arrival, suspicious now, I turn to see Mama pacing the circle, looking like she is waiting for someone else to come through. Why hasn't the circle vanished? Moved?

Keegan reaches for her, only to have her glare and step away. His hand falls to hang at his side. In the fingers of his other hand, I see a bone mask dangling—

"The plan was my plan and mine alone," she mutters, a pout forming on her lips. "And I want this to happen now."

He rolls his eyes. "I can see that but you're—"

A shriek bursts from Mama's lips, cutting him off.

"Shut up!" she shouts at him. After a brief moment of silence, where she takes several deep breaths, she seems to regain her composure and turns to me.

I'm scared of the malicious glee in her eyes. "Mama?"

Darkness pulses in her gaze then. "*Don't.* Do *not* call me that." She shoves me to my knees; the guard behind me grabs my shoulders, pressing down to prevent me from standing.

"I-I don't understand."

She scoffs. "You wouldn't. You were always a slow child, never quite understanding or seeing the world around you." Her lips peel back. "Always talking and playing with your beloved shadows or taking up all your Papa's attention."

The last part had my gut clenching. "I didn't want it." I try to block out the remembered sounds of his crying, his crooning, the feel of his punches and slaps.

"No, I suppose not," Mama sighs. "He never really did understand his obsession with you, either. But it was obvious to me. Once *she* died, nothing—no one—mattered but you and drinking and gambling."

"Once who—"

Anik cuts me off, "Mother, this really isn't the time."

"Stop protecting her!" she roars, a dagger appearing in her hands. When I see the red gem in its handle, I still. How had she gotten one of Agata's daggers? "Stop protecting this ... this freak." Her cheeks are damp with tears now, and she's sniffling. "She killed your sister, took your father away from us. She deserves this."

"I know she does," Anik agrees and my head snaps in his direction. "But not like this."

Her eyes burn brighter at his words. She motions the Vodihran guard to let me stand up, beckons me to come forward and stand before her. Her hand cups my chin, forcing me to look at her once I'm standing. I watch blood, black, drip from the corner or her mouth. She frees me for a second to wipe it away, laughing. Her stained fingers reach to grip my chin again.

"Oh, how long I've waited to do this—again."

There is a pause, a sudden stillness as her eyes widen and I—

The house creaked, settling on its foundations as she stepped upon each stair with care. Shadows watched from the walls; stalked close from behind. They were powerless to stop the events unfolding, powerless against her bitter and festering wrath.

She had waited so long for this. Had waited for the invitation to come to Wraith. For the means to fulfill her darkest desire.

Her face was devoid of emotion beneath the antlered bone mask she had been given upon stepping from the circle into Wraith. There was a quick kiss, a nip on her lip, then the mask latched on, molding to her features. She was pushed in the direction she needed to go.

So close. She sucked in a deep breath.

The dagger in her hand was out in the open for anyone to see. The mask was alive, practically begging for an audience—for witnesses. A scene in her mind played over and over, showing her the sweet revenge that was mere moments away.

Up ahead, she could hear a murmured conversation, a protest in a child's voice. The voices made the taunting in her ears louder and her hand tightened on the blade's grip. She began to hum—it was a song she used to sing for her daughter. The sound echoed in the folds of the cloak hood snug around her head.

There was a flash of white.

She followed the other woman, drinking in the surprise, then horror, that filtered across her face when she turned to face the doorway.

This was it. Her body a blockade that would fall.

"Wait. Please—"

The dagger jerked upward then back, breath caressing her cheek before the woman stumbled back into the room and crumpled to her knees.

High-pitched screaming came from the corner of the room just as a man's roar filled the downstairs. Goddric charged up the steps, meeting her at the doorway. His eyes fell on the scene before him, and she soaked in his devastation—the quivering of his lips, the sagging of his frame.

She turned back to the woman lying on the floor, blood pooling around her body from the hole in her stomach. Her hood fell back.

The blood crept outward, licking her boots, and she smiled.

The young child, no older than five, wailed louder from the corner she hid in; her hands dropped the blanket and pillow she held to bury themselves into the fabric of her night dress. She stumbled forward, tripping over a black leather book. Her voice was raw and broken as her eyes traced the blood that flowed forward, taunting her.

"Móðir?" the girl sniffed. "Mama?"

Jerking at the word, the cloaked woman realized she was still standing there calmly, the dagger dangling from her red-smeared palm and fingertips. It was not yet finished, her revenge not yet fully fed—it was hungry for more.

The woman had taken her husband.

The girl had taken her daughter.

More. More. More. The mask demanded it.

*"Jocelyn—*don't."

Deaf to the command, she straightened and stepped away from the body. Her cloak fluttered around her ankles, gathering blood in its hem.

"Jocelyn." There was a brush against her arm, fingers around the exposed skin of her wrist. And she reacted, slamming her fist first onto the arm that bound her, then into Goddric's nose.

"This is my moment. Mine."

Movements calculated and controlled, she motioned the child forward. When she was ignored, she reached out and yanked the girl into the open, forcing her to stand by her mother's body. Patiently, she then waited for the child's chubby, tearstained face to look up, for their eyes to meet. Her own eyes hardened against the tears on the girl's face.

A face so sweet.

So naïve.

Not her daughter's.

For a second time, the dagger was jerked upward, but this time, there was no twist, no jerking free, no dying breath because she was pushed away almost immediately after her blade connected with soft flesh.

She stumbled back, mesmerized at the sight of the dagger's gem, once white, turning red.

"No!" Goddric jumped, twisting to catch his daughter. They fell together in a heap, her body cradled in his arms, blood seeping around them.

The sudden silence was unsettling; no breathing, no cries, no dripping of blood.

Alarmed now, the woman watched darkness hover over the child's body. She watched as the pool of blood began to contort into nameless faces along the floor before seeping into the child's pale skin, her veins turning black.

"What have you done?" a woman demanded from the hallway.

"I—I don't know."

"What have you done?" I repeat aloud, the memory fading. Dazed, I don't have time to react before Mama steps forward and slams her blade into my stomach, burying it to the hilt. I hear myself gasp; there's a faint wail in the background.

Then there are the sounds of a struggle, a muted roar.

I hear Mama's satisfied moan of pleasure, feel the heat of blood as it trickles along my navel.

The events of the memory begin unfolding again.

"You weren't supposed to kill the girl," Agata snapped, rushing to kneel at Goddric's side. He was hunched over, rocking back and forth.

Reprimanded, confused, she ripped the mask from her face and let it hang between her fingertips.

I slump forward, Mama catching me in her arms. She flicks the dagger's handle and sends a pulse of pain crashing through my shock. One of her hands moves to cup my cheek; she begins stroking it, reminding me of how I used to crave her love as a child, love that I never got.

Was it even *her* love I craved?

I feel her breath on my ear, smell the staleness, the flowers as she breathes, "Pathetic." Spittle from her words lands on my lips and I turn my head away.

She lets go and I fall to my knees and hunch into myself, the pain growing. I fight the numbness as it works its way downward first. I'm cold, can't feel my knees in the grass and dirt.

"Rune, Rune stay with me."

I'm tilted backward, my eyes opening to face the approaching daybreak before a face obscures it.

"Weylin," I whisper and watch his face tighten; he nods. The red fading in his eyes.

"Breathe, breathe with me," he encourages, his voice breaking.

"Breathe, breathe with me," I demanded, staying at his side, my hand on his back as he fought the rage. "Come on, Weylin."

"Rune, focus on me," he pleads, and I blink only to slip away again. I'm cold.

"Focus on me, only on me," I soothed, stroking his back up and down. He gagged and I winced.

There is a flare of pain and I cry out, my back arching with the dagger as it's pulled out. I feel a burst of blood before the numbness spreads back in, eating the feeling away and I sigh—a small smile on my lips.

How odd. The dagger's gem is white. Had it always been that way?

Weylin tosses it away.

"Rune, please."

Skuggar are gathering around us. From my feet, I see a shadow form outside of Vodihr's circle, its figure skeletal and bald, bones barely covered by translucent flesh. It sniffs the air, its gaze coming to land on me. It begins to crawl toward where Weylin holds me, hunched over pressing on my wound.

Anik grabs one of my hands, squeezing it tight but I can't look his way. I feel all of his anger, his sorrow, his guilt.

'I know she does,' Anik had said.

Do I? Do I deserve this?

Gael moves to crouch at my feet, obscuring the skeletal skuggi still creeping across the ground, getting closer. Gael's words to my brother are lost—I'm too tired to pay attention to what he has to say.

Larken stares from over his brother's shoulder, his face crumpling.

Keegan's still here, and Mama, too, is at his side. His head is bowed low, the mask still dangling from his fingers. Mama smiles when our eyes meet.

A hot liquid presses against my lips and I gag, moving my head to the side.

Another glimpse of the shadow—it's closer now, crawling over the dead bodies of Vodihran guards. Its pace is steady and determined, its eyes completely black—fathomless. Tuffs of red hair dot its scalp.

"Rune."

Weylin fills my vision completely, blocking out the ancient shadow man. He turns my head back upwards, toward him. I take in his tears, the streaks of blood on his cheeks and neck. The still specks of red in his eyes. He chokes back words, strangled, and presses harder on my wound. I squirm in agony under the weight of his hand.

There's a flash of gold that catches my attention, it dangles from the leather around Weylin's neck. There's a ring hanging beside the engraved bone pendant I gave him. There's an engraving—*fritt*.

Free.

"Is that … ?" I stop and squint, everything going blurry again.

He tries and fails to laugh. "It's for you. I never … I never meant to leave you, Rune, at least not for long. I left you a letter. I went home to make amends with my fjölskylda to get this." His hand cradles the ring and I feel the sting of tears as the black onyx catches the light.

"I'm sorry." So much time was lost, so many things left unsaid. I fight to keep my eyes open.

"Don't be," he manages. "We will be okay—*you* will be okay."

I shake my head. "Mundu eftir mér," I beg and watch his eyes darken. *Remember me.*

I feel selfish, greedy, asking him to remember. It's unfair of me to have my shadow stain him when he should be free to live his life after … after I'm gone.

"Ég mun alltaf muna eftir þér," he utters, his words sounding like jagged stones. *I will always remember you.*

The skuggi creature is at my legs now, and I can feel its skeletal fingers wrapping around my ankle before it gives a tug. Darkness clouds my vision.

"I love you." I reach up to brush my fingers against his lips and let my hand fall to wrap around his, still holding the ring; I give his fingers a squeeze.

A raven caws in the distance.

His cry is the last thing I hear before I give in to the creature's second tug and am dragged into the darkness.

~~MISTÖK~~

MISTAKE

The Reaper waits for satisfaction to fill the marrow and gaps of their-*his* bones, waits for it to ignite his blood and create a fire of content. Waits for the mask to congratulate him.

Instead, the emptiness is suffocating. He fights against crushing dismay as Jocelyn moves past him without so much as a word, stepping over dead guards. Without looking back, she makes her way into the woods, sidestepping the circle of Vodihr.

She is humming faintly.

He shakes his already-muddled head. H-how did he get here? Hadn't he just been watching the girl earlier at the party?

He remembers Agata holding out his mask ... Remembers putting it on—

"Rune!" the pet roars, drawing his attention as saliva pools in the sides of his mouth. He is nauseous and doesn't know why. A headache is forming at the base of his skull.

His face feels heat and a breeze. Is it bare?

Wait. Rune ... Rune had been part of the Bloodletting and Goddric had been there. But Goddric was dead now. And the matriarch of Vodihr, the last witch ... She's dead, too. He'd killed her just before the ritual. Then they'd escaped, made a run for it. He'd turned back because someone was calling him.

Where is he now?

This wasn't the plan, the mask says. *She was supposed to be mine-ours.*

At odds with himself, he watches the pet ... No, not a pet. Not anymore. Weylin. He knows Weylin. Had been friends with him ... right?

Weylin is shaking Rune, demanding in broken slurs she open her eyes. His grip has to be bruising her as he presses harder on her wound, trying to stop the bleeding. And the blood: the red of her blood is mesmerizing to him. Rich and dark. It begins to clot; soaks the ground beneath her.

Her brother, no, Jocelyn's son, babbles on her other side, talking too quickly to make any kind of sense; he still holds her hand.

Reaper's mouth twitches, amused, even as another bout of nausea rolls through his stomach.

He feels another brush of a breeze and touches his face. It's bare ... Why is it bare?

He feels the wetness of tears on his cheeks, the press of terror in his mind.

The prince—the older one—assesses the situation quickly and gets to his feet. The younger prince is dragged to his side, still sobbing. "We have to go."

Weylin bares his teeth, red flooding the edges of his irises. His sudden movement, a twist of his torso to face the prince, causes Rune's head to fall Reaper's way—her pale cheeks, her long lashes.

He sees a newborn he is afraid to hold.

He sees a child of four, giggling as he, age nine, teases her from the doorway of the house. They'd been outside playing hide-and-seek.

He sees a child of eleven, bruised and cradling a broken wrist on the outskirts of Vodihr's woods as she cries for someone to help her. She doesn't know he is watching her, waiting to take her back.

He sees a sixteen-year-old girl, defiant as she faces Mistress Agata. The whip strikes her again and again.

And he sees his half-sister in the arch of her brow, the shape of her nose, the darkness of her hair. Her spirit is the same, her eyes a quiet gray. Why had he never noticed before?

But he had.

He had.

The mask made him forget.

She made him forget.

Bile burns his throat, his lungs contract. Skin crawling, he stumbles back, the prince's eyes cutting to him—

"Keegan?"

He thinks he catches a glimpse of his sister hovering at the edge of Vodihr's circle, a hand covering her mouth as she stares at her daughter, a deluge of colorless feathers falling from her fingertips.

"Gods ... what have I done?"

Keegan vomits, the bone mask slipping from his hands and onto the forest floor.

~~ÞRÆÐIRNIR HENNAR~~
HER THREADS

Weylin barely glances at Keegan when he vomits—his eyes are on Rune, denial already forming to burst past his lips. The beast within him roars in outrage, a need for revenge and blood.

He had decimated the Vodihran guards, but that wasn't enough.

He thinks then of meeting Rune in Vodihr, of their time together—of the defiant words, of stolen touches, shared smiles, of the pain, and love, and heartbreak, and confusion … Thinks of their escape, of her unwillingness to let him go until she thought he had left her. Thinks of his journey home and his father, his sister, and his brothers; of his mother's ring. Everything tangles in his head, his heart, into this moment—this *now*.

"Rune," he gasps, feeling her blood burn his palms. Still he stays steady, keeping pressure on the wound.

Rune!

He jolts at a woman's cry nearby. Looking up, he sees a figure hovering at the edge of Vodihr's circle. A hand covers her mouth, her eyes blank yet watery. She is dressed in a white shift, a wound on her stomach the same as Rune's.

She must sense his gaze, for when she looks at him, she nearly fades completely—a jumble of feathers falls from her fingertips before she solidifies again.

When he blinks, she is pointing at Rune, saying something he cannot hear. Weylin's head bows; one of his hands moves to stroke Rune's still-warm cheek.

Don't let her go.

Startled, Weylin looks up into the eyes of the shadow, her gray eyes wild but determined. She looks so much like Rune.

Don't let her go, she orders again, and she points to where his other hand rests against Rune's wound.

His eyes narrow at the nearly translucent gray threads tangling with his fingers, seeping over his hand and towards the ground.

"I won't," he mutters and from the corner of his eye, he sees the woman nod, her lips in a small sad smile before she fades.

~~SANNHET~~

TRUTH

CHAPTER TWENTY-EIGHT

une …

When I first open my eyes, I see nothing. Whatever space I'm in is void of life and I shudder at its stillness—instinctively knowing that touch and sound have no meaning here.

Sweet girl, ljúfa stelpa, it's time to wake up.

A light in the distance approaches, flickering in and out. I can make out the whiteness of a candle encased in a lantern, make out the jumping contortion of the flame itself. With the light comes a rush of shadows. They are dancing all around me, gleeful and sad all at once. Yet just as fast, they disappear back into the void.

"Hello, Rune."

The Zila stands before me; there's a pressure in my forehead, one that drags my gaze downward to the dirty helm of the Zila's dress.

"Am I dead?" I feel hollow at the question, a husk of myself. The pressure in my head grows, expanding to the backs of my eyes where it sits and pulses.

"Not yet," she offers and smiles. It is creepy and at odds with everything I know of her. I've seen her smile before, but not like this. But abruptly, before I can think on it anymore, the smile falters and she glances over her shoulder.

A mist trickles in, and with it, the sounds of laughter, crying, shouting. I hear voices that fluctuate in volume and dialect.

"Come."

"Come," the Zila commanded, motioning for me to step forward.

I hesitated, Anik's head falling down to rest on shoulder. I felt his slow breath against my skin as he whispered, "Ru? Ru, where am I? What—?"

Hushing him, I adjusted my hold on his waist and stepped forward.

The Zila nodded as the circle parted, repeating, "Come."

I was halfway through the circle when I heard footsteps behind me. Quickening my pace, I burst through the circle and startled the young woman prowling around the circle's outer rim. Her dark brown eyes met mine, widening when they landed on my brother.

"Take him," I said, shoving a sputtering Anik forward.

Stepping back, the scent of the forgotten sea and coconut teased my nose, I felt hands yanking at the back of my dress.

Shaking my head from the memory, common sense suggests sitting there, curling into a fetal position, and sobbing because if I'm not dead yet—or so says the Zila—then I know I will be soon. No living soul is allowed to enter the Skuggaland and that's undoubtedly where I am.

But it appears that common sense has deserted me, since I feel my legs shake before I take one step, then another. I grimace but follow my feet.

The mist swirls, pulsing with flashes of light. I'm transfixed by the colors and whispers it tempts me with. So many threads. So much life.

See me.

Look at me.

Rune …

One light fights with the rest, standing out as it twists and becomes a light lilac thread. It flickers, fading, and I step forward. When I stop, hand outstretched, and focus on it, I'm nearly blinded by its intensity. It vibrates, waiting.

Look, look, look.

Glancing up, I find the Zila staring at me, perplexed—unsure, even.

Fingers brush my arm, then my ankle. Something cold nudges the back of my knee and makes me think of Birgir. My chest tightens at the gentle chuff and brush of fur, but when I reach down, he isn't there.

"Once there was a child who spoke with shadows … "

To my left, the lilac thread is back, and a shadow takes the shape of an older woman. It's an abrupt but easy transition, the most fluid of any skuggi transition I've yet seen.

And in here, I can hear her aloud.

She moves to sit, hunching forward to lower herself into a cross-legged position, her back curved with age. Her skin is weathered, sagging from the years she's spent battling the trials of life. Rocking now, she mutters to herself, her hands hiding something that rests in her lap—a doll made of straw and bone.

"Grandma Bell?"

Her smile is blinding when she looks at me, and I try not to wince at the fact she has no eyes—only holes where they should be. A darkness chases across her features before she motions me over, impatiently waving with her hand to get me to hurry.

I sit in front of her, mimicking her cross-legged position.

"Rune, my sweet Rune. I have been waiting for years to show you this."

There's no time to ask what she means; her hand rises to tuck strands of wayward hair behind my ears, just as she had done when I was a child. Her touch is gentle, loving—her fingers moving to stroke my temple and press on the knot between my eyes.

It pulses and I sigh, leaning into her touch.

"Listen," she whispers. "Watch."

"But Mama," I whined in defiance. My lips shaped into a pout as I tried to mimic the look Anik gave to get away with anything. "Pleaseeee, I want to stay just a little longer. Grandma Bell was just about to show me her storybook—"

A hand slammed down on the table, causing me to jump back. I landed on my backside, the wooden floor cold and hard beneath me. Xavier hissed at me from under the table and I stuck my tongue out at him.

"Enough, Rune," Mama said then, wearily. "We have to get home; Papa is waiting for us."

Quickly, I avoided her gaze, knowing if she saw my unhappiness, it would only feed her irrational anger. I should have been grateful she at least remembered to come get me this time. Last time, she had forgotten about me and didn't send Anik to fetch me until the next morning. I had gotten whipped because of the inconvenience I'd caused.

"Yes, Mama," I whispered, keeping my head bowed.

There was a shuffling of feet, the thump of a cane, and then a wrinkled finger tilted up my chin. "Why don't you go grab the doll I made for you and let me speak to your mama for a second?"

I was already nodding eagerly, my feet swift as I raced to Grandma Bell's only bedroom and the doll I had put down for a nap. Already I was thinking of how I would beg Anik to play house with me.

My brow furrows. I remember this, though it is fuzzy. "What storybook?"

"Hush," Grandma Bell croaks, her fingertips pressing harder against my temple to the point I can feel the ragged edges of her nails.

She waited until Rune was out of sight before turning to face Jocelyn. "This has gone on long enough," she snapped, jabbing a finger into the younger woman's chest. "You cannot allow that child to continue growing up thinking she is someone else."

Jocelyn's eyes flashed, anger again darkening her expression. "You forget your place, Embela. She is my *child now and* mine *alone."*

Embela scoffed, thumping her cane once; her features changed, smoothing out, her hair elongating and darkening to pitch black streaked with gray. "So you've fooled yourself now, as well. Does Goddric know how delusional you've become? Surely he sees—"

"He only sees her *and will only see* her *because he is lost in guilt and pain," Jocelyn snarled. Spittle gathered at the corners of her lips.*

"Because you terrorize his daughter before him each day? Killing her mother wasn't enough? What happened to Tillie was an accident—"

"Say one more word and I will kill her." A tiny smile suddenly contorted Jocelyn's face. "I will kill her again, and this time, I'll make sure

she stays dead. I don't care what Agata says. We don't need you; I can find another witch to make her tonic. Coming here just hurts Goddric because you remind him of her." She sighed.

"Either way ... Goddric will suffer as he should. If he hadn't left me. Hadn't fallen in love with your daughter. Hadn't gotten her preg-nant. Married her when he was already married to me, home raising our three-year-old and pregnant again ... " Her voice trailed off as tears spilled down her cheeks.

"Mama! Mama, look!"

Jocelyn eyed Embela, her gaze full of warning. The witch let her body shift seamlessly back into Grandma Bell's, her face deepening into a mapwork of wrinkles, her hair growing shorter and white.

*"Say anything to her, Embela—*anything*—and you will never see your granddaughter again." Her face was tearless, her eyes cold and clear, as she turned away.*

The pressure of fingers fades and I open my eyes. It is Embela who straightens before me, her features smoothing out; hair long and white now, eyes clear gray and bottomless. The bruising, thick and dark around her neck, stands out like ink stains on parchment and I bite my lip.

Grandma Bell and Embela are the same person. How had I missed that? I think of Xavier, a cat who'd been alive as far back as I could see in my memories, but who had never aged. I thought of a cottage where I had always felt safe. Of a doll I'd left behind one day and had never seen again.

Of a woman who'd protected me when Vodihr wanted too much. Who had made my tonics, but who had still read me stories so I wouldn't completely forget.

But I still forgot.

My chest aches. I want to be angry. Why hadn't she taken me from Jocelyn? Or from Agata?

"Embela, I don't—"

"I love you, child."

She places the doll, once mine, in my lap and leans over to kiss my forehead.

I clutch it tight as she fades, taking her threads of lilac with her.

I'm alone, the fog covering my legs, my wet lashes sticking to my cheeks. Nothing is making sense. "But Amma, I don't understand."

CHAPTER TWENTY-NINE

I t's okay, Rune," a child's voice calls out.

A light yellow thread appears now, tangling itself around my hands still holding Embela's—no, *my* doll. I pick at the yellow thread, in awe of the softness of it against the bone and straw doll.

"Come play, Rune Nornwood," the little girl shrieks, her giggles bringing a smile to my face.

"Tillie Hansen," I call out, my voice much younger. Dimly, I'm aware of the change. "Where are you?" The thread unravels in my hands as I stand, the doll falling to my feet.

"Come on! Papa is waiting for us."

Experimenting, I give the thread a light tug and watch it fade before a little girl in the distance appears. She waves at me, skips ahead, and the fog rushes to hide her.

"Coming!" I shout and dash forward, panicked when at first she isn't there.

Then a little hand is grabbing my own; I look down into the child's face. The dried blood above her brow, dirt and a bruise I had missed before on her chin, the laziness of her one eye. The gaping of flesh. There are leaves and a few twigs in her dirty blonde hair.

She is the same child as before, the one from the forest.

"Who are you?" I ask, my voice soft and hesitant. I know I should know her, but when I search for her name, there is only buzzing.

Her face scrunches up unhappily, her lip quivering. "You don't remember yet? You just said my name … "

"I-I did?" I shake my head and she sighs in disappointment, her shoulders drooping.

Her face quickly clears, though, and her grip on my hand grows tighter. "That's okay, she said you might not remember me and I shouldn't be sad about it."

I frown, the earlier pressure returning to move from my fore-head and eyes down the back of my neck. "Who?"

The little girl laughs. "Your mōðir, of course!" At my stunned silence, she huffs and impatiently tugs me forward. "I'll show you," she says. "Watch."

"Runeeeeeee, no fair! You can't always win at hide-and-seek," the five-year-old whined, a frown on her face. "You're cheating!"

I stuck out my tongue. "Am not!"

"Are too!"

"Am not!"

"Are—"

A woman laughed, the sound clear and friendly, even if a little exasperated. "Let's agree to disagree, Tillie. My daughter," she glanced pointedly in my direction, "has some hidden allies that help her."

"Mōðir." I huffed and was going to say more, but the look on her face made me stop—her brow was raised like she knew exactly what I was thinking. "Fine."

Her smile grew and she reached out to gently tug a piece of my hair. "Good girl." The snap of a twig had her turning, her eyes lighting up as she shooed me away. "Now go play with Tillie."

Tillie raced off but I stopped to wave at Papa, who was still dressed in his forest green guard uniform. He winked at me before reaching for Mama and pulling her into his arms. They kissed and I muttered an "ew, gross" before running into the trees.

I stumble in the memory, my memory, jerking myself back and away from the shadow's—from Tillie's grasp.

Confused, she turns to look at me.

My eyes feel pinched, my nose clogged. I run a shaking hand through my hair and give it a tug, trying to relieve some of the pressure building within me. "I don't understand," I tell her, fear in my voice.

Tillie's eyes soften, and she holds out her hand for me to take. "Keep watching."

"Tillie," I called out, panting. "Just ... wait ... stop!" I groaned, bending forward at the knees. "You win, you're too fast," I complained.

Leaves rustled to my left and she burst forth, a wild shriek coming from her lips that had me jumping back, yelping in surprise. She fell into a pile on the ground, laughing.

Irritated, I crossed my arms and looked into the trees. At first, I saw nothing but dead leaves and some yellow patches of grass still cling-ing to a long-gone summer. Then, the first shadow appeared and, there, another. Soon, three little skuggar children stood around us, half-formed. They were watching and waving and whispering to me.

Can we play too? one asked.

Yes, yes, can we play?

I sucked in my lower lip, my teeth opening a scab. Mama had said to not talk to the shadows when I was playing with Tillie because she'd be afraid. But Tillie wasn't afraid of anything, she told me so. Would Mama get mad? Would Papa? Tillie and I had been friends for a few months now. Surely it would be okay.

"Rune, let's do something else," came Tillie's voice, her arm brushing against mine. She stood beside me and stared in the direction of where I was gazing.

From the corner of my eye, I saw her brow furrow. "Are you okay?"

I gave myself a shake, my lip popping free from the confines of my teeth. "Yup."

"Good!" she replied. "Because I'm not! I'm booorrreeeddd." Tillie dragged out the last word dramatically and I rolled my eyes.

The shadows edged closer, and I hid my grin. "Close your eyes, Tillie," I instructed. She eyed me warily but soon smiled and obeyed.

I motioned the shadows closer and they eagerly formed into their former selves: two little boys and one girl, all varying in age, now stood before us.

I didn't notice the places where their bones stuck through, nor did I care if they were covered in blood and bruises. One boy was a sickly shade of yellow from whatever disease had finished him off. But these were my friends, too, and I just knew Tillie would like them.

It would be so much fun, all of us playing together.

"Okay," I said, reaching and holding tightly onto the skuggars' strings, "Open your eyes."

Tillie did, and blinked once, twice. I watched the color fade from her face. Her mouth parted open on a gasp and then she started screaming.

I covered my ears, glaring. "Tillie, that isn't very—" She screamed louder when one of the shadows stepped forward, interrupting my admonishment.

There was an awkward pause, everything very still, before Tillie took off running.

Throwing an apology at the confused skuggar children, I took off after her, dropping their dimming threads. "Tillie! Where are you going?"

She didn't respond, only ran faster. I could barely make out her form as she stumbled and mowed down the straggly plants and branches in her way. Her elbow cracked against a tree trunk and I winced at her cry of pain. In the distance was our way home, to Vodihr—she was going the wrong way. Her home was in the other direction, the direction Papa often came from, a place called Laus.

I sped up and that's when I saw it. My eyes widened at the steep drop looming ahead of us—of her. "Tillie!" I screamed. "Stop!"

In the distance, I could hear Mama calling me, her tone frantic. "Rune!"

Then Papa called, "Rune? Tillie?"

I watched as Tillie tried to stop short of the ravine, but she had been going too fast. Her momentum carried her forward and she slipped, her limbs flailing to catch onto anything. The branch she grabbed broke in her grasp and her eyes met mine as she fell.

"Stop," I sob, burying my face in my hands. "Enough." I flinch from the light touch that brushes my shoulder. I remember my screams, Tillie's screams—the sudden silence.

I'm rocking back and forth. Glimpses of the memory bleed into my mind in chunks. Me, scrambling down the small ravine, my knees scraping on rocks and dirt along the way. Me, bleeding, crying, finding Tillie at the bottom, her head bent at a severe angle, blood flowing heavily from an enormous gash on her forehead.

Her eyes had been open, one rolled back, staring up at the sky. I knew she was dead the moment I saw her body; her shadow had been watching me from a few feet away in utter confusion before she disappeared in a burst of yellow threads.

"I'm Tillie Hansen," the girl of five said, holding out a tiny hand.

Shyly, I reached my hand out, too. "Rune Nornwood."

"We are going to be the best of friends."

I looked over to see Mama and Papa whispering to each other. Papa saw me watching and smiled.

I had sat beside Tillie's body, crying, my hands buried in the dirt as I tried to hold onto the last of her threads to no avail. Soon enough, Mama and Papa had found us.

"It wasn't your fault," Tillie whispers to me now.

I choke out a strangled sound. "I'm sorry, so sorry."

She shakes her head, gives me a warm smile, then fades away into the fog, a leaf falling from her hair to land on my knee.

The numbness spreads into my legs and I feel something wet on my stomach; the material of my dress is scraping at the raw skin of my wound. I stare at the endlessness before me. The fog has strengthened, and any wandering shadows are now completely out of reach—out of sight.

My doll is gone.

The stray leaf from Tillie's hair is gone as well.

Never have I felt so alone.

CHAPTER THIRTY

uddenly two threads appear before me, weaving themselves into patterns at my knees. One is black-gray, the other forest green.

Loss and confusion war inside me.

"Rune, I-*we* need to explain," comes Papa's voice. From beneath the curtain of my hair, I see his knees as he crouches in front of me. His hand reaches for my shoulder but stops short. "Will you let us?"

Swallowing, I tilt my head back and see a woman standing above me. I cannot stop the burning in my throat as I utter, "M-Mōðir? Mama?"

Tears flood her eyes. "Yes, ljúfa stelpa, it's me." She crumples to kneel at my side. Her hand begins a rhythmic motion up and down my back. "I'm so sorry," she whispers. When her arms wrap around me, the numbness inside me fades just a little.

I'm leaning towards her warmth without even realizing it, until I do and force myself to pull out of her embrace. "The truth,"

I demand. "I need the truth."

They exchange glances before both reach for my hands. My vision caves inward as the black-gray and forest green threads race up our joined hands, wrapping around my forearms.

"This is wrong," she muttered, but continued to unbutton the formal jacket of his guard uniform anyway. The buttons blazed against the little light that was left in the candle at their side.

"I know," he admitted. He trailed kisses across her cheek and down her neck. "I have to be back soon. The ship for Arden leaves at dawn. And then I'll head to … "

His words trailed off. At her silence, he whispered, "I love you," before he swallowed her cry with another kiss, his hands moving lower down her back.

She sniffed, pulling back to tug his shirt free of his waistband. "I love you, too."

The conversation fades and another memory takes its place.

"You have to push, Elowyn. Push!"

There was a muffled shriek, a curse, and then the wail of a baby.

"My ljúfa stelpa," Elowyn whispered from within Goddric's encircling arms. "Look at what we made." Her head tilted back and she smiled., The newborn was placed on her chest by her mother.

Goddric's eyes welled with tears as he adjusted his hold, the sleeves of the uniform he still wore rolled up on his arms.

"What will you name her?" Embela asked, her own eyes misty as she paused gathering the linens from the foot of the bed.

"Rune," Elowyn whispered.

Goddric's head bowed then as he placed a kiss against Elowyn's forehead. "Our little secret … our Rune."

More glimpses come, sporadic and distorted.

I see Papa, his eyes intent on the cards in front of him as the other Arden guards place their bets around the table. He is reaching for his coins when he freezes, seeing a young woman dressed in pink with long black hair appear in the doorway. She catches him staring and throws him a distracted pretty smile before moving towards the bar and the young boy of six playing with cards there.

Another where they are entwined in each other's arms, a sheet barely covering their bodies. A knock at the door sends them scrambling.

And another—

"Run away with me," Goddric pleaded. "I have enough money saved. We can find somewhere to go."

Elowyn smiled sadly, tears making her eyes shine too brightly in her wan face. "You know I can't." Her hand went to rest on the swell of her stomach. "Your family needs you … " She wiped her nose, adding, "and I need to be strong for our daughter."

"Goddric! It's time to go," a man called in the distance. "The ship's getting ready to leave."

The threads sink deeper into my flesh and I want to rip my hands away to cover my eyes. I don't want to see this, don't want to reach the final moments again that I'm starting to remember of my own accord. The pressure in my head is blinding, tears squeezing out from under my eyelids.

"She's beautiful, isn't she, Papa?" Elowyn asked, her hands twisted in her skirts as she watched her faðir holding Rune. Embela hovered nearby with Goddric.

The older man's face was carefully blank until Rune opened her gray eyes and smiled. "She is." His answering smile faded when he turned to look at Elowyn. "She has the gift."

"I know."

"It won't be easy for her; she won't understand."

She came to stand beside him and rested her head on his shoulder to peer at the baby in his arms. "She'll be okay." Her head tilted back as she looked first at her móðir, then up at her faðir. And lastly, at Goddric. "She has us."

"Make it stop," I plead.

"Not yet," they say, unanimous.

I was crying, rocking back and forth beside Tillie. Mama was at my side, her hands frantic as she checked me for injuries. I had pushed her away twice, hissing through my tears, yet she still tried to check, to comfort me.

"It's my fault," I shouted suddenly, causing my parents to stop their hushed conversation as they focused on me. "I let her meet my shadow friends ... I didn't think she'd be scared, that she'd run away from them—f-from me."

"Goddric—" Mama started, but Papa shook his head and came to pull me into his arms. His eyes, though, were on Tillie; I saw his tears, his heartbreak.

"Oh, Rune."

"She was my half-sister," I say wetly through the snot clogging my nose. "She was your other *daughter.*" I glare at Papa, his eyes downcast as he nods.

I wheeze a laugh; a sob. "I killed my sister."

"No," Mama says sternly. "It was an accident, you didn't know."

Already I'm shaking my head. "I did. Because I didn't listen to you."

Silence follows my words. "You had another family. A daughter, a son, a wife," I say next.

Papa looks away.

"Were you ashamed of me? You said I was your little secret … "

Mama closes her eyes; Papa sucks in a deep breath.

At their silence, I sigh. "Show me the rest."

The fog and my parents fade, the scene changing once more.

The woman was wailing, her arms wrapped around Tillie's body. Each shriek cut into me, each glare thrown my way damning me as I huddled further into Mama's skirts. I was shaking and shaking, so cold—not even Papa's cloak could keep out the deep, biting chill.

Eventually, the sun dipped below the trees and the shadows crept closer in curiosity. Most were tentative, though, only reaching out to touch my elbow or brush against my boots. They didn't understand what was happening and neither did I. One formed fully, taking shape, its eyes fathomless as it watched the scene play out with a dazed smile on its blue lips.

Papa was trying to console the still-wailing woman, who struck at him each time he got too close. She'd been throwing curses, threats, accusations, and blame his way for a long while—but now, only her tears and boiling anger remained.

"Jocelyn," Mama whispered, gently nudging me aside to step toward the woman. "I cannot begin to understand your pain—"

"Shut up, Elowyn!"

Tillie fell to the ground and I bit back a cry of surprise at the thunk her body made against the forest floor. I was torn between running to Papa and pulling Mama back when the woman, Jocelyn, got to her feet, her anger so tangible it was an entity all its own.

"First you take my husband. Then your ... spawn takes my daugh-ter. You can't *understand," she said, her voice low, "but you will."*

CHAPTER THIRTY-ONE

Some moments pass by, in a rush and out of order: the funeral, where I meet a strange boy with long hair and a snarl for a smile who likes to build boats; talking to Tillie's shadow, playing with her even when she can run through trees and is completely unaffected by the cold.

There are hushed arguments between my parents, accompanied by whispered prayers and the scent of incense.

A tri-colored raven, black, silver, and white, watches me from a tree branch high above as I scavenge for food, Mama—no, not Mama—*Jocelyn* having kicked me out of the house again.

Tonic after tonic. The shaking. The sickness.

Hours spent trying to understand my gift as shadows shift and speak and finally fade, leaving me alone, always alone.

Time is a funny thing here and I'm not sure how much of it has passed.

Or who I still am.

Then a new scene begins.

I was screaming in the corner of the room, Papa's roar coming from the doorway. Móðir lay on the floor, blood pooling around her body from the wound in her stomach. My fingers were nearly ripping apart the material of my night dress as they twisted and twisted, the storybook forgotten near the bed.

The blood, it rolled slowly toward me, my throat raw as I cried and cried. I was mesmerized by its progress, watching it through tears and hair; transfixed by the way it seeped into the wood and soaked up into the soft white material of Mama's nightgown.

Onward it crept, ever onward.

Her threads were darkening as they spread from her body, filling the room with the nebulous, tangled cloud of her shadow.

And Jocelyn was standing there, calm, the dagger still in her hand. She seemed unfazed by the blood dripping onto her skin from the hilt of her blade, by the body inches from her feet. Her cloak's hood had fallen back and her blond hair was in chaotic disarray; she still wore the bone mask, but it was crooked now.

I had been sleeping when the pounding on our door had woken me up. I'd stumbled from bed, clutching a pillow in one hand and my favorite blanket in the other. From my bedroom doorway, Mama had motioned for me to be quiet, to hide in my closet. I hadn't had a chance to complain, taking in the fear that lit up her eyes, the pinched twist of her mouth.

Something was wrong.

The floorboards had creaked behind Mama, she turned in the doorway, and—

And now I was no longer screaming, just watching Mama and wishing she'd get up. Her shadow slowly leached from her body. I itched to grab her threads, but I was afraid to touch the blood.

"I don't ... I don't remember what happens next," I say. But I do remember—it's hazy and elusive but I catch bits and pieces: a struggle, a woman's cruel laughter, the clank of a dagger ... A pain in my abdomen has me hissing.

Wiping the tears and snot from my face, I grimace as the threads on my forearms fade away and the silence lengthens.

My parents still hover at my sides, wordless, waiting. The pit in my stomach hardens, my hands clenching and unclenching as I try to take deep breaths. After another wipe of my face, I sit back.

"You started screaming when you saw your mother's shadow," Papa says, his voice deep and troubled; he shares a glance with Mama, who gives a little shake of her head. "Jocelyn knocked you out after that."

"Lies," I say. "I was stabbed, too." I think. I'm not sure.

A shadow mutters in my ear, *Careful.*

Listen closely, another cautions.

"No," Papa protests, though a bit weakly. "She-*we,*" he corrects, "took you back to my ... my other home and family."

"But before that—" I start then stop as a familiar bite of anger heats my blood. "Wait, you mean the family that *wasn't* actually mine? The family where *Mama* rarely spoke to me, criticized me any chance she got, forgot about me whenever she could ... Where my faðir wasn't ever home and when he was, he'd beat me for no other reason besides the fact I still breathed?"

"Wait, Rune—"

I scoff. "It was Hel." I turn to him, meeting his gaze. "You made my life Hel." And then I take a deep breath, "I wish I had died with Mama."

Papa looks devastated by my words. "You did."

At first, I feel a sense of satisfaction at hearing the truth, at being right and at finally getting honest answers.

I had died. I remember dying and the cold and the creature that greeted me at the wooden circle with blood-red lips. Death had been so dark, so quiet. I had been crying, so confused.

"Where am I?" I whispered. "Where is my mama?"

The creature's gaze was infinite.

"Where is—?"

She put her finger to her lips to stop the words building behind mine; I froze.

"I was sent back. The Zila sent me back."

"You aren't supposed to be here."

"Am I dead?"

Her laugh was deep, otherworldly.

"The gods may forgive you for what you have done, but I won't." I say, hoping my words cut as deeply as all the times he has cut me with his words, his belt, his hands. Oddly, there is a hint of surprise on his face. Why?

"You don't understand," Mama says. Her voice is hoarse.

"You're right. I don't." I shake my head. "So, what was the debt? The skuld?"

They both flinch. "Your half-sister's death," Elowyn answers, her words soft, troubled. And again, I feel like she is holding something back. "But Rune, what is this about your papa? I don't think—"

"You don't think what? That the man you fell in love with would be capable of abusing your child?" My laugh is cruel, the words condemning. "You don't need to think it because I *know* it."

Papa moves to sit in front of me, his hands loosely resting on his knees. I recognize the posture, remember it now; it's the one he'd assume when defusing a situation, usually between Anik and myself. I hate that seeing this familiar gesture is softening something inside of me. Hate that it reminds me of a time before he became twisted—before he became a drunkard and a liar. If he hadn't always been bad—wasn't all bad—did I still have the right to despise him? To deny him forgiveness?

"I know … " He stops, rubbing a hand over his face, then tries again. "I know you aren't going to believe this, believe me, but it wasn't *me*, Rune."

I scoff again, but he holds up a hand, a look in his eyes begging me to let him continue.

When I say nothing, he starts again, "After your mother died—"

"Was murdered, you mean? By your wife, your first wife you were still married to?"

He huffs a breath through his nose. "I bargained with Jocelyn to keep you, to take you into our home because I was afraid of the consequences. You weren't old enough to handle Wraith, the secrets it contained and the gods it fed, and I wasn't ready to let you go, either. I didn't want to lose you."

"But Jocelyn didn't want me. So what about my amma, Embela? She wasn't capable of raising me? What of my afi?"

Elowyn shakes her head. "Embela … as the town matriarch, the head witch, there were expectations of her. Demands on her time and responsibilities she had to Vodihr. It wasn't the right life for you. And your afi, he was a priest to the gods and the leiðtogi of the people. He had his own duties to attend."

"Sure, beating and degradation were much better alternatives."

I lean away when Papa leans closer.

"The older you got, the harder it was to face the truth. I saw your mother in you every single day—in your laugh, in your mischief. In the way you wore your heart on your sleeve and never hid it." His breath breaks on a sob.

"W-we drugged you, a potion Jocelyn would bring home. She'd never tell me, but it seemed to help you, so I had to accept it. It dulled your memories and as you aged, it was easier for you to just accept your life as it was, and you began needing the potion less and less."

"Grandma Bell," I answer. My lips form into a sneer. "Or rather, my actual amma, Embela. She'd make the potion. Jocelyn would take me there when my nightmares came back. When she caught me talking to my friends outside." I shake my head. "So you drugged me and beat me to make me forget what had happened? To forget your sins?" Bile was souring my stomach. "It didn't work—you failed. I remember *everything*."

And I did.

My two lives.

The lies. The secrets.

The pain.

"Papa, I didn't mean to break it." I pulled at the gloved hand that wrapped around my wrist. My bedroom door soon filled my line of sight and I winced, biting my lip to hold back more protests. I knew if he hadn't stopped by now, he wouldn't at all.

"Rune." His voice wavered, breaking and turning oddly higher pitched before smoothing out again. I saw his smile, the flash of his eyes—umber to hazel—before he pushed the door open.

I was pushed forward, then motioned to strip. I turned, my dress loose around my hips, the front of it scrunched against my chest. The air nipped at the bare skin of my back.

One ... two ...

Snap, *the belt cut deep, and I knew it drew blood.*

My head bowed, my toes curling into the wood.

"I'm sorry, Papa."

Snap.

Shuddering, I recoil from the hand on my shoulder. "Don't touch me," I seethe through gritted teeth. The memory still burns, the stinging in my back as fierce and persistent as the pain in my stomach. I feel a trickle of blood—real or just a part of a memory? My head lolls forward to hang and I close my eyes. The pain is too much; it's exhausting.

"I suspected she was beating you," Papa whispers; I feel his gaze on me, willing me to meet his eyes and understand. "I suspected it but didn't know for certain until a week before I took you to Vodihr."

A cracked laugh escapes me. "Took me? Ha!" I wave his words away. "*Sold* me. You *sold* me to the Vodihran's only brothel, to Agata. I became her pet when I was only ten and didn't escape until I was sixteen. For six years, I was beaten, drugged, touched against my will ... And where were you? Lost in another's skirts? Doing the bidding of the Ardenian king?" My eyes narrow on him, "Or maybe you were just numb from ale and gambling, passed out in a pub somewhere?"

I run out of breath and—wait. What?

'... *she was beating you.*'

She?

What he said before comes back to me, sending me reeling. I-I couldn't fathom the idea that Jocelyn had been the one behind the belt; had been the voice that spat each curse and threat.

Jocelyn detested me, I could plainly see that—her having killed me and all—it wasn't just that she didn't love me. That I wasn't good enough to be the daughter she wanted: I wasn't her daughter, I wasn't who she wanted.

I'd killed her real daughter.

She then killed my Mama.

She killed *me.*

It wasn't so far-fetched now to believe.

And Papa ... Papa had always seemed different, like he was wearing different masks, or he was two different people altogether. I never imagined there were really two of him ... I'd wondered when I was young if I really was so wretched that I was to blame for his violence and mercurial mood. Later, I blamed the alcohol. His gambling addiction.

But to believe this?

I relive every moment: slap, curse, rake of nails.

"Can you prove it?" I ask, my voice strained. "Can you show me it was Jocelyn who hurt me and not you?"

At his quiet "yes," I look up. His face is grim as he reaches to tuck a strand of hair behind my ear. His fingers lingering on my cheek.

"*What have you done, Jocelyn?*" Papa demanded, his large body filling the doorway. I took in his stance, the antlered mask hanging at his side. I flinched from the whip dangling in my face, and the leather lazily brushed my cheek, leaving a smear of my own blood behind.

"What I needed to do. Your brat never listens, Goddric. Never follows orders. Instead, she is out talking to trees."

"Shadows," I muttered, "not trees."

The whip came dangerously close to my face again and I braced for the pain, but a hand reached out and stopped it from connecting. I tilted my head back, my vision obscured by fresh tears. I could see Papa and Mama staring at each other—one of his hands was gripping the thong of the whip, the other was curling around my shoulder.

"I don't … " My vision blurred.

Mama flickered, like a skuggi but more solid. She was Papa, then Mama again. Two Papas. Then only one. Mama returned and her features twisted as she said, "She is my daughter to discipline. Especially when you are always away."

"She is not, nor will she ever be, your daughter."

There was a gasp, a flutter of movement; my eyelids felt so heavy now and I stifled a yawn as a door slammed. Someone began running their hand through my hair, humming a song that was familiar but not.

"Papa, I'm sorry."

The hand in my hair stopped for a second before continuing; the song was clipped, strained, before Papa said, "No, sá litli. I am sorry." He paused and I saw him move the mask he'd been holding a little further away from us. "I'll fix this. It's time."

I curled my body against his, feeling him lift me into his arms, careful to avoid my wounds. Sighing, I snuggled closer, burying my nose *in the space between his shoulder and neck. I smelled blood but ignored it. I felt too safe to care.*

I blink and the memory was gone.

"I reached out to the contact I still had in Vodihr and set it up for you to be taken to your amma there. She would take care of you until you were taken to a new home in Arden, away from Jocelyn and me, and the city itself," Papa says, then flinches. "I didn't know it had gone wrong. We were being watched at the trade, but it was supposed to be an act—"

"An act? Really? So you didn't know that your 'contact' didn't take me to Amma after you left? That they just dumped me at the brothel instead? I was in The House for six years! Where were you?" I growl.

I don't give him a chance to answer. "Is this some sort of joke to you—to both of you? Giving me my memories back—if they even are my memories—making my deepest wishes about being loved and wanted by my family come true, but only after my whole family is dead? After I'm dead? What's the point of it now?"

I can't handle the idea of being stuck here, not now; the possibility of it is pushing me just a little closer to the whispers in my mind, to this oblivion within the darkness.

There was a brush of movement, a whine and the nudge of a nose against my knee. I wrap my arms around myself.

But he's dead, too. Gone. Taken.

"You aren't dead," Mama says. Her gray eyes shine with tears and she glances at something over my shoulder.

"I'm not?"

She ignores my question, my ire and doubt and sarcasm.

"There is so much more I want to tell you … "

"Then tell me. What's stopping you?"

Her hand brushes my forearm.

"I want to make a deal," Mama said, appearing from the void. Her features were hard as she took in the sight of the creature standing before us.

"You know what I want," the creature crooned. Her smile widened, sharpened.

Mama looked at me. "I do, but she is too young. She doesn't yet understand her gifts."

The Zila sighed and stepped away from me. I blinked and saw her come to stand face-to-face with Mama. My breath froze in my chest. I was reaching for Mama when the creature's hand moved to cup Mama's face, the creature's long nails tangling in Mama's black hair. I watched the color start to run, strands going from black to grey to white.

"Then I suppose I'll have you first."

I screamed as Mama's face contorted. There was a flash of light, of feathers and silver eyes, before everything went dark.

"It was you," I say, my throat dry.

Mama's face gives nothing away when Papa glances at her in confusion.

"You made a—"

"Not now, Rune." Her tone is urgent, and I hear the footsteps behind me, too. I go to look but she grabs my chin. "Trust yourself, Rune. You aren't out of danger yet and I don't know what they will try next, what they have planned."

"They who?" I demand.

She shakes her head. "I'm sorry. Too much is still at stake.

They … " She is falling back, and Papa moves to grab her shoulders. "Be safe," she whispers to me. "Be brave." For a split second, her face is that of a raven's, tri-colored feathers reflecting in the darkness, and then her face is my mama's again. She bows her head and turns to find comfort in Papa's hold.

I feel a hand on my shoulder—a yank that causes the fog to shudder and the darkness to crumble. Looking up, the face of the Zila comes into view. Her lips are pursed, her eyes mirroring the swirling of the fog.

"No, wait," I plead, turning to look at my parents. I watch as they tremble, their skin beginning to peel away from their bones—I close my eyes, unable to stomach each hiss and crack of their transformation back into shadows. I feel a soft feather caress my cheek, followed by another yank backwards from the Zila.

"I'm not ready."

In the silence, something growls, followed by a whine and the clicking of nails. There is a sudden pressure of warm weight against my leg …

… then nothing.

CHAPTER THIRTY-TWO

Pain. It claws through my consciousness, demanding my immediate and undivided attention. From the tips of my toes to my eyelashes, there are aches and twinges and spots of agony. My stomach feels as if I've laid on a bed of hot coals for fun. My limbs are tingling, waking up slowly and agonizingly.

Keeping my eyes closed, I focus first on wiggling my toes. Next, rotating my ankles. I am relieved to find my feet are still attached to me. The same conclusion and relief follow with my wrists and hands.

There is a pressure on my arm, something I'm not yet ready to discover the cause of. And I don't dare try to move my middle— my stomach is already shouting at me that the skin has yet to scab over. Part of me wonders if I'd feel better if it stopped trying to heal and was just left a gaping mess. Perhaps the Zila needs an apprentice.

Snorting at that thought, I press my lips tighter together to keep back the hysteria building within me. I still remember everything: two different lives, the stab wound, the shadow world, my parents.

'Trust yourself, Rune.'

Behind my eyelids come a kaleidoscope of memories, feelings, smells, words, and I can do nothing but lay there and let it consume me.

'Be safe.'

The weight on my arm shifts and something tickles my skin. Grasping at the distraction, I finally open my eyes—only to slam them shut when my vision pitches and rolls. Eyes and stomach spiraling, I focus on breathing for a second—in and out—in and out. More movement on my arm and the feel of hair brushing against my skin prompt me to try opening my eyes again.

'Be brave.'

One blink shows the color of brown. Two blinks reveal the brown to be wooden beams. I then register the rocking. By blink four, I manage to gather I'm on a ship. The smell of the sea couples with the stale air of a cabin that has housed an injured, ill person for too long.

My mouth is dry, my tongue heavy and forgotten. I can feel each individual crack in my lips, and when I suck in a deep breath, the cracks shrivel open a bit more.

"Ouch," I hiss.

There's a quiet curse, a grunt, and then more silence. Wiggling my neck, I look down to see an ash-brown mass of hair tickling my arm. One strand of hair is stuck in a small cut and it burns, but I try to ignore it. The hair falls from a bun on top of the person's head and tears burn my eyes—I greedily follow the curve of his jaw.

"Weylin."

I can't take back my whisper, nor can I stop the tears. I'm not sure if I'm ready yet to face him, not after my sort-of death and sloppy goodbye—both of which I would've mocked anyone else relentlessly about.

But it doesn't matter if I am ready or not to face him; my whisper has his head jerking up, blue eyes blinking at me.

"Rune," he manages to say, my name distorted, rough with fatigue and disbelief.

My lips pull into a grin even as tears continue to wet my face.

He chokes on a laugh, surging upward and pressing a harsh kiss to my lips.

Another pain courses through me, one that is bittersweet and full of longing: our first meeting, our first kiss, our escape, his goodbye, his return, the ring. A barrage of memories and feelings threatens to drown me again. I reach up to grip his neck—and the movement pulls at the skin around my wound. I moan and Weylin jerks back, his lips hovering over mine.

We both stop to breathe.

I feel a light tickle at my feet and look to see the peering eyes of two shadows. They squeak and dart away.

"I'm sorry." I brush another kiss against his lips. Tasting salt. "So sorry." Another kiss that soon ends with me wincing and flopping back onto the mattress.

"Sorry for what?" he asks, a twinkle in his eye. "Sorry for getting stabbed? Sorry for saying you love me, then almost dying?

Sorry for ruining my surprise and seeing the ring before I was ready?"

I huff a laugh. "Uh, all of it, I suppose?"

He nods, looking serious, until a grin breaks across his face, at odds with the fresh tear stains he has. "Good. Apologies accepted."

My eyes mist at his teasing. I've missed this, these little moments where he isn't so on guard and I'm not so standoffish. I've missed the freedom that comes with having him close and the comfort of knowing he has my back, whether I'm being stupid or not.

Clearing my throat, I bury my regret. "So about the ring—"

The door to the room swings open and slams against the wall. I startle and fall back—I'd unknowingly been propping myself up to get closer to Weylin's lips again. I grunt in annoyance.

"Well, I was going to kick Weylin's arse for not resting, but it appears you're awake," a voice says cheerfully. "And now I can have the pleasure of kicking your arse instead."

I fight a grin, trying to look pitiful. "But Ailith, I'm injured."

"Injured. Right. That kiss of yours looked a lot like foreplay to me."

Weylin flushes. "We weren't doing that."

One of Ailith's eyebrows is raised, a little smile on her face. "Whatever you say, friend."

Snickering, I try to sit up—

Only to close my eyes against a wave of vertigo. When I open them again, two faces are leaning over me, both anxious and concerned. "I'm fine."

"Fine enough to clean the mountain of rags I used to stop you from bleeding out?"

"Nope, not that fine—still terrible and near death," I whine.

Ailith's smirk disappears. "Don't even joke about that." She leans closer, touching my forehead with the back of her hand. She frowns at the damp of my skin and goes to toss aside my blankets.

Weylin takes my hand closest to him, his grip firm and reassuring as she starts to poke and prod me.

I wince when she jabs too hard. "Bad?" I ask.

"No," Weylin says at the same time Ailith huffs out, "You'll live."

There's a shout from above us, followed by a bang and some cursing. My eyes go to the ceiling. "Someone appears to be partying too hard," I sigh. "I'm offended I wasn't invited."

"It's a 'get well soon' party held in your honor. It happened quickly, no time for invitations."

Laughing, I extract my hand from Weylin's and attempt to brace myself up on my elbows, trying to get a look at my stomach. Ailith has yet to reapply the cloth that covered it. I take in the red puffy skin, the bruising around the area, the stitches that ooze yellow pus. The smell hits me and I bite back from saying 'infection' out loud. If I can see it, then Ailith and Weylin do too.

"It's better than it was," Ailith says quickly, her eyes on my face. "It was touch and go. We weren't sure … when you'd wake up." Almost aggressively, she tugs a fresh cloth from the bag tied to her belt and pulls out a jar of some greenish paste that smells absolutely foul once opened.

"How long?" I ask between gritted teeth. The paste feels as bad as it smells.

"Three days," Weylin answers. He avoids my look of surprise when I glance his way.

Three days of being trapped in the Skuggaland. Three days of reliving memories that had been stolen from me. The anger comes suddenly, muting all the pain I feel.

"Where is Anik?"

Weylin and Ailith share a look before Ailith replies, "He's upstairs. He had been in here, too, but we sent him up with Gael for some fresh air." Her eyes shift to Weylin who actually looks sheepish now. "This one was supposed to go up, too, but apparently he has trouble understanding basic commands."

"It's more of a selective hearing," I offer offhandedly, struggling to sit up. "You get used to it."

Ailith laughs as Weylin grumbles something under his breath.

Both jump to my sides when my bare feet touch the floor and I sway. I close my eyes, gripping the sheets. Everything hums.

In and out.

Breathe.

"Rune," Weylin whispers and I look at him. He's crouching in front of me; his hands are on my arms, bracing my weight. I lean forward to press my forehead to his shoulder.

In and out.

Once the nausea passes, and the pain becomes more of an annoying twinge, I slide a little further off the bed and am able to stand upright.

"So far, so good," I mutter more to myself than to them. I grab hold of Weylin's hands after they slip from my forearms down to wrap around my sweaty palms. I flush, hating that he's seeing me this way but glad he's here, just the same.

"I've seen you much worse," he remarks. I look away so he

can't read my eyes again. "I want all of you—the good, the bad, the broken and whole parts," he whispers, letting go of one of my hands to tuck some strands of hair behind my ear.

We share a smile before I turn to Ailith who's hovering nearby. She masks her anxious expression. "Ready for some fresh air?"

"Are you sure she's ready?"

I groan at Weylin's question and answer for myself, "Yes. Yes, she is."

The walk from the captain's quarters to the stairs feels like an eternity. I'm shuffling along, half-slumped, leaning against Weylin. Ailith is silent on my other side. I see her motioning or pushing back curious crew members, but their whispers and looks are mostly lost to me. My gut hurts too bad to care about all that. I keep my gaze forward, and when the stairs enter my line of sight, I almost weep.

In the distance, I can hear the splash of the waves, the echo of the wind; I can smell the salty tang I've grown to both love and hate. Someone curses, a loud cheer accompanies it, and I smile at the sound of a child laughing.

"Is Larken okay?" I ask, stopping at the foot of the stairs to take a deep breath and steel myself for the ascent. The boat rocks and I steady my balance with Weylin's help.

It is Ailith that answers. "Physically, yes. Mentally? He screams from nightmares whenever he sleeps. Gael's been trying to get him to talk but he hasn't yet."

I nod. "It'll take time." My foot brushes the first step, but I pause to look at Weylin. "You should talk with him." His hand presses a little harder on the small of my back. He says nothing but nods to let me know he's heard me.

When I feel the gritty deck of the ship beneath my feet, I grin, tilting my face back to the sky. I needed this; the sun's haze, the wind's kiss. Even the flecks of saltwater splashing up from the waves about the hull to land on my arms and face.

There is a soft caw and I see a raven high above, watching from its-her perch of the crow's nest. Our eyes meet—a flash of black-gray thread dangles from her beak. When I blink, she takes flight and disappears into the sky.

"Mama."

"What?" Weylin asks, leaning closer.

"Nothing. Thought I saw something." A little shaken at seeing her and being reminded of my new knowledge from the Skuggaland, I turn away. And then I see what's transpiring at the *Tempest's* helm. "Well, well," I manage to say and point, "Ailith, you owe me twenty coins."

She looks in the direction I'm pointing, curses, then fumbles in her bag.

Gael and Anik are caught in each other's embrace, ardently making out. The crew is staring—some in surprise, some in amusement. Gael's guards just look resigned.

I can't help but wonder how long this has been going on. It's just another thing he's kept from me.

At the feel of cold coins sliding against my palm, I clear my throat. "Am I interrupting something?" Gael and Anik jump apart and I give them an idle wave, trying to hide my feelings of betrayal under nonchalance. I slip the coins Weylin's pocket. "I can go back to my death bed and come again later if you prefer."

"Ru," my brother breathes and takes a step toward me.

And immediately, I know the nonchalance isn't going to work. I hold up a hand, shaking my head. The betrayal is back, obliterating the happiness I feel at seeing him again, alive and unharmed after our escape. Anger sweeps through me, hot and nauseating. "Don't," I hiss. "You bastard."

There are murmurs at my words. Gael's eyes narrow. He steps to put a hand on Anik's shoulder when my brother sways on his feet, color draining from his face to pool in his cheeks. He knows, he must know or suspect where I've been, what I've learned. I smother my concern over the purple around his eyes, the green hue of his jaw, the puckered cut on the side of his neck.

"You knew," I whisper. "You knew the whole damn time and you never said anything." I feel the sting of tears and grit my teeth, my hands making fists. All the times he comforted me, the promises he made of a better future when I lay curled on my bed too terrified to move.

"But I deserved it, right? That is what you told Ma-Jocelyn. I deserved everything."

In my mind, I see his snarling face as he kicks dirt on Tillie's freshly dug grave. I come to stand beside him and he hits my shoulder hard.

Anik moves closer. "You don't understand."

"Don't understand?" I look away, roughly brushing the knotted hair from my face. We aren't kids anymore. It shouldn't hurt so much. "I guess you're right. I don't understand how someone who always tried to protect me, who said they loved me, could lie to me all along." I pause. "You were my brother."

And yet, he hadn't always protected me. I remember pieces of the first few days in my strange new home. I'm crying and no one answers me. No one cares if I'm hurt or hungry or hiding from the new shadows that taunt me. Papa is gone. So is Mama.

"I *am* you brother," he shouts, and I flinch away.

I feel the crew's eyes on me—on us. Some look uncomfortable and awkward, while some are greedily taking in the anguish on our faces, basking in the melodrama. I can tell some of them want to interfere—they have their hands on their weapons just in case a fight breaks out and they have to pick sides. I notice then that Larken is absent, below deck somewhere.

The next words feel like ash in my mouth. "No, Anik. You aren't."

I hate myself when he recoils. Part of me knows I'm being unreasonable. In truth, he is still my brother—half, at least—but I'm being ripped apart at the seams and he is the only one who knows why—the only one I can make my equal in this suffering.

'*... she deserves this.*'

'*I know she does ...* '

Gael steps between us, his eyes on Anik, who's breathing has become shallow and rapid. "Let's take this downstairs."

Weylin moves to angle himself between me and Gael, but I shake my head, moving around him. I look past Gael's shoulder and meet Anik's eyes. "There isn't anything more to be said. I'm done." I turn from Anik's anguish and face Gael, adding, "I did what you asked. I got your brother back, regardless of the consequences. I'll let you know what you owe me later."

CHAPTER THIRTY-THREE

I wake up to heat, Weylin's arm resting lightly over my hips. I wiggle further back into his bare chest, trying to ignore the flames in my stomach. Is the infection spreading? Am I sweating more than I had been earlier?

My eyes are swollen, crusty from sleep and the tears I shed while I ranted to Weylin. I told him everything from our escape three years ago, to what I had done after he left Arden, to what Gael had asked of me before we'd reached Vodihr. I barely managed to get out what I had learned in the Skuggaland. And by the time I got to my mama's deal to save me, I was a wreck.

I knew he was upset. I could tell by the tick of his jaw and his red-infused eyes. Still, he pulled me closer, holding me together as I fell apart.

While I wept, Ailith had brought in a lumpy cot, a handful of blankets, and a pitcher of water. Only after the tears and words were out of my system, when I began to pace in exhaustion, did

Weylin guide me to the cot and coax me to lay down. He'd changed my bandage and laid down beside me.

Lulled to sleep by the sting of green paste and the comfort of his presence, I had dreamed of my childhood—of Anik and me playing in a field of flowers, of Papa sneaking me treats after dinner, of a woman with beautiful ebony hair dancing with me under the stars.

Feeling the prickling sensation of eyes on me, I blink and see two shadows watching from the farthest corner of the storage room we've commandeered for ourselves. One waves at me, while the other shimmers before settling back into the dark worn timber of the floor. Comforted by their benign presence, I turn my attention to stretching out the kinks in my limbs and clearing the haze from my mind.

"Five more minutes," Weylin sighs into my neck, his breath tickling my skin.

"Mmhmm. Only if you promise to get us food."

He chuckles and my toes curl at the sound. "As you wish."

My hand buried itself in his hair, the other grasping his hip, my back arching at the press of his lips as they moved from my collarbone downward. "Don't stop," I hissed.

He nipped at the skin under my breast. "As you wish."

I bat the distracting memory away, a blush heating my cheeks. Weylin stretches, bringing me back to the present, and presses a quick kiss to the nape of my neck. When I look back at him, he winks before moving away and getting to his feet. He finds his discarded shirt, pulling it over the pants low on his hips, and heads for the door.

"Anything specific you want?"

"Mead."

"Tea it is," Weylin says, ignoring my disgruntled sigh and leaving before I can complain.

Settling back against the pillows, squirming a bit to get comfortable, I try to pretend everything is normal, that nothing has changed.

I'm closing my eyes when there's a hesitant knock on the door. I sit up too quickly and pain ripples through my midsection. The knocking comes again. Is it Anik? Ailith? Though neither would bother with knocking.

"Come in," I call, anxiously twisting my fingers in the blanket covering my bare legs.

The door opens slowly, sea-green eyes peering in, wide and full of nerves. I take in the faded hue of his skin, the bruises, and I motion him closer. "Hi, Larken," I greet. I try to keep my tone soft and unrushed. I don't want him to be scared.

"They-they said you were doing better and … " His words trail off as he steps fully into the room and shuts the door behind him. He stays there, hovering, awkward and unsure of himself. He rubs sleep from his eyes.

"I'm doing better," I soothe. "I heard you were—"

He squeaks. "I'm sorry," he wheezes, shutting his eyes. "I just … seeing you and then remembering … I thought they would fade faster than they are."

His words make my head spin, but I keep my frown to myself. "What would fade?" I ask. I'm sure I know what he's about to—

"The memories," he says, gasping for breath.

My heart aches for him.

'*He has nightmares whenever he sleeps.*'

I motion him closer, patting the cot. "Come here, Larken."

I see him struggle for a second. Finally, his breath leaves him in a rush and he flies to my side, burrowing himself as close as he can. His elbow connects with my wound, but I don't show the pain. Instead, I pull him close, rocking him as he cries.

"She was so c-cruel. Always making me ... watch her b-beat the others," he stammers through his sobs. "One day, she had-had me hold the whip after s-she beat Lettie."

I say nothing. I don't know who Lettie is, but I'm fully aware of the cruelty Mistress Agata is capable of. The things only she is capable of.

"How can she do that? Why doesn't my father stop it?" Larken cries. "Doesn't he know about it? Did he even look for me after I was taken? Does he even care?"

I give him a second to catch his breath, my hand rubbing up and down his back. "It's complicated," I say, not sure how to proceed. My shoulder's soaked with tears. "Vodihr and the Revelry have been around for decades but when the new pact was formed, it became a mandate for," I choked, "for sacrifices to be given in order to appease Vodihr and their gods."

"But why is it still allowed? As king, my father should be able to stop it."

Though I agree with him—it should be stopped and the king should be able to do it—I know it isn't as simple as that. Politically speaking, the treaty between Vodihr and Arden is loosely formed at best—based on a spoken agreement when Utlen was just beginning to modernize across the sea and Frumland stayed uncharted in its shadow. And while Vodihr remains an unclaimed territory, ripe for all to experience its eccentricities, Arden—or any other power, for that matter—could send more than just an advisor to check on the city if they ever felt like it. So, all I can do is shrug. "I'm not sure."

After a few minutes, he speaks again. "We'll arrive home tomorrow and I'm scared."

The confession hangs between us. Larken has stopped crying and now fumbles to wipe at his face. He glances to the corner where some skuggar have lazily begun to form into different shapes—one shifts into a rabbit and the other playfully pounces on it, their threads tangling before they break apart. Larken smiles a little, but then he sees me looking and turns his head away, schooling his face.

"You see them?" I ask, unsurprised. Children, I had learned, were more susceptible to their presence. The other pets I'd grown up with in Vodihr would often ask me about them until they reached a certain age and forgot.

"Yes," he admits. "They were all over Wrai—uh, Vodihr. One even tried to talk to me the first night I was there."

I make some noncommittal sound; I don't want to pressure him to tell me more, though I am curious.

"She was scary at first until she fully formed—then she was pretty like my mother. Her hair was dark, like yours, and she was thin, dressed in a white shift like my nursemaid would wear before bed." He sniffs. "She told me not to worry, that everything would be okay. That people were coming to save me."

I'm hot and cold at once. Mama.

"Rune?" Larken touches my hand, my other frozen on his back. "D-did I say something wrong?"

I feel his body start to quiver and I sigh. "No, no, you haven't said anything wrong, it's okay. I just … I know the shadow you speak of. I haven't … seen her in a while, that's all."

"Oh," he breathes, buying my lie. "She told me to be brave. Was I brave?"

'Be brave.'

"Very," I manage to say.

The door opens—Weylin comes in balancing two trays full of treats. While the smell is enticing, I find my appetite has since disappeared. Still, I try for a smile as Weylin looks first at me, then at a guilty-looking Larken who focuses on his hands in his lap.

Weylin takes it in stride, though, and plops himself by our feet. I tuck my legs in quickly to avoid getting burned by the trays he sits down.

"Good thing I brought extra," he says, nudging Larken.

The boy flushes and looks at me for permission before reaching for a pastry and taking a bite. His hum of appreciation has my stomach growling. I reach for a similar pastry and soon I'm making the same sounds, enjoying the warmth and flavor of fresh food.

Noticing the little prince's shoulders are still hunched and stiff, I nudge his leg with my knee; when he laughs, Weylin and I share a smile.

⁂

It's late by the time Weylin and I slip upstairs, our feet soundless as we walk the hallway. We left Larken asleep and tucked in on our cot after sharing snacks and stories for hours.

We even played a few rounds of guess-the-shadow-image with the shadows themselves, who readily joined in on the fun. I was a little reluctant to leave him at first, noticing the furrow of his brow as he dreamt, but the shadows promised they'd alert me if he was entering the throes of a nightmare. Plus, I was craving fresh air.

I take what feels like my first deep breath in hours as I move across the deck to the railing on the starboard side. The lone crew member in charge of manning the wheel the first shift of the night barely glances in our direction.

Bracing myself against the weathered wood, I tilt my head back and count the stars lazily until I lose track. The breeze feels amazing on my feverish skin.

"This reminds me of the night you left. It was so calm and quiet; I remember thinking how wrong it was," I say, startling myself. The ensuing silence becomes a dead weight between us. Gone is the easy peace of our first day reunited.

In my mind, I see myself standing at the beach, the rocks biting into the soles of my bare feet as I watched the ship sail away with Weylin, shrinking to a speck in the distance. I remember shivering, wrapping my arms around myself, staying rooted to the spot long after the ship was no longer visible.

I had wanted to scream, to wail under the crushing agony. The sounds of the Revelry were behind me, the sea before me. A raven had been there that night, too, I remember that now. The flash of its tri-colored feathers as its caws mingled with my cries. Birgir, still just a pup, was utterly confused. He stayed with me, though.

"I don't know how long I stood there," I admit to Weylin, and from the corner of my eye, I see him tense. "I just remember Vin coming and giving me a blanket and eventually I went back to the cottage."

"Vin." Weylin says the name with disgust. His frown mars his face and causes the scar across his right eye to flatten. "Vin was the one I gave the letter to." His words are careful, his eyes dark as he turns to face me. "I never just *left*, Rune. I wouldn't do that to you—never to you."

My throat and heart constrict simultaneously. How I want to believe him. To forgive him. And part of me already has, ever since he walked into my cottage acting like nothing had happened; acting surprised at my hate towards him when I had pushed him away. And I *had* hated him, cursed him, tried to forget him.

"I never got it."

He snorts, offering me a lopsided smile that disappears just as fast it formed. "I got that by now." He shakes his head. "What I don't understand is why he never gave it to you." His hands wrap around mine, the grip tight but not uncomfortable. He tugs me close. "Rune, if I had known what you thought, if I had written you before coming back ... "

My hands squeeze his when he flounders for something else to say, for a way to explain the want that hangs between us. Pain is clear in his expression, echoing what I had felt for months. Can I really just let this go? Can I just forgive him?

Have I already?

"Why did you leave?" I'm not sure why I ask this since he had already told me—even if had been a bit hurried and I'd been on the verge of death. My eyes travel to the valley of his shirt opening, focusing on his neck and dipping lower. I flush and look away, starting to pull my hands from his grip.

"No," Weylin says quietly, tightening his grip for a moment. "Don't—don't let go. Just give me a second to think. To explain."

And so I do. With our hands still locked together, I turn my gaze back up to the stars.

As a child, even before Mama's death, I would often escape outside and let the shadows guide me through the trees to a small clearing nearby. I'd lay down and they'd rest around me, their threads spooling serenely on the forest floor, and together we'd watch the stars. Sometimes I'd tell them about my day, random things. Sometimes I'd talk about my family. Often, I'd just bask in the silence and pretend I didn't exist anymore.

A squeeze on my hands has my eyes returning to Weylin's face.

"After we … escaped, I wasn't sure what to do. It took weeks to recover from the wounds and even longer to feel like I was worthy … of anything. Of being a person. Of being loved or happy." His voice breaks and he clears his throat. "Through it all, you were there for me—the panic attacks, the withdrawal, the nightmares, me pacing along the shoreline at all hours of the day. It wasn't fair to you. I kept telling myself I needed to piece myself back together, to be whole again."

He winces. "And I tried, and it worked for a time, but inside I longed for home, even while we worked on building a life together in Arden. It wasn't just make-believe anymore, escaping Vodihr, and it terrified me. I didn't know how to keep going."

"I was scared, too," I murmur. My eyes are stinging. "Every night after you fell asleep, I cried. I didn't even know why I was crying half the time. I felt dirty and unworthy."

""I-I know." The apple of his throat bobs twice before he can continue. "After that day at the market—when you had been looking at necklaces and tried on that ridiculous shawl that reminded me of my mother's favorite ceremonial robe—I knew I needed to go home. I needed to see my parents and brothers, my younger sister who I missed watching grow up. They needed to know I was alive even if I wasn't … wasn't me anymore. I couldn't help you, lessen your fear, when I was terrified myself. I wasn't strong enough."

I gave his hands a squeeze.

"So I went to the dock and found a tradesman who was leaving Arden the next night. He was going to be stopping by my tribe's village, along the west coast of Dýra, and was willing to let me work for passage. It happened so quickly, I barely remember shaking his hand and walking back to the cottage—by the time I got in you were already asleep." Tears wet his cheeks. "I wrote the letter to you that night and packed a bag … then I waited."

"Why didn't you just tell me? We spent the whole next day together." My words are raspy, a bit harsh, and without thinking, I yank my hands from his and hug myself tight, careless of my wound.

Weylin slowly shakes his head. "I should have. But I-I didn't want to ruin our last day together before I left. When I finally felt ready to tell you, that's when we found your wolf at the Revelry."

My heart sinks at the mention of Birgir, reminded for the hundredth time of his absence. When I first met him, he had been in rough shape, his left ear bitten and infected, wounds all over his small, thin body, his paws and nose scraped raw. I'd been so angry at the shape he was in, especially after seeing the ringmaster stab him with a hot poker, that I jumped onto the stage, grabbed the poker from her, and stabbed her right back. Weylin had had to drag me away before the guards showed up.

"You were mad at me then; angry I hadn't done anything."

I nod, staying silent. I had been, turning my anger on him and demanding him to get out of my sight because I couldn't stand to be around someone who wouldn't fight for what was right. "It wasn't fair to you. It just made me think of Vodihr." I sigh. "And then you left."

He runs a hand through his hair, causing it to spike up in some places. "I wandered after you locked me out of the cottage, headed back to the Revelry. I hadn't planned on going to the ringmaster's tent, but I found myself there, off to the side of the crowd as she showed them some exotic snakes—one rumored to be Loki himself."

At my snort, he shrugs.

"When I went to leave, the shadow wolf whimpered from his cage and I knew I couldn't just leave him there. So I," he chuckles, "I picked the lock and stuck him under my shirt. I must have looked odd with my shirt growling. The little bastard nipped at me constantly until I put him down on the road back to the cottage."

"He didn't run off?" I ask, slightly amused. I can picture the scene in my head, and it warms something in me that had been dormant.

"He did actually, three times. And all three times I bribed him back with food until we got to the cottage. I admittedly shoved him through the door before he could go for a fourth attempt. He wasn't very happy and seemed ready for a fight, but he got distracted when you moved in your sleep … or maybe it was a sound you made? Needless to say, I was worried. I thought he was going to attack you, but instead he hopped up on the foot of the bed and went right to sleep."

I wipe away tears, remembering waking up to a cold nose on my cheek. "I was pretty surprised when I woke up," I tell him, giving a watery laugh. "I was calling for you when he nipped at my fingers and I took him to the door. He bolted and I thought he was taking me to you, so I followed. He brought me to the shore and," I sniff, "I saw the ship and just knew. I knew you had left."

"Rune—"

I shake my head. "I thought I had pushed you too hard with our fight and that you just couldn't take it anymore."

"No, I wouldn't have just left. I wouldn't just abandon you, not after everything."

I glare. "I know that now! But then? Well, I didn't know what to think then." My eyes burn at the memory. "Anik had to deal with me for days just hiding in the cottage with Birgir until he got fed up, dragged me to The Wild Rose and left me there for my first shift."

Silence falls between us. I want to know about his family, his year with them, but I am afraid to ask. Maybe a little jealous to know as well.

"I told them about you."

Sometimes, I swear Weylin can read my mind; I shrug and fake disinterest, watching the waves as the *Tempest* soars through the night.

"I told my sister, Sasha, she's sixteen now, all about you—your fire, your laugh, your determination. How damn stubborn you can be sometimes." He sneaks a smile at me. "She told me about her life and how the tribe had looked for me for months until my mother grew sick. She died when I was away, died believing I was either dead myself or had not wanted to come home. No one knew, until I told them that I had been taken by an enemy clan and given to Vodihr as part of their sacrificial payment."

"Oh, Weylin. You don't have to—"

"After talking with my father, I went on a retreat. I'll spare you the details, but two weeks in the wild with little food or water can really put things in perspective. When I came back, the tribe welcomed me—it was my rebirth, my true return to them. I went back to my studies. I practiced hard, became the warrior I was supposed to be. But never," he looks at me again, his eyes flashing, "never did I forget about you. I couldn't. I missed you every single day."

He yanks at the cord around his neck. The pendant and ring appear, the onyx glittering in the moonlight.

"Sasha gave me the ring after we returned from a raid. She said, 'Stop wallowing, go back to her, and then come home.'"

The sound I make is half sob, half laugh. "I like her already."

"I can't wait for you to meet her; to meet the rest of my tribe."

It hangs between us, the unspoken of what is to come. I can see in his eyes what he wants, and it terrifies me. I can't help but think of the stories I've heard of Dýra shared among the traders over ale and hot meals. Of the wild beasts the land births. "Weylin, I-I don't know."

I don't know if I'm brave enough to leave, capable of being what he wants, what he deserves.

"This wasn't how I pictured this, but I can't wait any longer." Quickly he reaches up to untie the cord. The ring falls into his waiting palm, along with his pendant. I step back when his hand clenches around them, his knuckles going white. More tears wet his cheeks and his hand starts to shake.

I step closer, wrapping both of mine around his. I'm hot and cold; nervous and excited—still scared. All of our whispered dreams to get us through Vodihr have been leading to this.

"Are you sure?" I ask, clinging to the warmth of his hand in mine.

"Mundu eftir mér," he whispers, and I shiver. *Remember me.*

Hesitantly, I hold out my left hand, wiggling it after he stares at it for too long. We share a laugh that fades when he slides the ring on. It is solid and heavier than I expected. It gleams against my skin, and I feel this weight in my chest that bubbles and bursts. More tears slip free and I sniff, another laugh escaping that is both broken and joyful.

"Rune."

Just my name, but it holds a thousand meanings and one important question.

"Ég mun alltaf muna eftir þér," I whisper, moving so our breath mingles; he leans down as I reach up. "I'll always remember you." My lips ghost over his. "Always want you."

Sudden clapping breaks us apart. Behind us, the crew member who'd been manning the helm is grinning, his hands halfway together for another round of clapping.

"Ignore him," Weylin says gruffly, tugging me back around and against his chest. His hands move down to grip my waist and I grin impishly.

"As you wish."

His eyes darken, his head lowering.

CHAPTER THIRTY-FOUR

Word spreads fast of our engagement. Ailith is all smiles and fake swoons when we're summoned to gather on deck prior to our arrival at Arden. I'm not sure how I will feel seeing Arden, now that I remembered it was my father's homeland; I hadn't realized I had any deep connection with the place.

The skuggar aboard are watching Utlen grow closer with restlessness.

Larken moves away from the rail where he's been watching the port come into view. He tucks himself against Gael, the elder prince standing on guard by my brother. The young prince sees me watching and smiles, waving a little.

"Do you think we can slip away without them noticing?" Weylin asks me under his breath.

I snort. "Doubtful. Perhaps your eyesight is going bad with old age, but they already have guards stationed on the docks ahead, and the ones here are pacing by the gangway."

"I am not *old*."

I bite back a laugh at his disgruntled tone. But Gael's guards are indeed pacing back and forth. Their movements are anxious, their hands resting on the pommels of their swords. Something feels off—suspicious, even.

Though to be fair, the *Tempest* contains both heirs to Arden's throne, and that alone requires heavier precautions. Especially since one prince had already suffered a kidnapping.

"Think there will be trouble?" Ailith asks, appearing at my side. She plucks a small blade from her boot and begins idly picking at invisible dirt under her nails.

Shrugging, I eye the approaching dock, counting the number of guards waiting. "Likely. We have both princes with us, and I don't know what Gael told his father prior to our departure."

"Good. I need a fight after watching over you the past few days. You were a horrible patient," Weylin says. He grins, completely ignoring my glare.

"You really are, Rune," Ailith chimes in. "Absolutely dreadful, and the smell of that paste?"

"Oh, shut up," I grumble, giving her a light shove. "You're the one who made it." She's still laughing but my amusement quickly fades. The guards on board are watching us. They look on in distrust, one has his weapon halfway out of its scabbard.

On edge now myself, I step further away from the port side.

The crew is bustling about, preparing the *Tempest* to dock. The sails lower, only the jib left up. The riggings screech and clunk in tune to the burst of song coming from Anik's crew.

One of the crew aiming to toss a heaving line bumps into a guard and nearly gets skewered for it.

The skin on my nape prickles, my muscles tightening. Near me lurk two skuggar. One is under the nest, billowing in the breeze; the other sniffs around the guards, circling like a predator ready to attack. I click my tongue to catch their attention, and they both reluctantly fade to nearly transparent spots, their faint threads trailing along the dock.

The *Tempest* sways, rocking back and forth as it sloshes through foam.

"Steady!" Anik shouts from the helm. His eyes meet mine for a moment before he looks away.

"Have you talked to him?" Ailith asks, her voice low.

I shoot her a glare. "You know I haven't."

"Perhaps you should—"

Whatever else she was about to say is lost, for as soon as the lines have us secured and the plank is lowered, Ardenian guards on the dock flood the deck, weapons at the ready. The group splits. Some make their way to Gael and Larken—Anik is pushed back, the end of a sword in his face. The rest of the guards circle us.

The crew goes still. I blink at the swirl of colors as even more guards arrive. We're surrounded. Some of the crew nearby who've lost sight of Anik through the crowd look to Ailith for direction instead, and she gives them a subtle shake of her head, mouthing, "Steady."

Few relax but they still relay her command to the rest.

I whisper to Weylin, "You just had to say you wanted a fight."

Ailith laughs and two swords are abruptly pointed our way, stopping inches from our noses.

"What in the bloody Hel is this? I didn't give anyone permission to come aboard," Anik snaps, breaking the tension. Gael and Larken are nearly invisible behind their wall of guards and the *Tempest* is groaning under the extra weight she now holds.

A raven calls from above; tilting my head back, I catch a glimpse of black and silvery white. I wonder what she is trying to warn me about now.

"Just an extra precaution ordered by His Majesty for the safe return of the princes."

I can still see Anik from where I stand and I nip the inside of my cheek to hold back from laughing; Anik's face is priceless—a mix of shock, amusement, and irritation.

"And who exactly informed the king we were arriving in port, pray tell?" Anik asks, pushing away the tip of the blade pointed at his chest. His other hand rests on his own sword and I silently beg for him to not do anything stupid.

"Privileged information," comes the pompous reply and I can't help a chuckle from spilling out. I take in the shine of the guard's buttons, the cleanliness of his forest green uniform—I think of Papa before I can stop myself. This guard, however, is either an amateur or some high-ranking enough that he doesn't see a lot of action.

Both Anik and the guard are looking my way; I hold up my hands, trying to look innocent.

"Privileged as in you don't want to tell us, or you aren't even privileged to know?" Anik asks.

The high-ranking guard points his sword back at Anik and I sigh.

"Alright then," I call out, gaining their attention again. I hold out my hands and take a step forward. "You can tie me up and take me to the king. It's been awhile since he's seen me."

And he has seen me, once, a long time ago when I was just a girl and he was a masked hunter looking to lose himself in the Revelry, sampling some of the darkness Vodihr had to offer in their Bloodletting. Keegan had been his chosen pet that night; the same night I let the Other go. He may have visited Vodihr more, but I couldn't remember.

Anik looks at me like I've lost my mind; Weylin groans behind me. Ailith is the only one who shrugs and mimics me, holding out her wrists and faking compliance.

Two guards step forward to bind our wrists, but Weylin steps around us and blocks their path. It appears we have a stalemate. Anik hasn't said anything more and whatever Prince Gael is hissing to the guards around him doesn't seem to be swaying them much.

"Enough of this," Prince Larken cries suddenly, pushing through the guards and past Weylin. He stands in front of me with his arms crossed over his chest and gives the pompous high-ranking guard a fierce glare. "I want to see my father, *now*."

No one reacts at first and it is Gael who pushes through next, coming to stand at his brother's side. "Are you disobeying a direct order from the prince?"

"They seem to do that a lot," I offer and receive a glower from Gael.

The high-ranking guard looks around for a moment before giving a shallow nod. "Very well, Your Highnesses. We will escort you to His Majesty."

In a flurry of movement and a sea of green, the guards abscond with the princes. I see the look of longing between Anik and Gael before the deck clears. Once they are gone, Anik's head drops. I take an involuntary step towards him, but then I catch a glimpse of something on the shore—feathers and the flash of a cloak ...

A shadow points frantically in that direction, but I see nothing more. Another shadow pokes at my shin.

Weylin's eyes are streaking through with red because a lagging guard has bumped into him. I quickly grab his hand and tug him towards the dock.

"Ru, wait," Anik calls, walking our way. I stop on the gangway, feeling awkward. His face is beseeching, but I can't—I'm still angry. I turn away.

'You knew the whole damn time and never said anything?'

'But I deserved it, right? That is what you told Ma-Jocelyn. I deserved everything.'

'You don't understand.'

'I guess you're right. I don't understand how someone who always tried to protect me, who said they loved me, could lie to me all along. You were my brother.'

"Not now, Anik," I say, forcing a harshness in my tone I've never used with him before. The crew members closest to the port rail shy away, their eyebrows raising in surprise.

Ailith shakes her head, the disappointment clear on her face. She leads Anik back to the helm, beginning a rather loud discussion on the length of the crew's shore leave.

Weighted down with guilt and confusion, I step onto the docks with Weylin in tow.

'I am *you brother.*'

'No. *You aren't.*'

CHAPTER THIRTY-FIVE

ow do I cut it again?" I asked, my voice weak. There was a sigh and then a brush of featherlight fingers on my nape that sent a chill down my spine.

I forced my gaze back to the mirror and tried to steady my shaking hand. The dagger I held tilted dangerously close to my nose before my hand flopped backwards.

There was another sigh and the shadow stepped closer, her eyes—wide and unfocused—met mine briefly in the mirror. Her hand rose and mimicked slicing a blade through her own blonde locks. Locks that were uneven and stringy, hanging at odd angles around her forehead, neck, and ears.

"And this is what Mama wants? It will make her happy?"

A short nod was the skuggi's only answer. Her hands then jerked, one going to wrap around her throat, the other grabbing her hair. For a second, I worried she was choking; that she was the one who put those bruised fingerprints around her neck. The wildness in her features soon *smoothed out, though; her eyes glossing over again.*

I grasped a fistful of hair and brought the dagger up to just underneath my chin. "You can do this," I snapped, threatening my own timid reflection. "Mama won't be unhappy with you anymore. She won't."

I only nicked a single strand of hair before the room door opened and my brother stepped into the candlelight. At his appearance, the shadow flinched and dissolved, melting back into the corner from whence she came.

"What are you doing?"

I shrugged meekly, worried by his brittle tone and fierce expression. "Mama threatened to cut my hair … I figured I could do it for her and then," my throat tightened, "and then she wouldn't hurt me again."

"Oh, Ru." My brother prized the dagger from my hands and placed it on the washstand. "Mama didn't mean it."

I closed my eyes against the pity in his expression. "You always say that."

He didn't respond, but I felt him move closer. His hands grabbed mine and he tugged me over to the tub. At ten, he was able to lift my seven-year-old self easily, placing me in the cool brass oval before scooting me forward so he could climb in behind me. With my eyes tightly shut, I turned and huddled against him—this wasn't the first time I had hidden there with him.

Lulled to comfort by the sound of his heartbeat, I pressed closer.

"You forgot to take your medicine again."

I huffed, wrapping my arms around his middle. "It tastes disgusting. I don't know why I have to take it—Grandma Embela says I'm all better anyway."

"Who?"

"Grandma Bell, silly," I said, trying to cover my mistake. My dream the night before had been of a witch with a cat familiar who was always cranky. The witch and I had read stories together. Danced. Created potions. She was Embela, my grandmother, my amma.

After a day of fun in her cottage in the woods that would sing, a woman had picked me up and taken me home. The witch had reminded me very much of Grandma Bell.

Anik was silent. One of my hands was tugged away from his back and a small bottle was placed in it. I automatically raised it to my lips and forced down the chunky contents. Swallowing a gag, I shoved the bottle back into his waiting hand and glared, my expression likely mulish—or so I hoped. I had been practicing different expressions with the shadows.

"I'm scared, Anik," I confessed a minute later, already half-asleep. My vision was blurring, stomach feeling tight, my throat numb; all common after my medicine was taken.

"I know, Ru," he whispered, tightening his arms around me.

"Will you protect me from the monsters?"

I felt his lips press a quick kiss against my forehead and smile. "Always."

But I knew even Anik wouldn't always be able to stop Papa's wrath or divert Mama's disgust. Some monsters were too human to be defeated.

I'm strangling the pillow, its cover soaked with my tears. A hand presses on my back, another runs through my hair. I melt into the touch, my sobs slowing, quieting. I press my shaking limbs deeper into the bed. The ghost of a warm weight brushes my foot before settling against my stomach. I feel the phantom press of a wet slightly rough nose and stifle another wail—oh, how I miss my wolf.

"Another one?" Weylin asks.

My grip loosens just a little on the pillow I hold. "Yes, I d-don't know what's real and what isn't anymore." I inhale. "Was I wrong to hate my Papa all those years? Was Jocelyn the villain or someone else?" I shake my head. "Nothing makes sense."

Nothing is real.

But some things are, and I just can't accept it.

The hand on my back stills and I'm flipped over, pillow and all, to face Weylin. He tugs the pillow away, ignoring my protest. I must be a mess, my eyes puffy from tears and lack of sleep. My skin is stretching too tight across my cheeks—I haven't had much of an appetite since returning to Arden.

Weylin offers a small smile, his hand cupping my cheek before brushing back a piece of matted hair on my forehead.

"This is real. You, me, the cottage—all real. We will figure this out. You aren't alone," he says, his words thick and full of promise. He brushes my ring, then takes my hand, bringing it to rest against his chest. His head is lowering towards mine when there is a knock at the cottage door.

Weylin growls and I can't help but laugh, thinking of how similar his reaction is to Birgir's when someone came to the cottage. Just thinking of the wolf makes my heart hurt.

Sending me a playful glare, Weylin gets to his feet. The knock comes again and I watch him stalk to the door.

My lazy appraisal of his bare back abruptly ends when Prince Gael steps through the doorway. I sit up, resisting the urge to reach for the covers. Gael's eyebrows shoot up and I resign myself to the awkwardness of the situation. I keep my head held high as I get out of bed and tug Weylin's shirt down over my thighs.

"You Highness, to what do I owe the pleasure?" I ask, then add, "Not another kidnapping or debt to be paid, right?"

Weylin rolls his eyes at me and steps in front of the doorway, blocking the guards trying to follow Gael inside.

"Stand aside or I will arrest you for—"

"Enough," Gael snaps. "Just wait outside, this won't take long."

The guard says something under his breath I can't make out before bowing his head in reluctant acknowledgment. He then turns and motions for the other guards—I'd say five from what I can see in my current position—to move away and surround the cottage.

"They should be retrained. None of them really accept your command," Weylin remarks. "I could help with that."

"They are following my father's orders. They've been told to do what they think is best." Gael's attention focuses on me. "I wanted to see how you were."

"Oh please, you tolerate me as much as I tolerate you." I wave away his frown. "Why are you here, Your Highness?"

My mood and tone hastily send the skuggar in the corners shooting up the walls in search of hiding places. In the back of my mind, I'm arguing with myself if perhaps I should be more gracious. Part of me is actually happy to see him. But the other part—the bigger, more vindictive one—wants to spit on his polished boots and kick him out on his royal arse.

Him being here only reminds me of Anik, and I am not ready to face the reality of my broken family. A broken relationship with my brother—half-brother—whom I had once naively asked to keep the monsters away when he was one of those monsters.

"He is being eaten alive by guilt," Gael says then, and I feel my resolve start to crumble. Apparently, the elder prince is a mind reader, too. "But that isn't why I'm here." He steps forward to hold out an envelope he has produced from the inside pocket of his cloak.

"The King has decided to host a special … Revelry for Larken's safe return." He waits till I take it and break the seal before adding, "You both are invited to attend."

I scan the scripted words, the parchment almost translucent in the light of the cottage's low-burning lanterns. I hand it to Weylin, torn between hysterical laughter and wanting to scream.

"Are you serious? Does Larken even want a *party* to celebrate his return from Hel?" I surprise myself with how calm I sound while my mind rages.

Gael looks suspicious and a little resigned. "He would rather become fish fodder than attend, but our father believes it is just what the people need to settle things after … after the kidnapping."

"Right, because the Revelry wasn't responsible for his kidnapping in the first place. Because hosting a second Revelry is the perfect way to solve all the city's—no, *people's* problems," I hiss.

"Because the Revelry doesn't take boys and girls as payment each year in every village they entertain, and your father certainly doesn't condone it. Children that are then … " I yank the invite from Weylin's hands and toss it into the idling fire in the hearth. "Because the Revelry is only to appease the *gods* and is not at all beneficial to the depravity and greed of men."

I wait for the parchment to catch flame, the invite's finery no match for the heat, then turn back to face Gael. "Please pass on my apologies to the king. I'm afraid we cannot attend."

CHAPTER THIRTY-SIX

'm wiping down the bar and imagining that Birgir is near, sniffing at an unidentifiable spot on the floor before trying to sneak a treat from those I carry in my pocket—still carry, out of habit and useless denial. Around me, The Wild Rose carries on with its usual gossip and drinking, the occasional drunk picking fights until Hensley kicks them out.

Bits of conversation float by as I make my rounds. I'm a little slower than normal but at least my wound is healing. And I don't have to use any more of Ailith's awful paste.

"Did you hear that the Revelry is coming back?"

"I heard that the King is having an affair with the Revelry's Reaper."

"The same 'Reaper' who took the young prince?"

"Shut up, both of you," a retired fisherman cuts in. "I heard there's supposed to be a special act dedicated to Prince Larken."

It's been five days since Gael and his entourage of guards

showed up at my cottage with the invitation to the "party" in honor of Larken's return. A week since I left the *Tempest*. Twelve days in total so far, full of dreams, indecision, and the contemplating of murder. Needless to say, I'm going a little mad.

"Can I get another round for me and the boys, hon?"

Pausing in my cleaning, I turn to see one of the tavern regulars, Ed, standing with his hip leaning against the counter. My eyes flick to where Vin and his cronies sit, all deep in conversation, before shrugging. Vin was usually the one to get drinks.

"Sure, Ed. The usual or are you finally going to liven things up a bit?"

When he smiles, I can count all ten of his teeth still determinedly remaining in his gums. "Now Rune, you know us old folk don't like change. We can't handle those new concoctions you youngins prefer."

"Old folk my arse, Ed—you're in your prime. It's time to live a little."

He slaps a hand down on the counter as he laughs, and I can't help but chuckle myself. My laughter fades, however, when Vin's eyes meet mine from across the room. An uncomfortable pit forms in my stomach at the new lines on his face, the purple under his light green eyes matching the purple and green bruise on his chin from where Weylin had hit him upon arriving home.

Vin greeted me with a smile. "Rune! I'm so glad you're home. Hensley just doesn't have your touch while tending the Rose." He was standing, half-turned in my direction, my cottage at his back. In his arms was a basket of fish, the smell reaching me from where I stopped on the path.

I didn't answer. Instead, I was noticing small light scars that littered his face. Uneasy, my gaze focused on my little cottage. I could still hear muted conversation from the Tempest *at the docks.*

"Well, I'll be damned. You seem to have missed your cottage more than your favorite patron," *Vin mused. I glanced down, taking in his absent limp as he shifted his weight. His walking stick was missing from its usual spot in his right hand.*

"Don't be too offended. I got the same treatment and I was gone a year," *came a voice from behind me.*

Vin's sun-weathered face began to lose color at an alarming rate. He wheezed and stumbled back as I glanced over my shoulder. "To be fair," *I said,* "I did think you had left me without a word."

Weylin shrugged and came to stand at my side; his eyes hardened, mouth settling into a grim line. But still, his tone was light when he teased back, "Fair, I suppose."

"Weylin," *Vin managed to say.*

Quickly, I grab new glasses and fill them with ale to avoid Vin's unsettling gaze.

My head tilted to the side. I'd never seen the fisherman look afraid— not even when he faced a giant of a man who had cheated in cards two months ago. Yet here he is now, looking as if he may piss his pants.

"If it isn't too much trouble, Vin, perhaps you could explain to Rune why my letter—you know, the one I gave to you before I boarded Gaely's ship—why that letter never reached her."

I stepped forward, moving to stand between the two at the growl in Weylin's tone and the hint of red creeping into his eyes.

"Any reasonable answer will do: You lost it. A seagull stole it. It got ripped apart by a sudden hailstone falling from the sky. You were *so touched by its beauty after you opened and read it that you kept it for yourself." The silence lasted only a second before Weylin prodded, "Well, what was it?"*

Vin's face was unreadable. "You never gave me a letter. You left her and—"

Weylin's fist was wrapped around Vin's shirt collar before he could finish his sentence. "Think very carefully about what you'll say next. I don't take kindly to being called a liar."

The sea whispered in warning; shadows crawled from the rocky shoreline. "Vin, just tell us what happened to the letter."

Indecision flickered briefly on Vin's face and I held my breath as his lips parted to answer. The disappointment nearly crushed me when he said, "There was no letter."

Crack! Vin grunted, falling to the ground, his jaw cradled in one hand while the other gripped at the stone and dirt beneath him. Fish surrounded his prone body, the basket torn wide open.

"Wrong answer," Weylin whispered.

A throat clears loudly and I flush, hurrying to finish the last of Ed's order. I wave him away after I clank the last glass down and nearly trip over a fallen rag as I flee to the opposite end of the bar. The abrupt movement has me slightly disoriented, one hand clutching at my stomach, the other bracing on the counter beside a dirty glass I had yet to clear away.

I don't even realize I've been glaring at that glass until someone jokes, "I hope I'm not interrupting anything."

"You usually do but I'll let it pass this time." The words slip free, the friendly retort wholly automatic. The carefree feeling immediately dies. "What do you want, Anik?"

"No hello? No calling of your watchdog to chase me away?" Bitterness seeps from his words. "Where is he, did you send him on a walk?"

"He is working, actually. Got a job with the ornery blacksmith down the street." When I look up, I have to swallow a curse at his appearance. It is the most unkempt I have seen my brother in years, from his half-tucked shirt with a mixture of stains on it, to his wayward hair sticking up at all angles. His hands are gloved, a crumpled envelope forgotten beneath one of his fists on the counter.

'He is being eaten alive by guilt.'

A lone shadow leans over my brother's shoulder to sniff at his hair before going to lick an empty glass nearby.

"Anik ... "

He holds up a hand, stopping whatever I was about to say. His shoulders slump and after a second of indecision, he tosses the envelope my way. I catch a whiff of ale and hope it isn't coming from him.

"An invitation to the Revelry tomorrow."

I cough. "I'm special enough to warrant two personal invites?"

Anik shrugs, stepping back. "It would seem so."

"Well in that case, tell your lover that I again refuse."

He looks unsurprised by my response. "Alright," he replies, his tone mild, unaffected at my budding tantrum. "Shall I let Mother know you send your regards, as well?"

His words are like a physical blow, the air in my lungs becoming lead and wool. I gape at him. "Excuse me?"

"Jocelyn was invited to attend," he says nonchalantly. I almost miss the bite in his words, but it's there. "She is one of three representatives from Wraith. Agata is another."

I'm positive I'm hallucinating, the buzz of the patrons fading as a roaring fills my ears. Surely this is an elaborate joke? A trick? Why would the king invite—no, host—the very people who kidnapped his child? Not just the Revelry, but its Mistress? And how had Jocelyn become a representative of a place she so despised?

"So, the rumors are true," I manage after a minute, grasping at the safest thought. I want to ask how he knew she was invited; what had happened to her after she stabbed me—but I don't. "The king has lost his mind if he has invited the very people who stole his son not a fortnight ago to perform for him."

Anik's back is to me as he replies, "It would appear so."

I watch as he leaves through the tavern's side door without another word. Dumbfounded, I look down at the invitation on the counter: it's a replica of the first one. It's far too bright, too white, and too innocent against the darkness of the tavern's wood.

The red scripted letters have not changed.

You are cordially invited for the Revelry's return to celebrate ...

CHAPTER THIRTY-SEVEN

I f one more person touches my arse, I'm going to start swinging," I grumble, adjusting the mask sticking to the makeup and sweat on my face.

Weylin laughs, his elbow nudging my side. "What if I say that last time was me?"

"Be serious," I hiss, my lips trembling to suppress a grin. A woman glances at me with unease, her eyes going to Weylin before she hurries away.

"I always am."

A retort is on my tongue when a flash of bleached white catches my eye. Following the flash, the crude bone mask comes into focus. The antlers are bent now and one now hangs at an odd angle. I freeze. I can barely see the slitted eyes through the holes of the mask. The figure wearing it sways; a gloved hand moves upward, the index finger pressing against cracked lips.

The Reaper, a shadow hisses in my ear.

He comes for you, another moans. *He remembers. He wants.*

I feel a tug on my ankle, my knee buckling at the unexpected pull. When I regain my footing, I see a shadow's fingers are biting into my ankle bone.

The Reaper is gone.

And so is Weylin.

Out of sorts, I spin—the swirls, laughter, crude remarks, blending to create a chaos beloved only by the gods who stirred the seeds of madness in the Revelry. A couple brushes past on my left, the woman shooting me a look as I accidently knock the bracelets on her arm and send them clanking—*clink, clink, clink.* The man at her side laughs, dragging her along. His hand dips lower down her spine until she squeaks.

A drunk stumbles in front of me, leering.

My throat is tight. My wound burns.

Focus, a soft voice soothes. *Focus, my sweet girl.*

From the corner of my eye, there is a flutter of black, white, and gray wings, a raven's lone cry echoing in the darkness. Her shadow appears up ahead then, her figure hazy and indistinct as she holds out a hand.

"There you are."

I drop my outstretched hand, Mama disappearing. I turn to find Weylin once more at my side. Beneath his mask, his lips are stained with grease from the roasted boar leg in his hand.

His eyes narrow as they search my face. "Is everything—"

"I'm going to be sick," I gasp, nearly tripping over my cloak in my sudden rush to reach the outskirts of the square.

Mama reappears, beckoning me to follow her to the tree line;

people pass through her and she fades. Music groans a melody into the night. My knees hit the hard ground and I gag. People and skuggar alike scatter in disgust.

"It's okay, I got you."

One hand goes to my stomach, the other pressing against my chest. The acid burns. My stomach protests when I try to swallow back another heave.

Finally, I take a breath and end up facing the castle.

Even from a distance, the castle is intimidating with its jagged angles and washed stone. It's been around for centuries, additions being built under the hands of each new king. I want to be impressed, but I'm not. To me, it is a relic of the age where man became settled and rotted. The surrounding towns—the Isle of Utlen itself—give testament to a forgotten time, no more modern or enlightened than the provincial village of Laus, no more civilized or moralistic than the isolated degeneracy of Vodihr.

I miss the freedom of my home, the warmth of my blankets ...

It was all a lie. I was never loved. Never safe.

But I was at one time, wasn't I? Ironic that Vodihr had been both Hel and a haven for me.

"Something's wrong," I whisper, my vision blurry. Furs and leathers mingle with wool and silk as the people around me distort. I press my fingertips to my brow. "Weylin, we have to leave."

Leave, one shadow mimics; its threads dance among the fallen leaves. *Leave, leave, leave.*

They are coming for you, another sighs.

Weylin grunts suddenly, bending forward, an arrow protruding from his side. I gasp, reaching for him, but a voice stops me cold.

"I'm afraid, elskan, leaving is impossible."

Turning, Mistress Agata blocks the path, the Revelry alive at her back. At her side is Vin, a grim expression on his face—a face with more scars, more cracks than I remember. And the Reaper, his mask covered in fresh gore, stands a little behind them; he seems wary, unfocused.

"You wouldn't want to disappoint Prince Larken, would you?"

In the distance, a familiar ceremonial drum begins to beat.

It's time, a shadow—Papa—whispers to me. I feel his fingers wrap around my wrist, giving me a slight tug forward. *It's time.*

It's not just the Revelry. It seems all of Vodihr has come to Arden.

⁂

We are made to stand at the very front of the gathering crowd, the wooden platform before us emblazoned with burgundy, grey, and black—the colors of the Revelry and of Vodihr—and gold and forest green—the colors of Arden. Intoxicated whispers surround me as I watch Mistress Agata, Vin, and the Reaper talk at the steps before only Agata takes the stage. She smiles at me, her gaze victorious. What game does she play this time? What evil thing is she plotting?

At my side, Weylin nurses a minor wound; the smell of copper lingers and whispers of our shared past— of grunting, creaking, cruel taunts, harsh slaps.

Someone brushes my elbow and I'm ready to curse before I see who it is. Anik is dressed in black with a cape of forest green adorning his shoulders. On his face are the markings of war, a horizontal slash under each eye and a vertical one on his chin. It is an old custom of Papa's ancestors that I haven't seen in years. What does he know that I do not? Our eyes lock for a second, but then he turns to face the stage.

"Anik, what is happening?"

Before he can answer, a hush descends as the royal family joins the crowd and I fall silent, too. The queen and Larken are escorted onto the platform, but Gael and the king linger with another handful of guards by the stairs.

Gael looks at me, and his lips tighten when he notices Anik at my side. His grimace is clear as he brushes past two swooning ladies blocking the stairs, coming to stand next to Larken and resting one of his hands on his brother's shoulder. I can see the young prince shaking from here.

The king is the last to take the steps; he is calm, focused—looking every bit the ruler he was bred to be. When our eyes clash, his demeanor shifts in the slightest, eyes narrowing. I smirk, surprised and disgusted that he recognizes me. If only the city knew of the king's ... exploits when boredom dug its claws too deep.

"Aren't you a little young to be in a brothel?"

"Don't you have a kingdom to rule or something?"

We stared at each other as I held out the deck of cards he had requested. The girl on his lap was still, wide-eyed—her jeweled necklace must weigh a ton. Keegan was leaning against the chair on the king's other side, his eyes warning me to behave even as he forced a laugh.

The king shrugged and took the cards.

Ahh. So he was a regular of Vodihr. Interesting.

"Arden has graciously allowed us a boon, a chance to right a wrong that has occurred to both our kingdoms," Mistress Agata says. It's eerie how the crowd turns as one to watch her.

"Vodihr is a kingdom now?" Weylin mutters for my ear alone. "I didn't realize we had risen so far in status, what with scrubbing floors and bedding anything that paid."

"It's called arse-kissing," Anik offers dryly. "I heard it works wonders if done right."

A snort escapes me and Anik grins in triumph.

"As most of you know, young prince Larken had been stolen from Arden and taken to Voh-Wraith as one of the payments for the Revelry's services this year," Agata calls out, her expression reflecting just enough fake concern to move the crowd.

"It is because communications to my—to Wraith's Reaper were intercepted and new orders were falsified. When I was informed of the mistake, the prince had already arrived and was being conditioned for his role in the Bloodletting." Her voice trails off. She appears uneasy now; the crowd mirrors her.

"As if she didn't know when he arrived. She probably snatched him up as soon as her Reaper had him through the circle."

Weylin nods at my words.

On stage, the queen lets out a quiet sob, Larken tensing at her side. Gael looks ready to explode. Only the king is unmoved, stoic.

"While I could never right this grievous mistake entirely, I immediately summoned one of my most trusted servants to return to Wraith and escort him home."

Her eyes find me and she gives me a wave of recognition, wiggling her slender bejeweled fingers my way.

I'm speechless; appalled.

A shadow groans or maybe it's Weylin.

"But many of you have cried for retribution, as is your right, and graciously your-our," she coughs to cover her slip, "*our* king has permitted us to host a special Revelry just for Arden." She waits for the cheers to fade, then continues. "We have located the ones who interfered with official Wraith communications and arranged for the prince to be taken." She sighs and the crowd shifts impatiently—their thirst for disorder and bloodshed is clear in the twisting of their features.

"I'm afraid it is too long and too sordid a tale to get into tonight," the crowd boos and she hushes them, "but those who tried to harm the young prince and destroy the peace between Wraith and Arden will be brought to justice—tonight."

The drum begins an unhurried singular beat and the crowd stomps their feet in anticipation. From beneath their soles, skuggar scurry for cover.

I wait, anxious, uncertain, as the Reaper appears; he holds two ropes leading two hooded figures. Their appearances, though their faces are obscured, show signs of abuse: dirty, torn clothes, blood stains, fresh cuts on their arms. One has long blonde hair that hangs to their shoulders; it is matted with grime.

Both prisoners stumble up the stairs, yanked along by the Reaper. The crowd is screaming, still stamping their feet. Some spit, others curse.

"Tonight, Vodihr—" The king clears his throat and Agata amends, starting again, "Tonight, Arden and Wraith sacrifice to the gods for healing, for hope."

The Reaper keeps hold of the ropes in one hand and rips off one of the hoods with the other. My cry is lost in the crowd and the feverish beat of the drum.

322

CHAPTER THIRTY-EIGHT

Jocelyn stands there, blinking in the torchlight. Tear stains are visible on her cheeks. "I don't understand ... " Her voice fails and she sniffs. Her watery, confused gaze moves from Agata to the Reaper to the crowd. "This wasn't—"

"Silence," Agata snaps. "Your confession has already been recorded before myself and the king. You will answer for your crimes."

Anik hisses a breath, his hand coming to grip my elbow. Weylin moves closer on my other side.

Jocelyn's shoulders fold in on themselves; her head bows. "I did it for you," she whispers at Agata, "for us," her eyes narrowing on the Reaper, "for him because you promised that after we'd—"

Slap.

Skin on skin, red flesh flaring to life.

The crowd waits.

"Jocelyn Hansen, you have been found guilty of conspiring

to kidnap the prince, of attempting to break the treaty between Arden and Wraith, and of trying to murder your own daughter— my els-servant."

I taste bile, bitter and burning.

Jocelyn shakes her head, a bellow escaping from her thin lips; fresh blood stains her teeth. "She is not my daughter; my daughter is dead!"

Agata tsks, her eyes sweeping the crowd. She's restless when she motions to the Reaper and he rips off the second hood. Vin?

"Slavine Green, you have been found guilty of conspiring with Jocelyn Hansen to kidnap the prince and break our king-dom's most sacred treaty with Arden." From my spot, I can almost hear her gritting her teeth as she adds, "You have also been found guilty of unfaithfulness."

A man in the crowd booms with laughter before being shushed.

Vin's eyes find mine, his gaze tired, watery, but determined. His silence against the accusations is answer enough and I find myself unable to look away.

"Do either of you have any last words?" It is the king who speaks, his tone flat and unaffected. Gael winces but hides it quickly.

Jocelyn screeches and I look back at her, finding her pointing at me. "It was her! She killed my daughter, my husband. She is a monster among us—the gods have defiled her. Cursed her!"

The people closest to where I stand shift, inching away from me. Some play with their masks uneasily; some tug on their clothes; some fiddle with their jewelry. I feel the hot brand of Jocelyn's accusation, but say nothing. It's true, I did kill her family.

"I was wrong," Vin's voice rings out then. "I was wrong to trust who I did, to love who I did. I have lied and been lied to." He shudders when our eyes meet again. "I deserve my crimes and may the gods," his voice breaks, "forgive me."

Snickers from the crowd are drowned out by the drum's renewed beat. A sword is brought on stage by an attendant of the king—it rests on a virginal white cloth.

"This is wrong, w-why aren't Gael or Larken saying anything? They know the truth." I'm angry, the pressure building in my chest.

"We do, too, yet you haven't said anything."

Anik's words are a slap to my face and the shadows at my feet dissolve.

He's right—any protests are rotting somewhere between my chest and my lips. Through dry eyes, I stare at the wooden platform, tracking the shadows that crawl and shift along the edges. Their threads make a web among the cracks. Papa and Mama are nowhere to be seen.

"May the gods forgive me," I whisper hoarsely.

The attendant on stage shifts uneasily; he eyes first the king, who shakes his head, then moves to Agata, his chin lowering to touch his chest. The sword tremors on the cloth as it's held up. It is a well-practiced show of submission and obedience and Agata preens, in rapture over this recognition of her importance, her power.

She motions for another attendant to light the stone-cradled pyre in the center of the platform. As the fire crackles to life and gorges itself on the wood, the crowd moans an echo of the words Agata has begun to mutter in an ancient tongue. I can't catch what she says, but the fire flickers from gold to orange to white and purple.

Is she summoning him? a shadow whispers; it circles the flames.

She wouldn't dare, another responds. *Not after she failed to …*

Sshh, the first snaps. *She cannot invoke him—not here.*

Distracted by their words and the flash of black within the flames, I almost miss seeing Jocelyn being forced to kneel. Her guttural cries wrench the breath from my lungs. I don't want to watch, I can't. Still, my eyes widen and I follow the flash of steel as it is placed to hang above her neck, wielded by the Reaper. He raises it high.

"May Hel welcome you," Agata roars. She gestures, and the Reaper brings his sword down quick, the blade heavy and unerring.

Blood splatters my lips, my cheek. My vision drips red—and Jocelyn's head now rests inches from my face, teetering precariously on the platform's edge, tangled in beige threads.

"Do you promise?" she whispered, cuddling closer against Agata's naked body. They were wrapped up in a bed of fur and silk at The House. She still hated it here, but the smells and the sounds grew on her each time she snuck in to meet her lover.

"Promise what?" Agata stroked her back lazily.

Jocelyn's head tilted to the side as she stretched. Dawn was approaching and soon she'd have to leave. "That if I do this, we can be together?"

The flame of the candle flickered. Someone screamed in a room down the hall.

"Together, yes," Agata breathed and Jocelyn beamed at her. "Of course."

On the chair by the door, an antlered mask with fresh markings sat, pulsing.

I don't realize the keening I hear is coming from me until Anik tugs me back and into his arms. My face is pressed against his shoulder. I taste copper and sweat. I taste my tears. I inhale ash and the sea.

The crowd roars.

The flames whisper.

A second wet splat echoes against wood.

"Rune."

Yanking myself away from my brother's hold, I turn to see Vin's head next to Jocelyn's. Already, color is leaching from their skin; their eyes are bulging and their lips are sickly purple. Death has not been kind to either of them.

Rune.

At first, I am afraid one of the heads has spoken to me and I close my eyes—rejecting the sight, the crowd, the loss. My hands rise to cover my ears, but I can't block out the drum and the singing and the cursing surrounding me.

I should've said something.

But still, the words don't come, only hysteria bubbling behind my teeth.

Rune, Vin whispers again and my eyes open. His shadow appears before me, inches from my face. *Please, we must hurry.*

He blurs when his fingers, wiggling with loose brown threads, touch my cheek.

"What have you done, Agata?"

"You know what," she snapped, anger flooding her gaze.

There were footsteps behind them and Vin and Agata turned to see Goddric appear, holding the body of a young woman—

"Mama," I whisper. "Papa."

Mama's shift is stained with blood, her eyes empty of her laughter.

Grief flares within me.

Agata rushed to light the fire pit, murmuring to the flames in a garbled old tongue. A boy of maybe eleven or twelve slunk from the trees, his hands gripping a cloth bag. He stopped at the edge of the flames and kicked at the dirt.

Vin glanced at the fire, pacing. "Agata, you can't—"

"Goddric, bring her closer."

Goddric's eyes were full of torment; he gripped Elowyn tighter. "Will this work? Will he bring her back?"

"You cannot mean to summon—"

"Shut up, husband," Agata said with a sneer at Vin. "I can and I will." Ignoring Goddric who was weeping, she beckoned the boy closer. "Keegan, come."

Gaze on his feet, Keegan rounded the firepit and held out the bag. Agata snatched it from him and cradled it to her chest. Her lungs deflated.

Vin shook his head. "Give me the bag, Agata." He stepped forward. "This has gone on long enough."

"Now, Goddric! Before it is too late," Agata instructed, ignoring him. Her eyes were half-mast, gleaming in the light. She whispered a repetition over and over.

The hairs on Vin's arms rose. He reached for her hands and the bag she held, but she lashed out, slamming a burning stick on his knee.

He felt the bone shatter as he crumpled to the ground, screaming.

No one reacted.

Goddric's shoulders shook as he tenderly closed Elowyn's still-open eyes before placing her in the fire. Before he could move away, the flames licked at his hands and he cried out.

"Stop!" Vin shouted but Agata appeared at Goddric's side, swiftly cutting his burnt palm and squeezing for his blood to mix with flame and ash and skin.

"For him," *she crooned. "For him."*

Something shuddered within the flames, an infinite black mass that ate the wood away and tumbled to the ground. It heaved and creeped along the dirt.

Keegan yelped and ran to Vin, cowering at his side.

"Goddric." A weighted silence befell the clearing after Agata spoke. There was no sound of the flames' crackling.

Still crying, Goddric asked, "Where is she? You said—"

"Ssh." Agata walked toward him. She tugged his head lower, her fingers gripping the hair on his nape. "Ssh." She brushed his lips with hers and then pulled forth a gleaming white antlered mask from her bag.

"No! I won't—" Goddric's protest was muffled, cut short.

Vin's eyes were caught on the fire. Something, someone, was taking shape from the black mass and flames. It touched the ground, sniffed the air, then growled.

"What have you done?" Vin repeated, horror coloring his voice.

Agata had placed the mask on Goddric's face. Looking towards the flames too, she moaned a single guttural word:

"Master."

Disoriented, it takes me a second to realize I'm back at the

Revelry, staring at Vin's severed head—Jocelyn's is missing. I swear Vin's eyes blink, his lips opening on a heave as more russet threads pour out.

Again, the scene shifts.

I'm watching my ten-year-old self go ridged as I'm brought to stand in front of Papa, shadow creatures sniffing, prowling just behind us.

I fight the urge to cry. I don't want to relive this.

There is a sigh in the air; a glare on Papa's face.

The girl's hood fell back, revealing an uncombed tangle of ebony curls beneath. She looked so much like his sister-in-law, like Elowyn. He cleared his throat to stop the tears. "She is a pretty thing, just like you promised."

I bite back a curse. It was Vin. Vin who took me to Vodihr and Agata. How had I never noticed that? Never remembered his voice or mannerisms?

The girl jerked against Goddric's hold and Vin almost told him to let her go. He had to look away when Goddric's fingers bit deeper into her flesh.

Vin was doing this for Goddric—taking Rune away from Jocelyn, from Agata … Maybe even from Goddric himself. Rune was set to leave on the next ship to Arden in a week. Goddric had already booked her passage. She'd go to the king with Keegan, to be a servant to his wife.

There wasn't much time left—the madness from the mask ate at Goddric's will and sanity every day. And so Vin said, "Not as big as I expected."

Over Goddric's shoulder, he could see a shift, a glimpse of red.

But they knew this would happen. They knew they would be watched.

Both heads are gone. Gone.

There are shadows crying among the flames, a creature re-forming from their darkness—it grins.

I'm not ready for the scene to shift once more, brown threads cutting into my skin. Vin's shadow grows weaker, more distracted.

He stood at Laus' dock, the wood swaying beneath him. The seagulls cried above, circling for food. There was a chill to the air, one that spoke of seasons changing.

"You want me to leave?" His tone was harsh, but to no effect.

A feminine laugh came—shrill and equally as harsh—followed by the stomping of feet. "Yes. She escaped. I cannot allow her to be free."

"Haven't you done enough?"

Silence before a slap. *Agata circled him like the seagulls overhead. Her lips were twisted, her eyes serpentine. There was a strange distortion, a bleeding of black in her veins visible just beneath the collar of her cloak.*

He knew he could not refuse her. He was in too deep.

"I love you, I have always loved you." He then took the potion from her hands and downed it. His grimace smoothed out, as did the myriad of scars on his skin.

When he faced her, changed, she smiled: "It will never be enough."

"Enough," I plead, my palms digging into my eyes. "Enough."

Slowly, reality settles around me. There is a hand pressing against my back, the touch warm and firm. I realize how cold I am and gasp, shuddering as I nearly pitch forward. The hand moves from my back to my arm, then wraps around my waist. Before me, a face weaves in and out of focus—furrowed brows, moving lips, hazel eyes with dilated pupils.

"Anik."

He breathes a sigh, his fingers hesitantly touching my face.

A voice howls a command to my right and instinctively I turn, only for Anik to grab my chin. "Don't look, Ru."

"Don't look," Anik told me as he moved closer to the shivering bushes. I shouldn't have come along but I wanted to see how his hunting was going. The market in Laus was in two days. We needed something to sell.

"Anik … " I crept behind him, my steps muffled by the thick grass beneath my soles. The bushes shivered again and there was a short cry. I saw snapped branches before a flash of metal. Then Anik was pushing me away, his face drawn.

"Don't look."

The now-dead hare, its body grizzled and beaten by the trap that held it, mocked me as I cried out—too late.

The smell of burning flesh is overwhelming, ripping me from another memory—though this time, one of mine. I dig my fingers into the dirt.

"Don't look."

I nod and am helped to my feet. The crowd shoves and quivers and dances in a frenzy as Weylin steers me through them. Anik stays close and I reach for him, wrapping my hand around his. There is a sheen to his eyes that he blinks away; he gives our joined hands a squeeze.

A tug on my ankle trips me and I stumble, shooting a glare at the skuggi threads tangled on the ground. A hand forms, pointing back in the direction we came from.

He's here. The shadow wraps a hand again around my ankle. *Hurry. Run.*

I risk a glance toward the fire.

On the stage, Agata watches the flames in a trance, her lips parted, eyes lustful. The Reaper stands at her side, but his eyes are on me, his hands frozen on the edges of his mask.

The queen and Larken are gone, only Gael and the king remain.

And at the fire, a hulking mass prowls around the edges before it leans down to sniff the hand that hangs from the flames.

"Don't look," Anik repeats a third time. I shudder as a raven calls out nearby and the thud of a body disrupts the crackle of burning wood.

Too late.

A MOTHER'S REFLECTION

She stands too close to the fire, though unfeeling of its heat—its fevered touch. Her attention is on her daughter as she is guided by her half-brother and her mate past Agata's sigil wards, the barrier they form around the perimeter of the clearing not caging her in as intended—not even slowing her group down in the slightest; Agata will be furious. Her "master" even more so.

Rune is as oblivious to her freedom as the world of shadow is to the unsighted eye.

Sighing, Elowyn forces herself to face the beast that watches her, cruel flames dancing in its eyes. The gods have cursed them—sent a plague on Vodihr as recompense for her elder sister's greed.

The "if onlys" nearly bring her to her knees.

She thinks of Goddric and the way his eyes crinkle when he smiles.

If only she hadn't stopped by The Banshee that day to pick up her brother, Keegan. She was sixteen and Goddric was twenty-one when they met. When they fell in love and their story began.

She thinks of her mother, Embela, and how she'd tell her of the stars and worlds just beyond the circle of Vodihr.

If only her mother hadn't been named the Matriarch, the last witch of the old ways. They could have left. Could have gone far, far away.

She thinks of her father, Asper, who was chosen as the town's spiritual leader, their Leiðtogi.

If only her father hadn't taught his eldest daughter how to commune with the gods.

She thinks of a time when she and Agata played without hate, without jealousy.

If only Goddric hadn't caught Agata's eye, too. She had been engaged already to Vin, her faðir approving of the match. But Agata always wanted the best, regardless of the consequences.

And lastly, Elowyn thinks of Rune, a daughter she gave her soul to save … Who had no idea what horrors still awaited her. The gift she had that was in demand by both the humans and the gods.

"Bróðir, your continued moping is irritating me," Agata scolds from where she sits on the wooden platform's edge.

Turning, her black-gray threads whispering over the ground, Elowyn glances first at her younger half-brother, then at her elder sister. She reads the warnings in Agata, from her clenched hands to her blown pupils and the singsong quality of her voice.

Elowyn knows only more death is to come.

CHAPTER THIRTY-NINE

When I open my eyes, I see the Reaper sitting on the edge of my bed; Birgir is growling at my side, the hairs on his neck raised. I open my mouth to cry out, but the Reaper puts a finger to his lips. It is then that I noticed he is insubstantial, fading in and out—his face twisting from the effort to stay.

I reach for Birgir, desperate for his solidity, but he disappears, leaving nothing behind.

It takes me a moment to collect myself. "She killed you?"

The Reaper nods, casting his eyes downward to stare at his lap. His antler mask is half melted to his face, his skin burnt and hanging limp on one side.

"Why?"

Perhaps I shouldn't have asked because his eyes flash angrily and he leans forward with a growl. I hold up my hands in surrender, sitting back to rest against the pillows and wall behind me.

We stare at each other in silence.

I see a chunk of purple hair and the breath solidifies in my lungs. So it is him. I was right. His random disappearances, his erratic behavior, his loyalty to Agata … "Keegan," I say, "tell me what happened."

He flinches a little at his name, but then he leans forward further and I hold my breath. His fingers, entangled in orange thread, lightly brush against my forehead.

I smell ash and burning flesh.

"Bróðir, your continued moping is irritating me," Agata scolded from where she sat on the wooden platform's edge. In her hands was a sword stained with red. Her feet, now bare, dangled as she hummed to herself, staring at her reflection in the sword's blood-wet metal.

Keegan stood, his back to her, his gaze on the dying fire. He said nothing, just grunted. His hands were also stained red, rubbed raw from scrubbing them over and over with little success.

The mask was silent for once. And for the first time in years, he had full control of his mind.

"Did you know?" he asked then, his words deep, reproachful. He couldn't bear to look at her. She disgusted him. He disgusted himself.

She sighed, long-suffering. "Of course. You only needed to know the basics of my agreement with—"

"No," he snapped, one hand moving to reach for the mask still on his face. Even if he had his mind back, the thing was sucking the breath from him. "Did you know that Rune was … Did you know who she was all this time?"

The silence between them was tense and foreboding. He knew Agata didn't want to answer. But he needed her to. He ripped off the mask and turned to face her—and their shared look of pain surprised him. After everything she'd done, he would think her incapable of remorse. If she wasn't, the weight of her misdeeds would crush her, wouldn't it?

And then her pain disappeared quickly, buried beneath a dark smile. "Don't play dumb, my pet. You knew who she was and just didn't want to accept it."

"Keegan," I choke out, breaking from his memory's hold to look at him—to really look at him. The mask is gone, his face still like melted wax on one side but recognizable now. I don't know what to say or how to feel. I think of all the times we laughed together, of his playful taunts and his overbearingness. Then there were moments he was cruel. He never did tell me much about himself. Where he'd go. What Agata had him do.

Now I know why.

"Agata was your sister."

His fingers press harder against my forehead and my thoughts stutter.

"Lies. I didn't. I didn't know." Keegan looked away, angrily wiping at the tears on his face. "All this time, I thought she had been killed with Elowyn. That she was lost to us in Hel because of Goddric." He began to shake. "But she was with Goddric's family for years. And then she was in Vodihr, in your home and being used ... " He choked. "The things I said to her, the things I let them do—let you do—to her ... The things I did." His voice broke. "Oh gods, forgive me."

Agata's laughter caused a shiver to run down his spine. She was lazily moving her feet back and forth, letting them dangle in an almost child-like manner. Her head tilted to the side. "You really didn't see it?

The resemblance is uncanny."

"I-I had." His words faded and he frowned. "But I'd forget just as quickly."

"The mask's poison worked nicely then. Our father's books on shadow magic are a little outdated."

Keegan's watery eyes grew round and he looked in fear at the mask he still held, but before he could respond, she changed the subject—"You seriously think the gods cared about Elowyn? Or Rune? It's been years."

"Yes," Keegan whispered. "You still care, too, or else you wouldn't have lured her back." She glared but he went on, "You need her, just like you needed her before."

Agata waved away his words, standing, turning towards where he stood watching the flames. "You really are remembering, aren't you?" Her footsteps were soundless as she moved towards him. "Did you know that you were supposed to go with her to Arden? She was to be a servant for the queen, and you the king. Goddric, Embela, Vin, they planned it all. They tried to rescue you from me, too." Her hand moved up his back. "But I couldn't let that happen."

She weaved herself around him, wrapping her body against his. One hand stayed at the middle of his back, the other gripping the base of his neck. "And the second time, you were involved then, too—oh, how angry I had been. Goddric was fighting the mask and wouldn't bring her to me." She tsked, fiddling with his hair. "And you, you were talking more and more with my mother—abandoning me."

"I—" He stopped, unsure of what to say.

"Look at me," she whispered, but he fought her. "Look at me."

When his face tilted down, she leaned up and pressed her lips against his. He winced and jerked back, blood on his bottom lip. "No, no more.

This is wrong." He reached for his mask, placing it back on to hide his expression, to protect himself from her.

The anger that took over Agata's face then was something otherworldly, something evil. He saw a blackness in her veins as she pushed away. Her face was full of pits and wrinkled grooves that stretched with her building madness.

"You cannot turn on me, too. Not now. Not when I am so close."

"Close to what? When does it end, Agata?" He stopped to look up at the night sky. A fresh wave of tears blurred his view of the stars. "It's been a lie, all of it. I can see that now. Elowyn, Rune—you staged it all. The mask you gave Goddric, then me. Now Goddric's dead. I-I killed Embela."

Agata's hiss mingled with his cry of surprise. She had moved quicker than he thought possible, embedding the sword in his back from behind.

"Why? " His voice broke as he fell to his knees. He touched the tip of the metal protruding from his stomach. She jerked the handle and he roared, slumping forward to land face first on the hot coals of the fire, the unnatural flames melting his skin and cracking his bones.

The mask whispered a "hello."

"Agata was your half-sister," I say again. "Mama, Elowyn, was your half-sister, also." I'm reaching for Keegan before I even register my actions. I stop halfway, grabbing the blanket instead. "But if … then that means … " I fumble for words, fumble to make sense of what I had seen: the kiss, the confessions, his murder.

I'm the half-brother of Elowyn and Agata, Keegan intones, his voice crisp, blank in my mind. *I was seven when you were born, a product of a traveling norn that our father—your afi—took a fancy to when he and his wife, Embela, were at odds over issues in Vodihr.*

"So then you're my … "

Frændi, he says. *Your half-uncle that beat you, tried to break you …*

"Kissed me," I mutter, my hand going to my lips. It had been a long time ago, before Weylin was back in Vodihr. I had gotten drunk off the wine at a party Agata was hosting and was caught by Keegan. In anger, I had kissed him to prove I was old enough to handle myself.

How naïve I had been.

Yes.

I blanch.

A stray skuggi bares its teeth when Keegan shifts, moving to stand and pace the room, threads trailing behind him. *Elowyn was the first to accept me as part of the family; she'd heard Embela and Asper arguing about me one night.* He smiles. *She found me hiding in the butcher's shed of The Banshee where she worked a few days later. She confronted Asper, our faðir …* He stops and shakes his head. *Embela ended up taking me in, my mother had left me behind—I was five, small for my age and weak from a disease that had ravaged our travelling camp.*

His eyes darken. *Everything had been fine until Elowyn met Goddric a year later. I noticed that Agata was coming around more often, getting into heated discussions with Embela until one of them would leave the cabin. I didn't mind Agata's attention, when she looked for me, didn't even question when she got too physical—too intimate. I was too young and attention-starved to understand. And at nineteen, Agata seemed … otherworldly at times. She was the outcast of the family and was often prowling around at the shrine.*

He shrugs and I slowly get to my feet, crossing my arms over my chest. "Something's missing though. What aren't you telling me?"

I have trouble believing that Agata truly killed Mama out of spite alone.

Agata wanted your Papa first, which you know. She teased him, taunted him, and yet he only had eyes for Elowyn any time he came through town escorting Arden's trade convoy. It enraged her, and when Elowyn got pregnant with you in less than a year, Agata lost it. She started muttering to no one, lashing out at everyone—especially her charges—without reason. It scared me.

"So she always owned the brothel?"

He nods. *It used to be a halfway house for travelers that Vin's family ran until Agata was given it as a wedding present. She took it over and expanded.* He clears his throat. *Things were okay again, Agata seemed content—our father joked married life had settled her. Then, on the night of my seventh birthday, I found her bathing, the water pink with blood, and I confided in Embela what I saw. I didn't know what had happened, still don't, but one of Agata's newest pets had been missing the next day.*

"How did Jocelyn even find out about Papa and Mama?" I rub my forehead.

Agata was feeding her information—true and false—for years. I think they even became lovers later on. And when Jocelyn killed Elowyn … his voice breaks and my vision blurs. *I remember hearing screaming, though it was muffled by all the brothel's noises. Then it was just eerily quiet, like Vodihr itself froze. But Agata influenced it. She had to have.*

"Did you know? Did you know what she-they had planned?"

There is a brief moment of hesitation, enough to arouse my suspicion, before he shook his head. *I was supposed to be there that night; Elowyn had asked me to visit, had wanted to talk. She knew I was avoiding Agata, just not why. But I went to Laus to run an errand for Agata instead. When I arrived back in Vodihr, her party for the Slaughter Moon harvest was out of control.* His form waivers, mimicking his voice, as he admits, *I stole some ale and blacked out.*

My fingernails dig into the flesh of my arms. "What happened after?"

I don't know. I had woken up to a patron kicking me in the gut when Agata came in sobbing, barely able to speak. He sighs. *I was still drunk, so I don't remember much. I think she had me go to the altar to retrieve something.* He shrugs.

"In a memory Vin shared with me, Papa had been carrying Mama to a fire. You were there, and you brought the antler mask. You gave it to Agata."

Now I'm the one pacing.

I-I do remember that. The mask, it's evil. Goddric had it, had worn it till he fought, went a little mad … Then Agata gave it to me—I-I killed a lot of women, Rune, Keegan whispers, head bowed. The change in topic is abrupt and I feel ice in my gut. *I liked it. Their cries, their pain.*

I swallow reflexively. He can't hurt me, not physically. I need to focus on getting answers first. If the mask controlled him … "You said the mask spoke to you, right? Influenced you somehow?" At his nod, I continue, crossing my arms. "So then how did you—"

The door to my cottage thuds open and Keegan disappears, leaving behind one last thread:

"Go to her. Tell her your story," Keegan heard Agata say between the pops in his ears, the rush of flame devouring him. "Then bring her back to Vodihr. It's time to finish this."

"Who are you talking to?"

"No one," I snap, the memory fading. I turn to glare at Anik in the doorway who is looking around, a hand on the grip of his sword. "Just let it go."

My brother releases a huff of breath, from annoyance or confusion, maybe both. This isn't the first time he has caught me "talking" to myself. But he says nothing and closes the door.

When he pauses, I know he is experiencing the oddness of waiting for Birgir to bark, to demand a pat on the head. Or maybe he just doesn't know what to make of me talking to myself again.

I avert my stinging eyes, fully back in the present. I feel the pinch of his gaze and quickly start picking at my nails, working to get the dirt out from when I'd clawed at the ground the night before.

"Rune, we need to talk."

I sniff. My thoughts are a mess. I keep thinking of Keegan, of what I learned. I need my big brother back. "I know."

"I know you don't—" I glance at him and almost laugh at his dumbfounded expression. "You know?"

I nod.

"Oh, thank the bloody gods!" he cries, startling me at the volume of his voice. His eyes gleam with tears. "I thought you'd fight me a little longer."

"What can I say?" I manage, a hesitant smile on my lips. "I miss you."

He laughs and lets his head drop forward, one of his hands going to cover his face. His shoulders are shaking and I hug him around his middle, burying my face in his shoulder.

"I'm still mad at you," I mutter.

Anik's arms tighten. "I'm sorry, Ru. So sorry."

We stand there for a few moments and eventually I pull myself together. I break away from his hold.

"I'm ready to listen."

A little while later, we are cramming ourselves into the big brass tub I purchased when I first moved into the cottage. Anik and I sit facing each other, our knees touching—frankly, I'm surprised we fit at all.

"So, this wasn't exactly what I had in mind … "

His smile is full of embarrassment, adding to the flush already on his cheeks. He tugs at his shirt self-consciously. "We used to do this as kids and I just-just missed it I guess."

My throat tightens and all I can do is nod. It's been a long time. "Please tell me you take your conversations with Gael more seriously."

"Well, we do talk in the tub sometimes, but usually we are—"

I hold up a hand. "Nope, too much information. I'm good."

Snickering, he bangs his elbows against the tub's outer rim. I bite back a grin at his curse. As we squirm to get comfortable, the silence becomes awkward and we eye each other nervously. Now I'm the one tugging at my shirt before smoothing my skirt over my knees.

"I—"

"So—"

Biting my lip, I motion for him to speak.

"I knew when they brought you home, to Laus, that something had happened," Anik starts, and my hands clench in my lap. "Mother was frantic, unhinged even, as she bustled about. You were sound asleep in Father's arms. And every time he went to put you down, Mother started screaming." His head tilts back.

"Eventually, he handed you to me and dragged Mother to their bedroom. I remember holding you, studying your face, and having no idea who you were. The sound of glass breaking and skin hitting skin came from behind their closed door; you stirred but didn't wake. I was about to knock on the door when the wailing started." He huffs. "In truth, their fighting wasn't unusual, so I didn't think anything of it. But after a while, you got too heavy and when I knocked, it was Mother who opened the bedroom door. She told me to put you in Tillie's bed and to wait for her there."

Anik's eyes gloss over as he loses himself further in the memory. "I had been so angry at first when they told me what happened. Mother said it had been your fault that Tillie was dead. That your mother was who had been stealing Father away from us. She said she still expected me to treat you as if you were my sister … I hated it; I hated Father for his betrayal." He clears his throat. "I hated you."

My head throbs as a memory surfaces, one of a younger me cowering in the corner of a room, my hands over my face, my eyes squeezed shut as I rocked. Before me, a younger version of Anik stood, his face red, eyes bulging as he yelled.

"You aren't my sister. Stop pretending!"

"It took me a month to finally see what Mother was doing. Father was gone and she seemed well, happy even. Once a week, she'd disappear for hours and when she'd come home, she'd have a bag of glass bottles for you, and always, pink lipstick on her cheek. She told me you were a sick child and needed nightly potions from a nearby healer to stay healthy. They smelled so foul and you always threw up afterwards."

One of my hands goes to my mouth, a familiar taste hollowing my cheeks.

He pats my knee through my skirts and waits for me to calm down before going on. "I wanted to keep hating you," he admits to me in a whisper. "I wanted to blame you, but ... but then I found you in the tub crying, covered in bruises, wiping at your eyes with your dirty sleeves and holes in your dress. And when you looked at me, when you asked what you kept doing wrong—I just couldn't. You didn't remember Tillie. Or your real home. Or even our father at times."

I remember that night, vaguely. A broken plate. Jocelyn screaming. The lash of a belt. Clarity flitters on the edges of my mind, ghosting away when I try to focus too hard. Anik's voice holds conviction, but what if his words were wrapped prettily in lies? What if he still hated me?

Licking my dry lips, I nod for him to continue.

"You know what happened next. Father began drinking, gambling—between that and his duties to the crown, he was hardly ever home. When he was home, I'd sometimes catch him whispering to himself or to a mask I caught him holding once or twice before he pushed me from the room. Mother spiraled more each day but hid it well, was still taking care of the house and visiting friends. And we g-grew closer." He coughs to hide the break in his voice.

"Anik—"

"When he took you, when he came back without you, I didn't know what happened. I went a little mad trying to get answers. Mother said it was for the best, that a debt had been paid. I already lost one sister. I couldn't forget you—wouldn't."

His hands shake and he holds them out, palms upward. He pulls out a small pocket knife and slices his palm.

"Are you sure?"

His hand grabs mine in response, his threads reacting, the memory hitting hard—*"Where is she, Faðir?" Anik's fists curled tighter into the fabric of his father's soaked tunic.*

Only silence met his demand. A demand he had asked again and again over the last six years. His father was staring lifelessly at the floor, watching a puddle form at his feet. The rain pounded hard against the roof of The Wild Rose tavern.

Frustrated, Anik gave him a shake before pushing away, turning towards the door. He glared at Hensley, a retired guard and friend of his father's.

"What did you do to her?" His words were a muted roar as he looked back over his shoulder. The patrons—one in particular with a scarred face—watched him from around the room.

"She's safe," his father whispered, his eyes glossy from ale. "She's home."

I stare at our clasped hands. "I *was* home, in a way. Did you not know where that was?"

"I didn't. I was too young to know where Father went most

of the time. Where his 'duties' with Arden took him. Then later, it didn't matter, and I went to Arden." Anik shakes his head and I let go of his hand. "I'm sorry it took so long to find you, Rune. I'm sorry I never told you the truth even after I got you back," he whispers. "I never—not once—stopped looking for you, because to me, you *are* my sister, and nothing will change that."

"You agreed with Jocelyn before. Said I deserved it—deserved to suffer? To die?"

"I thought if I played into her delusion, like I've done before, that it would be enough to stop her, distract her at least. Weylin was getting ready to fight and I needed just a little more time ... "

His hands are still outstretched, and I stare at them. My eyes sting. Logically I know, or can understand, the dynamics of what had happened. Tillie's death, Mama's death, Papa's devastation and spiral, Agata's deceit, Jocelyn's self-destruction ... Keegan and what happened with him.

But where does Anik fit into this mess? As cruel as it is, I still want to hate him. I'm angry, so angry. He knew this whole time—had let Jocelyn hurt me, trick me.

But he protected you when he could, a shadow whispers in my ear.

And he had—all the times we hid in the forest, the closet, the tub. The times he snuck me food or had taken a punishment that was mine.

He loves you, Rune, the feminine voice chimes in again. Mama. I can't see her, but she's close. I know what she says is true, but why does it hurt so much? Why does my heart feel cracked? Why is breathing so difficult?

"I got you out," I mutter, more to myself than to him. "Agata figured out who you were, drugged you. I smelled the ale when we first talked, and then the drug on your breath when you dragged me into the hallway. The more you moved, the more sluggish you became. I barely got you to the circle in time."

"I remember—or some of it, I do. I remember seeing you, trying to get close without giving myself away … "

"It doesn't matter now," I say when words fail him. And it doesn't to me. It's in the past.

Anik curses, his hands shaking as they lower; our knees bump. He tries to hide his devastation at my words. He must think he is losing me.

"Yes or no, Ru?" Anik grumbled from the doorway, his hand outstretched.

In that moment, I see the little boy he had been, facing me as the belt hit his back. The teenager who made silly faces just to make me smile, even when his eyes were red-rimmed from holding back tears or staying up late to work for extra coin. I see the man who had made a deal with a prince to rescue me; who had fought his demons to help me fight mine.

I reach out and grab his hands.

Another memory comes to me—

"You smell of ale," Gael said, coming to stand by Anik's side by the wheel.

"I made a mistake," came a muffled reply, a sigh soon following. Anik's shoulders curved further inward.

Gael shrugged. "We all do." When no response came, he shifted a little closer. "Are you okay?" His eyes glanced to the lone Tempest crew member snoring in the crow's nest.

"Sure." He had found his father. Had thought just maybe he'd get the truth.

A strangled noise left the prince's throat, and he moved to grab Anik's shoulders, roughly jerking him so they were face-to-face. "Did you find her?"

"No."

Anik knew what the prince saw then: the tear tracks on his cheeks, the blackness cradling his eyes, the swollen lip he now sported after getting into a tussle at The Wild Rose.

"How can I help?"

Anik looked up at the stars, then to Gael. "Kiss me."

I lean back, letting go of his hand, our knees bumping again. I take in the slight flush in his cheeks and figure that wasn't a memory I was supposed to see. He quickly wraps his hand with a kerchief from his pocket.

"So, you and Prince Gael?" He groans and I throw my head back, laughing.

"I'm mad at him for what he did—for his own deal with you," he admits.

But I shrug, no longer angry. "I guess that's just a big brother thing."

And when he smiles, I smile back in relief.

"Yes or no, Ru?" Anik grumbled again and I smiled.

"Yes."

CHAPTER FORTY

You know, when I said I'd let you borrow my ship, I didn't mean for you to literally take it." Anik's voice floats from the direction of the dock.

Grinning, dagger blade between my teeth, I motion vaguely in his direction and work on untying the next knot on the ship's railing. "What did you mean then?" I ask, my words garbled. I sheath my dagger and try again, "Actually, what did you think I meant when I asked to borrow your ship?"

My brother flushes and it is only then I notice Gael, standing at his side, a hand on my brother's shoulder.

"I-I well … Uh … "

Rolling my eyes, I sheath my dagger, hands going to my hips. "Bróðir, say that again, I couldn't hear you through all that virginal stuttering."

His glare is answer enough, the flush on his cheeks darkening. Gael laughs. "I thought you and Weylin wanted some *alone* time!" Anik hollers.

The crew, who from the corners of my eyes I could see have been watching our conversation with rapt interest, bursts into whistling and raucous laughter. Ailith snorts, doubling over at the wheel—I turn and wiggle my eyebrows at her.

"As gracious as that is of you, we have many other places we can use." I wink.

"Make all the fun you want, Ru, but at sea it is a mind-blowing—"

"You say that, but the last time we were 'at sea,' you nearly cracked your head open, falling out of bed when we ran into some big waves."

Anik's scandalized gasp can be heard over a new round of laughter and I wheeze at how offended he looks. He whips his head to stare at Gael.

"That was supposed to be a *secret*. I had everyone believing the bump on my forehead was from a really vicious game of cards."

Rolling my eyes, I gave up on the knot and used my dagger to slice the offending rope before moving on to the next knot. "Gael, I changed my mind. I do like you. When I get back, I'll buy you a drink and we can chat."

"Get back from where?" Anik's question causes a sudden silence from the crew. My shoulders tighten; I feel his eyes boring into my face.

"Vodihr," comes Weylin's voice, his tone strained and unhappy. He leaves his place at the helm where he'd been talking with Ailith and comes to my side, pressing a brief kiss to my cheek.

"Vodihr," was my brother's dumbfounded reply.

"Wraith," I confirm and Anik begins pacing along the dock.

"I'm," Weylin clears his throat and I give him a quick apologetic smile, "*we* are going after Agata."

"Are you sure about this?" Weylin asked. He kept his back to me, his hands in fists at his sides. My eyes traced the scars on his back before looking out at the sea. The sand was soothing against my bare feet while we walked down toward the water's edge.

"I need to know all of it. There is something missing." I shake my head. "Agata just left. She sent Keegan to me and left. How did she know I would see him? Why would she give up so easily?"

"It's a trap. You know it."

I nodded. "Yes, but I don't have a choice. I need to finish this—whatever this is."

Weylin was silent for too long. I risked a glance at him.

"And you still have your debt to the Zila. Though you don't know what she wants yet."

I nodded again. "Yes, that too must be paid."

⁂

By the time we reach the outer edge of Vodihr, I know something is very wrong. So far, we've encountered nothing on our four-day journey, and I mean *nothing*. And after we reached the cliffs and the *Tempest* dropped anchor, the shadows on board dissolved.

No skuggar.

No raven.

The trek from the cliff and through the woods is silent. A handle of the *Tempest*'s crew comes along with Anik, Weylin, and myself. Ailith has been left to man the ship.

When we reach the circle of Vodihr, no Zila awaits us.

Everything is silent, save for us.

Anik and Weylin flank my sides, the crew at our backs. We step through the circle, easily and without payment, and onto the path to Vodihr. We walk with our weapons tightly held in our hands. I can hear each snap of a twig, each muttered prayer, each hiss of breath. Everyone is nervous and I can't blame them.

"Something's wrong," I finally say when we turn the last bend and the city comes into view. There is a lone column of smoke coming from the town's center—a dark mist that, when I squint, I can see faces in. Some are locked in silent screams, some weep— all of their eyes are wide with fear.

Anik snorts. "What gave you that idea?" he asks. "Whatever that smoke is over there? The fact the place is deserted?" Not even my glare stops his next remark. "Oh wait, you wanted a welcoming party where they carried poppets of us on sticks—"

"I'm afraid we don't have those, but I'll be sure to pass along your unhappiness to the Mistress."

Appearing from the alcove of the butcher shop, a masked figure, feminine and petite, steps into view. She curtsies, then waits, her eyes boring into mine. I don't know her but she clearly knows me.

Reluctantly, I return the curtsy, and her painted blue lips form a grin. "We've been expecting you," she says. "You're late."

"For what?" I look to the trees for a glimpse of a shadow, a sign of life.

There is nothing.

"The ritual, of course."

And then I hear the drums, a low baritone voice accompanying the droning beat. The hairs on my neck prickle in warning. "What ritual?"

My question goes unanswered except for her drawn-out sigh.

More figures appear, surrounding us—no, herding us as we walk towards Vodihr's heart. Every person is unfamiliar, their faces obscured with Revelry décor. The colors that adorn them are startling against the dull lifelessness of the city's current state. Their movements are odd, uncoordinated, as if they are caught in threads I'm not able to see.

The air hums.

The scent of bellflower blooms and grows heavy.

Suddenly a child appears before me. Her head is bowed, her bare toes curling into rock and dirt. I take in her long, knotted hair, her dirt-streaked, pale skin, and her threadbare dress, barely visible beneath the brown cloak she wears tied at her neck.

Acid burns my throat when she looks up.

Gray meets gray and my vision fractures as shadows come in a torrent, pouring from her tiny body. They fall from her open mouth—her wail lost among their cries. They come from her flaring nostrils as she breathes. They crawl from her feet and slip through her clenched fingers. She breaks apart, ripping at the seams.

I stumble back. "Not real," I whisper, my voice breaking. "Not real."

Once there was a girl who spoke to shadows …

"Stop."

Someone tsks. Agata comes forth from the crowd, black sludge dripping from her nose. "Are we having fun yet, elskan?"

"Go to Hel," I manage, forcing my lips to stop wobbling and curl into a snarl.

She laughs and my ears bleed from the high-pitched sound. "Oh Rune," she sighs, using my name for the first time in years, "we're already there."

As one, everyone—Anik, Weylin, the crew, the townsfolk, the pets, the performers—step back as if pulled by a master puppeteer's strings. I see the threads now in an array of colors, shimmering, almost translucent in the fading sunlight. Clouds roll in from above. More threads litter the ground, creating a rainbow webbing that travels up invisible walls, appearing to engulf Vodihr completely. Everyone's faces are carefully blank, their lips moving silently in some language, a prayer I can't hear.

Thump, thump, thump.

Shadows in various stages of formation crawl, walk, run among the crowd.

"What—"

"Ssh," Agata reprimands, "he's coming."

Directly across the pit, new flames erupt. Startled, I stumble back, bumping into Agata.

"Who is coming?"

My question goes unanswered.

I squint, seeing the Zila, Birgir at her side, watching, waiting from the other side of the pit. Her hand moves to fist in Birgir's hair, the wolf braced and ready to spring, her collar still at his throat.

"When the time comes, you will know what to do," the Zila said as she circled me. I was shivering, my grip growing weak as I held Weylin in my arms.

"What does that mean?" I demanded.

She shrugged. "You'll figure it out. Just be ready."

When Mistress Agata started to sway with the crowd, I knew she was lost. Her lips curved into a smile, her eyes graying at the corners.

Thump, thump, thump.

"He comes." The childlike quality of her voice causes a shiver to run down my spine.

And then the dance begins. I only learned it once, and by force. On my first spin, I see Keegan now on the edges of the bonfire. His eyes are gone, his face smooth, blank just like those that circle Agata and I.

One, two, three: I throw my hands up, palms outward. My actions are not my own.

Thump, thump, thump.

I toss my head back, wailing a warrior's cry from the past. Threads are tugging at my clothes, my hair.

This is a dance for the dead and for Death itself. Only high talas and priests are privileged with the knowledge of how to conjure the gods and each step and pivot I make breaks that special vow.

Inwardly, I weep.

For a third time, Agata speaks, her voice still childlike, shivering with anticipation. "He comes."

And I see him, there within the fire. His shape is twisting—he becomes one creature, then another. He falls from the fire, aflame himself, and on shaking legs stalks towards Agata and I. He pauses as he weaves through the crowd, sniffing at faces, curved nails grazing cheeks and life veins.

"Mama," I asked hesitantly. I didn't want to break the silence. We were sitting side-by-side, facing the old shrine in the center of the city. In front of us, others were kneeling, whispering.

We came to the city's center once a week to pay homage to the gods of old. There was talk that the shrine would soon be removed. Its rotting wood and engraved crumbling stone created a barrier between Vodihr and the new world. I didn't want to tell her that I saw fresh shadows amongst the stones each time we visited.

"Mama," I tried again, and an old man hushed me from my left. Chastened, I curved into myself, reaching a hand out to pick at the grass pushing through the pale stones. My fingers stopped to hover over a story depicted there.

A beast was crawling out from the flames—humans, in pieces, surrounded a black mass sitting in the center of the destruction. There was a young woman, naked, kneeling before the beast. In her hands, she was holding—

There was a gentle tug on my braid, and I blinked up into the face of Mama. Her eyes were sad. She looked to the unfinished story in stone and then at me. Wordlessly, she reached for my hand.

"What happened?" I asked in a whisper after she began leading me through the gathered crowd. I had seen the story before, or some of it, in the storybook that she read to me every night. But I'm not allowed to read that story, or not yet at least.

When the beast stops in front of Weylin, my steps falter and red eyes meet mine. The beast snorts, toying with Weylin's necklace for a moment before moving on.

"Nothing. Nothing happened to her."

"But the one picture uses the symbol of a debt. Gods don't forget the

debts made, Mama. Right?"

Twice, the beast—a god—circles Agata and I. On the third circle, Agata pulls me closer, her cool body melting into mine. My hands move down along her back, stopping at her hips. I feel metal pressing against my palm. We spin apart, snap back together. I feel her lips press against my collarbone; my own lips brush hers when she lifts her head. I move my hand a little lower to the slit at her hip, feeling the tip of the dagger's blade.

"No ljúfa stelpa, they do not."

"Then what happened to her?"

From the corner of my eye, I see Mama; she moves to sit by the shrine. She leans forward, her fingers gently tracing the stone before her. Her shoulders start to shake.

She shakes her head. "Nothing, Rune. Nothing."

As she takes my hand and leads me away, I wonder why she is lying.

"You were supposed to die," Agata whispers in my ear. Her eyes are on Mama, too. Her pupils grow each time she inhales, swallowing her emerald irises. "You, you were supposed to die but my sister ruined it all—*again*. I just wanted … " Her words falter.

I force myself to close my eyes, force myself to breathe. Fabric tears just a little as I wrap my hand around the dagger and tug.

I was nearly asleep, fighting a yawn, when I felt Mama's lips press against my forehead. Something wet slid down the side of my face and my nose wrinkled; I whined, squirming to get deeper into my bed.

When it was silent, I peeked to see her cheeks wet with tears. She is reading, the old black book with wrinkled pages crinkling each time she flipped a page. She stilled and opened toward the end of the book, to where the forbidden stories were held.

"Only Death can end this."

"End what, Mama?"

The storybook slammed shut.

And when my eyes open—when the god's nails caress my spine, I drive the dagger into Agata's chest.

The spell fractures, the dance stopping so abruptly and the flames roaring up to the sky with such force that I stumble back and nearly fall.

Death watches me. At its feet, shadows wiggle for mercy— half caught in its snare. Its teeth gnash together, its head tilting to the side.

The ceremonial dagger in my hand quivers, the red gem turning white just like the other had. I swear I see a flash of teeth in the gem's center before it dulls.

So it's you. The girl who speaks to shadows.

The inhuman voice in my mind startles me. "I—"

Death catches my gaze, studies me a minute longer, lips peeled back almost as if it is smiling before it shudders. Then, once more, it turns into flames.

A wheezed laugh brings my attention back to Agata. Her hand wraps around mine. Her eyes look to where Death had just stood. The dagger is buried in her chest and our fingers are coated in her thick black blood. Her other hand raises to her lips, as if she is surprised and unsure how to react.

There are many things I want to say in this moment.

That this is for Mama.

For Papa.

For Keegan.

The words feel weak, worthless, because this is so much bigger than me, than my hatred for her.

And when her inky black threads crawl over my fingers, she reveals everything.

"Agata, come sit with me for a bit," her father beckoned from his bed. He was shivering from the cool night air that came from the open window. Tomorrow, they would be moving him to the basement, to where the sunlight could not reach in and burn his fragile skin.

She turned from the small altar on his dresser, reaching and taking a crystal from where it sat in cleansing water. Pocketing it, she flattened her pink skirt and moved towards the bed. Her mother had tried to counteract her work, but not even her mother was strong enough against Agata's new master.

As she checked her father's chains, she thought of the bouts of madness he'd been having lately. That was her fault, mostly. She'd tweaked some of the words in his book and the consequences were still making themselves known. She hadn't realized how connected he was to Vodihr.

The crystal poked her skin when she sat down beside him. "How are you feeling, faðir?"

He smiled, his body almost hairless, tuffs of auburn sticking to his scalp from months of illness. His headaches had started when Agata first began dabbling with his old books, and the bouts of vomiting started after the first time she truly met her master. "Better. I think the gods are listening."

She had to look away, to cover her lips to hold back a laugh. She knew a god was listening—but to her, not him. Soon, her master would come. He was hungry and he had waited long enough.

"How is Elowyn? And my little Rune?"

Her breath left her in a hiss. She reached for his tonic to cover her reaction. "Fine. They miss you. Elowyn plans to stop by tonight."

"Good, I don't want the gods to take me until I see them."

Agata stroked his brow, tracing the old scar that trailed downward and over one of his eyes, leaving it milky and unseeing. "Oh no, Faðir, you cannot leave, not yet. The gods know that."

When Agata winces, I smile and pull back from the memory. My happiness catches her off guard and I take the dagger, drawing it out of her.

"You—"

I crowd her space before she can continue. Shadows now free of Death's hold come forth to poke at her legs, tripping her. Her bare feet connect with loose twigs and stones with each back-wards stumble she makes. I wait to speak until her heels brush against the wood and stone pit that holds the lifeless flames.

"Tell me, Agata," I croon. Her eyes meet mine and I reach out to cup her cheek.

For Mama and Papa.

For Amma and Afi.

For Keegan.

For Weylin.

"Are you afraid yet?"

She reaches out, her fingers gripping my wrist. Black threads nip again at my skin, slithering like snakes up my arms. I get more snippets of her life: A laughing child being chased by a younger girl. A naked young woman sobbing in the woods, a pink dress at her feet. The same young woman, muttering a spell as she slices her arms and watches the blood pool and smear her skin, a dead body at her feet. When she calls for the gods— for any god to answer—the memory solidifies:

"Do you know what you are asking?" The voice was ancient. It poured from the bowl of ingredients in a thick smoke, stretched thin along the walls of the low-lit shrine.

Agata nodded, her eyes greedily taking in the shape forming before her. This was the first time a god had truly answered her.

"There is a price."

Turning, Agata looked out the window at the crowded streets of Vodihr.

She saw herself in a gown made of pale pink, the center of attention as she walked among a gathered crowd during the party she had hosted the night before. A party to celebrate her niece's approaching birth. But Goddric still hadn't noticed her—had rejected her again when she lured him into the woods. He left her as if she were nothing, her gown undone around her breasts, because even offering all of herself wasn't enough.

She saw swirling lights, and soon, she was covered in glittering jewels, and could feel the bite of teeth moving down her neck before a kiss was pressed to her shoulder. The man morphed into Vin, her husband, who smiled lovingly at her, but still, he was not who she wanted.

She was worshiped, loved, feared.

It wasn't enough.

A woman wailed in the distance, a newborn soon joining in.

The hatred bubbled up within her, choking what little humanity she had left. She thought of Goddric there, holding Elowyn. Of their babe cradled between them. Of her mother taking care of them and her father waiting downstairs to proclaim the news to all of Vodihr.

"I'll pay it."

The bowl cracked in her hands, and blood splattered her face, the altar, the ground. For a minute, there was nothing but darkness and wailing and a rumbling beneath her feet as stone cracked and wood splintered.

Death smiled. "You have sixteen years to appease me. To pay your skuld." Its head tilted. "I am so very hungry. It has been a long time since one of your kind has called on me."

"But what do you want?"

They didn't answer at first. Instead, there was pressure, so much pressure. Then the Zila's face appeared in the congealing blood on the wall, an elusive creature who lived in the woods and fed on stray souls.

Death moaned, "I want to feed."

Shadows exploded from the cracks as Vodihr and the Skuggaland became one.

The Zila stepped forth from a slit now present in the veil between worlds.

I jerk back, Agata's blood smearing my skin. I feel dirty, tainted by the memory she shared; by the awareness that she was Vodihr's plague—had been all along. I could almost taste her anger and jealousy.

"You condemned Vodihr to Hel, to Death, for a man?"

It was after her deal with Death that the Revelry started. That the Zila was bound to this place, this world, to take payment, to be the keeper of Vodihr's gate, her freedom to wander stolen from her.

I look to her across the flames. She is stuck too, just like the skuggar.

Agata's threads still shift along my arms, more memories come: Her growth of power. Her budding corruption. The need for offerlings when Vodihr's residents fought the changes she implemented with each passing year. I see her collection of tricks: a promise to a sobbing Jocelyn for revenge, the first potion held out for her to take; a bone mask birthed from dark sludge, a magic not meant for this world, given first to Goddric, then to Keegan. There is Vin, whose eyes are full of love every time he looks at her.

It was all Agata's doing.

"How did you plan to keep this going?" I ask her, and suddenly, Death reappears behind her, waiting to collect.

Her eyes widen, black veins moving to the surface of her face and twisting it into a mask made of threads.

"I-I can't keep this up much longer. The people are suspicious, are tired of—"

Death growled and she abruptly stopped speaking. "And just what exactly do you want? Do you want me to leave? How rude of you, when you invited me—begged me to give you your deepest desires for so little in return."

"He doesn't want me. Will never want me. The people of Vodihr no longer worship me. They only fear me." Her voice grew shrill. "My sister is dead. My niece taken away. What is it that you want?"

The god shrugged. "So you want a new deal? One that frees you from your debt?"

At her nod, Death chuckled. "I want the girl, then. The one who speaks to shadows. The one with a gift I forgot still existed among your kind. She has been helping the skuggar pass on without even realizing it."

"She isn't here. " Agata paused—but she'd get Rune back, easily. Jocelyn owed her, loved her. And Vin, Vin would do anything for her. She'd think of something—there was the mask, her 'Reaper,' and Arden's

king owed her for his continued satisfaction of Vodihr's delights at a discounted fee and her silence at his adultery. Surely, she could make use of that ... "Done."

"But," Death began, and she turned to face the god, "if you don't give her to me, then I want—"

I break from the memory and push Agata back into Death's waiting arms; the god grabs her and together they melt into flames. The 'o' shape of her lips is the last thing I see of her.

A pressure fills Vodihr to the point I hunch over from the weight of it. The fire gutters out.

A black mass slinks across the ground, crawling to the shrine that's breaking in the distance.

Everything goes gray and a young girl—me—appears and walks the edge of the pit. She stares at the shrine, then back to me, smiling before she vanishes.

Then other shadows manifest, caught in various causes of death and states of decay. Some whisper to blinking townspeople, others find me and nod before turning to dust, returning to a world that was again solely and rightfully their own.

Embela's image is there for a moment, her eyes glistening with tears. She blows me a kiss, then is gone. Xavier, prowling at her feet, also turns to threads, then dust.

Vin waves goodbye next, his hands going into his pockets, his shoulders straighter than I have ever seen them.

Tillie is one of the last to appear, her smile bright even now. Her giggle causes my lips to quiver, but I smile and wave when she runs past me and into the trees before fading.

Mama appears next, Papa on one side and Keegan on the other.

She steps forward, hovering just out of my reach. Her black-gray threads wrap around my shoulders, my forearms—a sob breaks free before I can stop it. The love she radiates is overwhelming.

My sweet girl, her words are as weak as her image, *I'm so proud of you.*

"I didn't want to do it," I admit to her, my voice small and hesitant.

It'll be okay now, Mama promises. Her eyes are shining bright. *But I need you to do one more thing. I need you to set him free.*

"Who?"

Her eyes turn to a house, the one on the farthest edge of town that I had never been brave enough to fully explore. At a distance, I can see its state of decomposition and I shudder.

"I'm not sure if he's—"

He is, she answers at the same time Keegan says, *It's not as bad as it looks.* He smirks. *But then again, it looks pretty decrepit at this point, so maybe it is.*

Papa chuckles at that, but Mama just frowns at her half-brother. Then she says to me, *I know how it looks, but be brave. One last thing and then—*

The debt is paid, Papa interrupts. His words are gruff, tears wetting his cheeks.

"A debt ... I cannot pay ... "

Those words would've broken me once, and yet now, I understand—it has always been my debt, my skuld, my responsibility. The girl who can speak to shadows. The girl who can free them and leave Death to hunger on.

My arms wrap around myself as they fade, leaving behind

threads tangled in my fingers.

Only after I hear a raven's lone cry—one of farewell—do I hear Weylin shouting my name. I see him running toward me, Anik close behind.

The debt has at last been fulfilled, I am free, a voice says for my ears alone. There is a slight pause, then, *and your beast has missed you.*

I have only a second to prepare before a warm weight barrels into my knees, knocking me to the ground. My arms are suddenly full of a wiggling, heavy, furry body.

"Birgir," I choke out and he whines at my voice, moving to lick my face, nudging my hand with his wet nose. Every happy yip of his makes me cry harder. I grab fistfuls of his fur and bury my face in his neck. The collar that bound him is gone.

It takes me a second before I can lift my head. I turn to where the Zila waits on the path leading to and from Vodihr. She smiles before she lights her lantern and fades into the dusk.

It's time. I'm so weary.

I'm coming, I whisper back to the voice, catching sight of a lone wolf that sits, waiting on the path to the house.

"I'm ready to try again," I tell Weylin, tilting my head up to look at him. He's confused, his eyes taking in the disarray of crying and relieved laughter around us. Anik and the *Tempest* crew also look equally lost.

"To argue over decorations in the cottage, to meet your family. For our family to grow, to get married. " I sigh when Weylin reaches for my hand, pulling me to my feet. His thumb caresses my ring. "But first, I have one more thing to do."

EPILOGUE

The house on the edge of Vodihr has been untouched by light for years. It hides, covered by the shade of towering trees and overgrown brush.

Wordlessly I step around the shrine that is now gone; a pile of rubble is all that remains.

A story of destruction, or perhaps of rebirth, is written in that pile of broken stones and cracked wood. Yet it was always unfinished and will remain so. I could always find the storybook at Embela's cottage, but something tells me it is better for this story to be unfinished, rather than unearth older, even more dangerous truths.

I turn from the rubble and walk the lined stone path overridden by decayed leaves and weeds toward the house that waits. The shutters are broken and slanted over slouching windows. The paint has long since peeled to reveal the wooden bones beneath.

The grizzled sorrel-red wolf sees me coming and disappears.

I feel like Vodihr is holding its breath as I approach the door, but as for myself, I'm oddly calm.

"Are you sure about this, Rune?"

It isn't the first time Weylin has asked this, his steps sounding from close behind me. Just ahead of us, Birgir paces, his ears twitching. Like before, I don't bother to respond; I am following the tugging in my gut, a thread I can't see but know is there, guiding the way.

Hurry, please hurry. The voice is louder, more desperate.

The thread starts vibrating when I push open the door, which groans wearily under the weight of my palm. Tiny cracks form around where I touched. Instinctively, I know that soon this too will be a pile of wood and glass and stone.

"Will you tell me then what happened?" Weylin asks and I laugh. There was a lot to tell.

"Yes, after."

Floorboards protest under my steps but hold. I wander through the house, taking in the leaf-covered furniture, the glint of a wooden figurine on the floor amongst a nest of old clothing. There is a set of dishes in the corner, broken and covered in scat. Nearby a wooden chair is missing two legs.

The gray wolf with the auburn-peppered face reappears before the doorway to the cellar. Its head tilts towards the door, its ears twitching. Birgir snaps his teeth, but I hush him with a quick pat on the head.

Taking a deep breath, I reach for the doorknob and twist— only for it to break off in my hand when the door sways open. The shadow wolf chuffs before disappearing.

Amused, I blink at the tarnished metal in my hand before tossing it over my shoulder. I hear it land, a surprisingly quiet thump, but I don't bother to look back.

"Rune," Weylin cautions, his hand tugging one of my sleeves. I brush him away and start down the steps, into the damp earth that beckons.

The scent of decay hits me first—it is tenfold stronger down here than upstairs. Birgir presses into my side as we descend, his hackles raised.

When I reach the bottom, the thread in my middle pulls taut. I peer into the gritty half-light that shines in from a lone window in the farthest corner of the dirt-walled room.

Hurry, child.

Ru …

Rune.

The shadow's whispering stops suddenly as a figure stumbles into the light, twisting towards me. Its skin smokes when the light touches it. It is hunchbacked, completely hairless save for a few tufts of auburn on its scalp. Its skin is loose over ribs and bone. The only clear feature is its eyes—gray. I see the chains that bind it to the wall, the tattered clothes it once wore rotting on the floor.

I had seen this being once before, when it dragged me into the Skuggaland.

I take a step forward, my pulse racing. Birgir growls and I hold up a hand to hush him. Reaching down, I grab the stained dagger from my pocket and slice my palm open. Blood seeps across my skin to speckle the floor.

And then the gray-and-red wolf materializes directly in my path when I take a step forward. Of course. His familiar. It has a scar that runs through one eye. Gold eyes, one hazy and unfocused, study me a moment longer, flicking to a quivering Birgir, before the old wolf goes and sits by the twisted figure's side.

Now both wait for me to make the next move.

Hovering over the first chain, my hand outstretched, I lock eyes with the figure. Its face goes slack as it takes in my features. Its lips wobble, mouth parting, but no words come out. I try for a smile, my blood hissing against the metal chain. A fissure appears, running the length of the wall from floor to ceiling.

Only after both chains fall and the figure crumples into my waiting arms do I whisper, "Hello, Afi-Grandfather."

He and the wolf dissolve into ashen threads, some I reach for, smiling at the memories they share.

Vodihr sighs in relief.

It is done.

HER ENDING

*Once there was a girl who played with shadows,
Until someone made a pact to a god and
trapped a city in the shadows of Death.*

*There was glory and taint.
Riches and waste.*

*Then the girl died …
But the shadows—
saved her
and her mother sacrificed herself
to give hope.*

*The child was spared
but a debt gone wrong needed to be righted …
More sacrificed out of honor,*

love,
and desperation to rewrite their fates
and hers.
The girl had left,
only to be asked to remember.
She needed
to defeat her monsters;
to fulfill her debt and theirs.
To use her gift.

And when the time came,
the watcher of Skuggaland remembered—
it was ready.
The shadows were ready.

Once there was a girl who spoke to shadows …
Once there was a god who was called to be fed …
Once there was a city trapped with the dead.

Only in death could they all be free.

The Other recites the old nursery tale to herself, a vision she'd had a long, long time ago and had written down in a book passed down through the generations after her.

She watches now, a century later, from outside the dirty window of her old home, the glass cracked with age and distorting the scene within.

She feels Vodihr's loss and sadness and hope.

She knows she is finally able to leave.

Giving one last silent goodbye, she turns and sees the Zila waiting for her at the forest's edge, adjusting the twin daggers strapped across her back—

And the Other bursts into threads.

Frelsi …

… Freedom.

ENDIRINN

THE END

ACKNOWLEDGMENTS

THE JOURNEY of *Shadowspeak* was a long one. After years of not writing and of listening to imposter syndrome, the day arrived when it was time. And so it began ...

Thank you to my grandmother for nurturing my love of books and writing. This book is dedicated to you and your constant support of me throughout my journey. You never let me stop or give up completely.

To my grandfather, you didn't understand half of the rants I've had when you asked, "How is the writing going?" But you listened and that's what matters. The cancer took you too soon—I miss you so much.

To my mom, thank you for letting me steal your books and read and read and read! Every trip to the bookstore brought new books and new memories.

To my sister, Cheyenne, you get the fangirling, the book obsessing, the need to create characters that leave an impression. Thank you for brainstorming with me and listening to all the different plots I came up with while writing—even the ones that made no sense.

To my sister, Lakota, you may not be a reader, but you helped me create book promotions, film intro videos, and you were my photographer when I needed a photo that wasn't a selfie. I couldn't have done all the techie stuff without you.

To Atlas, I love you. You are the best dog ever. Thank you for putting up with me.

To Fox Pointe Publishing, publicist Kiersten Hall, editor Chelsea Farr, and designer Becca Hudson. You made this book a reality, and that is amazing in and of itself.

Kiersten, you have helped me so many times along this journey and answered any question I had, regardless if I asked it more than once.

Chelsea, your notes are spot on, your edits intense but needed. Thank you for the support and encouragement along the way, from my random texts to long-winded emails to me wanting to change things over and over.

Becca, you worked your magic through formatting and design work and made this all official with a beautiful layout.

To Nicole Deal, from the first time I came across your work on Twitter, I knew some day that I wanted to commission you for artwork. You capture each and every commission spot on and take my breath away by seeing my vision a reality.

To my beta readers, Elysia Lumen Strife, Candace Robinson, Jamie Stewart, and Mallory McCartney; from the beginning when Shadowpeak was just a fledgling draft, your feedback was greatly appreciated along the way.

And finally, to my readers, thank you for giving me and Rune a chance. ༄

ABOUT THE AUTHOR

RAVEN ECKMAN is an author, freelance editor, and overall literary fangirl. She always knew books were her passion, well before her grandmother's challenge to read a book a day when she was young.

She obtained her B.A. in English with a concentration in Creative Writing from Arcadia University. Since 2016, she's been working with a range of authors, both self-published and traditionally published, on short stories and novels from horror to contemporary in YA and Adult fiction.

Shadowspeak is Raven's debut novel. She is currently working on her second novel, as well as her first children's book.

She lives in Pennsylvania with her fluffy pup, Atlas.

www.ingramcontent.com/pod-product-compliance
Lightning Source LLC
Chambersburg PA
CBHW061053100726
47911CB00012B/209